Praise for Anne Emery

Praise for *Children in the Morning*

"This sixth Monty Collins book by Halifax lawyer Emery is the best of the series. It has a solid plot, good characters, and a very strange child who has visions." — *Globe and Mail*

"Not since Robert K. Tannenbaum's Lucy Karp, a young woman who talks with saints, have we seen a more poignant rendering of a female child with unusual powers." — *Library Journal*

"Emery paints a poignant portrait of a girl burdened by information she was never supposed to have, and of a tormented man who, at the most critical juncture, realizes that mounting a proper defence requires fumbling around in some very dark corners."
— *Quill & Quire*

Praise for *Barrington Street Blues*

"[Emery] is a master at creating a sense of place (in this case, her hometown of Halifax, N.S.) and developing characters — talents that place her in the same rarified circle as Margaret Maron, Marcia Muller, and Sara Paretsky. . . . Highly recommended."
— *Library Journal*, starred review

"The yin-yang of Monty and Maura, from cruel barbs to tender moments, is rendered in occasionally hilarious but mostly heart-breaking fashion. Emery makes it easy to root for Monty, who solves not only the mystery that pays the bills, but also the one that tugs at his heart." — *Quill & Quire*

"Anne Emery has given readers so much to feast upon . . . The core of characters, common to all three of her novels, has become almost as important to the reader as the plots. She is becoming known for

her complexity and subtlety in her story construction. . . . *Barrington Street Blues* should earn Anne Emery the right to fly first class from now on." — *Halifax Chronicle Herald*

"This is a wonderful yarn, full of amazingly colourful characters, dialogue that sweeps across the pages like a tsunami, a story that will keep you reading late into the night, and a plot as devious as a lawyer's mind." — *Waterloo Region Record*

Praise for *Obit*

"Emery tops her vivid story of past political intrigue that could destroy the present with a surprising conclusion." — *Publishers Weekly*

"Strong characters and a vivid depiction of Irish American life make Emery's second mystery (in a projected trilogy) as outstanding as her first. The Irish Catholic flavor is reminiscent of Robert Daley's books and will appeal to his fans." — *Library Journal*, starred review

"Emery has concocted an interesting plot . . . Her depiction of the gregarious Burke clan rings true . . . it is a pleasure to spend time with them." — *Quill & Quire*

Praise for *Sign of the Cross*

"A complex, multilayered mystery that goes far beyond what you'd expect from a first-time novelist." — *Quill & Quire*

"This startlingly good first novel by a Halifax writer well-versed in the Canadian court system is notable for its cast of well-drawn characters and for a plot line that keeps you feverishly reading to the end. Snappy dialogue, a terrific feel for Halifax, characters you really do care about, and a great plot make this one a keeper."
— *Waterloo Region Record*

"Anne Emery has produced a stunning first novel that is at once a mystery, a thriller, and a love story. *Sign of the Cross* is well written, exciting, and unforgettable." — *The Chronicle-Herald*

CECILIAN VESPERS

A MYSTERY

ANNE EMERY

ECW Press

Published by ECW PRESS
2120 Queen Street East, Suite 200, Toronto, Ontario, Canada M4E 1E2
416.694.3348 / info@ecwpress.com

LIBRARY AND ARCHIVES CANADA CATALOGUING IN PUBLICATION

Emery, Anne
Cecilian vespers : a mystery / Anne Emery. -- Pbk. ed.

ISBN 978-1-77041-023-7
ISSUED ALSO IN ELECTRONIC FORMATS:
978-1-55490-344-3 (EPUB); 978-1-55490-861-5 (PDF)

I. TITLE.

PS8609.M47C44 2011   C813'.6   C2010-907837-3

Cover and text design: Tania Craan
Cover image © Vincent Ricardel / The Image Bank / Getty Images
Typesetting: Mary Bowness
Printing: Transcontinental 1 2 3 4 5

Mixed Sources
Product group from well-managed
forests and other controlled sources
www.fsc.org Cert no. SW-COC-000952
© 1996 Forest Stewardship Council

This book is set in Garamond and ATSackers

The publication of *Cecilian Vespers* has been generously supported by the Canada Council for
the Arts, which last year invested $20.1 million in writing and publishing throughout Canada, by
the Ontario Arts Council, by the OMDC Book Fund, an initiative of the Ontario Media
Development Corporation, and by the Government of Canada through the Canada Book Fund.

 Canada Council   Conseil des Arts
for the Arts   du Canada   Canadä   ONTARIO ARTS COUNCIL
CONSEIL DES ARTS DE L'ONTARIO

PRINTED AND BOUND IN CANADA

ECW PRESS
ecwpress.com

Part One

Chapter 1

Pange lingua gloriosi
Corporis mysterium
Sing, my tongue, the Saviour's glory
Of His flesh the mystery sing
— Saint Thomas Aquinas, "Pange Lingua"

I

Father Burke appeared ready to burst into song, or at least into chant, as he tacked Saint Thomas's words to a bulletin board at the entrance to the building. He said, simply: "Let our work begin."

"Our work" was the inaugural session of the new Schola Cantorum Sancta Bernadetta, under the directorship of the Reverend Father Brennan Xavier Burke, BA (Fordham), STL (Pontifical Gregorian), STD (Angelicum). The schola was a kind of choir school for grown-ups, who would be learning or relearning the traditional music of the Roman Catholic Church. Gregorian chant and Renaissance choral music had been largely shunted aside over the past thirty years. For the church, the cataclysmic event of the 1960s was the Second Vatican Council, popularly known as Vatican II. It was a meeting of bishops and theologians from around the world, called together by Pope John XXIII for the purpose of opening the windows of the church to the modern world. When you open a window, fresh air may blow in, but something else may get blown out. In the opinion of Father Burke,

3

the great musical heritage of the church went out the window after Vatican II. In setting up his schola cantorum, he intended to do his part to recover what had been lost.

My law firm, Stratton Sommers, had done the legal work for the schola, but my involvement went far beyond that. My family and I — my estranged wife Maura, son Tommy Douglas, and daughter Normie — had been privy to Father Burke's anticipation, his anxiety, and his all-night planning sessions as he worked towards the realization of his dream. It was a lot of work but we were happy to assist in any way we could. We knew that if he succeeded in establishing the school, he would be making a permanent home in Halifax. Burke had spent much of his childhood in Ireland, most of his adult life in New York, and the past few years here in Nova Scotia. By this point we felt wedded to him, for better or for worse, and I know the lights would dim if he walked out of our lives. Not surprisingly, then, I was on hand for the introductory session.

"Now, Father, be mindful of the possibility that others in the group may have, em, views that differ from your own." The gentle warning came from Burke's pastor, Monsignor Michael O'Flaherty, a slight, white-haired priest who spoke with a lilting Irish brogue. "I know this is your show, but a bit of advice from your elders may not go amiss. Just remember to be patient, forbearing, courteous, and open to the variety of —"

"Michael," Burke interrupted, "when have I ever failed to be patient and forbearing?"

The older priest — who really was patient and forbearing, and who answered to "Michael" or "Mike" as cheerfully as to "Monsignor" — sent me a knowing glance, which I returned. He knew as well as I did that when the meek inherited the earth, Father Brennan Burke would not be among those on the podium taking a salute.

"Besides," Burke was saying, in a clipped Irish voice that could never be described as lilting, "these people know what they've signed up for. The fact they are here says to me that they have certain views on the Mass and on music that accord with my own."

"Oh, I wouldn't make that assumption now, Brennan. Not necessarily. Just keep caution in mind, my son." Michael turned to me. "Any advice for him, Monty, before he goes up there?"

"Somehow I suspect my words would be wasted, Michael," I answered.

We had reached the gymnasium of St. Bernadette's choir school, where the schola had its headquarters and the students were already gathered. Monsignor O'Flaherty and I took seats in the back. Burke went to the front of the gym and took his place at the lectern. Tall, with black eyes and black hair threaded with silver, Burke was a commanding figure in his clerical suit and Roman collar. He faced his inaugural class of just under sixty students. They were priests, nuns, friars, and a smattering of laymen and women from all over North America, Europe, and Japan. The term was originally intended to begin in September and wind up before Christmas. But, owing to the meddling of the priests' housekeeper, Mrs. Kelly, the notices and registration forms were several weeks late going out. The housekeeper, who had never quite approved of the worldly Father Burke and was not skilful enough to mask her disapproval, wrongly believed the papers had to be seen and endorsed by the bishop. By the time Burke discovered the error and set her straight in a blast that nearly blistered the paint off the walls, he had missed a number of publication deadlines. The first session had to be delayed, throwing the whole year's schedule off.

But the big day had arrived. It was Monday, November 18, 1991. Burke began his opening address: "Welcome to the first session of the schola cantorum. I am Father Burke, and I look forward to meeting each of you when we begin our work this afternoon. Your presence here suggests to me that you are looking for something deeper, something richer, something more, shall we say, mature than the liturgy and music you may be encountering in your home parish. I have heard the term 'do-it-yourself Mass' and that pretty well —"

"The phrase 'do-it-yourself' raises a red flag to me, Father! It suggests that you disparage anything but the old, conservative liturgy that held sway before the Second Vatican Council." The speaker was a heavy-set woman of middle age, with a large wooden cross hanging from a strip of leather around her neck.

"Well, you're right in part. There is much that has crept into the church today that I disparage. But people have the wrong idea when they blame Vatican II. None of that was envisioned by the Council —"

"Oh, I think you're being too kind there, Father, too kind altogether." An elderly priest struggled to his feet with the aid of a cane; he faced Burke, then turned to address the crowd. "In fact we can put the blame squarely on the Second Vatican Council for destroying the very essence of Catholic worship; some would say the very essence of Catholicism itself."

The first speaker was back before Burke could respond. "So some liturgical practices are not as good as others? Is that what you're saying, Father Burke? Are you admitting you're an elitist?"

Many a schoolteacher would have envied Father Burke at that moment; he may have been under siege, but he had the attention of every student in the room.

"We are members of the Roman Catholic Church," Burke countered. "That is not an institution founded on relativism, moral or otherwise. We need look no further than Saint Thomas Aquinas, who speaks of degrees of perfection. *Gradibus in rebus*, gradations in things. Thomas says some things are better, truer, finer than others. And that is certainly true of music. When you compare Mozart with, well, some of the tripe —"

"I was right," the woman asserted. "An elitist. Well, that approach leaves out great segments of our community, I'm afraid, Father. Not everyone can appreciate —"

"Who's being an elitist now?" Burke snapped. I was surprised he had held his temper this long. "I refuse to talk down to my congregation, as if the people are simpletons who 'don't get' the great music. I refuse to insult their intelligence with childish, jaunty, sentimental little tunes —"

"So we're going to be stuck with all the old music? I thought we were going to dialogue and workshop together to create some music of our own. There's a group of us here who have been sharing ideas for some new compositions for the Mass."

Burke's customary deadpan expression gave way to one of horror. How had someone who proposed composition by committee found her way into his schola, a bastion of traditional music?

He eventually got back on track and continued his address. The vast majority of the group were attentive and silent, but he was going to have his hands full with the disgruntled minorities in the student body. If things proved dull in the criminal courts, where I spent most of my days, I'd make a point of dropping in to the schola to observe the fireworks!

✝

That evening found me in Father Burke's church, where I was a well-established member of the St. Bernadette's Choir of Men and Boys. There were sixteen of us in the choir. The trebles and altos were young boys; the tenor and bass sections were made up of guys in their teen years or well beyond, like me. I was something of a crossover artist, since I usually did my singing with a bunch of scruffy characters who shed their day jobs at five o'clock, donned old frayed shirts and porkpie hats, lit up smokes, and did their wailing in my blues band, known as Functus.

The church, at the corner of Morris and Byrne streets, was a couple of blocks south of the city's downtown shopping area, and about a minute's walk from the waterfront. St. Bernadette's was a small neo-Gothic church with arched stained-glass windows. The Victorian-era rectory, three storeys high, stood beside it. Across the way on the west side of Byrne was a large stone building in the Second Empire style with a mansard roof, dormers, a crucifix on top, and a more recent brick extension. Wide stone steps led up to the double front doors. This building was home to the new schola cantorum; it also housed the children's choir school and a parish youth centre. I entered the church and took my place with my fellow choristers in the loft.

"*Gloria in excelsis Deo!*" The voice of an accomplished operatic tenor filled the church, and the entire membership of the St. Bernadette's Choir of Men and Boys moved to the rail of the choir loft to gape at the exotic figure below. The man wore an elaborate-looking soutane, the close-fitting ankle-length black robe traditionally worn by priests of the Catholic Church. It was unusual to see one these days. Over the soutane he had some sort of shoulder cape; the cape's lining flashed a lighter coloured silk as he extended his arms, turned, and intoned the "Gloria" again. He stopped to listen as the sound reverberated off the church's stone walls. A jewel flashed on his left hand as he raised it to his head. He was wearing an old-style flat black hat with a large round brim, a type of headgear I had never seen on a local priest. He whipped the hat off and shook out black and grey curls that swept back from a widow's peak. A prominent nose and curved lips gave the impression that he had stepped out of a Florentine portrait from Renaissance times. Father Burke emerged from the sacristy in his stark black suit and Roman collar. He greeted the man, and they seemed to be conferring on the subject of the church's superb acoustics. Burke pointed up to the loft, and the operatic priest bowed towards us with a flourish, then left the building.

Our choirmaster joined us. Burke did not allude to the stranger in our midst, but proceeded to open the rehearsal as he always did with a Latin prayer. He then announced that the choir would be joining the schola group for solemn vespers on November 22.

"As the boys from the choir school know, vespers is the church's evening prayer of thanksgiving. We chant or sing hymns, psalms, and antiphons. This will take place on the feast day of Saint Cecilia."

Burke looked at a little fellow named Richard Robertson, who was a bit of a rogue, which may have been why Burke was particularly fond of him. "Who is Cecilia, Richard?"

"The patron saint of church musicians, Father."

"Right. Now, we can't have the service here at St. Bernie's because there's a wedding that evening, so we're going to Stella Maris. A great old stone hulk of a church."

"It's spooky there, Father!" Richard said. "Me and my friend snuck over to that church one night because we heard there were rats there, and we wanted to shoot them with a BB gun. We didn't see them but we heard noises."

"Well, you'll be hearing the 'Magnificat' at vespers. About as far as you can get from the squeak of rodents. But you're right. It's quite deserted around there; the church is scheduled for demolition. I guess there are no parishioners nearby. All right, now, open your books to the 'Sanctus XVIII.' This probably dates back fifteen hundred years; some say longer than that. I'd like the full choir to sing it just to the 'Benedictus.' I want you young fellows in the front row — you're supposed to be in the front row, Richard, get down here — to carry on from there. The words are among the most beautiful in the Mass: *Benedictus qui venit in nomine Domini.* What's it mean, Ian?"

"Blessed is He who comes in the name of the Lord."

"Precisely. Let's hear those clear, young voices." He raised his arms and conducted the piece. The little boys sounded like angels as their pure voices soared to the heavens.

"Lovely. A little lighter on the higher notes. Let's hear it again." It was even more beautiful the second time. The priest favoured us with a rare smile, and gave credit where credit was due: *"Deo gratias!"*

When the rehearsal wound up an hour and a half later, Burke and I retired to the Midtown Tavern on Grafton Street. At the Midtown you got draft, you got steak, you got fries; nothing came with, say, a light mango-chutney mayonnaise on the side. The priest had shed his clerical collar, as he always did when we headed out for the night. He lit up a cigarette and sucked the smoke deep into his lungs.

"Big day for you, Brennan," I said. "How's it going so far?"

"O'Flaherty was right," he said. "How did he know all these malcontents would show up?"

"Monsignor O'Flaherty is a wise man. But, really, what's surprising about it? Ever since the Vatican Council wrapped up in 1965, preconciliar and postconciliar Catholics have been squabbling about whether it was good or bad for the church, whether it modernized things too much or not enough. Some of the more authoritarian aspects of the church needed reform. And surely not all the music composed in the past twenty-five years is bad."

"Of course not. I've heard some compositions and some choirs that are excellent. But there's an overwhelming amount of rubbish as well. If we don't do something about it, generations of Catholics are going to grow up without knowing anything better."

"Well, try not to fret too much about the students at the schola. There are just a few grumblers. And they're not all of the same stripe. You'll be attacked from the conservative side when they find out how liberal you are about everything except music and the Mass."

"This is about the sacraments, not politics! It's about beauty: the beauty of music, of language, of ritual. I've wanted this for so long and now . . ." He drained his beer and signalled for another. "What have I got myself into?"

I felt a bit guilty thinking it, but this was going to be fun to watch.

II

Et antiquum documentum novo cedat ritui
O'er ancient forms departing newer rites of grace prevail
— Saint Thomas Aquinas, "Tantum Ergo"

"'The most beautiful thing this side of heaven,'" Burke said to his class the next day. I had a chance to drop in to the schola between an early morning court appearance and my first appointment of the day. "That is Father Frederick Faber's timeless description of the traditional Latin Mass."

"So why did Vatican II outlaw the Latin Mass?" The voice was unmistakably American.

"Vatican II did no such thing," Burke replied. "Many changes were made, which were in fact not promoted, authorized, or envisioned by the Council. The only things that are official are those contained in the Council documents. Here's what the documents really say, and I'm quoting from *Sacrosanctum Concilium,* the *Constitution on the Sacred Liturgy*: '. . . care must be taken that any new forms adopted should in some way grow organically from forms already existing. . . . Particular law remaining in force, the use of the Latin language is to be preserved in the Latin rites.' Vatican II made that point in a paragraph all by itself. There is a subsection that opens the door to local languages in some parts of the Mass, but it is worded with great caution. Latin is the official language of the church. It is the sacral language of our faith, just as Hebrew is the sacral language of the Jewish faith. Active participation in the Mass was considered back in 1903 by Pope Saint Pius x to mean the congregation should be singing Gregorian chant. Subsequent popes agreed. Now let us observe two versions of the Mass."

The room darkened and a screen lit up before us, showing the exterior of a building shaped something like a saddle. The scene shifted and we were inside the low-ceilinged structure. A spindly cross was the only evidence that the place was a church. Two giant quilts depicting wheat sheaves hung on either side of what must have been the sanctuary. An earnest-looking man and woman stood at a microphone with guitars. A third woman raised her hands and urged everybody to sing the "gathering hymn." Few did, but the words came through loud and clear from the leaders of song:

> Come into the love! Come into the new day!
> His room is for all, a true meeting place.
> We are the ones He has called to the new way,
> We bring our light to the whole human race!
>
> All we in the love, all we in His peace,
> Will shake hands today with a peace that will bind
> All brothers and sisters. Divisions will cease.
> We are the light of all humankind!

Well, that wasn't going to get anyone inducted into the songwriters' hall of fame. They'd have to come up with something better than that if they wanted to be seen as light to the whole human race. But my attention was wrenched from the music to the centre aisle of the church on the screen, where I saw a procession of . . . clowns! Everyone in the procession, including the cross bearer and the priest himself, was, incredibly, dressed in the red, yellow, and green costume of a clown. They were carrying balloons and stopping to pass them out to children in the pews. We all sat, stunned, as the elderly clown-priest read the gospel, gave a sermon, changed the bread and wine to the body and blood of Christ. Every one of the priest's gestures reflected excruciating embarrassment.

Then I heard the ancient tones of Gregorian chant, and the screen was filled with the rich blues and golds of a magnificent church, with marble floors and stained-glass rose windows. The priest approached the altar wearing gold-trimmed white vestments and a biretta, a square black cap with three ridges and a tuft on top. He looked very European, yet familiar. A younger, somewhat heavier Brennan Burke without a trace of grey in his pitch-black hair, his handsome face less hawkish than it was now. In the film he followed a procession of altar boys dressed in black cassocks under lacy white surplices. One carried the crucifix; the others brought candles. In the priest's hands was a chalice covered with a cloth. I should have remembered the names of the items from my days as an altar boy. Purificator? Chalice veil?

When he arrived at the foot of the elaborate high altar, the Father Burke on the screen removed his biretta and handed it to an altar boy. He prayed *sotto voce*, then made a profound bow and recited the "Confiteor," striking his breast three times at the *"mea culpa, mea culpa, mea maxima culpa."* Incense rose to the heights of the vaulted ceiling, and bells rang out at the consecration. In a universally known ritual essentially unchanged since the days of Saint Gregory in the year 600, the Mass proceeded to the sound of Latin prayers and solemn chant.

When the morning class was over the present-day Burke stopped to chat with me in the corridor before the schola's next session began. The composition-by-committee woman, whose name tag read "Jan Ford," came up to him with a question: "Am I right? Were you the presider at the liturgy we just saw on tape, Father?"

"I was the priest singing the Mass, if that's what you're asking."

"Right," Jan Ford said, nodding, and she moved off down the hall.

"As if I'd sign up for a life of celibacy to be a *presider*," Burke remarked to me.

"I didn't see anyone leap to the defence of the clown Mass, Brennan. I've been to a lot of very beautiful and dignified Masses since the Council, so I assume you're using an extreme example of post-Vatican II experimentation."

"An abomination. Shows how far things can go if unchecked. It happened on more than one occasion, believe it or not. There were basketball Masses, cowboy Masses, all sorts of liturgical chaos."

"The Latin Mass was magnificent, of course, as I well remember from my altar boy days."

"You still have the look of an altar boy, Montague. The blondy hair, the boyish face, the baby blue eyes. You don't always behave like one, of course, but . . ."

"Yeah, yeah. I nearly didn't recognize you, though."

"It was a few years ago. When I was doing my graduate work in Rome. I'll be teaching the rubrics of the Latin rite to the younger priests who missed out on it; no doubt it will be a refresher for some of the older fellows as well."

"*Buongiorno*, Brennan! I am sorry to have missed this morning's sessions. I would explain but I do not wish to be indelicate. It is enough to say I was not feeling well." The man spoke with a strong Italian accent. It was the elaborately attired priest I had seen in the church just before the choir rehearsal. He and Brennan exchanged a few words in Italian, then turned to me. The stranger extended his hand, and Brennan made the introductions.

"Monty Collins, meet Father Enrico Sferrazza-Melchiorre."

"*Piacere, Signor* Collins."

"My pleasure. I saw you in the church. Where are you from, Father Sferrazza-Melchiorre?"

"Mississippi."

"*What?* Forgive me. I don't speak Italian so whatever you said sounded like —"

"You heard me correctly, *signore*. I live in rural Mississippi."

"Impossible!"

"Yes. It is impossible and yet, *è vero*, like the resurrection. It is the truth."

"You're not native to the southern United States," I insisted to the flamboyant European. "Surely I haven't got that wrong."

"I am a native of Rome. My mother's family is from Sicily."

"And what exactly did you do in Rome?"

"I worked for many years in the Roman Curia — the bureaucracy of the universal church — and taught at the Lateran University also."

"My question remains: what did you *do*? To get posted to the American south?"

"It is such a long story."

"I'm sure. Leaving that story — whatever it is — aside for now, what are the demographics down there? I wouldn't have thought the Catholic population was very large."

"Oh! You are right, of course. Only five percent of the entire state is Catholic. Even less so where I work, in Mule Run. Eh! What can you do?" He shrugged.

"Fit in well with the locals, do you?"

"Let us say there was a process of adjustment. There was, I recall, some confusion at the first seminar I conducted in the church hall. I thought it might be helpful to give people a little history of the Catholic Church. To dispel some false ideas. Striving for a popular touch, I advertised it as 'Introduction to AAA.' I was encouraged when I peered outside and saw many large vehicles roaring up to the building. But my set piece on Augustine, Aquinas, and Abelard was not well received by those assembled." He sighed. "I hope we shall meet again, *signore*." He turned and was off in a swirl of luxurious fabric.

I raised an eyebrow at Burke.

"Later," was all he said.

III

Great was the company of the preachers.
— Handel, "Messiah," from Psalm 68

"This is some information the insurance company requires," I told Brennan when I returned to St. Bernadette's rectory after work that day. "You're already covered, but they need this form completed and signed."

"Why? In case somebody arrives home and claims he wasn't taught the difference between a *punctum* and a *podatus* in chant notation? He's going to sue me for failure to deliver the goods?"

"No, it's in case somebody *doesn't* arrive home. Never makes it out of your course alive! Or goes home on crutches because you didn't clear the steps after the first snowfall. Typical liability insurance."

Burke scribbled his answers on the insurance form.

I was stuffing the paperwork back in my briefcase when Monsignor O'Flaherty came in and announced that he was going to the airport. "To pick up our final guest. Student, I suppose I should say, though it seems odd to apply the word student to people in middle age!"

"We could call them scholars but that sounds a little grand," Brennan said. "Or disciples, but I wouldn't presume . . ."

"Good of you, my lad."

"So, who is it you're picking up?"

"A Father Stanley Drew. Do you know him?"

"No."

"He's an American, apparently. Working overseas. That's all I know."

"Thanks for fetching him, Michael."

✝

That evening at the Midtown, the waiter had just placed our glasses of draft on the table, and Brennan had lit up his first cigarette, when Monsignor O'Flaherty appeared before us again.

"Brennan!" O'Flaherty was all out of puff. "Hello to you, Monty. Brennan, you'll be hard put to believe me!"

"Evening, Michael. Have a seat, and let us treat you to a draft."

"Thank you. I've an awful drouth on me, all the talking I've just been doing."

"How did you ever know to find me here, Monsignor?"

"Amn't I after following a star in the east? But no, all coddin' aside. Wait till I tell you! Thank you. Ah. Goes down like liquid gold." He smiled and put his glass on the table, then looked at each of us in turn. "You'll never guess in a million years who our latest student is!"

"Stanley Drew," Burke replied in a deadpan voice, "an American who's been working overseas —"

"No! Drew is just a pseudonym for —" Monsignor O'Flaherty paused for dramatic effect, then blurted out his news "— Reinhold Schellenberg!"

"You're having me on!" Brennan exclaimed.

It wasn't often I saw a dumbstruck look on the face of Brennan Burke. They stared at each other in amazement.

"How could we not have known he was coming? Why the false name?" Brennan asked.

"Security reasons!"

"What do you mean?"

Here O'Flaherty looked uncertain. "I don't know exactly. He wasn't all that forthcoming on the subject. But he's a lovely man."

"So what did he say when you met him? Did he identify himself right away?"

"No. Not till we were alone in the car coming into town. But you know, there was something familiar about him. I just didn't twig to it. He hasn't been in the public eye for a long time. He used to sport a beard, but that's gone now. He has only the slightest accent; his English is perfect. You wouldn't know right off who he was. Did you ever meet him, Brennan, during your time in Rome?"

"I attended a couple of lectures he gave, and saw him at a conference or two, but I never had a conversation with him."

"Gentlemen."

"Yes, Monty?" O'Flaherty turned to me.

"Who is Reinhold Schellenberg?"

"Do I take it that theology was not among the subjects in which you excelled during your illustrious academic career, young Collins?"

"You wouldn't be wrong in drawing that conclusion."

"Father Schellenberg is a noted theologian who became quite famous — infamous might be the better word — in the years immediately following the Second Vatican Council. He was a figure of some controversy in controversial times. It apparently got too much for him and he entered a monastic order. He hasn't been heard from in public since — what would it be, Brennan? — the early 1980s, or thereabouts. Ten years or so."

"What kind of controversy are we talking about?"

"His theological positions didn't sit well with some in the church."

"Didn't sit well with whom? Liberals or conservatives?"

"It's never that simple, Monty, but, em, he attracted criticism from both ends of the spectrum."

"How did he manage that?"

"He started off as what we'll call a liberal, at the time of the Council in the 1960s," Brennan replied, "pissing off traditionalists and other conservatives. Then he did an apparent about-face, renounced his liberal positions of the past, and pissed off his former adherents. But his ability as a theologian has never been in doubt."

"And now he's here to learn at the feet of the Reverend Doctor Brennan Burke at the Schola Cantorum Sancta Bernadetta."

"You find that surprising in some way, Collins?" Burke demanded.

"Not at all, Father."

"I thought not. Well, we'll have to make his visit a memorable one."

IV

Hora novissima, tempora pessima sunt, vigilemus.
These are the latter times, not the better times.
Let us stand watch.
— Bernard of Cluny, *De Contemptu Mundi*

Everything I had heard about the students of the schola and the controversies swirling around them made me keen to catch some of the show. So I popped in to the school two days later, on Thursday, when a client failed to show up for my last appointment of the afternoon. I headed down the hall and turned left, on my way to find Brennan or Michael, or perhaps the famous and now reclusive Schellenberg. Someone had set up a table and chessboard in a little alcove off the corridor, where two men were engaged in silent combat. They appeared to be in their late fifties. One had very pale blue eyes and greying blonde hair in a short military-looking cut. His opponent was a priest with fluffy white hair and rimless spectacles reflecting the light from the window at the end of the hall. The priest gave me a pleasant, if absent, nod as I stopped momentarily to observe the match. The man with the military appearance looked up, kept me in his gaze for a few seconds, then returned to the game without any change of expression. I felt I had been scanned, comprehended, and committed to memory.

I continued on my way and found Father Burke leading a seminar billed simply as "The Great Latin Hymns." I pushed the door open and took a seat in the back.

"The 'Dies Irae,' the Day of Wrath, is attributed to a Franciscan friar in the twelve hundreds. Walsh's book on the thirteenth century contains a description of the 'Dies Irae' as 'the greatest of all hymns, and one of the greatest of all poems . . . nearly or quite the most perfect wedding of sound to sense that they know.' The author concludes that perhaps no one with the exception of Dante or Shakespeare has ever equalled the 'Dies Irae' as poetry. Two verses will suffice to show he's right:

> *Recordare, Jesu pie,*
> *quod sum causa tuae viae:*
> *ne me perdas illa die.*

> *Quaerens me, sedisti lassus:*
> *redemisti crucem passus:*
> *tantus labor non sit cassus.*

"As for melody, Walsh tells us the creators of the great Gothic cathedrals developed music worthy of those magnificent temples. He means of course Gregorian chant.

"Now let's hear what is on offer in the hymn books of today:

> The lowly ones, they come to sup.
> The rich man, shamed, is drawing near.
> The lame, the leper, all are here
> To share His brimming, saving cup!

Burke gave a shudder, then turned a new page.

> Share the courage of the songfest.
> Join His dance around the table.
> If the proud ones come among us,
> Call them forth if you are able.

"Does that make any sense at all? Woe betide anyone I catch doing the shimmy around the altar in my church. This sort of goofiness is everywhere in the hymn books now. Along with all those songs in which the members of the congregation congratulate themselves end-lessly about being the light of the world, and aren't we grand? All this is yet another selective interpretation of the documents of the Second Vatican Council, in this case *Lumen Gentium*, Light of Nations. Which in reality did not replace worship of God with worship of ourselves.

"Ah. Mr. Collins. Thank you for drawing near. Come forth if you are able. May I present to you Montague Collins," he said to the class. "You may have seen him around. Not only is he the schola's wise legal counsel; he is also a member of the St. Bernadette's choir." I nodded to the group.

After the lecture I saw Monsignor O'Flaherty standing alone by the chessboard, looking down at the pieces.

"Are you a chess player, Mike?"

"Alas no, Monty, I can't even win at checkers."

"Who are the two men I saw playing chess here?"

"You haven't met Father Schellenberg yet, have you? That's who you would have seen at the chessboard. And a fellow by the name of Bleier, who's actually Colonel Bleier. He's a German policeman, *'Oberst der VP.'* The *Volkspolizei*! Retired now, apparently. They live in Berlin. She teaches there."

"She?"

"Doctor Jadwiga Silkowski is Bleier's wife. She's a leading authority on moral theology." He leaned forward, a mischievous look in his eyes "She told me she got in trouble on a couple of occasions. Ran afoul of the authorities."

"Government authorities?" I asked.

"Well, now that you mention it, she may have got herself in the soup there as well, considering that it was East Berlin they were living in till the wall came down. But I meant the church authorities. Some of the positions she has taken from time to time have not gone down well in Rome."

"I don't suppose the colonel could help her there."

"No."

"I wonder why Colonel Bleier and Father Schellenberg weren't in the seminar."

"Who knows?"

V

Judex ergo cum sedebit
Quidquid latet apparebit,
Nil inultum remanebit.
When therefore the Judge takes His seat
Whatever is hidden will reveal itself.
Nothing will remain unavenged.
— "Dies Irae," *Requiem Mass*

I called Brennan Friday morning to ask where the choir would be meeting for vespers that evening.

"We'll all go directly to Stella Maris. That way we don't have to arrange drives for all the little lads."

"That's what you have insurance for."

"Spoken like a true lawyer. We have insurance but we don't have the vehicles. So the parents will drop the boys off. We'll meet outside and have a procession. Put on a little show for Saint Cecilia."

"Right. She's the patron saint of . . . music, is it?"

"Church musicians. This is her feast day, November 22. Oh, and wear your surplice. You got it from the choir loft?"

"Yes, I did. I feel like an altar boy again."

"Good. That means I'm doing my job."

"When do I get an introduction to the great man?" I asked.

"We have a surfeit of great men here, Monty. To whom are you referring?"

"Not to you, you pompous arsehole."

"Ah. Could it be Father Schellenberg then? If so, you're in luck. Mike O'Flaherty charmed him into giving a lecture this afternoon. He had to be cajoled and he made it clear he does not want to speak on the subject of the Second Vatican Council. His topic will be the divine office of the Latin rite, the prayers sung at various hours of the day. Matins, lauds, vespers, compline, and so on. Schellenberg is a Cistercian-Benedictine monk, so he knows whereof he speaks. And after his lecture you, too, will be qualified to speak on the matter. If ever you're asked."

"Good. Some new opening lines for my next visit to a pickup joint. Hey, baby, have you heard this one? A lawyer and a monk go into a bar. Only it's time for compline, so the monk says —"

"It's always worked for me."

"I'm sure."

"Anyway, O'Flaherty had lined up a bus trip for the group, to Peggy's Cove; the tour will be postponed for an hour or two so people can hear Schellenberg first. Be here at two o'clock."

I returned to my office on Barrington Street, dictated some letters on a medical malpractice case, and tried to line up my witnesses for an upcoming drug trafficking trial. Then, just before two, I headed over to the schola for the lecture by Reinhold Schellenberg. But I was out of luck. I would not be meeting the renowned theologian after all.

"Father Schellenberg came to see me," Monsignor O'Flaherty explained. "He was most apologetic. But something came up, and he had to go out. Where he'd have to go, and him a stranger in town, I don't know. I didn't ask. Anyway, he promised he'd give his talk next week. So I called the bus company and got the Peggy's Cove trip back on schedule. I packed them all onto the bus, and they're gone. But, Monty, you'll meet Schellenberg this evening at vespers."

"Yes, our choir's first performance for the schola."

"A beautiful ceremony, the peaceful closing of the day."

✝

Stella Maris Church had not been used, as a church at least, for fifteen years. It was the scene of occasional manoeuvres by the police, putting the run to squatters who used the place for their own purposes. The massive ironstone building, with its twin Gothic spires, sat high on the northwest tip of the Halifax peninsula, above what is now the Fairview Container Terminal. Overlooking the waters of the Bedford Basin, the church had been built in the late nineteenth century to assert the Catholic presence in the city; it was a landmark visible to those approaching by boat or by train from the north. Now, commuters coming in on the Bedford Highway could see only the tips of the spires, behind the massive structures of the container terminal. Very few people lived in the area; it was strictly industrial.

The church's day was nearly done. Stella Maris was scheduled for demolition the following week, and in fact a twentieth-century addition at the back had already been torn down, except for one jagged stone wall. The stained-glass windows would be saved, as would the pews, the font, and all the other fittings. Brennan had mentioned his desire to have the ornate old altar transferred to St. Bernadette's, where it would be used for the weekly Tridentine Mass.

Now, in the dark of a moonless November night, robed figures gathered before the blackened wooden doors of the church. The scene was indistinguishable from one that might have taken place in the early Middle Ages. We were far away in time from modern-day Halifax. Priests in vestments, monks in cowls, nuns in habits, choirboys in white surplices, we processed into the nave and down the aisle. A candle in red glass flickered on the altar; our golden candles were the only other light. The only warmth. Incense wafted back to us from the front of the procession. Two by two we genuflected before the Blessed Sacrament present on the altar and took our places in the sanctuary for the Office of Vespers, by which we would consecrate the end of the day to God. Father Burke chanted the opening prayer:

APERI, Domine, os meum ad benedicendum nomen sanctum tuum: munda quoque cor meum ab omnibus vanis, perversis et alienis cogitationibus.

OPEN my mouth, O Lord, to bless thy holy name: cleanse also my heart from all vain, evil and distracting thoughts.

In the company of friars who sang Gregorian chant as part of their everyday lives, choir and clergy made their voices one; the ancient psalms floated upwards like the incense. All vain, evil, and distracting thoughts melted away, and I felt myself at peace in a way I had never known.

The peace was shattered by a scream.

We all whirled towards the sound. One of the sisters stood clutching her heart; her other hand groped wildly for support. Her mouth hung open; her eyes were fixed on the south wall of the sanctuary. "Mother of God, Mother of God," she whispered over and over.

"What is it?" Burke demanded, making all too clear his annoyance at the breaking of the spell.

"He's dead! He's been . . ." Her voice faltered but her trembling finger pointed to the scene.

With a swish of robes, the whole group rushed to see. There, slumped against the wall, was a figure in white vestments and a Roman collar, drenched with blood. The blood was everywhere, on the wall, the floor, and all over the man's body, which had been nearly severed from his head. What was that on his leg? I shifted slightly to get a better view in the dim light. There were three or four cards showing hearts pierced with arrows — valentine cards! And something else; it appeared to be a swizzle stick for stirring drinks. The top of it was shaped like an anchor. I saw no sign of a murder weapon.

"It's Father Schellenberg!" a woman cried behind me. "Oh God in heaven! Who would do this?"

A few feet shuffled towards the scene, and someone said: "He should be given the last —"

"Stop! Do not approach the body!" The voice was German. Colonel Bleier, the former East German police officer. Bleier's voice was calm, and it carried the weight of authority, but his face was ashen. "Everyone move back to your places," he instructed. "We will not further interfere with the scene. Is there a working telephone in the building?"

"There wouldn't be, no," Burke answered distractedly. He turned towards the dead man and began to pray aloud in Latin.

"Does anyone have a car telephone?" Bleier demanded. Nobody in the group was on the cutting edge of 1990s technology. "One of you will go and call the authorities. You will exit the same way you entered, and return that way also."

I was already on my way. "I'm going for the police." I turned to make sure I'd been heard; I saw Bleier making a count and writing something down — names? — in a small spiral notebook.

I got into my car and drove at top speed to Jenny's Place Beverage

Room on Lady Hammond Road, where I used the phone to alert the Halifax Police Department. When I returned to the church, I saw that the traumatized group had broken into small clusters, though, in strict obedience to the resident officer of the *polizei*, none had left the sanctuary. Some, such as Father Sferrazza-Melchiorre, knelt in prayer; others sat with eyes downcast as if in shame. An aggressive-looking man with red hair stood with his hands gripping the pew in front of him; he stared at the body and seemed to be unaware of anything else. It was too late to mark anyone's immediate reaction to the discovery. If someone had made a ham actor's effort to look surprised, I had missed it. We had all been gaping at the dead man. I joined Father Burke and Monsignor O'Flaherty, who were on their feet, eyeing the scene and conferring with Colonel Bleier.

"Ah. Monty," O'Flaherty said. "We were just saying that there's a swath of clean floor leading from the body to the sacristy. The killer must have wiped up after himself."

"I wonder how long the body has been there. Any idea?"

"I would say a number of hours," Bleier answered. "Was the church door locked when you arrived, Father Burke?"

"I can't say for sure because I was given a key to the side door and used it. I was able to push open the front doors — they have those bars you push down — so I don't know whether they were locked when I pushed on the bar or not."

"I came in the front just now. It wasn't locked. Or, at least, it hadn't locked behind us when we all came in."

"I see. When was the last time you were here, before this evening, Father?"

"Yesterday afternoon. I brought the . . . the Blessed Sacrament and placed it in the tabernacle. The place was bathed in light, and there was nothing amiss."

"The church is not used, am I correct?"

"That's right. It's going to be knocked down next week. Young people, homeless people, sleep in here sometimes. But the place was empty when I was here yesterday. I looked around and I locked up."

"Would there be tools in the basement, I'm wondering, Brennan?"

"Don't know, Michael. I'd say not. I imagine everything's been removed."

The local police arrived then and took charge, securing the scene, examining the body and surroundings, and taking our statements. Colonel Bleier and a tall, balding man I had not met watched the police activity with interest. Monsignor O'Flaherty tended to the flock of schola students, reassuring them that the killer would be brought to justice and that counsellors would be available for anyone who would like to use their services. The schola's director, Father Burke, was too shell-shocked to respond. Even if he were his usual self, he would not have thought of counselling. And he would undoubtedly have sworn to bring the killer to justice himself. For everyone on the scene, it was a long night.

I went to the rectory with Burke and O'Flaherty after the police were finished with us. We stood together in the parking lot of St. Bernadette's before I headed home.

"Let us hope and pray this slaughter had nothing to do with our work here," O'Flaherty pleaded. "Some other motive was in play, surely —"

"It happened on the feast of Saint Cecilia, Michael. Patron saint of church musicians."

"That could be coincidence, Brennan. The killer knew we would be going to Stella Maris and so —"

"Nothing about this looks like coincidence to me, as much as I would like to go along with you, Mike."

"How did Saint Cecilia die?" I asked. "Was she a martyr?"

"She was indeed," O'Flaherty replied. "She didn't die a happy death, God rest her soul. Now, as for details . . . Let me do some quick research. I have a number of works on the saints' lives. Are you coming in, Monty?"

"No, it's long past my bedtime."

"I'll be back in a jiffy."

O'Flaherty's face told half the tale when he returned. "Not a happy death, indeed not. Saint Cecilia's killers —"

"Who were they?" I interrupted.

"The Roman authorities of the second or third century. The true date is unknown. They tried to suffocate her in her bath. But she survived that attempt. They then sent a soldier to cut off her head! Three times he hacked at her neck, yet he couldn't separate her head from her body. They left her like that, the poor young girl. She lived for three days before she finally succumbed!"

"Nearly, but not quite, decapitated. Just like Reinhold Schellenberg."

Part Two

Chapter 2

Liber scriptus proferetur
In quo totum continetur,
Unde mundus judicetur.
A book, written in, will be brought forth
In which is contained everything that is,
Out of which the world shall be judged.
— "Dies Irae," *Requiem Mass*

Michael O'Flaherty had friends in the police department and, the Monday after vespers, one of his cronies gave him a call. Michael phoned me that morning to fill me in. The autopsy had provided no surprises. The priest bled to death as the result of a massive wound to his throat. The murderer's weapon had nearly severed Father Schellenberg's spinal column. Blood and tissue samples did not show any alcohol, drugs, or toxins. He had been vested as if for Mass at the time, and wore his black clerical suit underneath. He had a wallet containing a few dollars in cash, and some identifying information. There was loose change in his pants pocket. The report described the odd collection of items I had seen: a swizzle stick from a local bar and a bunch of crumpled valentine cards. There were no names on the cards and no printed greetings, just the front flap with a heart and arrow picture.

At lunchtime I grabbed a pen and notebook and took a run over to St. Bernadette's to see if there were any new developments. I found Brennan in the auditorium of the choir school, sitting at the piano. He had a pair of half-glasses perched on his nose and a pencil clenched in his teeth. He picked out a melody and a few chords, then made notations in a music dictation book. Composing a new setting for the

Mass. I had heard some of it before. Now, I noticed, the music had a darker tone than I remembered.

I walked up to him and watched his fingers on the keys. "How have you managed to make such a seemingly ordinary series of notes sound so plaintive, so dolorous? What key are you in?"

"C minor. This is the 'Kyrie.' I'll repeat the progression in the 'Miserere Nobis.'"

If he had turned to his music to escape the concerns of this world, it was clear that he hadn't travelled very far. The tragedy was colouring his composition. Not surprising, perhaps: the "Kyrie" is a plea for God's mercy.

"How are the other people holding up?" I asked.

"They're going around like the walking wounded, which is to be expected. But they're determined to carry on with our program. I'm grateful for that, so I'll have to pull myself together and get to work. Come over to the rectory. Mike O'Flaherty went to the police station in the hopes of getting some more information. He'll be back any minute."

We left the school and crossed the street to the parish house. I followed Brennan into the priests' library, and sat down with him at a long cherry-wood table. Bookshelves rose to the ceiling along three walls of the room. I took out my notebook and uncapped my pen.

"So give me an outline of the day. What were people doing on Friday, leading up to vespers?"

"Does this mean you're on the case?"

"Aren't I always? Besides, what's the alternative? Sitting on my butt wondering what the real story is!"

"Well, that's a relief, because I can't see myself interrogating the very people who have paid to attend my college. Our lawyer, on the other hand, has no need to be so delicate."

"Exactly. So, tell me about the day of the murder."

"We had Mass in the morning, at nine. I had the impression at the time that the whole group, or nearly the whole group, was there, including Reinhold Schellenberg. Then everyone had a free day until it was time for Schellenberg's afternoon lecture. Which, as you know, he never gave because something came up. If we knew what came up, we'd be more than halfway to the truth about his murder. Anyway, most of our students went to Peggy's Cove on the bus, and we didn't see them again until vespers."

"Any unusual behaviour that morning?"

"Nothing I noticed."

"What about Communion? Did everyone receive? Would it stand out in a group like this if someone didn't come forward for the sacrament?"

"I see what you mean, but I simply didn't notice if there was anyone like that."

"Well, let's hope the police have a handle on who was where at the crucial time. Here's Mike. Good afternoon, Monsignor!"

"Good day to you, Monty."

"What did they tell you, Michael?" Brennan asked.

"The good news is that the vast majority of our students can be eliminated from suspicion. Of the fifty-six participants at the schola, only eight missed the bus trip to Peggy's Cove. Reinhold Schellenberg, six other men, and one woman."

"How many of the seven can account for their time in the afternoon?"

"None of them, unfortunately."

"Don't be telling us that, Michael!"

"It's true," O'Flaherty replied. "No, wait, one of them was in a tavern at the time of the murder, and has a witness to prove it. The estimated time of death was between two and four in the afternoon. The bus left for Peggy's Cove at one-thirty, with forty-eight of our students on it. The others were either in their rooms alone, or out shopping or walking by themselves. Or so they claim."

"Who are the seven besides Schellenberg?"

"William Logan, Father Enrico Sferrazza-Melchiorre, Father Fred Mills, Colonel Kurt Bleier, Brother Robin Gadkin-Falkes, Jan Ford, and Luigi Petrucci."

"I've met Sferrazza-Melchiorre and Bleier. Who are the others?"

"Well, you may have seen Jan Ford on opening day. She expressed some views on the liturgy and music that diverged somewhat from those of the director of the schola, our Father Burke here."

"Right, I remember her. Brother Robin? I never met him. Or Mills, Logan, and Petrucci."

"Brother Robin is a monk, as you can guess from the title."

"Same order as Schellenberg?"

"Well, a Benedictine, but not of the same stripe."

"Okay. Mills?"

"Fred Mills is a young priest who is a former student of Brennan's, when Brennan taught in the seminary. Somewhere in New York."

"So Brennan can fill us in on him."

"Fred Mills wouldn't kill a spider if it was advancing on his mother's handbag," Brennan avowed.

"Good. Logan?"

"A priest who left to marry. He taught with Brennan at the sem."

"Is his wife here with him?"

"Yes, though I haven't met her."

"So she wasn't on the bus trip."

"No, she must have been with Logan, wherever he was."

"And Petrucci?"

"I don't know anything about him, except that he's the one the police say was having a wee drop to drink at the crucial time. His nephew vouched for him. Petrucci is not a priest. He's a layman, obviously someone keenly interested in church music and liturgy."

"Surely some of the other six schola people have an alibi!" Brennan insisted.

"All but one of the others, anyway!" Michael said. "Well, I shouldn't assume. Perhaps there was more than one of them in on the killing."

"Kurt Bleier is here with his wife," I remarked. "Where was she that day?"

"On the bus trip."

"But he didn't go."

"No."

"Where is everybody staying, Mike? I know you have people spread out around the city."

"If Mike ever gets tired of being pastor to the flock at St. Bernadette's," Brennan said, "he can get a job as a logistics expert with the military. He's got people billeted in rectories, convents, college dormitories, private homes, and maybe cathouses for all I know. Need to find housing for an army of thousands? Call Michael O'Flaherty."

"Now, Brennan, it's only sixty people. Fifty-six."

"Well, you found places for them. I didn't even know where to begin."

"All right," I said. "Reinhold Schellenberg was staying here at the rectory." Mike nodded. "What about the other seven people you named?"

"Father Sferrazza-Melchiorre, Father Mills, and Brother Robin Gadkin-Falkes are also staying here. Jan Ford has a room at Mount Saint Vincent University. Colonel Bleier is at a bed and breakfast on Gottingen Street, and Mr. Petrucci is staying with his nephew in one of the south-end apartment buildings. William Logan has an arrangement out in the suburbs somewhere. House-sitting, perhaps. He and his wife set it up themselves."

"A key point," I said, "is that Stella Maris is not within walking distance of any other place in the city where people would normally be. There are a few businesses nearby, and the container pier. So Schellenberg had to have been driven there, either by the killer or by cab. The police will obviously be checking the taxi companies."

"Oh, yes, they're doing that."

"If he took a cab, he may have said something to the driver about why he was going there. Or, if not, there's always the hope the cab driver saw somebody, or something, of interest when he got to the church."

"Let us hope so, Monty."

"Now, about Father Schellenberg, Mike. What was his role in the Second Vatican Council?"

"He was a *peritus*, a theological adviser to one of the bishops from Germany. Many of the bishops leaned quite heavily on their theological experts when it came to formulating their positions. So these *periti* — some of them anyway — wielded a great deal of influence behind the scenes."

"Who was Schellenberg advising?"

"Bishop Rodl."

"What do you know about him?"

"He's dead now. Died probably fifteen, twenty years ago. He was among the group of Germans, Dutchmen, and Austrians who wanted significant changes in the church, in the Mass, and so on. They wanted a more ecumenical Mass. Less Catholic, is what they meant!"

"And Schellenberg provided the theological underpinnings?"

"To an extent, yes."

"So traditionalists might tend to blame him for what they see as the falling away, or the chaos, of the church after Vatican II."

"They might. But don't forget: he had a change of heart. Once he saw what was happening — much of which, to be fair to the Council, was neither foreseen nor intended — he started to backpedal and take up much more conservative positions on matters relating to the church and liturgy."

"Opening him up to an attack from the left."

"Afraid so, Monty." O'Flaherty nodded. "Did you know this, now, lads? There was a Saint Reinhold."

"Is that right?"

"Yes. I thought there was, so I looked him up."

"What did you find out?"

"He lived in the tenth century. Until they fished his body out of the Rhine River."

"He drowned?"

"No." O'Flaherty leaned forward. "He was murdered!"

"Jesus the Christ and Son of God!" Brennan exclaimed. "What do we have here? History repeating itself? Who killed him?"

"Construction workers."

"Construction workers. Why would they do that?"

"A dispute over a building project, I believe it was."

"Some things never change," I said. "Our firm has storage rooms filled with files on construction disputes. Was the saint in the building trades himself?"

"No. He was a Benedictine monk."

"Another Reinhold, another monk. This gets more bizarre by the day."

"The history of the church, Monty, is littered with people who died in the most macabre ways imaginable! Anyway, I'll take my leave of you gentlemen. I'm due for my rounds at the infirmary." He went on his way.

Brennan said: "We have to find out, obviously, who was seen with Schellenberg, who engaged him in conversation. Where do we begin?"

"We talk to everyone. We may get some useful information from the innocent, and some telling behaviour on the part of the guilty."

"Kurt Bleier strikes me as a very observant sort of a fellow. Perhaps we should start with him."

"Keeping in mind, of course —"

"That he may be the killer himself. But if he is, he's carrying around some religious baggage that is not evident to the senses. He was a police officer in East Berlin, part of an officially atheist state. If Bleier's the one, why do it here, where he sticks out like a square pri— like a sore thumb? And, a man like that, if he wanted someone out of the way, wouldn't he be cognizant of all sorts of lethal manoeuvres that would be much quicker and more — I don't know if discreet is the proper word but —"

"Discretion is not what this killer was after, Brennan. He was making a statement. A religious statement. That doesn't necessarily rule out an enforcer of an officially atheist regime in Schellenberg's native land."

✝

"Don't you look distinguished today, Collins!" It was Burke, who had just caught me coming out of a criminal trial in the Nova Scotia Supreme Court at the end of the day on Wednesday, decked out in my barrister's gown and tabs.

"Black and white becomes you as well, Father."

He shrugged as if to say *I'm always well turned out.*

"What brings you to the law courts?"

"There's been an arrest."

"Really! Who?"

"Brother Robin. You never met him."

"What does he look like?"

"Tall beaky fellow. Robin Gadkin-Falkes. As if you couldn't tell from the name, he's a Brit."

"How did the arrest come about?"

"Apparently, he was the last person anyone could remember talking to Father Schellenberg, shortly before Schellenberg went off on his own. The police questioned Brother Robin and obviously were not satisfied with what he had to say for himself. There's some physical evidence as well. I don't know what. He was arraigned this morning, and sent to the Nova Scotia Hospital for a thirty-day psychiatric assessment."

"No surprise there. When was he arrested?"

"Middle of the night."

"Good. So what do you know about this monk?"

"Not a thing. I can put a face to the name. That's it."

"No outbursts from him in the classroom?"

"No."

"Did you see him with Schellenberg?"

"Can't remember one way or the other. But somebody did."

As soon as they heard the news, Father Burke and Monsignor O'Flaherty had informed the schola that Brother Robin Gadkin-Falkes had been arrested and charged with the murder of Reinhold Schellenberg. The announcement was greeted with relief mixed with consternation that there had been a killer in their midst for the first week of the course. They rallied, though, and reassured Father Burke that they were willing and able to return to their work. Classes got underway again; Masses and prayers were said for the victim and the accused man. The international news media descended on the place and they were a nuisance, but everybody seemed to cope.

Brennan and I conceived the idea of inviting the schola people to a gathering later that week, in the hope that a social event might help ease the stress. It would be much more convenient for everyone if the locus were within walking distance of the school. At my old house, for instance, which was a short walk up Morris Street from St. Bernadette's. This meant negotiating with the mistress of the house, my estranged wife, Maura MacNeil.

I pulled up in front of her — formerly our — grey nineteenth-century house on Dresden Row. She met me at the door with a scowl on her face and a yellowish-brown stain all over the front of her white shirt.

"Did I come at a bad time?"

"Stuff it, Collins. I've had a long day. The baby has been fussing —"

I walked past her into the house. I did not want to hear about the baby. Not today, not ever. But I would have no choice. There he was now, a squalling bundle in the arms of my little girl, Normie.

"Hello, Normie sweetheart. Got your hands full, I see."

"Daddy! I got a hundred on my math, and Mrs. Vickers is giving me extra work! A grade ahead!"

"Well done, angel. I always knew you'd be a math whiz."

"Just like my grandpa, right?"

"Right."

"If Dominic ever stops crying I'm going to try to teach him some arithmetic. It's never too early for them to learn, you know."

"Well, three months is a little young, probably."

"Not when your own grandfather was boss of the whole math department at Saint Mary's University!"

"The university was Dalhousie, but you're right. My dad was chairman of the math department." *You're confused, though, about young Dominic's lineage.* I was not the baby's father. "Is Tommy around, sweetheart?"

"He's in the kitchen. Lexie was here." Normie lowered her voice and imparted some news. "She has new glasses. She says she doesn't think these frames suit my face."

"Is that right?" My son's girlfriend would no more criticize my daughter's glasses than my wife would welcome me at the door with a big wet kiss.

"Well, she agreed with me that even if they look nice there are lots of other kinds of frames that would go with my face."

Tom came in then. "Hey, Dad."

"Hi, Tommy. How's the lad?"

"Great."

While our daughter, Normie, didn't look like either parent, with her auburn curls and big, near-sighted hazel eyes, our son Tommy Douglas was a shorter, younger version of me, with dark blond hair, blue eyes, and a deceptively mild-looking boyish face. He was seventeen; she was eight. Normie's real name was Norma, after the Bellini opera; never make crucial decisions while you're still intoxicated — by music, or anything else. We never called her anything but Normie, though her big brother sometimes called her . . .

"Klumpf, if you want one of Lexie's brownies, you'd better come get one. There's only two left."

"Don't call me Klumpf. And can't you see I'm busy with the baby?

Save both brownies for me because you guys pigged out on all the rest. Go put my name on the tin!"

Klumpenkopf, so-called because of the clumps of tangles commonly found in her hair, glared at her brother until he went into the kitchen, presumably to identify the remaining brownies as the property of his sister.

My wife left the room, then returned, dabbing at her shirt with a wet towel. Maura was well above a size twelve and looked good that way, with dusky brown hair that fell to her shoulders and grey eyes that turned up at the outer corners. Laugh lines were visible by her eyes but she wasn't laughing now. An unexpected pregnancy at the age of forty-two would throw anyone off stride, even the formidable Professor MacNeil.

"Should you be wearing white?" I asked her.

"Is that a dig about my character, Collins?"

"I meant: shouldn't you put your white shirts away for the duration of your maternity leave? They're all going to be stained. You should remember that. I do."

"Yeah, yeah, I know."

"Mummy, can I put the baby down?" Normie pleaded. "He won't settle. Even for me. He usually calms right down when I hold him, Daddy, not like Tommy Douglas. Tommy's not much good with babies, I'm sorry to say." She didn't look sorry.

"I'll take him," Maura said, and carried him from the room.

Normie took something out of her jeans pocket then. "Daddy! Look at the pictures I took! You have to sit down to see them."

"Sure."

We sat side by side on the chesterfield, and she produced her snapshots. They showed Normie and the baby; Normie and her friend, Kim, dressed in devil costumes for Halloween; Tommy looking cool, wearing black-framed sunglasses and playing his guitar; and . . . what was this? A man holding the baby against his shoulder. Both were facing the same way, caught in profile, with the baby's little head nestled under the man's chin. They were both unaware of the camera. The baby's hair was almost as dark as the man's, which was shot through with silver on the sides. The man was Brennan Burke.

That brought back memories that were as embarrassing as they were agonizing. Memories of me in a tense, drunken moment following the announcement that my wife was pregnant by another man, me striking out at Burke, punching him in the eye. Up till then, I had never struck another human being in my life, except in self-defence. But those days and weeks after the announcement, which brought to a screeching halt my efforts to reconcile with Maura, were times of drinking, brooding, and recrimination. I was ninety-five percent certain the father of her child was her sometime paramour, Giacomo. So why had I lashed out at Burke? Well, it hardly mattered now. Except that whenever I looked at him I could see the damage to his left eye. I hoped he didn't think of it every time he saw himself in the shaving mirror. The eyelid turned down a bit at the outer corner. It gave him a certain tortured-artist look, which I suspected would not be unattractive to women — if he were looking for a woman — but I would go to my grave before I'd be fool enough to say so.

I shook myself out of it and returned to the present, and the reason for my visit: a social evening for the Schola Cantorum Sancta Bernadetta, in the wake of the brutal murder of its most illustrious guest. As it turned out, it wasn't difficult to talk Maura into hosting the party. She had heard enough from me and Brennan about the cast of characters to be convinced they warranted a close examination. What cinched the deal was that I would come over beforehand and fill the freezer with party snacks, so no cooking would be required on her part. Tom had already promised to take Normie to a movie that night, so they would miss the festivities, but otherwise it all clicked into place.

I stopped in at the rectory to finalize the plan with Brennan. When I got to his room he was on the telephone, and he waved me inside. "What?" he said to the person on the phone. "I don't know now, Bill. It's not often I'm called upon to supply the women for a party. Things didn't lighten up *that* much after Vatican II. I'll see what I can do."

"What was that about?" I asked when he had hung up.

"Billy Logan, here from Cleveland in the U.S. Have you met him?"

"I don't think so."

"A former colleague. We taught together at Sacred Heart Seminary in upstate New York. I began teaching there in 1979."

"Logan's the priest who left to get married?"

"Right. He has been 'laicized,' as they say."

"An ex-priest."

"Thou art a priest forever; the sacrament of Holy Orders imprints an indelible spiritual character on the soul. But, informally speaking, you're right. He left the priesthood a couple of years after I met him. He and his wife are here, staying in the house of a friend in the suburbs somewhere. So. Did you approach MacNeil about having the party at her place?"

"Systems are go-all-go. What were you saying on the phone about women?"

"Logan thought it would be nice if the schola people got to meet a few locals while they're here. I guess it didn't escape his notice that the students of the schola are predominantly male. That must be why he stressed women, to even things up. Not a bad idea. I'll pass the word around to some of the women at the church."

"MacNeil and I could invite a few of the people we know."

✝

So that Saturday night, the last day of November, I was answering the door of my old house as if I were still in residence. I admitted Brennan, who was in his clerical suit and collar. He arrived bearing several bottles of wine. Maura joined me in relieving him of the burden.

"Sacramental wine, I presume, Father?"

"All of nature is a sacrament, Professor MacNeil, and the vineyards of Tuscany are particularly rich in God's grace."

"Not in civvies tonight?"

"Had to meet a troubled parishioner and didn't have time to change."

"We'll have that collar off you before the night is done. Excuse me. I have to go down and get the finger food out of the freezer. I forgot to thaw it out."

She headed down to the basement. Her baby chose that moment to start whimpering and, within seconds, he was crying as if his little heart had been broken. After a few minutes of this, and a glance in my direction, Brennan went to the corner of the dining room where Dominic lay in his crib, reached in, and picked up the squalling baby. The child's dark hair was damp and his face red from crying. I could almost feel his frustration: an early lesson in "nobody understands me."

I wanted to go to him myself. It's hard not to fall in love with a baby, especially if you've been through the baby stage as a parent yourself. But the circumstances of his birth were, to put it mildly, a sore point. The pregnancy wasn't planned; that much I knew. But that did not make it any less painful for me. My wife now had three children, the last of whom was just as precious to her as my own. Try as I might, I could not see myself getting past this. Not that little Dominic was to blame, obviously. He was a sweet baby, and I often felt the urge to pick him up, play with him, get to know him. But so far, I had not been able to make the move.

Now, in Brennan's arms, the infant ceased his wailing. He gave a little gurgle of contentment, then fell peacefully asleep. Brennan placed him gently in his crib, and tucked a blanket around him.

The doorbell rang, and I found Father Sferrazza-Melchiorre on the doorstep, garbed, as always, in a soutane with a cape. He looked like a sinister figure from another time, making his entrance on the operatic stage. Two young boys struggled in his wake, burdened with overflowing bags. I recognized the kids as choirboys from St. Bernadette's. Before I had a chance to greet them, they had dumped their load and scarpered. I turned to see Maura coming up from the basement with two plates full of the frozen, store-bought food I had provided. She gawked at Enrico.

"You!" she began. "You make *him* —" she pointed to Brennan, standing in the hallway, looking as imperious as ever in his Roman collar "— look *so* low church! Who *are* you?"

"Permit me to introduce myself."

"Oh, I insist!"

"I am Father Sferrazza-Melchiorre. Please call me Enrico." He held out his hand, on which there was a large, ornate gold ring; he gently took her own hand and brought it to his lips.

"I'm Maura MacNeil."

"Piacere, signora!"

"Come in, Enrico. Are those bags full of groceries?"

"Yes. I have here all the ingredients for Italian antipasti. Hors d'oeuvres. If I may take command of your kitchen."

"I won't stand in your way." She turned to Burke: "Brennan! Were you telling tales about my cooking skills?"

"Em, no. Well, I may have said your training in Italian cookery was cut tragically short with the arrival of your latest child."

"Right. So maybe I should put this stuff back in the freezer."

"Allow me," Burke said, and relieved her of the platters.

She helped Enrico carry his bags into the kitchen, and left him to organize his purchases, then came over to me and whispered: "What's the story on this guy?"

Brennan joined us and answered: "There's a streak of, let us say, decadence that runs in his family. He's descended from a long line of Roman aristocrats. That's one side of the family. The other is Sicilian. He's an expert in ecclesiology. History of the church."

"Sounds dull," Maura said.

"That shows you haven't been paying attention, MacNeil. Church history is blood-curdling. War and scandal and schism, popes kidnapped, popes fathering large broods of children. Magnificent art and mendicant friars and warrior monks. Picture the Roman emperor Theodosius at the end of the fourth century, begging Saint Ambrose for absolution for his sins. The most powerful man in the world, stripped of all the accoutrements of royal power, bowing before an unarmed priest in his church. There's nothing insipid about any of it. The history of the Catholic Church is the history of Western civilization. Rumour has it Enrico's mother is descended from one of the Renaissance popes, but nobody knows for certain. Ask him; he just shrugs."

The object of our interest came by then, and I spoke up: "Father Sferrazza-Melchiorre, tell me. How on earth did you end up in Mississippi?"

"Eh, well, I had always felt that my family had been given so much. And others had so little. As a boy, I burned with the desire to become a missionary. But instead, I became a careerist. I did my studies, I received my doctoral degree, I was a teacher at the Lateran University and a bureaucrat in the Vatican. There was an incident — best forgotten — and it was decided that I should spend some time away from Rome. I seized upon this as an opportunity. This was God working in me, to bring me to the mission lands where I had always yearned to go. Alas, I did not have — *come si dice?* — the tolerance, the constitution for the equatorial rainforest. I was ill the whole time I was there. The local cuisine — No, I would rather not remember.

"But the African experience was valuable to me. And to my vocation. Because I met there a man and his family who were missionaries from the U.S., from the state of Mississippi. They belonged to one of the breakaway sects, and I found them so well-intentioned but also so . . . so deficient in their learning and in the message they sought so manfully to articulate to the African people." He shook his head. "Just a man and his Bible. You would think that would be sufficient, but no. Without tradition, without the church Fathers, without the centuries of philosophy and scholarship and interpretation, what do you have? Before I was airlifted out, too weak to raise my head, this man and his wife were kind enough to visit me in the infirmary. I asked him about their home and about the Catholic presence in Mississippi. The expression on his face was all the answer I required. The state of Mississippi was itself a mission land!"

"And how has it turned out?" Maura inquired.

"My work is far from accomplished."

"Oh, yeah? What's it like running a Catholic parish down there in — what's the name of the place?"

"It is called Mule Run."

"Oh, God," she muttered.

"Our church is at the end of Main Street, well, quite far out of the village really. But I see the local people frequently. I buy my provisions in the general store. They regard me with suspicious eyes there; they peer at me from the gun shop across the street. I am always made to feel like a stranger in the town. I did some work restoring the church, a small white wooden chapel. Charming in its own way. I brought over from Italy a little frieze of naked cherubs and I placed it over the door. One of my cherubs — a boy — soon came to grief. Someone must have attacked him with a chisel or perhaps the butt of a gun. There have been other desecrations. But —" a shrug "— hasn't it always been so?"

"How's the food?" Maura asked. "Do your parishioners have you over for Sunday dinner?"

He closed his eyes and a delicate shudder ran through his elegantly clad body. "One is always conscious that one is far, far from Rome. *Di più*, this place is what they call a 'dry town.' I had never heard of this custom but apparently some years ago they held a plebiscite, and decided there would be no spirits, no beer, no *wine* sold in the town! Wine, the drink of Jesus Christ himself! This is beyond my understanding. But of course the markets are overflowing with vegetables and meats so, when I have the time, I make a good Italian dinner for myself and my guests. Kind friends in Rome have kept me supplied with *vino rosso*."

"You're settling in then. You have people to talk to."

"Oh yes, there are wonderful people in the town, certainly. The language barrier can be daunting at times."

"But your English is perfect," Maura assured him.

"My English, yes, thank you. I studied English for many years. But the English spoken by the nativ — the local people, I find it difficult to interpret. They have a strong regional accent, you see. I wonder if you have ever been exposed to it. I hoped to find a few children who might wish to learn Italian, but I had no students. In fact, I have rarely even heard my name pronounced correctly there."

"Is that right?"

"Difficult for you to believe, Maura, I agree. Do you know what they call me? And I find I must accept it with graciousness."

"What do they call you?"

"My name is Enrico. The equivalent in English is Henry. I now know that the diminutive for Henry is Hank. So I am not Father Sferrazza-Melchiorre, but Father Hank."

Maura did her best to hide a smile, and patted him on the arm. "I'm sure you bear up better than most of us would."

A couple of Maura's friends came in, and more people arrived from the schola; some I recognized, some I didn't. The sleeping infant was a matter of interest to the guests, as I heard when I entered the dining room and caught part of a conversation among Sferrazza-Melchiorre, Burke, and a man I had seen but could not identify.

"Lei ha due maschi ed una femina," Burke said. I took that to mean he was telling Enrico how many kids we — no, Maura — had.

The third man looked at the baby and then pointedly at Burke. "If that little black-haired kid grows up with a great voice, you'd better get outta town."

Burke laughed. Uncomfortably, I thought.

Enrico Sferrazza-Melchiorre excused himself to start the party treats. I chatted with him for a few minutes, then went into the living room.

At the far end of the room, several people were gathered around a petite, skinny woman with big hair in a shade of ashy blonde; her face was tanned and creased. I heard her introduce herself as Babs Logan. Then she asked a question: "How many people in this room could use an extra fifteen hundred dollars a month?" People looked at each other uncertainly. "Could we have a show of hands? Don't be shy!"

When there was no response, she sought out a familiar face. "Brennan!"

His delayed reaction suggested his mind was far, far away. "Mmm?"

"Where's your clicker?"

"My what?"

"Your remote."

"My remote what?"

I stepped in with some crucial information. "Brennan doesn't have a television, Babs, let alone a VCR or anything else that involves the use of a remote control."

Babs stared at him in astonished disbelief. "No television? How do you talk to folks around the water cooler? What do you do with your time?"

He turned to me and muttered: "We'll never get *this* time back again, Collins."

"You may want to try somebody else, Babs," I suggested.

"Yes, well, okay. How about this young lady?" A woman nodded. "Where is *your* clicker?"

"Uh, I don't know."

"Bingo! We never know where our remotes are because when we're through with them we toss them on the couch, on the coffee table, on the floor. Or we put them on top of the TV. Where's that darn remote? Right?" Nods from a few of the guests. "So. Perfect example of where an accessory can save the day. I have a line of zany but practical remote holders that can be attached to a reclining chair. Others sit on the floor. The floor models, William?"

I could now put a name to the man who had advised Brennan to leave town. William Logan was short and wiry, with bristly reddish hair brushed back from his forehead. His posture, his jawline, everything about him suggested he didn't take any crap from anybody. I remembered seeing him at vespers. Now the ends of his mouth jerked up in the form of a smile, and he drew a number of items out of a carton.

"Vesuvius?" he asked.

"Yes! Let's start with Vesuvius! This is one of our most fun products. A remote holder that looks like the volcano at Mount Vesuvius outside of Rome!"

"Naples," Burke mumbled. Then he caught sight of the garish plastic object, blinked, looked again, and dropped his head into his left hand. He massaged his temples and contemplated, I suspected, the advantages of a well-timed volcanic eruption.

"We also have one — and this will be really popular with you folks — shaped like a monk's robe. Lift up his hood; out comes the remote. We've got one shaped like a cigarette pack —"

"Next time one of us gets up for a refill, we'll bring the bottle in," Burke said to me with quiet urgency.

Why wait? I got up, went to the kitchen, grabbed the bottle of Jameson's Burke and I were sharing, poured myself a shot, and downed it. I returned to the living room and filled his glass, then my own.

"— and fun, imaginative garage door opener holders as well," Babs was chirping. "My husband is in garage doors, and he can show you his brochures on those. William?"

William addressed the assembly. "How many of you can honestly say your garage door adds curb appeal to your home?"

The guests looked from one to another.

I spoke up again. "I think, William, that most of the local people live downtown. It may be that nobody has a garage at all. I can't speak for the visitors who are here for the schola, of course."

This prompted no response other than a pissed-off look from Logan to his wife. But Babs carried on. "That's okay! Not everybody has the space that comes with suburban living. But here's something everyone in this room can have: any product in my catalogue for forty percent off. Everyone also has the opportunity to sign up now to become an Accessoreez consultant, so you can host parties in your home state, wherever that may be. And make quick, impromptu interventions at other gatherings like the one tonight — we call these 'partymercials.' We like to say: Pitch your tent, make your pitch, and shut down before they pitch you out! So, get on board and earn extra income for that new patio furniture or little Johnny's college education! Those of you who are priests may not want to take up my offer, though it's too bad — I imagine you could use the extra income! But some of you ladies have the opportunity of a lifetime. If anyone wants to talk about a bright new future in home sales, give me a call or come see me at twenty-nine Loftingdon Mews."

Apparently nobody had ever heard of Loftingdon Mews, but Babs had a map ready, showing its location in a new suburb west of the city. "This is the home of one of my fellow consultants. We met at a sales convention in Vegas. She and her husband are spending the winter months in Florida, so she offered us their home while William is at the choir school. You can see she's done well! The advantages of a truly international sales organization!"

"*Gesù mio!*" The entire party turned as one, to see Father Sferrazza-Melchiorre staring dumbfounded at the Vesuvius gadget.

Brennan turned to him. "Better get out there and rattle those pots and pans, Enrico. They're trying to sell us a bunch of knickknacks — *ninnoli*. Now I know why he wanted me to round up some locals." He spoke *sotto voce*, but he was not quiet enough. William Logan had overheard, and the embarrassment on his face was excruciating to see.

Enrico returned to the stove, and the house soon began to smell like a fine Italian restaurant. People were drawn to the kitchen where the master chef had several pans and several conversations going at once without missing a beat. Finally, he pronounced himself satisfied, arranged his concoctions on their plates, and handed them around. We were offered salted cream puffs, gnocco fritto, salmon canapés, and truffle crostini. There was no prohibition in effect in this town, and we drank gallons of Italian wine. All of this breathed new life into a plan Burke and I had cooked up and which surfaced whenever the wine was flowing: he and I were determined to take a road trip in Italy, if we could both get away at the same time.

After we ate, we sat around in a blissful stupor until I saw Father

Hank looking at the door. I turned to see Monsignor O'Flaherty coming in. His face was a ghostly white, and he looked almost fearful as he peered into the room. I went to greet him.

"Evening, Mike! You missed a magnificent spread, but I'm sure we can come up with a few scraps for you."

"Who's here, Monty?" he whispered.

"Oh, well, quite a few from the schola, if that's what you mean. William Logan, Enrico Sferrazza-Melchiorre, lots of others whose names I've forgotten."

"The German?"

"No, he didn't come. Is everything all right, Mike?"

"Is there somewhere we could talk, with Brennan?"

"There's a little den upstairs."

So up we went, to a small room fitted with a comfy chesterfield, a television, and shelves overflowing with books. The room had a five-sided dormer with a banquette, which Normie had fashioned into a playground for her dolls, with a toy swing set and a merry-go-round. I gently put the toys aside so I could sit facing the two priests on the couch.

"What's wrong, Mike?"

"I've been to see Brother Robin."

"Really! Over at the hospital?"

"Yes, he's there on psychiatric remand."

"Right. And?"

His eyes shifted away; he seemed to have trouble getting started.

"Michael!" Burke exclaimed. "You're just after meeting the man who, apparently, murdered Father Reinhold Schellenberg at solemn vespers here in Halifax. And now you've nothing to tell us?"

"Why did you say 'apparently' just now, Brennan? Have you had some doubt about the, em, situation?"

"No, I just meant he hasn't been tried yet. And we've a defence lawyer in our midst! What's troubling you, Michael? Have you some doubt yourself?"

This was not the Monsignor O'Flaherty I had come to know: gabby, sociable, and more than a little fascinated by lurid crime.

"Why were you concerned about who's here tonight?" I asked him. "Why did you ask about Colonel Bleier? You don't think Brother

Robin is guilty, so one of the people in this house tonight could be the real killer? Is that it, Mike?"

He avoided my questions. "Perhaps you should go over and see him yourself, Brennan. And Monty, unless, well . . ."

"Unless he wants to confess to Brennan whatever he confessed to you. Which in some way has led you to question his guilt."

"I'm not saying that!"

No, the monsignor would not come out and say it. He couldn't. A priest can be excommunicated for revealing what he hears in confession.

"Who is representing him?" I asked.

"Saul Green."

"Saul would pay solid gold for a tape recording of whatever Gadkin-Falkes told you tonight, Michael."

He looked down at his hands. After a few moments he asked: "Are the children here tonight?"

"Tom and Normie are out. The baby is here. We should cut this short, you're suggesting."

"I don't know what to say, Monty. But I have to get back to the rectory. There are some things I want to do. Go over to see Robin," he urged us again, before making his exit.

"Jesus! What do you make of that, Brennan? Why isn't this Robin Napkin-Forks, or whatever his name is, raising holy hell over there if he's innocent? If he is and if he knows who really did it, and is protecting him, then that's the connection we should be looking for. We have to find out what's going on."

We went downstairs, and soon the party drew to a natural, uneventful conclusion.

But we didn't get in to see Robin when we tried to arrange a visit on Sunday. He had left instructions with the staff of the hospital that no one was to be admitted to his room.

Chapter 3

Quid sum miser tunc dicturus,
Quem patronum rogaturus,
Cum vix justus sit securus?
What then shall I say, wretch that I am,
What advocate entreat to speak for me,
When even the righteous may hardly be secure?
— "Dies Irae," *Requiem Mass*

The police had their suspect. But, as far as I was concerned, Michael O'Flaherty's nervously imparted hint was a bombshell: it was clear he had reason to believe Brother Robin was not the killer. The case was wide open. There was no doubt I'd be drawn into Burke and O'Flaherty's attempts to solve the murder, and not just because I was the schola's lawyer; my own curiosity would impel me to look into it. So I was anxious to start searching for another suspect before the trail got any colder.

I couldn't do that, however, until I dealt with suspects of my own, two clients who had been ordered by the court to have no contact with each other and who had just been arrested together in connection with the robbery of a credit union. I succeeded in getting them released from jail, but I had no confidence that they would comply with their bail conditions this time, any more than they had in the past.

When I finished with them on Monday, I stopped in at St. Bernadette's rectory long enough to collect the notes O'Flaherty had made of his conversations with the police, and read them as soon as I got home. There wasn't much to go on. He had already filled me in on the autopsy results, and on the schola students who had not gone to Peggy's Cove on the afternoon of the murder.

The notes told me that the police had established who had rented a car upon their arrival, who had been picked up by Burke or O'Flaherty, and who had taken a cab or bus from the airport to wherever they were staying in Halifax. Of the people without an alibi, only Kurt Bleier had arranged for a car, a black Japanese compact he picked up at the airport when he flew in on November 16. He returned it two weeks later. William Logan and Luigi Petrucci both drove up from the U.S. in their own vehicles. All our other suspects had relied on taxis, public transportation, or lifts from the locals.

I saw an excerpt from a police interview with the taxi driver who carried Reinhold Schellenberg to the scene of his death:

> *Yes, this is the fellow I picked up at St. Bernadette's rectory on Friday. I thought he was either Dutch or German.*
> *What time was this?*
> *Two-thirty-five in the afternoon.*
> *What did he say to you?*
> *Just asked me to take him to Stella Maris Church. I said: "Are you sure you got the right church, Father? That place is closed down." And he said it was right, that sometimes solitude is what a person needs. So I said: "You're going pretty far out of your way to be alone!" He kind of laughed and told me it wasn't him that needed peace and quiet. It was somebody else. And no, before you ask me, he didn't say who.*

The police interviewed everyone working near Stella Maris, at the container terminal and the handful of businesses close by. Nobody saw anyone at the church. Cars went in and out of the parking areas but this was normal, and no one reported anything exceptional. There was one woman who at first looked promising. Clara MacIntyre. She had parked in a lot near the church so she could take her dog for a walk along the top of the peninsula. She thought perhaps she had heard something in the church but, on questioning, she could not provide the police with any information they could use. I picked up the phone, rang Mrs. MacIntyre, and asked if I could pay her a call. I didn't have much hope of a breakthrough; it's just that we didn't have anything else.

Clara MacIntyre was in her early sixties and lived in the Hydro-stone area of the north end. If you look down on the neighbourhood from the Needham Park hill, the row houses with their chimney pots and narrow back lanes will make you think of England, especially on a soft rainy evening like this, the first Monday in December. Mrs. MacIntyre had one of the big stand-alone houses at the end of the street across from the park, a location ideal for a dog owner. She walked her little cocker spaniel, Dewey, several times a day in the park or around the neighbourhood. But every once in a while she treated Dewey to a jaunt through Point Pleasant Park at the southern tip of the Halifax peninsula, overlooking the Atlantic Ocean, or Seaview Park at the northern tip, overlooking the Bedford Basin. The salt air perked him up, she said. The dog sat at her feet, and she rubbed his silky ears as we spoke.

I explained that I was the lawyer for the Schola Cantorum Sancta Bernadetta, and that I was doing a bit of investigating on the schola's behalf.

"But they got the person! Are you looking for someone else?"

I didn't answer her directly, but said: "We'd like as complete a picture as we can get of the circumstances surrounding the murder."

"Okay."

"So, on Friday, November 22, you and Dewey went to Seaview Park."

"Yes, we did."

"How did you end up near Stella Maris Church?"

"Well, there was what I call an irresponsible pet owner on the loose at Seaview Park that day. He had two Rottweilers, lovely dogs if they'd been properly brought up — I don't fault the dogs — but they came bounding after Dewey. I thought they were going to have him for lunch. This was the second day in a row they were there. We had been up there Thursday afternoon as well, and we enjoyed our walk until this man and his dogs appeared and ruined our outing. We left. We tried again on Friday. But no, the Rottweilers bore down on Dewey again. I scooped him up and glared at the owner. He laughed at us.

54

That was it for me. But it was lovely and sunny out, and Dewey and I weren't ready to call it a day. On the way back to my car I looked up, noticed the spires of Stella Maris, where I'd made my first communion as a girl. I said to Dewey: 'How about a walk around God's house on the hill?' That sounded just fine with him, so off we went." She smiled down at the dog.

"So you parked where, behind the church?"

"No, there's a small parking lot behind a white building, a city building of some kind, at the top of the hill. From there I walked across the grass to the church."

"Then what?"

"We went for our walk down by the church and along the hill there."

"You didn't go into the church."

"Oh, no. I assumed it was locked. Even though they're tearing it down. What a shame. But no, I just walked around it."

"And you heard something?"

"I thought I did. I thought I heard voices."

"Coming from the church."

"Well, I thought so. But when the police questioned me I had to admit there were voices I could hear from the container terminal. And someone was unloading a truck at one of the businesses nearby. So now I have to wonder whether the voices I heard came from the church at all."

"I understand. Could you make out any words?"

"No."

"Could you tell anything about the tone?"

"It seemed they were speaking loudly but it wasn't loud to me, if you understand what I mean. It was windy, and there were other noises, so the voices were faint by the time they reached my ears, but it sounded like yelling. Does that make sense?"

"Yes, I think I know what you mean."

"But, as I say, it could have been from somewhere else. And I couldn't catch the gist of it anyway."

"Was it English?"

She looked up from petting the dog. "I don't know. I didn't even think about it. I'm sorry."

"That's all right. So then what happened? You had your walk and went back to your car?"

"Yes, I heard the voices when I passed the church the first time. We had our walk around. Dewey found an injured seagull farther down the hill so that occupied him for a while. Then we returned to the car."

"How long were you there, do you think?"

"Twenty minutes maybe."

"What time was this?"

"Three, three-thirty or so."

"And you didn't see anything unusual around the church on your second pass by."

She shook her head. "No, just got in the car and started for home. I nearly got hit, but that could happen anywhere."

"Nearly got hit by —"

"Another car in the parking lot. I had just backed out of my space and was getting ready to leave the lot. He pulled out in front of me. I guess he didn't see me, with the sun in his eyes. And the wipers flapping."

"Wipers?"

"Yes, it was funny. The sun was so bright, it reflected off his windshield when he pulled out. That's probably why he didn't see me driving out of the lot. He was in a hurry and for some reason he had his windshield wipers on."

"Maybe he was cleaning the windshield."

"I don't think so. It was a nice, clean car. And he didn't have the water spraying or anything like that. Just had his bright lights and his wipers on, in the blinding sun!" She shrugged. "But we didn't collide. No harm done. I got Dewey home and fixed him a nice supper after his outing."

"Thanks, then, Mrs. MacIntyre. I appreciate your speaking with me."

"Sorry I couldn't be more helpful."

"That's quite all right."

I gave Dewey a pat on the head on my way out.

✝

I called Brennan after work the next day, Tuesday, gave him a quick précis of my talk with Clara MacIntyre, and asked him how we should approach the people we had come to regard as suspects.

"Let's start with the least likely, simply because I know where he is right now."

"Who is it? Why do you say 'least likely'?"

"Because I've known him for years. Fred Mills. The schola is finished for the day, so who knows where the others are. Which makes me ask myself — not for the first time — why the person guilty of the murder would stay around."

"Because to leave would immediately cast the person in a suspicious light. I know a couple of students left the program — it was in the police notes Mike gave me — but they were people who had been on the Peggy's Cove bus trip, so they were above suspicion. The guilty party feels he has to stick around in order to look innocent, but he must find it agonizing to do so."

"He or she."

"Right. And the person may also feel compelled to monitor events as they unfold here, see how the case against Brother Robin holds up. Who knows? Anyway, let's go find your 'least likely' suspect."

"Fred said he was going to watch the children rehearse for the Christmas pageant, so let's meet up with him there. This is no doubt the first time in his exemplary life that Freddy will have been asked for his alibi."

"Maybe so, but we have to check him off the list."

†

The rehearsal was taking place in the basement of St. Bernadette's Church. Breeze block walls were painted a glossy beige, the floor was a streaky brown, blue, and cream-patterned linoleum, there was a small stage at one end and a kitchen at the other; the room could not be anything other than a church basement. We were nearly knocked off our feet by a little boy with a white and green hotel towel on his head, a shepherd's crook wielded like a sabre in his hand. He looked up in alarm at Burke and kept on running. Then we were hailed by a trim, athletic-looking man in his mid-thirties, with cropped blond hair and the handsome, friendly face of an all-American boy. He wore a tan cardigan over his clerical shirt and collar. He waved us over to a row of grey metal folding chairs, where the audience would be sitting on the big night.

"Monty Collins, Father Fred Mills. Fred was a student of mine at the seminary in upstate New York."

"Lucky you!" I exclaimed.

"You should have known him in those days," Mills said. "Before he mellowed with age."

"Let me see if I have this right. You knew a version of Brennan Burke that was less mellow than he is now and yet you willingly came to see him again."

"I'm not the only one. Even Billy Logan showed up. Bill was teaching at the sem when Brennan arrived there," Fred explained to me. "I sent Bill the schola's brochure with an invitation to sign up, tongue-in-cheek. And he's here! Well, have a seat. The drama is about to begin."

It couldn't hurt to catch a bit of the show. The alibi would hold for a few minutes longer, if it held at all. A young woman stood beside a cardboard replica of a stable. She called a blue-veiled girl and brown-blanketed boy to their places. "Kayla, come sit by the manger. Zachary, stand beside her. Beside her! Don't be shy." The blessed couple moved into place, as half a dozen shepherds abided in the fields of linoleum.

The names were new — in my day, Mary and Joseph were Mary Eileen and Timmy — but otherwise there was nothing new under the sun. Or was there?

The woman stood to the side, opened her Bible, and began to read: "The king, the one who they called Augustus, made a rule that there would be a numbering of all the world."

"Hold it right there," Burke demanded. "It's Mrs. Kavanagh, do I have that right?"

"Yes, Father."

"Was the one *whom* they called Augustus one of many kings of Rome at the time? Whatever happened to 'There went out a decree from Caesar Augustus'?"

"I don't know, Father. This is the Bible they gave me to use."

"Who?"

"The parish council."

"Well, I'll have a word with them. It's no fault of yours, Mrs. Kavanagh. Carry on."

Things went from bad to worse when the baby was born. "And she wrapped him in bands of cloth, and put him in the place where the animals had their food."

"I have to stop you again there, Mrs. Kavanagh." Burke's eyes swept the scene, taking in all the children. "Who can tell me why Mary would wrap her baby in bands of cloth? Why not put him in rugby shorts and a T-shirt?"

"I know, Father, I know!"

"And what would your name be?"

"Jeremy."

"All right, Jeremy, tell us why."

"Because they weren't invented yet!"

"Exactly. What did they wrap the newborn babies in two thousand years ago?"

"I don't know."

The catechism teacher jumped in at that point and said: "They don't know what swaddling clothes are or what a decree is, if that's what you mean, Father."

Wrong thing to say. "You know what they are, don't you, Mrs. Kavanagh?"

She laughed. "Yes, I do."

"I do, too," Burke said. "How do you and I know all that, Mrs. Kavanagh?"

"We're grown-ups, Father."

"We didn't learn this stuff as grown-ups, though, did we? Somebody explained to us when we were very young children what the words in the Christmas story meant. And that's what's going to happen here. So instead of not teaching them, and then removing the words they haven't been taught, and pretty soon having no words at all we can use, we're going to teach them the words and put those words back where they belong."

"Um, well, I only have the children for another half hour, Father. Then I'm not in again until next week. But I could —"

"I won't trouble you about it any further, Mrs. Kavanagh. This is a situation not of your making. I'll take the children myself for an hour after Mass on Sunday. Then we'll go out for hot fudge sundaes to ruin their lunches and get their mothers' knickers in a twist." Apprehension turned to joy among the cast. "And when you see them next week they'll know all about Caesar Augustus and swaddling clothes. And that the animals had their food in something called a 'manger,' as in 'Away in a Manger.' And I shall provide you with a Bible that tells the story in language we can all be proud of."

"That went well," Fred Mills remarked when the rehearsal was over, and the teacher had shepherded the children out.

"If they want things to go well," I replied, "if they want the Father Burkes of this world to remain benign and good-humoured and stay out of everybody's hair, they should never attempt to dumb down the Bible. Or the liturgy. Or the music."

"Now they know. So, what brings you gentlemen to call on me today?"

"My lawyer and I are doing a bit of investigating," Burke explained.

"I thought that was all done. Brother Robin under arrest, end of story."

"That's probably it, you're right," I agreed. "But it will help wrap things up if we can account for everyone else's whereabouts that afternoon. That will make the case against Robin all the more solid."

"I see."

"Right. So we're trying to place everyone the day of the murder."

"You want my alibi."

"Alibi is merely a Latin word that means 'elsewhere,'" I responded.

"And that's where I was. Elsewhere."

"And that's all you're going to tell us?"

"No. I can also tell you I was nowhere near Stella Maris Church that afternoon, and I did not take an axe to Father Schellenberg."

"And that's it?"

"That's it. Now, let me give you a little vignette or two about your friend Father Burke."

"He knows more than enough about me already."

"He was never a student of yours, Brennan, so he doesn't have the full picture. We were all getting along just fine at Sacred Heart Seminary. Then we received distant early warning signals about this hard-ass priest who was coming to terrorize us. And we also heard absolutely hair-raising tales about his father! Everything from organized crime connections to Irish Republican derring-do. Don't know how much of it was true." He looked at Brennan and waited. Nothing. "Have you met his father, Monty?"

"Mm-hmm."

"Really! So, what's the story?"

"My lips are sealed."

"There is something behind it. I knew it! Anyway, back to the sem. If we thought things were lightening up in the 1970s, we had reckoned without Brennan Burke."

"And a proper thing too," rejoined Burke.

"The first thing he did was start quoting from the *Summa Theologiae* in Latin."

"*Summa Contra Gentiles.* You obviously weren't listening."

"There was hardly anybody in our class who could understand you."

"As I discovered. Don't get me going on what passes for education these days."

"We won't."

"I'm on my way out," Burke announced, and stood up. "Have to see some of Monty's clients at the Correctional Centre."

"How many times do I have to tell you, Brennan? If they're in jail, they can't be clients of mine. What kind of a defence lawyer would I be if I let my clients be sent to jail?"

"You're delusional, Collins. But I could be wrong. The same was said of the great mystics, and they've stood the test of time."

"You still minister to prisoners, do you, Brennan?" Fred asked.

"Yeah. Keeps me out of the hospitals, ministering to the sick! I'm sure there's nothing left to be said about me, so ask Fred about his former calling."

"What was that?"

"Fred is brilliant on the baseball diamond."

"Oh?"

"Yeah, I played a season with the Kansas City Royals before I followed my true calling."

"Are you serious? Must have been hard to give up a major league baseball career."

Mills shrugged. "This is where God wants me."

"I still say you could have done both," Burke said.

"Not this again." It must have been an old argument between them.

Burke gave us a farewell salute and started up the stairs. He nodded to a man who was on his way down — William Logan.

"Freddy! I heard I could find you down here."

"Hi, Bill. Come have a seat."

He sat and turned to me. "Have we met?"

"Briefly. At the party at my wife's place. You and Mrs. Logan put on a little, um, product demonstration."

"Yeah, yeah. Babs gets these ideas in her head. What a flop. So what's up?"

"Fred was recounting his first meeting with Brennan Burke. You used to teach with Brennan, I understand, Bill. When you were Father Logan."

"Yeah, I have all the luck. Things were pretty laid-back at the sem in those years. The guy Burke was replacing was the kinda guy who'd let the students do self-evaluations, mark their own papers. Don't worry about how they're written, that sort of approach. Then, in mid-term, he was out and Burke was in. Burke had Freddy quaking in his boots."

"True. I was given the task of introducing him to the other semi-narians but I hardly dared speak to him. To me he was intimidating and almost — I don't know, I guess 'exotic' isn't quite the word — anyway there I was, little Fred Mills from middle America, never been anywhere, and here was this big black-Irish *force* thrust upon us. Someone whose family was said to have fled Ireland in the middle of the night, and emigrated to Hell's Kitchen in New York. And he had that clipped sort of accent that made me rethink everything I had ever heard about the twinkling-eyed, charming Irish. What was he going to do, shoot our kneecaps off if we faltered in the fourth con-jugation of our Latin verbs? One guy stood up to him, though, that first week —"

"Yeah, me. I stood up to him, in case nobody remembers."

Fred continued as if Logan had not interrupted. "It was another Irishman, wouldn't you know? Father Burke was berating us for being slack in our work, and this Irish guy in the class, Fingal MacDiarmid, let fly at him in a tongue I had never heard. Irish Gaelic. Well! Burke's eyes absolutely bored holes into him. He ordered MacDiarmid to stay behind after class. When Fingal tried to leave with the rest of us, he heard a bark from the front of the room. 'MacDiarmid! Sit!' Fingal kind of hesitated, then put on a brave front and sat right on the corner of Burke's desk. Burke told him that, like most Irishmen these days, he had only a smattering of the old language but he wanted to learn more.

"'That's where you come in, MacDiarmid. That's your assignment this term.'

"'You mean I'm going to teach you?'

"'You are. Yes.'

"Of course MacDiarmid thought this would be in place of some of his other work, but no such luck. 'We're not children here, Mac-Diarmid, and life's not fair. My room, Wednesday evenings. I'll bring the Irish, you'll bring the Gaelic. Off you go now.' And he said something in Irish that even Fingal had never heard. But he put it together. It was something vulgar, and Fingal turned around and stared at him. Burke just laughed and waved him off. Anyway, they got together on Wednesday evenings, drank copious amounts of Irish whiskey, and Fingal taught him some Irish. Burke returned the favour and tutored him in Latin."

"MacDiarmid was an asshole!" Logan asserted.

"Why do you say that, Bill? He was a great guy."

Logan left the subject of MacDiarmid and took a swipe at Burke instead. "Brennan was such a throwback!"

"Oh?"

"Yeah. Most of the guys teaching at the sem were letting their hair down, wearing jeans, cowboy boots. And there was Burke, always in a soutane or a clerical suit and collar. Like, what year is this, Brennan, 1979 or 1279? He's one of these guys who thinks the way the church does. In terms of centuries. What was good for the church five hundred years ago? What will be good for the church a hundred years from now?"

"Maybe he thinks some things don't change. Or shouldn't," Fred replied. "Anyway, I have things to do. Nice to meet you, Monty. See you later, Bill."

"Listen, Freddy. What I came down here for — Do you want to go out for a beer and a bite to eat tonight? Babs has some of the neighbours coming over. I can't stomach another sales party. So what do you say? Boys' night out?"

"Sounds good, Billy."

"So, why are you here, Bill?" I asked after Fred had left us. "I wouldn't think this program would be of much interest to you. And if you don't like Burke —"

"Oh, I like him well enough. He's a character, no question. As for the program, hard to say why I signed up. Maybe I just find the old rituals entertaining. And some of the music is gorgeous. No getting around that. I'm between engagements right now."

"What have you been up to since you left the priesthood? Do you have a family?"

"Don't talk to me about family! I'm divorced, my ex has the kids, and my new wife is starting to get a wistful look in her eyes whenever we pass the baby boutiques in the mall. Women! You can't live with them and — take it from one who lived the life — you can't live without them."

"No regrets then, eh? About leaving the priesthood?"

"No! God, no. So, how long have you been practising law?"

"I'm past the twenty-year mark."

"Like it?"

"It has its moments. Has its aggravations too."

"Must be a few bucks in it."

"It's all right. But I do a lot of criminal work, so it's sometimes hard to collect my whole fee. And I've given up most of my night and weekend work to be with my kids."

"Yeah, well, there's more to life than the almighty dollar, I always say. Burke likes the smell of money, if I remember correctly."

"What? Are we talking about the same guy? He couldn't care less about money. Anything he gets, he gives away. 'Bible tells me so' is his attitude."

"You wouldn't say that if you'd seen him kissing up to Carson Whitehead."

"Who's he?"

"He's a very wealthy man who lives about two miles from the seminary where Brennan and I were teaching. Made his money — still does, I suppose — manufacturing all kinds of unsavoury products used in law enforcement around the globe. Whitehead hosted this extravaganza at his country club. Invited everyone from the area, including the priests and seminarians. I left as soon as I could, but not before I saw Burke topping off Whitehead's glass and treating him to his Irish charm. It made me sick."

"I've never seen Burke suck up to anybody, rich or otherwise."

"You had to be there."

"Okay. While I have you here, Bill — I'm the lawyer for the schola and I've been helping Brennan and Monsignor O'Flaherty, trying to gather some more facts about the murder."

"How come? You've got a Limey sitting there in a straightjacket, police say he did it. That's good enough for me."

"Well, as you say, he's in a psychiatric hospital. We'd like to be sure his version of events will stand the test of time."

"Oh, Christ, don't tell me you think he didn't do it!"

"Oh, he probably did. We're just trying to tie up loose ends. Make sure everyone else can account for their time."

"You mean you're checking for alibis."

"Just a formality. So, what did you do that day?"

"Went out and about. Ate lunch, did some exploring."

"On foot or by car?"

"I was with my wife in the car."

"Where did you go?"

"Around. Looked at the city, did some shopping."

"Where did you shop?"

"Downtown. And a mall."

"Which mall?"

"I don't frigging know. Just a mall like all the other damn malls the wife drags me into."

"Did you buy anything?"

"Spent money left and right. The usual crap people buy and don't need."

"Like what?"

"To tell you the truth, I don't remember. What's the difference?"

"None, if you didn't get an axe or something else that can be connected with the murder."

"I sure as hell didn't. I just bought some trinkets for my kids. They want this, they want that. Always something."

"Where's the stuff you bought?"

A hesitation, then: "I mailed it home."

"That day?"

"Yeah. No, I think it was a couple days later. I don't know exactly. Anyway, I have to get a move on. See you later."

I hadn't made much progress. I didn't have the resources to check the malls and every shop downtown to see whether anyone remembered William and Babs Logan. I wondered how much of this the police had done. Not much, I guessed, before they homed in on Robin Gadkin-Falkes.

✝

That evening I got a call from Brennan and I recounted my conversation with Logan.

"That's why I'm calling. It could be Logan, it could be any one of the people who can't give an account of their whereabouts. We should question them all, definitely. But every one of these people is from overseas or the U.S.A. How much can we realistically expect to learn about them?"

"We can't do background checks or anything like that. We don't have the resources the police have, Brennan."

"I know, I know. And, from their point of view, they've got their man. So what can we do? Do you know of anyone who can help us?"

"Why don't you have a word with Monsignor O'Flaherty? He has friends in law enforcement circles."

"I'll do that."

"If he can't come up with anything, I'll see what I can do."

✝

I was not satisfied with the answers Fred Mills had given us with respect to his whereabouts the day of the murder. In fact he had not provided an answer at all. So I wanted to try again. But I would lead with another subject of conversation. Thursday morning I found Fred bent over his books in one of the classrooms in the choir school.

I said to him: "I got quite an earful from your old friend Billy Logan. He took the opportunity to sound off about Brennan, and I have to say I didn't even recognize the man he was talking about."

"What did he say?"

"He tried to suggest Brennan sucks up to the high and mighty. Which I find hard to believe. He doesn't try to curry favour with the bishop, I know that much. And money is not a motivating factor in his life, so —"

"I suppose this was the Carson Whitehead wingding at the country club."

"That's right."

"Billy went around telling anyone who would listen that Burke was toadying up to Whitehead. He neglected to mention the outcome."

"Which was what?"

"We had all been invited to the dinner and dance. The priests, the seminarians, the butchers, the bakers, the candlestick makers. Whitehead was strutting around, playing the squire. He laid on this party for the whole town. He's virtually a teetotaller, likes to stay in control at all times. But Burke had him hammered by the end of the night. Fetching him drinks, telling him tall tales about growing up poor and starving in Ireland. To hear him, you'd think the Burke family was reduced to eating grass."

I didn't respond. From what I knew, the Burkes had not been starving in Ireland. Mills laughed when he saw the confusion in my face.

"Not the way you heard it, right?"

"Well, I know they had it rough for a while when they washed up in Hell's Kitchen, after their hasty departure from the old country."

"I never knew what prompted that departure. Do you?"

"I can tell you this much. Brennan's father is a formidable man. If you met him, you wouldn't want to meet the kind of guys who would propel him from the country in the middle of the night."

Fred's eyes were wide; he was longing to ask for more, but discretion held him back. When I was not forthcoming, he returned to his story.

"So anyway, Brennan was telling Carson Whitehead how poor they all were in his village."

"His village being the city of Dublin."

"Not the way Carson heard it. The villagers were all so 'porr' that, if it hadn't been for the man in the Big House — the kindly Anglo-Irish aristocrat in the stately home on the hill — all the 'childer' would have wasted away for lack of nourishment. But this one good man, Lord Sun-Shines-Out-His-Arse, set up a food bank on the grounds of the estate, fed the people, and fed them well, too! No thin gruel for the good people of Ballybegob. They ate nearly as well as himself, and were glad of it, bless his soul! Brennan worked on Whitehead till he came around to Brennan's way of thinking."

"About what?"

"Whitehead's newly conceived charitable donation and tax write-off."

"Burke dunned money out of him for the church."

"No, not the church. We wouldn't be seeing a cent of it. It was a soup kitchen and food bank that the area sorely needed. Whitehead woke up the next morning convinced of two things: he'd never touch alcohol again, and he was the great white hope of the local poor. Brennan had done such a job on him that he — Whitehead — believed the food program was his own idea. And the cream on the top was the way Brennan had appealed to his vanity: Whitehead would put on the best spread in town. So not only were the poor going to eat; they were going to tuck in to a feast. The local gentry, and ladies who lunch, would be dishing it up alongside Father Burke and some other guys he dragooned into volunteering. It was a master stroke on Brennan's part."

"That's what Billy Logan missed. Or, more likely, chose to ignore. Bill was kind of the cool guy on campus, till Brennan showed up and didn't give a damn about being cool and got all the attention anyway. Billy wasn't there when Burke came down from the head table, sober as a Baptist, and said out of the corner of his mouth: 'My work is done.' Then he muttered a little comment about Whitehead: 'Feckin' arsehole thinks the famine was in *nineteen* forty-seven.'"

"That sounds more like the Brennan I know." Now, down to business. "Fred."

"Yes?"

"Where were you on the afternoon of the murder? You must have given the police your whereabouts."

"Yes, I did, and they haven't come after me with handcuffs, so they were obviously satisfied."

"Exactly. Why don't you tell me, and I'll get out of your hair."

"I was at a lecture, at the Atlantic School of Theology."

"Oh. Beautiful spot they have, eh? Right on the water."

"The wa — yeah, on the water. Though we didn't have much time to admire the view. There was a series of speakers, and we got deeply into the subject of the apostolic succession, the Petrine primacy, the deposit of faith, and all that stuff."

"Why didn't you tell me this in the first place?"

"Because I'm innocent. I didn't think there was any need to belabour the point."

"All right. Thanks, Fred. Appreciate it."

"Okay, Monty. See you later."

I left the school and went back to my office, where I settled down once again to the day's quota of legal work. The two guys I got released on bail Monday had breached their conditions already, and were back in the slammer. I was fed up with them, and made a call to a younger lawyer to handle the next bail hearing. I had just completed the arrangements for that when I got a call from Monsignor O'Flaherty.

"Good day to you, Monty!"

"Morning, Michael. What's up?"

"Brennan is concerned about us being out of things with respect to the investigation; he's thinking I can help out with my contacts in police circles. And indeed I can! I've asked Moody Walker to give us a hand."

"Oh?" Sergeant Emerson Walker had retired from the Halifax Police Department a few years before. He and O'Flaherty were cronies and met frequently for coffee.

"What did Brennan have to say about that?"

"Em, well, he remained tight-lipped, shall we say."

That wasn't surprising. Walker once suspected Brennan Burke of a very serious crime. Burke had moved to Halifax two years ago. A few months after he arrived, two young women were murdered. For various reasons, Moody Walker's suspicions had led him to Burke. I was hired to defend him, and I secured an acquittal when I tracked down the real killer. I had run into Walker a few times since then in Tim Hortons and other places, and we had never alluded to the murder trial.

"We need another set of eyes and ears, Monty," Michael O'Flaherty said now, "and Walker tells me he's going into business as a private investigator. The police have Brother Robin. So they won't be following our lead in other directions, at least not right away. Moody can open doors for us that we can't open ourselves. He has contacts with overseas law enforcement agencies, for one thing."

"Yes, I see what you're saying."

"So, em, Moody is coming over this morning to have a look around. To 'eyeball some of the suspects,' as he put it. Could you, perhaps, accompany him for awhile today?"

"Sure I will, Mike. I'll be free in an hour or so."

Chapter 4

Emerson "Moody" Walker, our retired sergeant, was a compact man in his late fifties, with cropped greying hair and seen-it-all brown eyes. Early that afternoon I escorted him to Stella Maris Church, the murder scene, which was no longer cordoned off. The demolition had been postponed because of the investigation.

"You were doing what over here, Collins, when the body was discovered?"

"It was a prayer service. Chanting, candles, incense. The usual."

"Usual. Right. Why can't the RCs just have someone bawling at them from the pulpit on Sunday and leave it at that, like everybody else? He was found here?"

"Yes." I described the scene, and what I recalled about the various participants. When Moody had seen enough, we departed for the schola.

"What's the name of this place again? The schola? Couldn't they just call it a school?"

"It's Latin, Moody. You know, like 'Nova Scotia.' This might be a good time to see some of the suspects for yourself. They've all signed up for a series of seminars. We can sit in and observe."

"Yeah, I might learn something. Like whether putting a statue of the Virgin Mary in a bathtub on your lawn is a mortal sin or a ticket to heaven."

We seated ourselves in the back row of the classroom and tuned in to the debate.

"I know we'll never agree, Father Burke, on the knowability or unknowability of the *Ding-an-sich*," an intense-looking young priest was saying, "but —"

"You can't just say 'but' and move on," Burke interrupted. "You have to stop and grapple with what you're implying here. If we follow Kant in saying that the ultimate reality is the *Ding-an-sich*, the thing-in-itself, and that the Kantian categories of the mind apply only to the phenomenal world — the world as it appears to us — then we can have no knowledge of reality. It leads to what Jacques Maritain called the abdication of the mind. The philosophy of common sense, on the other hand, was synthesized in the thirteenth century, and we'd do well to heed what Thomas Aquinas had to say. Aristotle and Thomas teach us that the thing-in-itself *is* knowable. Being is intelligible to the human intellect; in fact, being is the formal object of the intellect."

"But the ideas of Kant pertaining to —"

"Be careful with that word 'ideas,' now, or we'll be back to Plato," a middle-aged woman admonished with a wide smile.

"By ideas, do you mean ideas *id quo* or *id quod*?" Burke asked.

"I don't know what you're saying," the young priest protested.

"Another reason to restore the teaching of Latin in the seminaries. I just meant that ideas are that by means of which — *id quo* — we know, and not that which — *id quod* — we know directly. But back to the propositions you raised . . ."

I turned to Moody Walker and raised an eyebrow.

"What the hell are they talking about?" he rasped, the picture of bewilderment. We were a long way from the Virgin in the bathtub.

I smiled, then took out a notebook and wrote down the names of the students who had not been on the bus to Peggy's Cove at the time of the murder. I pointed to those on the list who were in the room: Sferrazza-Melchiorre, Logan, Mills, Ford. No Bleier. Maybe he had an intuition that Immanuel Kant would be given short shrift in the seminar. Next to Petrucci I wrote "alibi of some kind."

The discussion wrapped up a few minutes later, and I waited to introduce Brennan to our investigator. As far as I knew, the men had never met, either before or after Burke was cleared of the murder charges.

"Brennan, this is Moody Walker. Sergeant, retired, and now working as a private investigator. Moody, meet Father Burke."

Burke gave him a terse nod. "Sergeant."

"Father Burke. This time I'm working for you, not against you."

"Glad to hear it."

"One thing Moody is going to handle is the international component of the investigation. He has police contacts in Europe and the U.S. We can't get that information ourselves and we don't know what the Halifax police will do in that respect."

"Right."

"I've given him a list of our possible suspects, and he's going to see what he can learn about their backgrounds."

"All right," Walker said. "I'll go and make some calls. See what I can dig up." We said goodbye to Walker, and he went on his way.

"There's somebody I'd like to interview myself while I'm here, Brennan. Mike O'Flaherty tells me the police have spoken to all the priests and staff except Mrs. Kelly."

"True. She took the janglers so bad they couldn't get a sensible word out of her. So they're coming back for her."

"They're takin' her in?" I asked.

He didn't speak but brought his hands together in prayer and looked up at the heavens. Poor old Mrs. Kelly. She hadn't done herself any favours when her meddling delayed the inauguration of the schola cantorum. She had always been nervous around the formidable Father Burke, and it was clear he did not fit her image of the ideal priest of the church. This was as obvious to Burke as it was to everyone else, but he had let it all run off his back. Till now.

"Let's go see her."

He sighed and jerked his head in the general direction of the rectory. I followed him across the street and into the kitchen.

"Mrs. Kelly."

The woman leapt away from the dishwasher as if Burke might have

73

rigged it with explosives. "Merciful hour! I didn't hear you come in, Father!"

"We'd like a word with you."

Her eyes darted from him to me. "What about?"

"What Father Burke means, Mrs. Kelly, is we're hoping you'll be able to help us out. Perhaps you could tell us how some of the people at the schola acted with Father Schellenberg. You haven't yet had a chance to offer your impressions, and we were wondering if we could sit down with you and hear what you have to say."

"Well, I . . ." Her hand went up and fussed with her faded blonde hair. "I don't know anything."

"People always know more than they realize. You must have noticed that sometimes."

"Yes, I suppose I have. Like the time when my sister was taking spells. I thought back over the years and suddenly it clicked. Whenever she took a turn, it was when she had a little sweet. And I said: 'Sure, she has diabetes!' And she went to the doctor's and, sure enough, that was it. Now they've got her on —"

"Exactly. People suddenly remember that they did notice something. So if we could just have a seat, and you could think back to the time when Father Schellenberg arrived at the schola —"

"Tea, Mr. Collins?"

"That would be lovely."

"Father?"

"N — yes, sure. Thank you."

She bustled about and then led us to the Victorian parlour of the rectory. After she got us all settled with tea, Burke began: "So. Who —"

I interrupted: "Now, Mrs. Kelly, you must have had a great deal of work to do getting ready for all these people to arrive. Some are staying here at the rectory, I understand."

"Oh, yes. Some of the priests are staying here."

"A lot of work, are they? Priests? Pretty high-maintenance group?"

Her eyes shot over to Father Burke. "Well, they —"

"I mean, you have rooms to make up, all kinds of new people at mealtime."

"Oh, yes. A lot of work. I thought I wouldn't be able to get it all done by myself. But I persevered. I think I have things organized pretty well."

It was my turn to shoot Brennan a look. He caught on. "Very well organized. Couldn't have been better, Mrs. Kelly."

"Thank you, Father," she said with prim satisfaction.

"Now, who was here when Father Schellenberg arrived, do you recall?"

"Well, Monsignor brought him in and introduced him to me. There was nobody else here. I knew some of the others were gathered over at the school, so after I showed him his room and offered him tea, I took him over there. I introduced him around."

"Who all was there, do you remember?"

"Well, now, there was Father Serr — Sver — the Italian. And Brother Robin. Father Mills. And the German and his wife."

"How did those people react to his arrival?"

"Let me think now."

"Were the greetings friendly?"

"Oh yes. At least those that greeted him at all."

"What do you mean?"

"Well, most of them said hello, they were pleased to meet him. Some said they were honoured. He was a famous man, in his day. So they seemed excited. Except, uh . . ."

"What is it?"

"Nothing, probably."

"You said a moment ago 'those that greeted him.' Were there some who didn't speak to him?"

"Just the German. And he never says much anyway, far as I ever heard."

"What did the German do? Mr. Bleier."

"He looked at Father Schellenberg with hardly any expression on his face. But that's what he looks like every time I see him. He made kind of a slow nod of his head, and that was it."

"Did you happen to see the expression on Father Schellenberg's face when he saw Mr. Bleier?"

"I thought he kind of did a double take. As if he found it queer. That the German was here. Or he may just have been surprised to see another German in the crowd."

"But Bleier didn't speak."

"That's true. Maybe it was just that the man had a German name."

"Speaking of Colonel Bleier, why exactly is he here, Brennan?"

"He's here with his wife, Jadwiga. She's signed up for the program."

"What about him? Did he sign up?"

"No, but —"

"So what does he do all day? Does he hang around the choir school? Go sightseeing? What?"

"He's here a good bit of the time. Sits in on some of the sessions."

"For free."

Brennan shrugged. Money was not the driving force in his life, or in his music program apparently. "What sessions has he sat in on?"

"I don't know, Monty. I haven't kept track of him."

The phone rang then, and Mrs. Kelly jumped as if she had never heard the sound before. She grabbed the receiver.

"St. Bernadette's. Oh! Your Grace!" She turned partly away from us to shield the important call. "No! I'm sorry, Your Grace. Monsignor's not here, but I'll see if I can find him. Oh." She turned back reluctantly until her eyes found Burke. No doubt about it; he was here. "Well, yes, he is, if you're sure you don't want me to look for Mons — Certainly, Your Grace." She pressed the receiver against her thigh. "Father! His Grace on the phone. He wants to speak to Monsignor but he says he'll speak to you."

Burke took the phone. "Dennis!" Mrs. Kelly's lips contracted into a thin line of disapproval.

Dia is Muire duit! You don't say! O'Flaherty? Transferred where?" The colour drained from the housekeeper's face. "Oh, pardon me, Dennis. I thought you said — My hearing must be going. Not enough vitamin A in my diet. Or is it vitamin B? What's that? I know, I know. And I will confess it. Now, you were saying, Bishop. I know he'd be happy to. And if he can't, I will. Though you know my Irish is not as good as Michael's. Ah. Yes. Well, we're not much further ahead. I —" He interrupted himself to ask Mrs. Kelly to fetch him a notepad and pencil; then, when she had departed, he said rapidly to the bishop: "Michael went out to see Gadkin-Falkes. I think he made a confession. Naturally Michael didn't say. But my feeling is the man didn't do it at all." Mrs. Kelly bustled back into the room with pencil and paper, and handed it to Burke. He nodded his thanks, put the items down and returned to his conversation with a higher power. "I will. Yes, we've been fortunate in one respect, anyway. Our school is still in operation, despite the catastrophe of Father Schellenberg's death. Several of the students have told me they want to persevere with the program precisely because Reinhold Schellenberg supported it." He paused to listen. "Tomorrow? Enrico Sferrazza-Melchiorre is giving a brief history of the music of the Vatican itself, St. Peter's, the Sistine Chapel. My own topic will be 'The International Style: Architecture, Liturgy, and Music, the War on Decoration.' Well, arguably, it's all of a piece. Bare ruined choirs and all of that. Oh? That would be grand, Dennis; drop in any time." Mrs. Kelly tensed in her chair. "No, no need to call ahead. Stop in at the parochial house here, or at the school. We'll be happy to see you. Bye."

He hung up and turned to me. "Are we off then, Monty?"

"Father," Mrs. Kelly began, "is His Grace planning a visit here?"

"What's that, Mrs. Kelly? Ah. Yes, he may be dropping by."

"When would that be now, Father?"

"Oh, he's not sure. We'll see him when we see him."

"But, did he narrow it down at all?"

"No — well, he may attend one or two of our sessions tomorrow. Anyway, we won't take up any more of your time, Mrs. Kelly. Thank you for your help."

He left the room. I repeated our thanks, assuring the housekeeper that her information was helpful, before following him out.

"You're a real prick, Brennan, the way you were needling that poor woman."

"First the bishop, now you."

"The bishop gave you hell?"

"Well, he suggested her lot would be inheriting the earth some day, and I might not want to rack up any sins against her."

"She's terrified of you."

"A woman who nearly jumps out of her hide whenever a man appears shouldn't be a housekeeper in a rectory full of priests."

"She's not terrified of men; she's terrified of *you*."

"No need to be. Amn't I the most harmless of God's creatures? When I first arrived I was the soul of patience with her. But everything I do is not the way my predecessor, Father Shea, would have done it. Then she didn't send out my notices of the opening of the schola because of some half-cracked idea that the bishop had to approve them. I thought I had her sorted after that. But no. There were a couple of times the woman pretended she didn't know I was in the building when the bishop called; she thinks his voice is for O'Flaherty's ears alone. And this affectation of being nervous around me —"

"Do you suppose it could be your manner? Have I ever mentioned — I believe I have — that you can be a little brusque at times —"

"Oh, yer bollocks."

I waved goodbye, and left for the office.

✝

Just before the close of the workday I had a visit from Moody Walker.

"Come in, Moody. Don't tell me you have something for us already!"

"You're not paying me to sit on my butt doing nothing. I did a criminal record check on all the people who didn't go on the bus trip."

"Great. Did any names pop up?"

"Petrucci. You told me he has an alibi? Too bad."

"Why too bad?"

"Because he torched a church back in 1979."

"No!"

"Yeah. Arson conviction. Set fire to Santa Chiara's Church down in New Jersey. Served just over a year, then got out on good behaviour. Nothing else on his sheet."

"That's enough, I'd say. I'll have a word with him, alibi or no alibi. Anybody else?"

"Janice Gwendolyn Ford."

"Jan Ford has a sheet?"

"Disturbing the peace. A protest in Tallahassee, Florida. It was only two years ago so I called the local police to see what they remembered. Not much. Just that she caused a ruckus at a demonstration. Cop said she hit somebody with her sign but she must have pleaded to the lesser charge."

"What was she protesting, did the guy say?"

"The death penalty. They were about to fry some death-row inmate. Big crowd gathered outside the prison. Ford must be one of those people who hate killing and violence, but doesn't see any problem clobbering people who don't agree with her!"

"I'll see what she has to say. Any more criminals in the choir school?"

"No. Or nobody else who got caught anyway."

✝

I found Jan Ford that evening in her room at the Mother House, the massive grey stone building that is home to the Sisters of Charity at Mount Saint Vincent University. The Mount has an enviable location, high over the waters of the Bedford Basin.

Jan was doing her homework. Spread before her were a music dictation book, a pitch pipe, and a hymnbook. I recalled a time during choir rehearsal when Burke caught sight of a copy of that same hymnbook on a shelf in the loft. He stopped the music, marched over, picked it up by two fingers, gave it a look that should have rendered it a smoking ruin, and dropped it in the trash can. The choirboys were agog. Good thing I had left him behind when I set out for this interview.

"Hello, Ms. Ford. We were never formally introduced but —"

"Monty. The lawyer. Yes, I've seen you around. Have a seat." She cleared a chair for me. "Give me something that rhymes with Jesus."

"Ephesus."

"No, that's not how it's pronounced."

"Oh. How about 'pleases'? That would be damning with faint praise, though, wouldn't it?"

"No, it could work:

> Come to Jesus, He will please us.
> Sister, brother, child of light.
> Hail the dawn as His love on us.
> We are pleasing in His sight.

What do you think?"

"It does rhyme. How do you like it out here? There's a good view of Stella Maris Church across the Basin."

"Yes, and I try to banish all negative thoughts when I look towards the peninsula and see the church. But it isn't easy to maintain a positive frame of mind. What's happening with the murder investigation? Did the monk really do it, or are they covering something up?"

"Why do you suppose they would do that?"

"The church authorities are masters at keeping unpleasant truths under wraps. That's probably what's happening here."

"Is there someone in particular you think they're covering up for?"

"Well, certainly if it's someone who's in favour with the current regime, they might not want word to get out."

"Who, for instance?"

"Oh, I'd say look around for the ones who are most intent on suppressing any kind of progressive reform in the church and you'll be halfway to finding the killer."

"So your theory is that a conservative killed Father Schellenberg? Why? He had taken a conservative turn himself in recent years. Wouldn't they be on the same side?"

"Too little too late, from their point of view. The few inroads we've made in opening the church to a more ecumenical, pluralistic position can be attributed in part to Reinhold Schellenberg in his younger, more progressive days. Many in the church, at all levels, have never forgiven him for that."

"How did you feel about Schellenberg?"

"I disagree with what you say, but I defend to the death your right to say it! That was my position."

"Interesting choice of words."

"Not my choice. I'm quoting — who? Voltaire?"

"I understand. But I'm wondering if there might have been someone else who felt they had been silenced by the current climate in the church, and took 'defend to the death' literally."

"If you're suggesting that someone in the open, forward-looking, life-affirming wing of the church would do something like this, you're way out of line."

"I may be, but we have to look in every direction. Before we leave that subject, though, I have another question for you."

"What kind of question?"

"I understand you had a bit of trouble down in Florida."

"I won't even ask how or why you have that information about me. In the age of Big Brother watching, nobody should be surprised if her privacy is invaded."

"That's what happens when you get convicted of a criminal offence."

"Speaking of offence, I find you a little offensive today, Monty. What are you suggesting, that because I defended my freedom of expression and got hauled off to jail by a bunch of uniformed thugs who should have been standing at my side rather than making their arrest quota, this makes me a killer?"

"Did you hit somebody?"

"Did I hit somebody with an axe and leave him in a pool of blood in a church in Halifax, Nova Scotia? No. Anything else I ever did is none of your business. End of story. If there's nothing else you want to harass me about, I'll get back to my composition."

But I wasn't finished with the interview yet. "What brings you to the schola cantorum? You must have known it would be a centre of very traditional music and liturgy."

"Are you saying I should have been kept out? Not welcome in the club?"

"No, of course not. I just wondered."

"Because if that's what you mean, or if that's what's going on here, let me tell you I am willing to storm the barricades to make sure I and other like-minded persons have a seat at the table."

"We already know that."

"I'll ignore that little jibe. And let me tell you something else. I did not appreciate the attitude of your friend Brennan Burke in our seminar the other day when I presented the choreography I was working up for the spring, but which I decided to share with the group. I don't know how familiar you are with liturgical dance."

"I, um —"

"No, I suppose you don't know a thing about it. Well, don't wait for Father Burke to introduce you to it. Anyway, Kyle, Tamsin, and I performed my 'Ballet for the Birthing Season' for the workshop. I admit I'm not the most graceful dancer but that's not the point. I caught Burke exchanging looks with that guy Sferrazza-Melchiorre from Rome. Well, of course, you can't expect the boys from the Vatican to appreciate creative movement. It was almost as if Burke was saying: *Can you believe this?* Between you and me, I think he feels threatened."

"Who?"

"Burke."

"I've never known Burke to look, act, or feel threatened by anything or anyone."

"Well, I wouldn't expect you to admit it. But I think he feels threatened by strong women and their voice in the church."

"I can tell you without reservation that, whenever I've seen him with women, it's precisely the strong women he likes the best — those who don't take any crap from men, including him. You've got him wrong on that score."

"Right. Macho men sticking together. As usual."

"Well, Ms. Ford, I am sensitive enough to suspect I've overstayed my welcome." And sensitive enough to the mood to know I'd get nowhere at this point asking where she had been at the time of the murder. "I'll let you get back to your work."

"Which I probably won't get to perform. At the Father Burke School of Music."

"Which makes me wonder yet again why you signed up."

"I wouldn't expect you to understand. Goodbye!"

✝

I stopped by St. Bernadette's before work on Friday to fill Burke in on the previous day's developments. I caught him just as he was leaving his room with a stack of books under his arm.

"What's this, amnesty day at the library?"

"I'm giving a lecture on Saint Gregory to the theology students. Atlantic School of Theology."

"I should go with you. Not to listen but to walk around the grounds. They're blessed with one of the most beautiful, and valuable, properties in the city, overlooking the waters of the Northwest Arm."

"It wouldn't hurt you at all to come along. Broaden your education, Montague. Feel free to seek my guidance at any time."

"I'll do that," I said. I sounded flippant but in fact I had often thought of seeking his priestly instruction. I was a highly educated man in some fields of knowledge but I was embarrassingly ignorant in others, notably the finer points of religious thought.

"The theology school is Fred Mills's alibi," I said. "I can't remember if I told you. He attended a lecture there."

"Alibi for what?"

"November 22. The killing of Kennedy."

"Ah. That makes sense. Just don't be telling me it's an alibi for the killing of Schellenberg."

"Why do you say that?"

"There was nothing happening at the theology school on November 22. I got a call from one of the faculty members that day, asking about the planned lecture by Schellenberg. A crowd of them were going to come over for it. The building's electrical system badly needed work, so they decided to send everybody over to hear Schellenberg and get the work done that afternoon. They turned off the lights and shut the place down. Everybody had the afternoon off once the Schellenberg lecture was cancelled."

"So Fred Mills lied to me."

"That's hard to believe."

"I'm sure it is, but there you have it."

"Fred must have been up to something else. He's the last person in the world I can see as an axe murderer."

"None of them strike me as being axe murderers, Brennan. But one of them is exactly that. Anyway, your trip to the theology school appears to be legit, so I won't keep you." I gave him a quick rundown of my talk with Jan Ford and Moody's discoveries about Ford and Luigi Petrucci.

"Santa Chiara's. I know that church. At least I've seen it from the outside, driving by. Never heard about the fire, but I wasn't around there in '79."

"What kind of church is it?"

"It's a beautiful big stone place with a dome and columns in the front. Something you'd see in Rome. Or Dublin. It's still standing."

"An old-style church? Sounds magnificent. I wonder what Petrucci's problem was with that. What do you know about him?"

"He's not a clergyman or a church musician, but he's an arch-Catholic. Goes by the name of Lou. Works as an electrician in New

Jersey. His nephew is here, son of Lou's widowed sister. The young fellow came to Halifax to play football for Saint Mary's, so Lou drove up to see him and attend the schola. Somebody told me he's bringing his wife and the lad's mother up here after Christmas. The nephew, Giorgio, is the alibi; they had lunch at the Lighthouse Tavern. The police tracked Giorgio down at his girlfriend's place. He wasn't one hundred percent sure how long he and his uncle were together, but it sounded as if they were there till three-thirty or so. Petrucci looks clean."

"Sounds it. But with the church-burning conviction in his background, we'll have to check him out."

We walked down the stairs and saw Mrs. Kelly emerging from the kitchen. It wouldn't hurt to hear what she remembered about people's whereabouts on the afternoon of the murder. I said goodbye to Brennan, and asked the housekeeper if I could direct a few more questions her way.

She sat me down at the kitchen table, gave me a cup of tea, and pushed a plate of tea biscuits in my direction.

"Thanks again, Mrs. Kelly. What's your other name? Mrs. What Kelly?"

"Mrs. James Kelly. My husband passed on twenty years ago, God rest his soul."

"I'm sorry. Well —" I stopped to sample the biscuits. "These are delicious."

"Thank you, Mr. Collins."

"Call me Monty."

"Okay."

"Why don't you have a seat? If I need a refill, I'll get up. We've already covered Father Schellenberg's arrival. Now, let's go through what you remember about the day he was killed. Do you recall anything about him that Friday?"

"No, Mr. Collins — I mean Monty. Sadly I cannot remember one thing about him that day. He may have come and gone through the front door. We never use it, but some of them don't know that, so they use it."

"Mmm. Did he get any phone calls?"

"I don't know. The calls go directly to their rooms. If they don't answer after four rings, the calls get rerouted down here."

"How about some of the others? Most of them went on the bus trip but a few stayed behind. Let's begin with Brother Robin."

"I'm pretty sure I saw him a couple of times but I can't say what time, whether it was morning or afternoon. I've tried to remember, but I just didn't take any notice on the day."

"All right. Father Sferrazza-Melchiorre."

"He was in his room. I heard him playing music up there after Mass in the morning. Then he went out."

"What time was that?"

"Lunchtime, or early afternoon."

"Anything unusual about him when he left?"

"I don't know. I didn't actually see him. Just heard him say something in Italian to someone else as he was going out the door. Front door. We don't use that door."

"Do you know who he spoke to?"

"Um . . ."

"Did the person answer?"

"Yes, he did. I remember now — it was Father Burke. He answered in Italian."

I couldn't help asking: "Does that mean Father Burke was using the front door?"

"I certainly hope not! The lock's queer on that door, and you never know whether it's secure or not. Plus, I don't want to be answering two doors all day!"

"Right. How about Billy Logan? Was he around?"

Her lips tightened. "He's not staying here, of course. A spoiled priest, is what I heard about him. But he was in and out of the choir school that day."

"When you say in and out, what times are we talking about?"

"He didn't arrive in time for Mass. I was there and he was not. But I saw him come out of the choir school just before noon."

"Anything notable about him?"

"No. Except for the fact that he looked like he'd swallowed a bitter pill. But I find he always looks like that. He got into his car. His wife was in the passenger's seat, and the car was piled to the rafters with stuff."

"What kind of stuff?"

"I couldn't tell. Maybe it was in garbage bags or boxes — I didn't pay that much attention. Anyway, he peeled out of the parking lot and leaned on his horn. He must have been angry with another driver. There's no need for such noise, especially on church property!"

"Did you see him again that day?"

"No, I didn't."

"Did you see Mr. Bleier?"

"No. He's not staying here, either. I believe he is staying at a bed and breakfast run by Germans. I suppose it's natural to want to be with your own kind."

"So you didn't see him. How about his wife, Dr. Silkowski?"

"No."

"Father Mills."

"He went out early in the afternoon. Said hello to me before he left."

"Do you know when he came back?"

"No, I didn't see him again."

"I'm nearly finished here, Mrs. Kelly. What about Jan Ford? You know who I mean?"

"Yes. She is staying at Mount Saint Vincent but she was here that day. She and another lady — she may have been a sister, hard to tell these days — were on their way to a restaurant, and they were kind enough to invite me along. They were going to compose some music over lunch. Said they were working on a 'song cycle,' whatever that is, about Joan of Arc. And I could contribute if I wanted to. But I had a bird to put in the oven for supper, so I couldn't go. I saw the two ladies stop in the parking lot and have a word with Father Mills. Then I got back to my bird."

Mrs. Kelly was of the generation that believed it took six hours in the oven, and a lot of fussing in the kitchen, to roast every last molecule of moisture out of a turkey or a chicken. I kept my own counsel on that.

"One more question and I'll leave you in peace. Do you know where Mr. Petrucci is staying?"

"Petrucci? Who's he?"

"One of the people at the schola. Not a priest. Just someone keen on the music, I guess."

"Well, he should be on the list then. Father gave me the phone numbers in case he wants me to make some calls for him." She got up and thumbed through a stack of papers by the phone. "Here it is. Petrucci, L."

"Would you mind if I called him from here?"

"No, go right ahead."

I dialled the number and waited. A young woman answered and told me Lou had driven up to Montreal for a few days. Did I want to leave my number? No thanks, I'd try him again another time.

✝

I had a visit from Moody Walker later that morning at the office.

"I made a call about Bleier."

"Oh?"

"Yeah, I have a buddy over there, in Hamburg. Gunther Schmidt. He's a cop I dealt with a few years ago when there was some suspicious container traffic plying the waters between Hamburg and Halifax. He knew all about the Schellenberg killing, needless to say. He'd never heard of Bleier but he ran the two names through his computer. Didn't come up with anything about Kurt Bleier, except that he was on the police force in East Berlin till the wall came down. There wasn't all that much about Reinhold Schellenberg. He was a priest in a town called Magdeburg, he was an adviser at the Second Vatican Council, he taught at a couple of universities in Germany. And he was detained briefly after some kind of political demonstration in the 1970s."

"Another protest gone wrong! I guess it's trite under the circumstances to say we've got a lot of people here with strong opinions."

"Yeah, whoever went at Schellenberg with an axe certainly had strong opinions about him."

"Too true. Any indication Schellenberg and Colonel Bleier knew each other?"

"No, but there may be a connection of some kind. There was a Schellenberg in the same prison camp as Max Bleier during the war. A camp outside Berlin."

"Is Max related to Kurt?"

"His father. Max was a commie too, in the 1930s and 1940s. That's why he was targeted by the Nazis."

"Who was the Schellenberg?"

"Schmidt doesn't know. He's going to call me if he's any relation to our victim. Schmidt was more than a little curious about Bleier being over here when the hit was done. Not much I could tell him, except that he's here with his wife. All the way over here from Germany to learn music? Nobody would ever call me a culture buff, but even I know you don't have to wear out your shoe leather before you find a bunch of choir boys around an organ over there."

"True, but the same could be said for others in the group as well. There are people here from France, Italy, England —"

"And a queer-looking bunch they are, some of them."

"You think?"

"Who's that flamer in the cape? I'd like to know where his two-thousand-dollar shoes were standing at the time Schellenberg was getting axed."

"Why don't you ask him?"

"I thought you just wanted me for the information you can't dig up yourself."

"No reason you can't come along while I have a chat with the man. How about now? We'll see if he's in."

Walker shrugged, and we left the office for the rectory at St. Bernadette's.

We rang the bell — of the *back* door — and waited. A face peered out at us through the window before the door was opened.

"Hello again, Mrs. Kelly." The housekeeper looked as if she needed an emergency hook-up to a Valium drip. "Is something wrong?"

"Is . . . Is His Grace out there?" she asked in a quavering voice.

"I don't see the bishop out here, no. May we come in?" She opened the door halfway, and we sidled in. "Sergeant Walker and I are going to head upstairs if that's all right."

"Oh, I don't know . . ." Her eyes rolled upwards. "Do you hear that?" I heard singing then, opera perhaps. "That's been going on for —" she looked at her watch "— ten minutes now. And His Grace said he may be coming to visit! Imagine him hearing that! I'd better stay here to keep an eye out."

As Walker and I approached the staircase we heard a tenor voice soaring through the building at full volume; the piece was a fulsome "Ave Maria" I did not recognize. We climbed the stairs and approached the source: Sferrazza-Melchiorre's room. His door was ajar. We found him singing to a portrait of the Virgin and Child, Mary's naked breast grasped in the hands of her son. The priest was, as always, in full regalia, in his soutane and cape. His arms were flung out in a gesture of operatic passion. A bottle of *vino rosso* stood half-empty on his table. I turned my attention from him to Sergeant Walker. The retired cop was goggling at the caped figure as if it was his first day on the job as a rookie policeman. The priest turned and directed the last bars of the hymn, with no *diminuendo*, to me and my stunned companion. He raised his arms as he declaimed the amen.

"Monty!" he cried, when the song of praise had ended. "*Buongiorno!* You have brought me a visitor. Wine?" He gestured towards the bottle with his jewelled hand.

"None for me, thanks. Enrico Sferrazza-Melchiorre, this is Sergeant Walker. He's helping us with the investigation."

Walker gave him a wary nod. Enrico grasped his hand, and said: "*Piacere, signore!* Make yourself quite at home."

We sat across from him, and he filled his wineglass, took time to savour a mouthful, then asked: "In what way can I help you?"

"We have to find out if anyone saw anything out of the ordinary on the afternoon of the murder."

"Everything is out of the ordinary for us, Monty. We are all strangers here."

"What did you do that day?"

"I went to our Mass in the morning, I returned here to my room, I went out to lunch."

"Where?"

"I do not remember the name, a small place. Then I walked and walked around the city."

"Were you dressed in any, uh, distinctive kind of way that day?"

"No." The priest shrugged his caped shoulders. "I just wore what I always wear."

"Right," Moody Walker said. "If you were out there, it shouldn't be too hard to find people who noticed you. Why do you think Schellenberg was killed?"

Again, the shrug. *"Chissà!"*

"Come again?"

"I say: who knows?"

"You seem a little blasé about the death of one of your compadres."

Enrico didn't respond, but pointed to a poster he had on the desk before him. There was a pair of scissors beside it, and some trimmings from the borders. "Are you an admirer of Jacques Villeneuve?" he asked Moody.

"Sure. That's the Reynard Alfa. Where did you get the poster?"

A hesitation. "I found it blowing along the street, and I brought it here. Villanova, he is on our F3 team now. But he will be F1 some day."

"You follow Formula One racing?" Walker asked, barely masking his surprise.

"Oh, yes. I was at Monza last year."

"Really! Watching the Ferraris?"

"The Ferraris were driven by Prost and Mansell, placing second and fourth. I follow Riccardo Patrese. He is a cousin of mine. He was driving for Richards."

"Patrese came in about a minute behind Mansell. What were they, fourth and fifth?"

"Yes, but it was not a minute. Mansell's time was one hour, eighteen minutes, fifty-four seconds. Riccardo came in at one hour, nineteen minutes, twenty-three point one five something."

"Were you at Monza in '78 when Ronnie Peterson was killed? They blamed Patrese for that. Even brought charges against him."

"He was cleared of blame! By the Grand Prix Drivers Association and the courts!" Enrico's face had reddened. "It was a tragedy for all concerned. We are thankful that Riccardo's career recovered. He won the San Marino Grand Prix last year."

"He went over to Richards when?"

"In 1988, and was cursed by those not-turbo-charged engines. They went to the Renault engine the next year, then the 1990 victory."

"You obviously follow this closely."

"Not as closely as I would like to. They have a form of racing where I live now, but —"

"Where's that?"

"Mississippi."

"What do you mean, Mississippi?"

"I now live in the southern United States."

"You're puttin' me on."

"*Che cosa?* Anyway, they have a form of racing there. I was joyful when I heard it being discussed by some in my congregation, and I attended a race. It is not the same thing at all."

"You went to a NASCAR race? I wish I'd seen that! You sitting there with all those good ole boys in the south."

"Please don't misunderstand me. It provides entertainment for those who . . . who are less fortunate than others, but one could not properly compare it to, say, the Grand Prix at Monaco." He shook his head, then looked at us as if remembering why we were there. "I am not keeping you from your rounds, I hope, Sergeant. Are you seeing others today as well?"

We hadn't planned on it, but it might be a good idea to pretend otherwise. "Yes, we are. Thank you for help, Enrico." We left and closed the door behind us.

"Well, he sure spilled his guts there, Sergeant. How do you do it?"

"Piss off, Collins. He wasn't going to give us anything. He says he was out walking. If he isn't lying, somebody will remember seeing him in that outfit."

†

I spent half the afternoon in the office, dealing with a young guy who had just blown his chance to have a future outside the walls of a prison. He had committed an armed robbery, and he had two particularly aggravating factors working against him: he had carried a sawed-off shotgun and worn a mask. All of this meant five to eight years behind bars, if he got sentenced as an adult. The Crown had offered him a chance to avoid that. If he pleaded guilty, the Crown would not apply to have him sentenced as an adult. He would serve less than two years as a young offender, some of it already served. The client ignored my advice, refused the deal and, as predicted, was found guilty at trial. Now he had the gall to ask whether we could go back to the Crown and salvage the deal. *No, we cannot.* People don't listen. It was a relief to turn to a client who was not guilty, the doctor I was defending in a medical malpractice case. He had failed to diagnose a rare neurological disorder in his patient. Was there a failure to diagnose? Yes. Did this amount to negligence? No. I was hard at work on my pretrial brief when I received a call from Moody Walker.

"I heard from my man in Hamburg. Schmidt. He was able to identify the Schellenberg who served time in the same Nazi prison camp as Kurt Bleier's father. It was Johann Schellenberg, a priest. Uncle of our Reinhold Schellenberg."

"Well! Did they know each other at the camp? Or before the camp?"

"Schmidt didn't have anything on that, one way or the other."

"Interesting, to say the least. Maybe it's time to have a talk with Kurt."

"Definitely. I got something else too. I asked around some of the downtown businesses to see if anybody noticed the Caped Crusader window-shopping the day of the murder. I spent two hours and all I got was no, no, no. Nobody saw him. But then one of the girls in Mills Brothers said he sounded a lot like a guy her husband told her about. Husband works at the Jaguar dealership on Kempt Road. An Italian 'in spiffy clothes' test-drove a Jag that day but didn't buy it. I took a run up there and the salesman wasn't in, but guess what? Sferrazza-Melchiorre took the car out at one-fifteen on November 22 and didn't bring it back till nearly four o'clock."

"No! Did he give them his real name, credit card, and all that?"

"Yeah, he did."

"Well, then. He must have known we could find out."

"I suspect this princeling doesn't think the way you and I do, Collins!"

✝

I drove to Kempt Road after work in my non-Jag and went into the showroom. It took a few minutes to get through to the salesman who had signed the car out. He was an Englishman in his early thirties; who better to market an upscale British car? I explained why I was there. Yes, Nigel Soames remembered Enrico. He had test-driven not a Jag but an Aston Martin. And he had cut quite a figure in his obviously costly ensemble.

"Was he dressed as a priest, European-style?"

"A priest? No, he was in very pricey-looking Italian clothes. He wore a fawn cashmere topcoat with a yellow scarf wound round his neck, and he pulled on a pair of driving gloves when he took the wheel."

"I see." Enrico had lied to us about where he was, and what he was wearing. "Was he alone?"

"Yes. At least he was when he took the car out and when he brought it back."

"He had the car out for quite a while, I understand."

"Yes, he was gone for a good three hours."

"Were you concerned?"

"Normally, I would be if a car was out that long. But he had told me he wanted to drive on the highway and on some twisty roads. That too would have concerned me but we had quite a chat about cars and driving. He's something of an expert. Chaplain to the Grand Prix set perhaps! We had some Jacques Villeneuve posters on hand, and he took one of those. Anyway, all in all, I expected him to be gone for awhile. And I had his credit card for a damage deposit."

"Were you expecting a sale? After all, he was clearly not local."

"Well, he was Italian of course, but his current address was somewhere in the United States. Missouri or something."

"Mississippi."

"Quite right, yes. So it didn't seem too much of a stretch to think he might purchase it here and drive it home."

"True. Was there anything out of line about the car when he brought it back? Any damage or soiling?"

"No, apart from a bit of dust and dirt from the roadway, it was in tip-top shape. The only thing was that he had moved the passenger seat back and couldn't return it to its normal position. So I helped him with that. It was a bit stiff, actually; I don't think it had been moved in a while."

"Why did he move it?"

"He didn't say. There was no sign anybody had been in the seat. But, then, there wouldn't be, really."

"Was there anything unusual about him when he returned?"

"Not that I can recall."

"Can you remember him being calm or agitated?"

"A little excited perhaps. I was hoping that was about the car. He did say he might be in touch again."

And that was that. Enrico may have been excited, but it may have been about the car. He may have had someone as a passenger, or he may have had some other reason to move the seat. I might ask him about the drive or I might not. If past experience was any indication, I would be no wiser by the end of the interview.

Chapter 5

Thou hast heard their reproach, O Lord,
and all their imaginations against me.
The lips of those that rose against me,
and their device against me all the day.
— Lamentations 3:61-63

It was Friday night, December 6, and a gentle snow was falling. I enjoyed the snow from the warmth of my old house on Dresden Row. Sitting by the fire with my feet up, watching the flakes float down outside the multi-paned windows, it was as if I'd never left home. But the cry of my wife's new baby jerked me back to the present day. Maura had plans to go out and, since our son Tom was not around, I was going to look after our little girl for the evening.

"My homework's all done!"

"Let me see it, Normie."

"Aw, Daddy! You're no fun. It's as if it's done 'cause I know everything I have to do."

"So do it already! Then we'll play."

"Okay, okay. We'll play Scrabble and Clue and read stories."

"Sounds good."

Maura came into the room with the baby resting against her shoulder. His whimpering sounded like the prelude to a full battle cry. His mother looked exhausted, in desperate need of a break.

"Okay, Normie. Bedtime doesn't change just because Daddy's here.

Oh, sweetie, could you go get me the diaper bag? It's in my room. I'll change him just before we go, but I'll still need a couple of spares."

Normie left to get the bag.

"Where are you off to?" I asked MacNeil.

"Dinner at the Silver Spoon with Fanny and Liz."

"Wouldn't it be a bit more relaxing for you to have dinner with your two best friends without the baby?"

Did she take him with her every time she went out? Where was the father, I wondered for the thousandth time, thinking simultaneously that I'd like to punch his lights out if he did show up.

"No, it's fine," she said. "He's used to going out on the town, aren't you, Dominic?"

He let fly with a scream then, and I saw her eyes clamp shut. She was on the verge of tears.

"Leave him here with us," I said.

"No, he'll be good. He just lies in his basket and sleeps beside the table."

"Leave him. In fact, why don't you sleep over at Liz's? You've got the baby on a bottle now, right?"

"Yeah, but nobody's pretending this is your problem, Collins. God knows, we've been through that."

"Whose problem is it?"

No answer.

"Where's the baby's father?"

A hesitation. Then: "He's not around much."

"Listen. Pack a bag and take a night off. We'll handle things here, won't we, Normie?" I said to my daughter when she came back with the baby's gear. "We're having a sleepover and Mum's going to stay with Liz."

"Really? Great! That means I can add to my list of things we're going to do!"

"Go right ahead."

MacNeil packed her bag and headed out for the night with a lighter step than I'd seen in months. She looked like a little teenager going to her first sock hop.

Normie played with the baby while I made pasta for supper. The minute she left him alone he started to wail. "Oh, Dominic!" she cried.

"Leave him for now, sweetheart. He'll be all right. Eat your supper."

The infant continued to bawl, and Normie invented an urgent errand upstairs. She'd obviously had enough for a while. I realized it was the first time I had been alone with my wife's son. Red-faced and miserable, he cried at full throttle. Well, I couldn't go forever without picking the little fellow up. And nobody was here to see how I did. I reached into his crib and gently lifted him out. I put him against my shoulder and patted his back. That used to work for Tom and Normie. Not for this one, though. He just screamed louder. I persisted for a good twenty minutes, checked his diaper, offered him a bottle, then gave it up and laid him down.

I popped open a beer, threw another log on the fire, and sat on the chesterfield. The doorbell rang, and the crying stopped. Before I could get to my feet, Normie was down the stairs and at the door.

"Hi, Father! Oh, good! My books on the saints. And, oh, right, angels too. Thank you!"

"You're welcome, Stormie."

"You're the stormy one — you've got snow in your hair. You know, Father, I hate to say this but you remind me of the boys at my school."

"Oh yeah? How's that?"

"It's snowing out. You're wearing the same jacket you wear in the spring; it's not buttoned up, and you don't have any mittens on. Your mother would be mad if she saw you."

"She would indeed. I'll shape up. Is your own mother home, or are you the châtelaine now?"

"What's the châtelaine?"

"The lady of the castle."

"No. Daddy's here."

"Ah."

I went to greet him. "Evening, Father. Are you here to bring Mass to the shut-ins?"

"Well, since it's you and there's no sign of herself, perhaps I should be hearing confessions."

"Come in."

"I just stopped by to bring Normie some books."

Did he feel he needed to explain his presence at the house? That was not like him at all.

"Have a seat. I'll get you a beer." I went into the kitchen.

Normie came in behind me and whispered: "I asked him for books about saints in Scotland and Ireland, so he wouldn't know it's the angels I'm after."

"Good thinking."

My daughter had got it into her head, for some reason, that Father Burke might be an angel. This had been going on for months now, ever since she first saw him celebrating Mass in his white vestments. She said there were spirits all around him on the altar. Normie had a touch of second sight, or so I'd been told by her maternal relatives in Cape Breton. She had not yet come to a conclusion about Burke; apparently there was still a great deal of research to do.

"Ah," sighed the angelic one as the first sip of Keith's India Pale Ale slid down his throat. "Nectar of the gods."

The howling started up again. Burke looked over at the crib, then at me. "Don't you think you should pick him up, Monty? You're not without experience in that regard."

"He won't settle," was all I said.

Finally, Burke put his beer on the table and went to the crib. "Evening, Dominic. How's the little lad?" At the sound of Burke's voice, the baby fell silent. Burke picked him up, cradled him in his arms, took the corner of his blanket and used it to wipe his face. The baby smiled and kicked his legs. "That's more like it," Burke muttered to him, and stood there, irresolute. We were saved by the arrival of Normie, who announced that she would take the now placid baby to his room.

My own son arrived then, his blond hair curling out from under a black fedora, a skinny tie askew against his white shirt; this signalled that he had just come from a jam session with his band, Dads in Suits. We chatted a bit about the blues-rock direction his group was going in, then I asked him: "How would you like to earn a few bucks, Tommy?"

"Wouldn't say no. What do I have to do?"

"Research. Go through some old newspapers on microfilm. I won't pretend it's exciting work."

"Do you pay by the hour, so if it gets boring enough for me to fall asleep I get more?"

"I'm afraid not."

"I'll do it! I won't fall asleep!" his sister exclaimed, when she came back into the living room.

"We'll find a job for you, Normie, don't worry. But this one's for Tom. He has to go to the library and stare into a machine reading newspapers in German."

"I can learn German!"

"First lesson," Tom commanded. "When I say *'Fraülein Klumpen-kopf,'* you say *'Jawohl, mein Herr!'"*

"You don't know any real German. You only studied it in school."

"Well, he knows more than I remember from my own studies, so he's the man for the job. Get the reels showing *Die Welt* in the 1970s. Look for anything about Father Reinhold Schellenberg. I'm sorry I can't be very specific. I heard something about him being detained or arrested during a political demonstration of some kind, so I'm especially interested in that."

"You're letting Tom investigate the murder! I don't get to do anything."

"We'll get you out there in a trench coat yet, Normie, like the old-time detectives used to wear."

"Good. Father, make sure he keeps his promise."

"Don't I always keep my promises, sweetheart?"

"Well, yeah, but maybe not this time."

The four of us played cards for a while, then Burke went home. My kids and I hit the sack early. The baby woke up twice to be fed and changed. The first time, at two, was fine. I had forgotten how brutal that second awakening was just before seven o'clock.

✝

Maura came home just as the kids and I were clearing up after breakfast. She looked refreshed, and chatted to me quite pleasantly about her evening out. I drove Normie to her friend Kim's and dropped her off. With a free day ahead of me, I decided to take a run over to the choir school in case there was anyone I could buttonhole for information. Things were quiet until I approached a classroom at the far end of the main corridor. I heard raised voices and I peered in through the window of the door at the back of the room. I opened it and slipped in unseen. I had walked into an argument. Jan Ford was seated behind a desk, brandishing a hymn book in the direction of Father Sferrazza-Melchiorre in one of the chairs. How she thought she would be able to convert Enrico to her way of thinking, I couldn't imagine. But this was the same person who had expected police officers in Florida to side with her in her protest against the death penalty. She was not a woman who would go down without a fight. William Logan slouched in another seat, bored and above it all.

Jan had the floor. "Music should be accessible, user-friendly —"

"Will you please speak English!" This from Father Sferrazza-Melchiorre.

"— music that the people understand, that makes them feel good about themselves, even if the music does not come up to the old elite standards —"

"The music you speak of is trash! Melodies designed to appeal to the nursery! Babyish words and sentiments. All you hear in North America is this talk of people feeling good about themselves, whether they have done anything to merit all this good feeling or not!"

"Did it ever occur to you that we, as liturgists, have a role to play in moving people to that feeling? To let them know they are welcomed and empowered in their faith community?"

"All I hear from you, *Signora* Ford, is about the people. Congratulating themselves in these embarrassing songs. Have you forgotten God? Did you not hear Father Burke yesterday when he spoke of abandoning the self to God in worship?"

"I'm not surprised that Burke would dismiss the self, the very personhood of the faithful, in his form of worship. I suspect the phrase 'self-actualization' is not even in Burke's vocabulary."

You got that right. I realized they still did not know I was there.

"Get with the times, Enrico," Ford continued. "You're stuck in the past."

"You say that as if you mean to insult me, *Signora* Ford, *ma sai una cosa?* — I am not insulted."

"Right," William Logan put in. "You can't be insulted. Hundreds of years of aristocratic breeding make you immune to the opinions of the common people!"

"The church is for all," Enrico countered, "the common people and those of the privileged classes. The church is universal. And she is timeless. Her past — her long tradition — is a treasure of immeasurable value."

Jan Ford leaned forward and slapped her hymn book on the desk. "And so we should be saddled with the liturgy that was set in stone by the Council of Trent in 1570? If it's an unchanging ritual, it's just *there*. What are the people supposed to do while all this is going on?"

"The sacrifice of our Saviour being re-enacted? Is that what you mean by 'all this is going on'?" Enrico's voice had risen in pitch and volume. "The Holy Mass is, or should be, an act of adoration and mystery!"

"Adoration and mystery went the way of the horse and buggy!"

"Am I hearing you correctly, *signora?*" Enrico shouted at her. "It is out of fashion to adore the Supreme Being? God is out of style? How dare you call yourself a Catholic!" He was standing now and glaring down at her.

"That's you all over, Enrico! Some of us just don't count as Catholics. Well, I don't happen to agree with you. I see the church as a fellowship, a gathered community —"

"This is a fine example of fellowship," Logan interjected, a note of amusement in his voice. "And people wonder why I left the priesthood. This is exactly —"

Sferrazza-Melchiorre whirled on him. "You are being dishonest. This is not why you left the priesthood. You left because you wanted ease and comfort! You were not strong enough to endure the rigours of the consecrated life."

"Oh, yeah? How well have you endured those rigours yourself, Sferrazza? Have you kept to your vows since the day you were ordained?"

"I have not been without sin. But I pray for God's grace and His guidance every day in order to continue to serve him as his priest. Men like Father Burke and —"

"Burke! Funny you should mention him," Logan sneered. "The priesthood suits him just fine and dandy, thank you very much."

"What are you saying now?"

"I'm saying Burke's in it for himself, to gratify his own ego. He knows he looks damn good up there on the altar, and sounds damn good too!"

"You are outrageous, Logan! If Brennan Burke had his way, all you would see of him would be the back of his head. Because he would be offering the Tridentine Mass every day, and priest and congregation would all be facing the same way, towards the Blessed Sacrament. And have you forgotten the principle of objectivity in worship? In a sacred ritual the priest conforms to the rubrics, speaks or chants the words as they are written — the ego is subsumed, and he becomes the representative of all of us. One does not show off one's vocal flair in chant; one does not add trills or a big finish! Brennan could find less onerous ways to 'look good' as you say it. His youthful ambition was to be an architect. Prayer in stone! He could be a man with a wife and a family and a few dollars in his pocket, and some magnificent buildings to leave to posterity. But he chooses to use his talents to serve God. It does not commend you, Logan, that you cannot or will not understand that. I think you are a bitter man. A jealous man."

"You don't know what the hell you're talking about, you Italian fop!" Logan rose from his seat, and shouted into the priest's face. Jan Ford stared at the two in alarm. "You've been handed everything your whole fucking life. You don't have to get out there in the business world and scramble to make a buck, and look over your shoulder every minute to see younger, hungrier guys coming up behind you, ready to take it all away from you. I'd like to see you dropped down in the middle of the United States of America and have to fend for yourself like the rest of us. See how long you'd last there, you and your —"

"As a matter of fact, Mr. Logan, I have been dropped in it. Is that not the expression?" The anger had leached out of Enrico, and he regarded the enraged Logan with amused detachment. "I now live in America and I grant you I do not feel as if I belong there. The people of Mississippi seem to regard me with wariness, and I —"

"You in Mississippi! I'd give my left nut to see that. You and a bunch of good ole boys. You in a pair of shoes that cost more than they make in six months, guzzling wine and bellowing opera, and trying to tell them why the Assumption of the Virgin Mary into heaven is an infallible doctrine. You're probably the only Catholic in spittin' range. They probably think you're the Whore of Babylon."

"They do! They inscribed those very words on the front door of my church! Spelled incorrectly, but that is clearly what they meant. I have a lovely photograph of the Holy Father, encased in glass, at the entrance to my church, and they despoiled it with the words you said. And yet I feel it is my mission to bring these poor, disadvantaged —"

"If anybody should be a missionary in Mississippi, it's her." Logan turned and jabbed a finger in the direction of Jan Ford. "Her namby-pamby, everybody feel good, let's not be too Catholic, let's play the spoons at the offertory and clump around the altar and wail like it's a hoedown kind of fellowship might have a place in rural, Bible-belt Mississippi."

"Well!" Jan exclaimed. "At least I know where you stand, William. I can't expect anything better from *him*, stuck as he is in the sixteenth century!"

I tried to slink out, but my jacket snagged on my chair; the chair tipped and fell on the floor, making a bang and announcing my presence to the combatants. They turned as one and gaped at me. They looked as if they had been caught in flagrante delicto. I raised my hand in farewell and left for the calm, rational world of criminal law and litigation.

✝

"Father Schellenberg was beaten up by the police in East Berlin."

"The *police* beat somebody *up?*" When you're eight years old, there are still many, many facts of life you have not yet learned, most of them painful. Normie stared at her brother in horror as Tommy delivered the results of his research. The kids were at my house, across the water to the west of the Halifax peninsula, and we were sitting at the kitchen table on Sunday afternoon.

Tom tried to soften the blow. "It was in Germany a long time ago, 1971."

"I wasn't even born then!" Normie replied, her worries instantly assuaged. What could you expect from the creatures who roamed the earth in the dark ages before she existed?

"I went through the old editions of *Die Welt*. I found a few stories mentioning Reinhold Schellenberg at this or that church event, or giving a lecture. And being an adviser at the Vatican Council. But I also got the story of his arrest, or his 'detention,' by the police in East Berlin. He was involved in a protest when Leonid Brezhnev, the Soviet leader, visited Berlin at the end of October 1971. He wasn't just detained; he said he was beaten by the police. There weren't any other details. A couple of lines and that was it."

"Good work, Tommy. I'll pass this along to the other private eye we have working the case."

I picked up the phone and called Moody Walker. We agreed to have a word with Colonel Bleier that evening at the bed and breakfast where he and his wife were staying. So, after making sure Tom was studying for his exams and Normie was out of his hair, I left to meet Moody outside the Göttingen Gasthaus situated, appropriately, on Gottingen Street in the city's north end. The turreted Victorian house looked more Anglo than Saxon but a sign promised *Zimmer mit Frühstück*. The Göttingen's young blonde receptionist, Ulrike, rang Bleier's room and announced our arrival; he came down to the lobby to join us. Jadwiga Silkowski was not in, so we had Kurt Bleier to ourselves. I made the introductions. Sergeant Walker wasted no time on small talk.

"What were you doing on the afternoon of November 22?"

"I was walking."

"Where?"

"From one place to another."

"From where to where?"

"Around."

The two cops stared at each other, neither giving in.

"You don't strike me as an aimless kind of guy, Colonel Bleier."

"I am on holiday, Sergeant. A holiday of my wife's choosing."

"Make like you're not on holiday. Make like you're working a case. And help me put all the facts in the file. Where were you the afternoon of November 22?"

"Not in church."

"Would you consider an abandoned church, scheduled to be torn down, not to be a church?"

"I am not a Jesuit; I am not trying to trip you up with words."

"Good. How long did you know Schellenberg?"

"Why do you assume I knew him?"

"We know you did. For how long?"

"I did not in fact know him. I believe I met him on one or two occasions in Germany. That is all."

"Quite a coincidence, you and Schellenberg meeting on a couple of occasions in Germany, and then finding yourselves here in Halifax at the same time."

"As you say. Coincidence."

"Did you buy into that kind of coincidence as a cop in the German Democratic Republic, so-called?"

"If the facts implied coincidence, I inferred coincidence."

Walker stared into the unblinking blue eyes, then asked: "Did your father, Max, keep in touch with the priest Johann Schellenberg after they left the Nazi prison camp?"

It hit home, but Bleier quickly recovered. "My father tried to forget the camp. He had no interest in reliving those times."

"Did they get in touch again, yes or no?"

"My answer suggests no. If it was otherwise, I am not aware of it."

"Was your father a Communist Party apparatchik after the war?"

"My father was a party official."

"Was Reinhold Schellenberg ever taken into custody by the East German authorities, either the Stasi or the Volks Police?"

A hesitation. "I believe he was. Briefly."

"Were you involved in that?"

"I was on duty. I was not involved with his — with detaining him."

"Why was he detained?"

"I believe he was involved in an illegal gathering. It was a long time ago. I do not have the details."

"What happened to him as a result of that?"

Bleier shrugged. "He was released."

"After how long?"

"I don't know."

"Why are you here?"

"To answer your questions."

"Why did you come to Halifax?"

"To accompany my wife to the schola."

"Enjoying your time here?"

"I was."

"Where were you on November 22?"

"I walked along the waterfront."

"From where to where?"

"From the park at the south end up to, I don't know, the end of the city centre."

"The naval dockyards."

"I believe so."

"Take any photos?"

A hesitation again. "My wife asked me to shoot some photographs."

"Photos of the navy ships and facilities?"

"A ship maybe, if it presented a pleasing picture. Now I must go. I am meeting my wife for dinner. Good evening, gentlemen." With that he rose, nodded, and left us in the lobby of the inn.

"Well?" I asked Walker.

"Spying on our navy."

"So?"

"So nothing. He knows as well as we do there's nobody stopping you from taking pictures of navy ships. It's not as if he got into the nerve centre of Maritime Command. But maybe he's still conditioned to think that kind of activity is *verboten*, and the information worth passing along. To someone. Do you suppose he still thinks that way?"

"I doubt it, Moody, but he wants us to think he does."

"He wants us to think he was nervous about it, and that we wore him down and found out why he has been so secretive."

"When in fact it's something else he's hiding."

"That was my take on it, for sure."

Chapter 6

Ingemisco tamquam reus,
Culpa rubet vultus meus.
Supplicanti parce, Deus.
I groan like a guilty man.
Guilt reddens my face.
Spare a suppliant, O God.
— "Dies Irae," *Requiem Mass*

"Are you going to be home for a while?" It was Brennan on the phone, after I returned from the Göttingen Gasthaus.

"I'm just about to drop Tommy Douglas and Normie off at MacNeil's."

"I'll meet you there."

"What's up?"

"You'll see."

I bundled the kids into the car and drove straight downtown to Dresden Row. Burke was sprinting up the street when we pulled in.

"Brother Robin has confessed his guilt!" he announced.

"Confessed to —"

"The police."

"No!"

"Wait till you read this." He waved a sheaf of papers at me. "Evening Normie. Mr. Douglas."

"Hi, Father."

Maura greeted us at the door, and Brennan tapped the papers. "News," he said.

"When did this happen?" I asked when we got ourselves seated in the living room.

"Earlier today. This is Robin's statement to the police. He sent a copy to Mike by courier! But he wouldn't take Mike's call afterwards."

"Let's see it," I urged. Maura and I leaned over his shoulder.

"Rather than have us fighting over it," she said, "why doesn't Brennan read it to us?"

So he shifted through the typed papers and began to read. And, for the occasion, he spoke in an upper-crust British accent, which I inferred was the way Robin Gadkin-Falkes would have sounded if he were speaking to us directly.

> *That he had to go is beyond dispute. That his death has all the appearance of a ghastly aberration may be put down to the deplorable fact that the others of his ilk — and they are legion — have eluded earthly justice. They will not elude the Just Judge on the Day of Wrath. The Holy Catholic and Apostolic Church is — need it be said? — the One True Church. Founded by Christ Himself and His apostles, the Roman Catholic Church has endured in all its truth and splendour since that time, nearly two thousand years ago. It endures, it is meant to endure, it will endure — despite the fact that there is no one in the See of Peter, no one in place to carry out the Petrine Ministry. In short, the chair is empty! Nobody there, don't bother looking! The line of succession remained unbroken from Peter to the Year of Our Lord's Tears, 1958, when our Holy Father, Eugenio Pacelli, Pius XII, joined our Lord in Heaven and left a vacancy that has never been filled.*
>
> *Never been filled, you say? And you dutifully recite the litany of names — litany of shame! — of those who have pretended to the throne of Peter since 1958. John XXIII, Paul VI, John Paul I, and now John Paul II. "Have you had your head in the sand, Brother Robin?" you ask me. "Have you been living in the desert, has history escaped your notice? Are you mad? There is indeed someone sitting in the chair; I see him," you say to me. "He's dressed in white and has all the trappings of a pope; ergo, he is a pope." No, my dear. No, no, no. You are misinformed. That man sitting there is*

a heretic. And a heretic cannot be pope. Since 1958 we have had nothing but heretics in the See of Rome.

Brennan reverted to his normal voice. "So our man is a sedevacantist. It means 'empty seat.' These are people who maintain that the recent popes were not true popes at all. Needless to say, I consider these extremists to be beyond the pale! I wonder if he claims to be the true pope himself. We'll soon see."

"They'll never let him out of the psych ward if they hear that!"

"Oh, no, it's a regular sport among some of these factions. There are numerous anti-popes who have been crowned by their followers. But let's get back to Brother Robin:

> *That some will judge me a madman, I have no doubt. But hear me! And seek ye to understand. (May I add in parentheses that many of our Lord's most faithful servants were judged to be mad — or drunk! — when they proclaimed the Word of God. I do not number myself among the prophets, but stay ye and hear me for awhile.) Where, you may be asking by now, does Reinhold Schellenberg fit in with my insights into the heresy of the recent so-called popes? Simple. It was he who whispered in the ear of the man who had the ear of the man known to the unsuspecting world as Pope John XXIII. The soi-disant pope listened to Rodl, excuse me, that's Bishop Franz Rodl of Germany. And Rodl listened to Schellenberg. And what Schellenberg poured in the bishop's ear was pure poison. Heresy. Next time you're at what passes for the Holy Mass in this day and age, take a good, long look and think "Schellenberg." Look at that table which everyone gathers round so sociably, shuffling about and grinning. And I do mean everyone; really, the ragtag and bobtail, they're all up there now. And in the most frightful garb, some of them! Why does a priest even bother to vest these days, when he has to stand beside the unconsecrated in their mucking-out-the-stables or trolling-the-singles-bars attire? But there they are, the People of God, gathered round their table. It could be called the Protestant table, or the Schellenberg table.*
>
> *What used to be there, do you recall? The Holy Tabernacle, the Altar of God! But not any more, not with the priest — excuse me,*

the presider — with his back to it. The Tabernacle has been moved. Even the postconciliar liturgists were able to discern that it was unseemly to keep the Blessed Sacrament there now that Father Chuck has his bum facing it. What to do? Turn Father Chuck around again so we are all facing the same way in adoration of our Lord? O my dear, no, not at all. Let us instead shunt the Tabernacle off to the side! There, the Real Presence is out of the way, and we can all clomp up to the table for our meal. Used to be a sacrifice, The Sacrifice, but now it's chow time. I once heard a story of a Muslim visiting a Catholic church with a friend. He asked the friend why he genuflected. The friend explained the Catholic belief that Christ is really present in the consecrated Host. And the Muslim said: "If we believed God was truly present here, we would never get up off the floor." O, that we have much to learn, even from the Mussulman!

"Then he gives out about the changing of the words of consecration and whether the new form is valid or not. He talks about the reduced emphasis on the supernatural. And about the diminished role of the priest, the minimizing of his power with respect to the sacrifice, bringing about through himself the Eucharistic Presence. Priests are now like social workers, don't need to be celibate for that, no wonder so many left. Et cetera. He quotes extensively from the 'Ottaviani Intervention.' That was an attempt by cardinals Ottaviani and Bacci in 1969 to convince Pope Paul to save the traditional Mass, the true Mass according to the cardinals."

"What about you, Brennan? Where do you stand in all this?"

"You know where I stand. I say the old Tridentine Mass as often as I can. I don't go so far as to say the new Mass is invalid. Obviously. I wouldn't participate if I thought so. The new Mass is usually — thank God! — conducted with dignity and reverence. And I don't think everything about Vatican II was bad. My view was that they should have lightened up about all kinds of other things — birth control comes to mind! — but left the Mass and the music alone. I haven't seen fit, however, to commit murder over the issue. All right. Robin. Here he gets down to brass tacks:

Yes, yes, I know. Reinhold Schellenberg merely went along with others in the Teutonic world in trying to make the Mass a little more . . . accessible. Accessible to whom? Protestants? Children? Members of other, shall we say, cultural communities? Do you know what one of the experts said at the Vatican Council? In an effort to come up with a Mass that would attract the Japanese? That we shouldn't make the sign of the cross so often. The sign of the cross! Well, Jesus of Nazareth didn't die of hara-kiri. That's just the way it is!

We are told that the people should have a liturgy they understand! True. So, explain it to them. Last time I looked, my missal contained the sacred Latin text and a translation alongside it for my simple Anglo-Saxon brain! Read the translation, go to catechism class, et voilà, liturgy explained and understood. Again, we could learn from others. Do Jews say: "I'm not going to the synagogue because I don't understand Hebrew"? No. They have Hebrew school. They instruct their children in their own sacral language and in the holy texts. Exactly as we should do.

And then, you say: "But poor old Schellenberg changed his mind. Once he saw the imbecilities that took place in Catholic churches around the globe, and all the other madness and chaos that followed Vatican II, he got back on the straight and narrow, and tried to put things back to rights." Too little, too late, is what I say. A man is presumed to intend the consequences of his actions. Imagine the case of a man who murders his wife. He regrets it later. Often the case, I'm sure. Does that mean he should escape justice? Obviously not.

Finally, I must address the question: "Why Schellenberg and not all the others?" The answer is simple. You may find it chilling, but here it is: because the opportunity presented itself! Fate delivered the man right into my hands. We were brought together for one purpose. Matter and anti-matter. Church and anti-church. Pope and anti-pope. I had to destroy him.

We sat in silence for a few moments, each of us trying to assess the monk's extraordinary confession.

"I don't buy it," Brennan said at last. "My opinion is no doubt coloured by whatever he told O'Flaherty after his arrest. We didn't hear what it was, but Michael came away from that session with serious doubts about this fellow's guilt. My take on the confession is that it's too clever to be genuine. He's up to something, obviously, and this statement may be the product of a disturbed mind. But I get the impression he's not deranged enough to take an axe to someone on a sudden whim."

"I can't agree with you, Brennan," Maura said. "If he's intelligent enough to come up with this statement, he's smart enough to know that he may not be able to disentangle himself once the machinery of the state goes into gear against him. Why would he do this, risk spending the rest of his life in prison, for something he didn't do? I say he did it, though he may be found NCR."

"*Non compos . . .*" Brennan tried.

"Not criminally responsible. Insanity defence."

"What do you think, Monty?" Brennan asked then.

"I just don't know. I see too much guilt in the run of a day to be able to write the monk off as a suspect. On the other hand, I wouldn't have any trouble seeing the other suspects as guilty too. I'd like to see this guy in person."

✝

Brennan called me the next morning at the office. "Can you get away? Mike has persuaded Gadkin-Falkes to see us at the hospital. I've given the schola students a writing assignment that will sharpen their minds and keep them busy for the morning. How about you?"

"It would take more than that to sharpen the minds of my criminal clients, God love them, but none of them need me this morning. None of them are up on Monday mornings anyway. Give me an hour to do some paperwork, and then we'll go."

I got my work done, then called Burke to say I was ready. He picked me up outside my building. I was going along for the interview. But if there was a confession of the sacramental kind, I'd be out of the room and would never get to hear what was said. I would worry about that later.

"What kind of evidence did the police turn up against Robin?" I asked Brennan as we headed onto the Macdonald Bridge to Dartmouth. "Do you know?"

"He had some papers belonging to Schellenberg and he tried to burn them."

"That doesn't look good for him. What papers?"

"Notes of some kind. The remnants, or some of them at least, were found in a public rubbish bin a few blocks from the school."

"How do they know the stuff came from Robin?"

"There were other things with it, which belonged to Robin. And there were ashes. Or something of Robin's was scorched. I'm not sure. The waste can in Robin's room was empty; none of the other rooms had had their trash taken out. Now we have a confession, which I don't find convincing at all. And when Mike arrived at the party that night, he was obviously of the view that Gadkin-Falkes didn't do it. The monk told him something that threw it all into doubt."

"But the police were convinced by the evidence even before he confessed."

"The police aren't Robin's priest. Anyway, we'll go pull his chain."

We drove out Pleasant Street past old wooden houses until the street gave way to more commercial properties. When we got to the Nova Scotia Hospital, which sits overlooking Halifax Harbour, we took a moment to admire the view of the city we had left behind. An enormous cruise ship had just docked on the other side, partly obscured by George's Island.

We went through a bit of rigmarole with the hospital personnel, then we were shown into the room of Brother Robin. The monk, whom I now remembered from vespers, was tall and bony with a prominent nose and a thin, sardonic-looking mouth. His hair was sandy and he was bald on top; I didn't know whether this was a tonsure of some sort, or just male pattern baldness.

"Ah, visitors! How lovely. Father Burke, have you come to bring me my lesson books for the classes I've missed? And you are . . . Mr. . . . no, I'm afraid I don't remember your name." He did indeed have a posh English accent; Brennan's impersonation had been right on the (old) money.

"This is Mr. Collins."

"How do you do? I am Robin Gadkin-Falkes."

"We've come to have a word with you."

"Have you indeed, Father? Do sit down. I'm sorry I can't offer you anything. The gelatin dessert has been taken away. Untouched."

Burke wasted no time. "Who killed Schellenberg?"

"My, my, aren't we direct. Forgive me for saying so, but you lack the circumlocutory Irish charm of your co-ethnic, Monsignor O'Flaherty."

"I'm not O'Flaherty and you're not the killer, so let's get on with it."

"I don't for a minute believe O'Flaherty revealed to you anything I said under the seal of the confessional, so I can only infer that this is an exercise of your own deductive powers. Well, your powers have failed you. So why don't you go off and leave me to come to terms with my remorse over killing the good German father?"

"You didn't kill him."

"Of course I did. I've told the bill how and why. End of story."

"I suspect the police haven't closed the file quite yet. Sure, they have your statement, such as it is, but I wonder how compelling their other evidence will be if they start to second-guess your confession."

"My arrest in the middle of the night was quite compelling, I must say."

"They claim you burned something belonging to Schellenberg."

"Yes, I did! Or tried to. Have you ever tried to burn away all traces of a document in an ashtray? Not as easy as it sounds."

"What were the papers?" No reply. "Why would you burn them in your room?" Still no reply. "Why be the only fellow in the rectory with his waste can emptied out after the murder?" There was no answer again, and Burke raised his voice: "Where's the murder weapon?"

"I told the police I threw it into the harbour!"

"I didn't ask what you told the police. I asked you where it is."

"What a bizarre experience this is. Trying to maintain my guilt whilst being interrogated by someone who insists I am innocent! I don't know if you've ever been under extreme stress, Father, but people do not always act logically in those circumstances. I have no idea what I did. I panicked. I've admitted the killing; I never claimed I committed the perfect crime."

"Let's cut the shite here. You didn't commit the crime — at least, not the murder. No doubt you're guilty of fucking around with the police during a murder investigation. But never mind that for now. Tell me this: why would you put yourself through all this — getting banged up in a mental institution, and then it will be a murder trial —"

"Which you don't recommend, I presume."

"— for something you didn't do. Whom are you protecting?"

"You flatter me, Brennan. May I call you by your Christian name?"

"Suit yourself. Robin. Now, what are you up to? You've got O'Flaherty spooked. He didn't reveal anything confidential, but it's clear he thinks there's a killer on the loose across the harbour."

He changed course then. "Did it ever occur to you that I may just be seeking attention?"

"If so, you've succeeded. Now if you've had enough, perhaps you could deliver yourself of the truth and let us bring the real murderer to justice. Rather than leaving him free to lop someone else's head nearly off its post."

"I must correct you, Brennan, if you will permit me. You say I have succeeded in attracting attention to myself and, to an extent of course, I have. But I have not yet had my day in court. I have not yet been presented with the opportunity to make a speech from the dock, a practice honed to brilliance by your own countrymen facing execution for various crimes against the state. Or against their colonizers."

"You strike me as a man well able to expound his views without resorting to the criminal process. Write an article. Write a book. Write a letter to the *Times*."

"I in fact did write articles. I doubt if they've survived. The Gadkin-Falkes by-line appeared in a publication called the *English Catholic*. I played at being a journalist whilst in my early twenties and so I was selected to cover the final session of the Second Vatican Council in 1965. If my work is still extant, it will support my motive for killing the former Vatican II busybody."

"Well, then, why didn't you just dust off your outpourings on the subject, and get up on a soapbox in Hyde Park?"

"I would have done, I suppose, if I'd given old Schellenberg a thought before I left the sceptred isle. But he wasn't even in my thoughts, until he made his startling appearance here at your worthy institution. The opportunity presented itself and the rest, as they say —"

"The opportunity presented itself for somebody, but not you. Now who was it?"

"All right, Brennan, all right. Have it your way for a moment. Let us say for the sake of argument that it wasn't me. And let us think about this purely hypothetical killer. Somehow I doubt that the sort of person who would do this — someone not in control of his emotions or his actions — would be able to withstand the ordeal I am about to undergo with such admirable sangfroid. Put me in the dock, throw me in the nick, bang me up here among the barmy — it doesn't inconvenience me in the least. After all, I've been in a monastery for twenty-two years! Could have been worse, I suppose. I could have gone into the army, like my poor nephew, and been posted to Northern Ire —"

"What made you choose the religious life, Robin?"

"I am a servant of the Lord. Like yourself, Brennan."

"Why a brother and not a priest?"

"Oh, I agree. You have a higher calling than I, but —"

"Why not set your sights on being Robin Cardinal Gadkin-Falkes, Cardinal Archbishop of Westminster?"

"I could ask you the same. Why not Archbishop of Armagh? But I think I know the answer. Your ego, let us say, is sufficient unto itself. You do not crave or need the affirmation that comes from a position of leadership. And you most certainly do not need the aggravation. My imagination fails me when I try to picture you dealing patiently with the administrative cock-ups of your inferiors."

The man may have been mad as a hatter but he had Burke pinned with uncanny accuracy; no doubt he saw in him qualities he himself possessed. Burke, true to form, ignored the exchange.

"So I guess we'd better get the police on the line, Robin, and set them straight."

"Oh, I'll deny this little exchange if you report it to them."

"It's our word against yours."

"Very well then. I'll admit to the conversation but come up with a very convincing tale about why I engaged in such a fanciful discussion."

"You won't have them fooled for long, particularly if the physical evidence against you doesn't hold up."

"The evidence will hold up. It may not be the evidence of a professional criminal. It may in fact be the evidence of someone who wanted to draw attention to his crime in a rather ham-handed fashion. But I am an amateur, and have never pretended otherwise."

"Robin. You've virtually admitted you're not a criminal at all. You're not making any sense here."

"It must be the environment, Brennan! It is a psychiatric hospital, after all. Now, I must ask you gentlemen to leave me in peace. I'd show you out of the building, but I have no idea where they hide the exit. Good day to you both."

We drove to the rectory to see Michael O'Flaherty, but Mrs. Kelly told us he had been called to the Victoria General Hospital to attend to a dying parishioner. Burke and I stood discussing our loopy conversation with Robin Gadkin-Falkes, then Burke said goodbye and went up to his room to prepare for his afternoon classes.

"Not making any headway, Mr. Collins?" Mrs. Kelly came up to me as I started for the door.

"Not as far as I can tell, Mrs. Kelly. Unfortunately."

"Well, if there's anything you'd like to do here . . ."

"Sure, if I think of something I'll ask. Thanks."

"Like look around anywhere. The rooms or whatever."

"Uh-huh."

"They say you can learn a lot about a suspect from his room. Of course the police have been through Brother Robin's room already. Still . . ."

It was hard to miss the hint. "It wouldn't hurt me to have a look around in there, if you have the key."

"Let me see. Is this it? No. Wait . . . I think it's this one."

"Perfect. Thank you."

Robin Gadkin-Falkes's room was on the top floor of the three-storey building. His bed was still unmade. One black robe was slung over a chair; another hung in the wardrobe. There were two suits with shirts and ties, a pair of casual pants, and a sweater. There was nothing but underwear and socks in the bureau drawers. A small CD player sat on top of the bureau; his collection included chant by various monastic choirs, choral music by the Tallis Scholars, and a collection of works by Hildegard von Bingen. He had brought a small library with him. I noted Newman's *Apologia Pro Vita Sua* and an ancient book titled *The Great Standing Army of Rome: Monks in England before the Suppression of the Monasteries in the Time of Henry VIII.* I smiled when I saw a video of *Monty Python's Flying Circus*; whatever else could be said of Robin Gadkin-Falkes, he was not without a sense of the absurd.

But what was it Mrs. Kelly thought I should see? Something the police had missed? And why was she being so indirect? I continued my examination.

The monk had a cardboard briefcase containing materials from the course at the schola, and a scribbler full of notes made in black ink during class. He had drawn little cartoons in the margins. I guess when you're a mature student, you don't worry about having your knuckles rapped for doodling in your notebook. One of the drawings showed a man with a halo over his head; circles or spirals were drawn around the figure. It gave the impression he was turning. This was in the margin beside the words "Enough Palestrina!!!" There was a blue question mark next to the picture. I got the impression the question mark was done by someone else. In reply, Robin had written: "St. Charles spinning in his grave!" The blue ink answered: "True!" Must have been an exchange with the student at the adjacent desk, provoked by someone else saying he or she — Jan Ford perhaps? — had had enough of Palestrina, the great sixteenth-century Catholic composer. Obviously, Robin, his classmate, and Saint Charles did not agree.

The room contained more secular items as well. A bottle of gin stood half empty on a table, beside a kettle and an assortment of exotic-looking teas. There was nothing connecting Robin to Schellenberg, but I hadn't expected to find anything.

When I opened the door to leave, my foot hit something on the floor. I bent over and picked up a small rosary. It had red and white beads, and an oval religious medal at the end of the chain where a crucifix would normally be. There was a note attached to the chain with a paperclip. The note was printed on high-quality marbled paper, and had been torn from a longer sheet. It read: *"Fac me tecum plangere."* Let me cry with you? I would run it by Burke to make sure. From its position on the floor, it appeared to have been shoved under the door. I dropped it into my pocket and headed for Brennan's room. Then I thought I'd better find out what had set Mrs. Kelly on my heels.

I tracked her down in the kitchen. She looked at me and asked: "Anything there? Maybe not . . ." She tried for a tone of idle curiosity.

I drew the rosary from my pocket and held it carefully by the edges of the medal at the end. "I found this."

"I saw it there! That note might mean something."

"I'm going to assume it does."

"The police must have missed it!"

"Could be." But I doubted it. I inclined to the belief that it had been slipped under Robin's door after the police had searched the room. Placed there by whom? "I'm going to take it to the police. They'll try for fingerprints. Thanks, Mrs. K. This could be very helpful."

"You're welcome."

"Do you have an envelope?" She brought me one, and I placed the rosary inside.

"I'll see what Brennan has to say about the Latin."

Her face clouded over. The fact that she had told this to me and not to Burke — or the much more approachable Monsignor O'Flaherty — suggested that she felt she had been remiss in her duties somehow. I wondered if she had noticed it a while ago and failed to mention it. Whatever the case, I wouldn't allude to her involvement.

"I'll just say I decided to search the room. That will make me look as if I'm on the ball!"

Her relief was obvious. I headed up to Burke's room, and found him sitting at his desk with a stack of books and a writing pad. From the stereo came the glorious soprano voice of the woman of his dreams, Kiri Te Kanawa. She was giving him an incomparable version of "Vissi d'Arte."

Sempre con fè sincera la mia preghiera ai santi tabernacoli salì.
Always with true faith my prayer rose to the holy shrines.

I pressed the pause button and got down to business. "Have a look at this. It's a rosary I found on the floor just inside Gadkin-Falkes's room. Someone must have slipped it in there after the police were finished." I shook it out on Burke's table and began to caution him about handling it as little as possible. The look he gave me was meant to convey that I might be an imbecile but he was not. He didn't touch it.

"It's not a rosary; it's called a chaplet. A set of prayer beads for a certain saint. This one is —" he bent over the table and peered at the medal "— Saint Philomena. I don't know what significance the number of beads has but I'd say the three white ones symbolize virginity and the red ones, thirteen in all, symbolize martyrdom."

"What do you know about Saint Philomena?"

He shrugged. "We'll consult Michael. But I'm more interested in the note, as I'm sure you are."

"How do you translate *plangere*?"

"It means to beat your breast or your head in lamentation. A sign of grief. So whoever wrote this is saying: 'Let me grieve with you' or 'Let me share your grief.'"

"Someone sympathizes with his plight, his wrongful arrest."

"Or someone thinks he actually did it, and is expressing solidarity with the deed, or whatever drove him to it. Makes you wonder whether the writer of the note has more information than we do about our man Robin."

"Right. I'm going to take it over to the police station now. Maybe they'll get some prints off it."

"Maybe so. But the only one who'll have fingerprints on file to compare them with . . ."

Burke's voice trailed off. Robin Gadkin-Falkes wasn't the only person whose prints were on file; Burke himself had been fingerprinted at the time of the wrongful murder charge that had propelled him into my life.

"Yes, well, I'll leave you to your lesson plan." I picked up the chaplet by the edges of the medal and returned it to the envelope. Burke was lost in his own thoughts and didn't say goodbye. I pressed the button on his stereo, and Kiri resumed her lamentation:

Nell'ora del dolor perché, perché, Signor, ah, perché me ne rimuneri così?
In the hour of grief why, why, O Lord, ah, why do you reward me this way?

I drove directly to the Halifax Police Department on Gottingen

Street, presented the chaplet, and left it to be fingerprinted and cata-
logued with the other evidence. Then I went to the office for my
afternoon appointments. As usual, there was bad news for some of my
clients over the weekend. Two of them had talked to the police when
they should have exercised their right to remain silent; neither of the
confessions was as eloquent as that of Robin Gadkin-Falkes.

After my last appointment, my mind returned to the murder of
Father Schellenberg. I pictured the murder scene, Reinhold
Schellenberg's blood-drenched corpse with the head nearly severed
from the body. I thought of the near-decapitation of Saint Cecilia, on
whose feast day the murder had been committed. I recalled the police
reports showing the killer had mopped up after himself or herself,
eradicating the bloody footprints he might have made on his way out
of the church. The reports showed he had left a bloody towel and two
plastic grocery bags by the door; the police believed he had used the
bags to cover his shoes. There were no prints on the bags. If he had a
covering over any other part of him, he had taken it with him along
with the murder weapon. Schellenberg's wallet had not been taken,
but that meant nothing; nobody was pretending this was a robbery. I
wondered what to make of the valentine cards left on the body, and
the swizzle stick. The police had not been able to find any shop selling
valentines at this time of year, so the cards could not be traced. The
police had, however, located the source of the swizzle stick: the Wheel
and Anchor Beverage Room in Dartmouth. They had shown
Schellenberg's photo around, but nobody remembered seeing him in
the bar. Had they shown any other photos to the staff there? I couldn't
remember what the report said, but I knew which of the schola participants were without alibis for the time of the murder. So I decided
it couldn't hurt to collect their pictures and interview the waiters
myself. It was Monday, which meant blues night, when my band
Functus got together to wail and blow the harp and play slide guitar,
but it wouldn't be bad form to arrive late, especially if I had the perfectly acceptable excuse that I was coming from a bar.

Monsignor O'Flaherty had gone about snapping photos at the
reception held for the students on their first evening in Halifax. I
found him in residence, borrowed what I needed — I had snapshots
of Robin Gadkin-Falkes, William Logan, Fred Mills, Luigi Petrucci,

Enrico Sferrazza-Melchiorre, Kurt Bleier, and Jan Ford — and took the Macdonald Bridge across the harbour to the Wheel and Anchor on the Dartmouth waterfront. The west-facing wall of the pub was all glass, overlooking the city of Halifax and the harbour in between. It had a nautical theme, with massive anchors, ropes, wheels, and other ship's paraphernalia displayed around the room. The wait staff were togged out as sailors. Nobody on the day shift recognized any of the faces in my photos. The bartender suggested I come back later and, if I had no luck then, again on the weekend. I thanked him and headed off to join my band for an evening of the blues.

†

"They found fingerprints on that rosary, or whatever you called it, the chaplet I found in Robin's room." I had heard the news from Moody Walker on Tuesday morning, and was now on the phone to Brennan, filling him in. "Actually, the prints on the beads and medal weren't good enough to use. But there were identifiable prints on the note. Are you ready for this? The prints belong to Enrico Sferrazza-Melchiorre."

"What? Why would he give a note like that to Gadkin-Falkes? It doesn't make sense. And if he did give it, when? It must have been slipped under the door after the arrest, so how would Enrico expect Robin to get it? Or was he hoping someone else would pick it up?" He paused. "But, more to the point —"

"How come his prints are on file with the police?"

"Right. Interpol, or whatever it would be."

"Guess we'd better ask him. Where would he be this time of day?"

"Here in his room, as far as I know. Come on over."

I got snagged by a client on my way out of the office but I got him settled down, then drove to the rectory. I went upstairs, met Brennan, and followed him to the room of Enrico Sferrazza-Melchiorre. He came to the door wearing a smoking jacket of crimson satin with black lapels; he greeted us and bade us sit.

We made a bit of small talk, then I opened the questioning: "Enrico, did you send a note to Robin Gadkin-Falkes?"

The expression on his face didn't change. "No."

"Are you curious about why we're asking?"

His elaborate shrug brought into motion his eyes, mouth, shoulders, and hands. *"Va bene,* I will ask you: why are you asking?"

"Because somebody wrote a note to the monk, and attached it to a set of prayer beads, and your fingerprints are on the note."

That produced a reaction. He leaned back defensively. "My fingers on it? How can that be?"

"I was hoping you could answer that question for us."

"No, I cannot. This note, what does it say?"

Brennan joined the conversation. *"Fac me tecum plangere."*

"Perché 'plangere'?" he asked Brennan.

"I don't know why. I suppose a person could be grieving for a colleague who had fallen into mortal sin by taking the life of a fellow human being. Or it could be grief over a false charge of murder. Do you think he did it?"

"How could I know? I was not there."

I said to him: "Whoever wrote the note is not the object of any suspicion. It's just that, if the person knows something about Brother Robin and the killing of Father Schellenberg, it would be enormously helpful if that person came forward with information."

"I know nothing. And I did not write the note."

"Enrico, may I ask why your fingerprints are on file with the authorities?"

His hands made a graceful gesture of dismissal. "A small thing, an inconvenience. Monty, it would put you to sleep if I annoyed you —" he looked at Brennan "— *noia?"*

Brennan replied: "Boring. If you bored him."

"If I bored you by telling this long, foolish story. A misunderstanding is all it was. So. If you have no more questions about this strange English monk, I must dress for my day at your schola, Brennan." We took our leave.

"What do you make of that?" I asked Burke. He answered with a very Italian shrug. "Well, I'm certainly not satisfied with what we heard in there. I wonder how significant the prayer beads themselves are. If the guy just wanted to send a note, why attach it to the beads?"

"We'll assume the chaplet is significant," he answered. "I'm not familiar with Saint Philomena. I meant to ask Mike. Let's see if he's in."

Monsignor O'Flaherty was not in, but his room was open so we went inside. "He has Butler's *Lives of the Saints*. There it is." He pointed to four faded red volumes on the shelf.

"So," I said, "Philomena. Starts with P. I'm guessing volume three." I picked it up.

"It may be number three or it may not. The collection isn't organized alphabetically but chronologically. Liturgical calendar. If you don't happen to know what Saint Philomena's feast day is, pick a volume at random and start looking. The indexes are in the front."

It took us a while but we found her, and she was indeed in volume three, month of August.

"I never expected to see a four-volume book of the saints so well-thumbed and dog-eared," I remarked.

"This edition was published in 1956, and I can believe Michael's been reading it every night since. Let me see it." He removed it from my unconsecrated hands, and skimmed over the entry. "Philomena. Martyred as a young girl in Rome. Miraculous cures attributed to her." He closed the book, and we left the room.

"Brennan, just how much of a factor are the saints these days? I can't say I've heard much about them in recent years!"

"Montague, what people *these days* think or talk about, with their brains addled by television, has no bearing one way or the other on the eternal realities. In the murder case before us, we have a Saint Cecilia death scene and a Saint Philomena chaplet. To ignore the saints as a possible factor would be to ignore the evidence. You wouldn't want to do that, would you?"

"No, Your Honour."

"Thank you."

"So, who's your saint?" I asked him. "Are you devoted to any one in particular?"

"You figure it out."

"Thomas Aquinas."

"Of course. The Angelic Doctor. I've named my new Mass after him. Now if I could only get it to sound the way I want it. The 'Agnus Dei' just doesn't work. I hope to have the premiere in February, towards the end of the schola session, but now I don't know. Anyway, Saint Thomas is my main contact in heaven. And Saint Gregory. Whatever role he played in gracing us with Gregorian chant must have landed him at the right hand of God. There's a beautiful statue at Chartres Cathedral, the Holy Spirit in the form of a dove perched on Gregory's shoulder, whispering in his ear. Bestowing the gift of Gregorian chant. I'm not a weepy fellow normally, but I was moved to the point of tears when I first saw that."

"So where did the Philomena beads come from, I wonder? One of the priests may have had them on hand. Or he may have gone out and bought them especially for the occasion. There may be something in the miraculous cures, a tie-in with the reference to grief. Is it time for another chat with the accused? How about tonight?"

"Why not?"

✝

Robin Gadkin-Falkes was sitting in a chair facing his window; he was wrapped in a blanket.

"Good evening, Robin," Brennan said.

He turned to see us. "Good evening, gentlemen. What can I do for you? Or would you like to ask first whether they're making me comfortable here?"

"Are they?"

"They are most kind. And exceedingly tactful. Perhaps I'm considered a sensitive sort. I am rather a hothouse rose, I must confess. Oh, shouldn't bandy the C-word about carelessly, should I? Do sit down, Father."

Brennan sat in the only other chair.

"Here, Mr. Collins," the monk said, rising.

"Monty."

"Monty, take this chair. I shall take to my bed like the poor invalid I am. So, gentlemen, what brings you to me today?"

"We found something in your room," Brennan told him.

"Oh! Nothing embarrassing, I trust."

"Someone sent you a message."

"Best wishes for an early verdict of insanity, perhaps?"

"I'm afraid not. It's a note attached to a chaplet of Saint Philomena."

There was a jolt of recognition before he tried to cover it by fussing with his blanket.

"Would you be kind enough to enlighten us about it?"

"I'm sure you need no enlightenment from me, Brennan. You've seen the thing. I haven't."

"Oh? I thought perhaps you had."

"No. So, do tell me. I am intrigued, and not a little bored in here."

"Have you a particular devotion to Saint Philomena?"

"Can't say that I have, no."

"Let's move on to the note, then. It says: '*Fac me tecum potare.*'"

Robin couldn't hide his surprise. That was not what he was expecting to hear. He recovered as best he could. "Someone has a sense of humour. Must be trying to jolly me along through my ordeal. Well, if you find him, tell him I should be delighted to drink with him, as long as it's his treat. Nothing to swill in this place."

"Oh, forgive me," Brennan said then. "I had it wrong. It's '*Fac me tecum plangere.*'"

"Ah. We've gone from boozing to grief. A reversal of the natural order of things."

"That's right. I'm asking myself whether the writer of the note is grieving with you over your plight today, or whether the grief refers to something else. What do you think, Robin?"

I expected another flippant reply. But no.

"I lost someone." He looked away from us towards the window. "I understand grief all too well." He faced us again and continued. "Forgive me, if you will, for descending to melodrama. I lost my own mirror image, the other half of my soul. She was the love of my life, and I mean my entire life. From the instant of conception to this day and if God chooses, I shall but love her better after death. Let me show you."

He got up, opened his overnight bag, and gently extracted a photograph in a leather frame. "Here we are at fifteen, the year before she died."

The black-and-white photo showed a boy and a girl, slim and attractive with short blond hair. He had his arm around her shoulder, and they both were gazing intently at something to the left of the camera. Apart from the fact that one was male and the other female, they were identical.

"Twins, as you can see. My sister, Louisa. We were one. We shared the same womb, the same cot in the nursery, the same bath. We never grew apart. We never needed anyone else. For anything. When she was taken from me, I tried to go with her. Tried to top myself, you see. Didn't succeed. Here I am."

Brennan had lapsed into silence, so I asked: "How did your sister die?"

"My parents took her to South Africa, where we had family. I didn't go because I was in high dudgeon about something my father had said. If I had gone, Louisa would never have contracted her illness — or I should say infection — because she would not have gone into the wilds of Africa on an adventure with my half-wit cousins. They struck out into the jungles, where all manner of writhing, biting, stinging creatures lay in wait. I ask you, really! What civilized person — Had I been there, Louisa would have stayed with me and we'd have contented ourselves with the shops and art galleries of Jo'burg. Instead of boarding a private plane — I would have lashed myself to the propellers to prevent that! — and going off to the jungle. Anyway, she died out there. I never saw her again. After my own unsuccessful attempt to follow her into death, I underwent years and years of tedious therapy. How many times can you hear the word 'narcissism' before you want to scream and fall upon your therapist with a blunt and heavy object? 'Could it be that you were in love with yourself, Robin?' We were in love with each other! And with ourselves! It was all one and the same. Why be tiresome about it? Forgive me, I must be boring you. Brennan, you have been silent all through my little scene. Is it just too tawdry for you? Should I fall to my knees in the confessional yet again?"

Brennan looked over at him, not unsympathetically, I thought, but still did not speak.

"Where did religion come into all this, Robin?" I asked him.

"It was not just a reaction, a retreat from the world, contrary to the trite thinking that characterized just about everyone I ever met subsequently. My sister and I had always been — I won't say 'pious' and I certainly won't say 'saintly' — perhaps I could say 'spiritual.' We came from an old papist family. Shunned by many of the 'best' people on account of it, needless to say. I had always toyed with the idea of entering an order. I knew I would never marry. Even what passes for the aristocracy in England these days would not have condoned the only marriage that I ever wanted to contract. So, no interest in settling down with a wife. There went the biggest obstacle to religious life for me. I joined the Benedictines and spent my days tilling the fields, tending the garden, chanting my office, and praying to God to take me home where I could see Him, and Louisa, face to face."

"I am very sorry about your sister, Robin," I said. "Is there a connection of some kind between her death, your grief for her, and the death of Reinhold Schellenberg?"

"Not that I can see. Can you? I thought we were talking of this note you found in my room."

"We were. But naturally I wonder whether a message sent to you, the man accused of the murder of Schellenberg, is in some way connected to the case."

"Can't help you there, I'm afraid."

"How well do you know Father Sferrazza-Melchiorre?"

Robin raised his eyebrows. "How well could a simple monk like me know a worldly figure like Sferrazza-Melchiorre?"

"You tell me."

"I have lived a monastic life. Our sartorially splendid *sacerdos* clearly has not. *So* Mediterranean! I had never heard of the man until I arrived at the schola cantorum."

"Did you become friendly with him during the course?"

"We exchanged pleasantries from time to time. That is all. Why are you asking about him? Is he a suspect? I hope he is, if you'll forgive me for saying so. The jailhouse and the mental asylum would bring him into intimate contact with the least of our Lord's dear brethren. A new dimension to his vocation, I daresay. And a new, pared-down wardrobe instead of all that clobber he's usually got on. Now Logan, the American, poor devil, not even a Roman collar could dress him up."

"Don't be thinking you can mulvather us with all this chit-chat," Brennan admonished him. "Let's get back to —"

"My dear chap, I've never heard you speak in your native patois, and I must say —"

"Don't you 'my dear chap' me. You seem to be getting a little too much enjoyment out of all this and your central role in it. Well, I for one have had my fill of you." Suddenly, Burke bolted out of his chair and leaned into the monk's pale face. "Did you, or did you not, kill Schellenberg?"

Gadkin-Falkes reared back, clutching his blanket in front of him. "Leave me! Get out!"

A nurse rushed into the room. "What's going on here? Are you all right, Brother Robin?"

"Yes, I'm quite all right, thank you. Though I do think it's time for these men to leave."

"Brother Robin needs to rest now," she told us, and stood aside for us to leave. Burke glared at the man in the hospital bed. But the invalid refused to meet his eyes.

"Mulvather?" I inquired.

"Bamboozle, confuse. Trying to get us off track with all this shite about Enrico's wardrobe. About the confession, Monty — I'm thinking we should keep it to ourselves for a bit. Leave the other suspects wondering whether we think Gadkin-Falkes is guilty or not."

"Mum's the word."

We drove back across the harbour to St. Bernadette's.

"I have to prepare tomorrow's lecture on the sacred music of Mozart. How would you like to fill Michael O'Flaherty in on our conversation with Gadkin-Falkes?"

"Sure. I'll give him a quick rundown before I head home."

I found Michael in the priests' library and described our encounter with the Englishman.

"So we know a bit more about Robin now, Mike. We know he's well aware of the prayer beads, though he refuses to admit it. And he denies any particular interest in Saint Philomena."

"The chaplet was the only item in his room that related to Philomena, was it, Monty?"

"As far as I could see, yes."

Mike said: "So that reinforces the impression that the Philomena reference is about someone else."

"Right. The only other reference I saw to a saint was a little drawing of Saint Charles. Whoever he is."

"What did the drawing look like?"

"It depicted the saint spinning in his grave. Somebody in one of the schola classes apparently announced that he or she had heard enough of Palestrina. Sacrilege, in the opinion of Robin and the saint."

"Well now, that would be Charles Borromeo. Sixteenth-century Italian saint. A contemporary, and a champion, of Palestrina. Charles is a particular favourite of clergymen, including Pope John XXIII! If my memory isn't fooling me, it seems to me Pope John arranged to have his papal coronation on the feast day of Saint Charles."

"So this saint might be associated in some minds with John XXIII, who set in motion the Second Vatican Council."

"Now I wouldn't be reading too much into that, Monty. Any more than I'd suspect you because Saint Charles was a lawyer!"

Chapter 7

Omnes sancti Sacerdotes et Levitæ, orate pro nobis.
Omnes sancti Monachi et Eremitæ, orate pro nobis.
Sancta Cæcilia, ora pro nobis.
All ye holy priests and Levites, pray for us.
All ye holy monks and hermits, pray for us.
Saint Cecilia, pray for us.
— "Litany of the Saints"

"What are you looking at, Bleier?"

"Is this the part of the movie where I am to be beaten by your fists, Logan? Or shot with a pistol? It seems I have looked at you in the wrong way; we all know what happens to those who do that."

"I'm glad you find things so funny here. Which leads me to the obvious question: what are you doing here, Bleier?"

"I am an invited guest."

We all were. I had joined Brennan and a few people from the schola for lunch Wednesday at the Gondola on South Street. We had just ordered our meal, and received our drinks, when Kurt Bleier walked in and drew the ire of William Logan.

"You know goddamn well what I mean, *Colonel.* Why are you at a school for traditional Catholic music? You know, that just doesn't compute for me."

"I might ask you the same question, Mr. Logan. What attracts you to such a traditional Catholic program? Did you not leave the church many years ago?"

"I never left! I am a Catholic! I am now living in the lay state and

I have my disagreements with the church, sure. But why am I answering to you? If you had your way, there would be no church. No religion. No belief in —"

"If you had your way, Mr. Logan, what kind of church would there be?"

"What the hell do you mean by that?"

"Just a question. What kind of church would you like to see?"

"I don't see how that's any of your business, considering how you guys worked to suppress religion at every turn."

"On the contrary. You will find that in the German Democratic Republic, the church was left largely to its own devices, as long as it —"

"As long as it toed the party line!"

"How could it do that? If, as you suggest, the party line was atheistic materialism, a church that toed the line would hardly be a church. And yet Christianity survived in democratic Germany. In fact, churchmen were always free to practise their faith."

"Free! Your system is the very antithesis of freedom. You would have liked nothing more than to overthrow the government of the United States, the very Land of the Free. What are you smirking at, Brennan? You think this is funny? Come to think of it, you never were actually Americanized, were you? You in your little Irish ghetto in New York. But this isn't about you. This is about Colonel Bleier and his late, lamented commie state, where nobody even had the freedom to take a piss without checking with the party first."

"Freedom is a mantra for you Americans, I realize," Bleier replied. "But what I see in America is freedom run amok. When it comes to the point where the citizens are free to buy guns at will and kill each other with them, have you not taken freedom beyond its logical extreme? Are you not on your way towards a society in which the freedom of the unarmed will be trampled by those who are armed with weapons, where you will not be free to step outside your house without the fear of being attacked?"

"I'm glad you mentioned killing, Kurt. That goes back to my original question. Why are you here? How many religious institutions have you attended in your life? Besides whichever ones you infiltrated so you could spy on them, I mean. Is this the first time you were struck with the inspiration to go to church? Did this inspiration coincide, by any chance, with the fact that Reinhold Schellenberg was coming here? A fellow German, who no doubt opposed everything you stood for and tried to do?"

"Were you not in opposition to Reinhold Schellenberg yourself, Mr. Logan? Did he not represent a retrenchment to a position for the church that you could not abide?"

"Are *you* accusing *me* of Schellenberg's murder?"

"Pardon my poor manners. I thought for a moment you were making the same accusation against me. Without any evidence or grounds on which to do so."

†

An uneasy truce was established, and peace reigned. Until I got to my office. I walked in to find one of my criminal clients badgering our receptionist about my absence. He was looming over the reception desk, and Darlene was clearly uncomfortable.

"What's the trouble, Duane? Move away from the desk."

"I'll stand wherever I fucking well want to, Collins."

"Darlene, maybe you'd like to go for your coffee break now."

"Well, I —"

"Go ahead." When she was out of harm's way, I said: "All right, Duane. Let's have a seat and see what's bothering you today."

"You're never fucking here when I want you. I got a trial coming up, remember?"

"I do remember. All you have to do is make an appointment and I'll be here. As it happens, I have a file full of copies of letters I've written to you, asking you for names of witnesses and other information I need for your defence. I've called you and left messages. You never call, you never write. You're the one who's going to jail if I can't put on a decent defence, but I need help from you —"

"If I go to jail, Collins, you die the fucking minute I get out. Hear me? So you get to work on my case and do a good job on it. Or you're dead. Got it?"

Out of the corner of my eye, I saw someone come into the reception room. I heard the person pick up the phone and punch in some numbers. I heard a man's voice, one of my partners. "Yes, I'd like to report a criminal offence. Uttering a threat. I'm calling from the Stratton Sommers law office on Barrington Street . . ." Duane bolted from the room.

So we dealt with that. Once again, I had made myself unpopular not only with a client but with my fellow lawyers at Stratton Sommers. Not everyone looked kindly on the addition of a criminal law department — me — to this long-established corporate law firm.

✝

"Who was it who said: 'Let's kill all the lawyers'?"

I had decided to absent myself from the office after the uproar with Duane. Something with a little more tone, like a lecture by a visiting professor on the counterpoint of Johann Sebastian Bach, was a fine corrective. I stayed in the classroom after the lecture and regaled Brennan with the tale about Duane.

"'Kill all the lawyers,'" he repeated. "I'm sure that's been said in every part of the world, in every age."

"Thanks, Burke. But some of us do the work of the angels. Not to blow my own trumpet, of course, but . . ."

"But what?"

"Nothing. I was fishing for a compliment. Hoping you'd butt in and assure me I'm doing good works. Mike O'Flaherty even came up with a saint who was a lawyer. Can't remember the name."

"Could be any of a number of people. There were many lawyer saints."

"There's hope for me yet. This guy was the patron saint of Pope John XXIII, or no, John was crowned on this saint's feast day. Saint Charles somebody."

"Must be Carlo Borromeo."

"Yes, that's him."

"One of those many and varied instances you're talking about, where somebody said: 'Let's kill all the lawyers.'"

"Why do you say that?"

"Somebody tried to do him in."

"What?"

"There was a plot to assassinate him. They shot him while he was

134

kneeling at the altar, saying evening prayers with members of his household. He commended himself to God and instructed the others to finish their prayers. But he survived the attempt and lived for another fifteen years."

"This happened during evening prayers. As in our case of an attack during vespers. Who tried to kill him?"

"A group of nasty priors."

"Priors?"

"High-ranking monks."

"Why?"

"He tried to rein them in, I suppose. Reform their order."

"Which order was it?"

"They were called the *Umiliati*. I don't know much more than that."

"Well, try to know a bit more about it next time we speak!"

"Monty, if someone here is devoted to Charles Borromeo, who was the victim — not the perpetrator — of an assassination attempt, chances are the fellow would take a dim view of those who try to pick off members of the clergy. There's no reason to think he'd take up arms against them. That would be like saying a devotee of Saint Thomas Aquinas would suddenly try to imitate the actions of his brothers in abducting him, holding him captive, and sending a hooker into his room. It doesn't make sense to think —"

"What? What are you talking about now?"

"Don't you know the history of Saint Thomas?"

"I know something about his times, and his thought, but what's this about a hooker?"

"Thomas's family — they were nobility, with a military history and royal connections — had become resigned to the fact that Thomas's future lay with the church. So they tried to make the best of it. They paved the way for him to become a monk and then, eventually, the abbot of Monte Cassino. But Thomas was having none of it. He was determined to become one of the Begging Friars, in the new order founded by Saint Dominic. Well! The fur was flying when he brought this news home. Not long afterwards, when Thomas was travelling on a road near Rome, he was waylaid by his furious brothers, who seized him and locked him up in a castle. They sent in a painted hussy to tempt him. He put the run to her and settled down to his life's work."

"And here I thought all this ecclesiastical mayhem was an aberration! We could have wild-eyed, murderous factions on all sides of this and never penetrate to the truth."

"It doesn't admit of an obvious solution."

"Borromeo was a favourite saint of John XXIII," I mused aloud. "And our victim, Father Schellenberg, was active in the Council set up by John in the sixties. But then he turned against John. So —"

"Who said he turned against John? Don't forget, Pope John died just eight months after convening the Council; it went on for another two years after his death. It's just as likely Schellenberg thought the changes in the church, as far as they went, would have offended John had he lived to see them. So he may have thought he was being true to John's legacy by backtracking in his positions. You can't take this train of thought to any logical end."

"So it seems. What are you going to do now?"

"Try to compose a few suitable bars of music for my Mass."

"Good luck with it."

"I'll need it. See you later."

He headed for the auditorium, and I started for the exit. Michael O'Flaherty and Fred Mills were chatting in the doorway.

"Did you know Father Mills played baseball in the major leagues, Monty?" Michael asked.

"I heard that. The Royals, was it, Fred?"

"That's right."

"When did you play?"

"Mid-seventies."

"With George Brett and Amos Otis!"

"Yeah, them and Mayberry and Patek. I taught them everything they know!"

"What position did you play?"

"Second base. If you watched the games on television, you probably saw a lot of Cookie Rojas on second. But if you kept watching, you'd see me once in a while."

"And he had a pretty nice batting average," Michael put in. "What was it, Fred?"

"It was .281."

"Good for you. Must have been hard to leave it behind."

"Well, yeah, but I knew I had a vocation, Monty. Brennan thinks I should have stayed on, and become a major league baseball chaplain or something."

"You could have heard their confessions."

"Didn't have to — I was on the road with them!"

"Some wild times, I'll bet."

"Not for me."

"Well, I should be off," I said. "Suppertime."

"I could use a bit of nourishment myself," O'Flaherty commented. "Mrs. Kelly is away today. Gone to visit her sister. So I'll make a foray into her kitchen and see what she left for us."

"Never mind that, Mike," I said. "Let's go find a bite to eat in one of the local guzzling dens. Especially since you missed lunch at the Gondola. My treat."

"Oh, now, doesn't that sound tempting!"

"How about you, Fred? Are you up for a brew?"

"Sure. I'd love a beer and a bit of pub grub."

"We'll take my car," I said. "Do you want to change first, Mike?"

"No, no, I'll keep my collar on. It helps to keep my head straight!"

"Sound advice for us all," Fred agreed.

"So, Fred, what kind of parish are you in?" Michael asked, as we walked to the parking lot.

"Parishes, Mike, in the plural. Too many, and not the one I want. They won't give me Saint John Vianney, which is a very dynamic young parish named after my favourite saint. There's a cranky old priest ensconced there, and he won't retire. And how can they force him out, with the situation the church is facing these days? There's a real shortage of priests where I am, in Kansas, so I'm run ragged. I had to plead and beg to get time off to attend the schola. But I had not had a vacation in six years, so the bishop finally took pity on me. As long as I brought some of my paperwork with me."

"Yes, we've lost a great number of priests in the last twenty-five years. Ever since Vatican II. There was good and bad about the Council, for sure. Don't tell Brennan I said so, but not every single piece of post-Vatican II music is bad! And the Mass is still beautiful in its own way, as he well knows or he wouldn't say Mass at all! It hasn't all been liturgical chaos since 1965. As for our fellow priests, however, I say they should have worked through their problems and stuck to their vocations. Holy Orders isn't something a man takes on lightly. But who listens to an oul fella?"

"I agree with you entirely, Mike. There's a homey expression where I come from: stick-to-it-iveness, and I wish more priests were blessed with it."

We got into my car, Michael in the front passenger seat, Fred in the back.

"Where to, Monsignor? The Midtown?"

"Oh, I do enjoy the Midtown. But if you have another place in mind, take us there. We're up for an adventure, aren't we, Fred?"

"Adventure is my middle name."

"Then let's go all the way to our sister city and sample the grub over there. I know a place where they pour a decent pint, and they have a splendid the view of the harbour lights. It's right on the water."

"What's this?" Fred asked. "Where are we going?"

"Overseas," I answered. I made my way to Gottingen Street and continued north towards the turnoff for the bridge.

"Really, where are we going?"

"You can probably see it from here if you look across and to the south," I answered.

"Let me out."

"What?"

"I didn't know you were planning to — to go so far. I thought we were going to a place near the choir school. Have a quick bite, down a beer, and then back home."

"This isn't far at all, Fred. Less than five minutes and we'll have glass and menu in hand."

"No!" His voice had risen. "I can't take this much time off tonight. Just stop and let me out."

"Time off from what?"

"I'm preparing a report for the bishop back home. It's long overdue. So let me out!"

"Okay, Fred. I'll turn around at North Street and take you back to the rectory."

"No, no, it's all right. I'll —"

"What's the matter, Fred? Have you been to this bar before, by any chance?"

"No! Brennan can vouch for me on that score. In fact, I've never been anyplace over there."

The light turned red at the North Street intersection. I stopped, and Fred Mills jumped out of the car. He skipped over to the sidewalk and began the trek back downtown. Michael was twisted around, looking at the young priest's back. "I guess we'd better leave him be, Monty. We'll keep going and have our pint. Or two. Though I suspect he needs it more than we do. Brennan speaks very highly of the lad."

"Yes, he does." Though he wouldn't be able to vouch for the young priest's whereabouts every minute of every day, as much as Mills might like us to believe otherwise.

We continued on to the Wheel and Anchor. Michael and I sat by the windows, ordered food and drink, and admired our hometown across the harbour. The water was absolutely still, and the lights cast a perfect reflection. It was a different bartender from last time, so I pulled out the crumpled photos from my wallet and gave my spiel again. He didn't recognize any of my suspects. A young waitress came by then, with a fistful of anchor swizzle sticks like the one found on Father Schellenberg's body, and I showed the pictures to her. She looked at them intently but, in the end, shook her head.

"Sorry I can't help you. I don't remember seeing any of these guys, but they look pretty clean-cut. Put a ball cap on somebody and have them go for a day without a shave, and it's a different story. I know because I did a makeover on my boyfriend. Cleaned him up before introducing him to my mum and dad! If any of these guys came in looking a little rougher, I wouldn't recognize them from these pictures."

"Too true," the bartender agreed.

They went back to work, and Mike and I returned to our meal. Mike kept me highly entertained with stories of his life as a fledgling priest in some of the small villages outside Halifax. Hearing what he went through in his years as a man of the cloth, I could well understand his disappointment with those who failed to stay on the path on which God had set them. We finished our beer and returned to Halifax.

139

†

Burke and I had dinner at my house the following night. I steamed the salmon; he provided the wine. Now the plates were off the dining room table, and I was sitting with my case file and a legal pad in front of me, a pencil in my hand.

"All right, Father. Let's hear about the saints. If I write it all down, maybe I'll see a connection. Start with Saint Charles Borromeo."

"He is sometimes called 'Apostle to the Council of Trent.' He participated in the Council, which took place in the sixteenth century, and he played a significant role in enforcing its decrees. He was an important figure in the Counter-Reformation."

"The Council of Trent, which formalized the Tridentine Mass. The Council that many feel was betrayed by the Second Vatican Council four hundred years later."

"That's right," Brennan replied as I scribbled notes. "And to be more specific, Charles was involved in the reform of the church's music. Some say it was Borromeo himself who commissioned three Masses from Palestrina, including the incomparable *Missa Papae Marcelli*. The date of the composition of that Mass is a matter of dispute, but that's a debate for another day."

"So, we have Robin Gadkin-Falkes devoted to the saint who is most closely associated with the Council of Trent, the very saint honoured by Pope John XXIII on his coronation day. And —"

"And Reinhold Schellenberg was an adviser to an adviser to John XXIII, and then seemed to revert to the Council of Trent after witnessing the problems associated with John's own Council, and it goes back and forth and gets us nowhere."

"All right. What other saints do we have? Fred Mills mentioned someone, his favourite saint. It will come to me —"

"Saint John Vianney. Fred has been devoted to him since his seminary days. John is a patron saint of priests. Known as a great confessor. Heard confessions sixteen hours a day, according to some accounts."

"There could be something in that."

"Could be. Or not."

"I'll write it down. Saint John, Fred. He who lied to us about his alibi. Oh, and he jumped out of the car yesterday rather than go to the Wheel and Anchor with me and Michael! Said you'd vouch for him, that he's innocent nonetheless."

"I do. He is. Move on."

"All right, all right. Who else have we got by way of saints? What did I hear about Jan Ford and a saint? She's writing an operetta about somebody."

"An operetta," Burke repeated. "Spare me."

"Joan of Arc, that's it. And it's a song cycle, not an operetta. Mrs. Kelly was telling me she was invited to add a few lines."

"Are you demented, Montague? You're not making sense here."

"I know, but the point is Jan Ford is interested in Saint Joan of Arc."

"There may be good news in that somehow. Who's got more backbone than Joan of Arc? If Ford prays to her often enough, the warrior saint may cure her of her wishy-washy music."

"Hope so. And then we have Saint Philomena. Of particular interest because of the prayer beads and note found in Brother Robin's room. He denies any knowledge of the note, which would make sense if it was delivered after his arrest. But you'll recall his jolt of recognition, so it's hard to know what to think. He claims he has no particular interest in her as a saint. Have we found anyone else here who is devoted to her?"

"Not that we know of."

"But the fingerprints of Enrico Sferrazza-Melchiorre were on that note, though he dismissed out of hand any suggestion that he wrote it. He has a little shrine in his room, but that's to the Virgin Mary. You should have seen the face on Sergeant Walker when we came upon Enrico serenading a portrait of the bare-breasted virgin!" Burke gave a snort of laughter. "Has he got a saint besides Mary that he favours?"

"I didn't see anything — oh, he did mention Saint Andrew Avellino at one point. I don't recall how the subject came up."

"Avellino? Who's he?"

"I know very little about him. I'll see what I can find out."

"Next in the litany of saints? Saint Cecilia, obviously, given that the murder was committed on her feast day, November 22. Patron saint of church musicians like yourself."

"What did we decide about the manner of Father Schellenberg's death when compared to Cecilia's?"

"Mike O'Flaherty told us Cecilia's killers had tried to suffocate her in her bath. I don't recall anything about our case corresponding to that. But hold on while I dig out my crime scene notes." I found them and placed them on the table. "Nothing about a bath. The victim had a couple of odd items on him. A swizzle stick from the Wheel and Anchor. The police checked the bar, and nobody remembered Father Schellenberg being there, but of course nobody could say for sure that he hadn't been. Same with my efforts to find someone who recognized any of our suspects from their photos. And there were the valentine cards, pink hearts with arrows through them. The police couldn't trace the valentines. Card shops say they are typical of the cards you'd find in a boxed set. The victim had some loose change in his pocket. Nothing remarkable about the coins. He had a wallet with the usual items in it. Anyway, back to Saint Cecilia. According to Mike, she somehow survived the drowning or suffocation attempt, so they went at her again. They took three whacks at her neck, trying to decapitate her. But they couldn't get her head off. She managed to live for three days after all that. It appeared as though our killer tried to sever Schellenberg's head from his body; he very nearly succeeded. So, some similarities. The scene may indeed have been staged to correspond to Saint Cecilia."

"Which may bring us back to music as a motive."

"How far would you go in the name of great music, Brennan?"

"I can't count the times music has nearly driven me to murder!"

"Nearly, but in the end you stayed your hand. Seriously, though, do you think someone would kill for music?"

"'Music is the harmonious voice of creation, an echo of the invisible world.' That is a quotation from Giuseppe Mazzini, a nineteenth-century Italian. Monty, think what your own life would be without the music you love: blues, opera, all the other kinds of music you play or listen to. Imagine if someone had the power to deny it to you forever. Imagine a concert pianist or a blues guitarist if someone took a hammer to his fingers . . . Well, let's not dwell on that. Remember too that if this person is a churchman, the Catholic Church thinks in terms of centuries, millennia, not decades or years. Do you know what the Second Vatican Council said about music?

This may surprise you, given the schlock you've heard in the church ever since the Council. But the Council itself wrote that the musical tradition of the universal church is a 'treasure of inestimable value, greater even than any other art.' Meaning it's greater than Michelangelo's *Pietà*, greater than the immense Gothic cathedrals with their priceless stained-glass windows. Music is pre-eminent because it forms a 'necessary or integral part of the solemn liturgy.' The Council document goes on to say that Gregorian chant is the music specially suited to the Roman liturgy, and that chant should be given pride of place in the Mass and other services. The tones that were adopted in plainchant are the tones that were sung in ancient Jewish times, the time of Jesus and the apostles. Polyphony, too, was mentioned in the Council documents. Think of the Renaissance polyphony we sing here in the choir. Play in your mind the melody and words of Victoria's 'Reproaches': the soaring line of the 'sanctus immortalis,' the descending notes through the 'miserere nobis.' What could possibly be more beautiful, more holy than that line of music?

"If someone thinks all that will die out forever as the result of decisions that were made or of vulgarities that were allowed to creep in, and if he is the type of personality who can cross the line you or I would never cross, you know as well as I do somebody would kill for music."

We were silent for a few minutes. I thought about music and the other great art associated with the Catholic Church. The sculpture, the stained glass, the great cathedrals. And it reminded me of something I had meant to do. I had not yet managed to interview the man who had set fire to a church in his native New Jersey some years before.

"Hold on a moment while I call Mrs. Kelly," I said. Brennan raised his left eyebrow in an unspoken question. "We're just good friends," I assured him.

She answered on the first ring. "Mrs. Kelly, this is Monty Collins. Could you give me the phone number for Luigi Petrucci again?" I waited for her to retrieve the number and I wrote it down. "Thanks."

"You haven't seen Father Burke, have you, Mr. Collins?"

"Father Burke? Is he among the missing, Mrs. Kelly?"

"His Grace was here. And not a priest in the house to greet him!"

"Oh? Did they know the bishop was coming by?"

"Well, no. He dropped in unannounced!"

"Look at it this way: it's a good thing he didn't drop in and find Monsignor O'Flaherty and Father Burke loafing around the rectory doing nothing. I'm sure they're out doing good works, and the bishop will be pleased."

"Well, I suppose it's possible," the housekeeper allowed, "though His Grace made a little joke."

"Oh?"

"He said: 'Where's yer man? Out at the Midtown Tavern?'"

"The Midtown! The bishop said that?" Burke's eyes bored into me from across the desk. "About Monsignor O'Flaherty? Good heavens!" Burke gave a bark of laughter.

"No, no," Mrs. Kelly hastened to explain, "he wasn't talking about Monsignor!"

"Oh, not Monsignor. Right. I'm sorry. Anyway, I'll let you go. Thanks, Mrs. Kelly."

"You're welcome."

"Ever the defence lawyer," Brennan remarked after I had hung up.

After he departed, I dialled the number of the apartment where Lou Petrucci was staying. A young man answered and said he was expecting his uncle home in half an hour or so.

I was waiting outside the Park Vic, a big apartment block on South Park Street, when a black American sedan with Jersey plates pulled up in front. The man who emerged was compact and middle-aged; he wore black-framed glasses and had thick dark hair brushed back from his forehead. Luigi Petrucci. I hailed him, walked over to his car, explained who I was. He greeted me in a heavy New Jersey accent.

"Lou, perhaps you know why I'm here."

He gave me a wary look. "You're asking everybody where they were when the priest was killed?"

"There's that, of course. So tell me: where were you that Friday afternoon?"

"I was having lunch with Georgie. My nephew, Giorgio."

"Where?"

"The Lighthouse Tavern."

"What time did you get there?"

"Maybe twelve-thirty, one."

"And how long did you stay?"

His eyes on mine were wide, unblinking. "I can't remember exactly. We were there for a couple hours, a few hours, something like that."

"You had some trouble in the past, Lou."

No reply.

"We've had to do some background checks on the people here. You understand, I'm sure."

"The fire."

"Right."

"I was crazy."

"But you did time in prison, didn't you? You were found guilty."

"Yeah, what happened was, it made me crazy what they did to that church."

"Which was what?"

"You know who built that church? Three generations of Petruccis, that's who. It took nearly twenty years to complete the project, from the 1890s to 1912. My great-great-grandfather started on the stonework the same week he arrived on American soil from Italy, my great-grandfather finished it. My grandfather was called whenever the walls needed repairs. My family built Santa Chiara's! That was our parish, and our lives revolved around it. You should have seen that building as it was then. A knockout. Bowl you right over when you walked by it. House of God? Oh, yeah, big time. And inside, *Madonn'*. Gorgeous high altar. You know, the altar and the elaborate kind of structure built up behind it, all white spires and pinnacles and things. Reaching up to heaven. It's called a reredos. They took a jackhammer to it, those pricks! Tore it right out of there. Goodbye, Charlie."

Petrucci's voice had risen, and so had the colour in his face.

"The church had columns and a big high ceiling, not arched but rounded. You may have seen Italian churches with ceilings like that. And it was decorated with frescoes. Fuck 'em. Gone. Well, I rescued the statue of Santa Chiara. Saint Clare. Beautiful statue — I'll bet she was a babe in real life. Anyway, know what they did to the church? Lowered the fucking ceiling, put in a new one made of acoustic tiles. About ten feet up. You may be wondering what they put up in front, once they hustled the altar out of there. One of those cheapo wooden tables was shoved out into the congregation, and behind that the so-called sanctuary is all covered over with cheap wood panelling. Looks like some guy's rec room. You expect to see a bunch of bowling trophies. But they didn't stop there. They yanked the pews and the kneelers out and replaced them with folding chairs, all at angles facing the chintzy table where the Mass is celebrated. Yeah, big celebration. You know when it starts 'cause that's when you hear the guitars and the tambourines, and the liturgical dancers start swivellin' their hips up at the front. Oh, and you see the plus sign coming in. You can't say it's a crucifix because Jesus isn't on it, and you can't recognize it as a Catholic cross because the sides are all the same length. A plus sign. They bundle it out of there after Mass, so, as far as I can tell, there's nothing in the interior of that building that looks like a church.

"And that's the way they want it!" Petrucci pointed a trembling finger in my face. "I did some reading after the desecration of that church and I found out the whole plan was to renovate or build these places that wouldn't look like churches! Places that could be used for all kinds of other meetings and stuff. That's why the cheap, moveable seating. You had these guys who weren't even Catholic, and who didn't like Catholic art or architecture, making up theories about what new Catholic worship spaces — I kid you not, *worship spaces* — should look like. And what they shouldn't look like was the house of God. I'm not imagining this stuff. You can look it up! That's why I fucking torched it!"

"And you'd do it again."

"No, I wouldn't do it again! If I did it again, I'd do more jail time. My wife would pack up and leave me. And those committees would just put it all back together the way they had it. No sweat, it's just cheap materials after all. Not like replacing the Sistine Chapel. I never want to see Santa Chiara's again. We go to a different church now, a great old Gothic place. They're threatening to close it. Over my dead body!"

"When did all these renovation theories come into play?"

"When do you think? The sixties and seventies. And it's still going on."

"So it started after Vatican II."

"What? You think I'm the guy that whacked Father Schellenberg because he was Vatican II?"

"It doesn't look good for you, setting fire to a church because you didn't agree with the new policies."

"The new policies were shit. They were more nails in the coffin for the church after the Vatican Council. People can't even worship properly in these places. They aren't kneeling there in adoration of God, they're sitting around having a meeting with each other. Hunkering in under that low ceiling. And Santa Chiara's isn't even the worst of them. There are churches out there that look like clamshells. I saw a picture of one that looks like a golf ball. I think it's up here in Canada. But guess what? It's not the Vatican's fault. Look at the papers from the Council. Nowhere did they call for all this trashing of the churches. They said the opposite. Churches and sacred art were to be preserved, not thrown on the garbage heap. So I don't blame Vatican II for any of that."

"Do you blame Reinhold Schellenberg?"

"Schellenberg wasn't the man in charge; the buck didn't stop with him. Now, are you finished? You've got me steamed and I need a drink."

✝

"So," I told Burke on the phone, "things won't look good for Lou if his alibi doesn't hold up or if the police find anything tying him to Father Schellenberg. He'll need a good lawyer."

"Someone other than you. Bit of a conflict of interest there. Speaking of lawyers, you'll be interested to hear that Andrew Avellino, the saint favoured by Enrico Sferrazza-Melchiorre, was a lawyer."

"Another one! Like Saint Charles Borromeo."

"As a matter of fact, he was a friend of Borromeo."

"You're making this up!"

"No."

"These guys all knew each other?"

"These two did. And there's more. I did some quick research. Like Charles Borromeo, Andrew was attacked by people who were pissed off by his efforts at reform. He survived."

"Who was being reformed this time?"

"You'll love this, Monty. There was, in Naples, a convent that was something of a hoor house."

147

"A brothel run by the nuns! I'm going to write the screenplay!"

"I'll do the soundtrack. Anyway, Andrew succeeded in restoring celibate discipline to this convent of ill repute, and was beaten by a crowd of men who had been thrown out."

"If all these scandalous events made it into the Sunday sermons, the churches would be full."

"No doubt. This Andrew was apparently a handsome lad and was beset by female admirers, so he shaved his head. Or, to be more correct, he took the ecclesiastical tonsure. This was before he became a lawyer, and then a priest. He was Sicilian."

"Enrico is part Sicilian. Which may account for his affinity with the saint."

✝

"Break time," I remarked to Brennan the next day, as we enjoyed a lunch of lobster sandwiches at the Bluenose Restaurant. It was Friday, December 13, the last day of classes at the Schola Cantorum Sancta Bernadetta until January. "Do you think your students can get their home choirs in shape in time for Christmas?"

"With what they've learned at my school, they'll sound like the heavenly host."

"So. What do we do now?"

"Now we act as if the murder is solved, the case closed. I think we should announce to the group that Gadkin-Falkes has confessed. It's Christmas. I intend to leave them all with the impression that they have nothing more to fear. Let the innocent sleep soundly in their beds, and the guilty believe he is off the hook. With the pressure off, new information may float to the surface."

"It will be interesting to see who returns for session two after Christmas. Or, should I say, who doesn't come back."

"Yes. As I've said before, I find it curious that the killer didn't slip out of the country immediately after the murder."

"We have no idea how that individual's mind works, whoever he is."

"Interestingly enough, all of the students have told me they're coming back. Including those without alibis. But then, with one exception, those without alibis are innocent! A couple of them aren't even

148

leaving for Christmas. Billy Logan is staying on. He didn't say as much, but I got the impression he and his wife have nowhere else to go right now. They may even have lost their house in the States; it's not clear. But they have free rent here for two more months. And Kurt Bleier is staying in the province. Apparently, he has family in Lunenburg and will be spending the holiday there. Petrucci is coming back whether he wants to or not; he's already committed himself to bringing his wife and his sister — she being the mother of the Saint Mary's football player — to Halifax for January and part of February. So, we'll see what the rest of our suspects do: Enrico, Jan Ford, and Fred Mills. If Freddy surfaces in Argentina, we'll know we've got it solved."

"Of course, if one of these people is the killer —"

"What do you mean, Monty, *if*?"

"Well, there's always the possibility that the murder was committed by someone who's not at the schola."

"Who, for instance? Someone from the Saint Cecilia Concert Series? Or is it a random hit you have in mind, a lowlife who just happened upon Schellenberg in the church, fell upon him in a rage, and inadvertently recreated a saint's death scene?"

"All right, all right, Father, I hear you. As I started to say, *assuming* one of the schola suspects is guilty, wouldn't we all be better off if he disappeared forever?"

"If he doesn't come back, we'll never solve it."

"If he doesn't come back, he won't kill anyone else here."

"You and I both know Reinhold Schellenberg was a unique target. I'm betting the killer won't go after anyone else."

"That's my thinking as well. Let's hope we're right. But, Brennan, don't get yourself too excited about solving the murder. The killer's hatred of Reinhold Schellenberg didn't take root here in Nova Scotia; the motivation comes from another time and another place."

✝

The next morning, Saturday, I picked up Normie for breakfast. I had promised to take her to Jimmy's Homestead Restaurant for pancakes. Really, she was angling for one of Jimmy's prescription-strength chocolate milkshakes. When we headed out in the car, she reminded me that I wasn't the only one who had promised her something. Father Burke had told her he had a collection of holy cards — cards featuring prayers and pictures of saints, angels, and other upholders of the faith — that he would be happy to give her. Just drop in anytime. Anytime could mean right now, couldn't it? I was powerless to resist the imploring eyes of my little girl. We pulled up outside the rectory, and I knocked on the door. Mrs. Kelly appeared.

"Is Father Burke in, Mrs. Kelly?"

"Well . . ." She looked uncertain. "I think he's still up there."

"He may be sleeping in. He doesn't have Mass till noon, I know. We can come back later, right Normie?"

Disappointment was written all over her face. "Aw!" She leaned towards the housekeeper and lowered her voice: "I have Father Burke under investigation."

The housekeeper's jaw dropped. "For *what?*" Her eyes swivelled to me in alarm.

"To see if he's an angel," Normie confided.

"An angel? Father *Burke?*"

"Why ever not, Mrs. Kelly?" I couldn't help but ask.

"I . . . I don't . . ."

"It's a surprise," my daughter said urgently. "He doesn't know, so please don't tell him. He promised to give me some old-fashioned holy cards with angels on them. I pretended — I didn't lie — um, he doesn't know I want to study them as part of my research. Right, Daddy?"

"Sure, sweetheart."

Mrs. Kelly looked lost in a world not of her own making. Then her body jerked spasmodically. "Oh! Father!"

The angel of the Lord had appeared amongst us, groggy, barefoot, and unshaven, wearing old black jeans and an ancient grey T-shirt that barely stretched across his muscular frame. "Mrs. Kelly."

"Yes, Father?"

"Is there something wrong with the water here today? It was cold when I took my shower, and I had to go back under the bedclothes to recover."

That's not all he's recovering from, I said to myself. He saw us then. "Normie! Are you here to see me?"

"Kinda. And Daddy wants to see you too. To, uh, invite you to breakfast."

"Father," Mrs. Kelly began, "about the water. There are workmen in the basement, so maybe they turned off the water heater. I don't know . . ." Her voice trailed off.

"Ah. Now Normie, why don't you give me about five minutes to get dressed."

"And wear something warm. Bring your gloves," commanded Normie, motherly instincts finely honed already. "There's a chance of flurries, and wind gusts up to forty kilometres an hour!"

"Right. And wasn't I supposed to be finding something for you?"

"Holy cards. No particular reason. I just like them."

"That's it. I know exactly where to find them. I'll bring them down. Breakfast, Montague?"

"Yes. You look a bit peckish."

"I'll be right back."

Twenty minutes later we were sitting in Jimmy's Homestead having breakfast. Normie had guzzled her milkshake; her pancakes sat untouched on the plate. The holy cards, about four by two inches in size, with white borders, were spread out in front of her. She eyed Burke surreptitiously as she studied the images. One, with a pale pink background, showed the figure of a woman in a voluminous cream-coloured robe, cinched at the waist; there were white feathered wings on her back; she had long brown hair and she gazed lovingly at a boy and girl playing at her feet. Another card depicted an androgynous figure with long, wavy blond hair and translucent green-white wings suspended in a blue sky with fluffy clouds around him or her. I did not see anything that resembled the black-haired, black-eyed, unshaven, unambiguously masculine figure across the table from me. He lit up a smoke; was his hand a bit shaky?

"A little too much of the water of life last night, Brennan?"

"Daddy, you're bad. You're saying Father Burke was drinking too much booze! You know that's not true."

"Of course not, sweetheart."

"But," she said, examining Burke, "you do look a little, well, like a tough guy today, Father."

"Don't you be worrying now, Normie, I'll be all tidied up by the time of the noon Mass." He turned to me. "Speaking, though, of priests gone bad, I came upon another interesting fact about Enrico's favourite saint, Andrew Avellino. I told you that, in addition to being a priest, he was a lawyer."

"Right."

"But he gave up the law after he committed perjury in court."

"Didn't any of these saints just sit around being holy? Have we got any perjurers in our own case yet?"

"The closest thing to perjury is Brother Robin's probably false confession to the police."

"You say 'probably.'"

"I haven't written him off entirely, Monty. There's something there, I don't know what."

"Something symbolized by the prayer beads and the note."

"The note with Enrico's prints on it. Enrico, devotee of the Sicilian priest, lawyer, and perjurer Andrew Avellino."

"I can't figure any of it out on an empty stomach."

We turned our attention to the bacon and eggs and pancakes and toast and juice and coffee in front of us. We listened in as Jimmy at the counter quizzed one of the other regulars, a judge I used to work with when he was a legal aid lawyer, about the judge's recent trip to Italy. He gave captivating descriptions of the meals he ate, the wine he drank, the music he heard, the people he met; he ended by describing how he tracked down a reclusive uncle in the Trentino region and found out why the man had been out of touch with his family for thirty years. "If I'd stayed on my butt here in Halifax, I never would have known. Now? *Mistero risolto!*" Mystery solved.

That's all it took. Burke looked at me and I looked at him. Here it was, after months of late-night, boozy, inconclusive plans. The schola was on break, and things were winding down at my office. I smiled. Our long-desired road trip was on. We were going to Rome.

"How long a trip are we talking about?" I asked.

He gave a Sferrazza-Melchiorrian shrug. *"Chissà?"*

"What trip?" Normie broke in. "Nobody talked about a trip!" I patted her hand and directed her attention to her pancakes. "Is it Rome? Can I come? Please, Daddy?"

"Not this time, Normie. But we'll go another time."

"Aw! Father Burke, remember when you had that T-shirt on that said 'Angelicum,' named after that guy you called the Angelic Doctor —"

"Right. My college was the Angelicum, named for Saint Thomas Aquinas."

"And you said . . ."

"I promised to get one for you, didn't I, Normie?"

"Yes, you did."

"I'll bring one back for you. Count on it."

"Okay!"

"What's your work schedule like at this time of year, *Signor* Collins?"

"It's manageable. I could hand a few things over to other lawyers. This trip won't be all Vatican City, will it?"

"I imagine we could dip into a bottle of Chianti and admire a finely turned ankle in the more secular parts of the city."

Yeah, I thought, *it might be fun to be a couple of assholes over there.* I pictured the two of us in Italian silk suits and sunglasses, following a cluster of Roman beauties in high-heeled, soft leather Italian shoes. I smiled at the image.

"I'll let you know later today if I can swing it. I have a friend who's a travel agent; maybe she can get us a last-minute special. Though we're pushing it, trying to get a flight right after Christmas!"

†

It wasn't much of a deal, but my agent came through with a red-eye flight to Frankfurt and a connecting flight to Rome. We would have one night in Frankfurt on the way back, and that gave me an idea. I called Moody Walker and asked him to get in touch with the police officer he knew in Hamburg. I wondered if there was anyone he could hook us up with on our night in Germany, someone who could shed some light on the enigmatic Colonel Bleier. Moody said he would work on it.

The downside was that Burke and I had to endure some pointed remarks from Professor MacNeil. "Let me see if I have this right. The police have arrested a suspect, they're satisfied with the evidence as far as we know, the suspect has confessed, he has hired Saul Green, one of the top criminal lawyers in the province, who has contrived for reasons of his own to extend the accused's stay in a psychiatric hospital, which makes me think Saul knows the guy is nutty enough to have committed the murder and Saul will likely get him off for reasons of insanity. Yet you guys are claiming that it wasn't Robin, it was somebody else. Who? Uh, we don't know. But we can find out if we — if we what? — take off together on a road trip to Italy! Yeah! That's where the answers are. Coincidentally, that's also where the best food and the most plentiful wine and the most beautiful women and art and opera and all the other worldly pleasures are. Well, you may be fooling everybody else, boys, but you're not fooling me."

Apart from that, I enjoyed the Christmas season. We walked to midnight Mass from the house on Dresden Row. Tom, Normie, their mother and her baby, some cousins and me. Snow was falling, church bells were ringing, and St. Bernadette's Church glowed with warm coloured light in the white stillness of the night. I joined the choir when I arrived; my family sat in the nave. Brennan sang the high Mass, and the music was magnificent. We all went back to Maura's afterwards to eat, drink, open gifts, and sleep. I pretended we were still a family; I just didn't look too closely at our numbers.

Part Three

Chapter 8

These that survive let Rome reward with love.
— William Shakespeare, *The Tragedy of Titus Andronicus*

We arrived in Rome the afternoon of Friday, December 27. Burke and I had two rooms reserved at the Hotel Alimandi, just outside the Vatican walls. It was a four-storey hotel with a roof terrace over the entrance, where one could sit and soak up the Roman sun when it wasn't December. We were both greeted by the manager as *"signori"*; *Don* Burke, dressed in civilian clothes, did not correct him. No sooner had I unpacked and flopped down on the bed than Burke was in my room, urging me out the door.

"Appointment at the Vatican. Mustn't keep the good sister waiting."

Twenty minutes later we were standing in the monumental Basilica of St. Peter, specifically at Peter's foot, where we had been instructed to wait for Brennan's friend, an Irish nun. The right foot of St. Peter's statue was worn down by centuries of kisses from devoted pilgrims.

"Ah. Here she is now," Brennan announced. Sister Kitty Curran appeared to be in her early fifties, short, plump, with a fresh open face and reddish curls going grey. Brennan greeted her with an extended hug and kiss.

"Not here, Brennan, *acushla*. People will talk." She hailed from Dublin and had brought the accent with her. She stepped back and appraised him. "A bit of grey there now but no less striking a figure for that." She peered up at him. "There's something about your left eye; it turns down a bit at the outer corner. I have to say it gives you a sort of moody Irish look. What happened?"

The mark of Cain, I thought. My mark on him. Would it never go away?

"Oh, there was an incident, Kitty. During one of my many lost weekends. It's best forgotten."

"Is it now. And who's this fine fellow you have with you?"

"Monty Collins, Sister Kitty Curran."

"One of ours, would he be?"

"Montague Michael Collins — otherwise an astute student of history — exists in a state of woeful ignorance about his Irish heritage, Sister. And there's the blood of an Englishman mixed in there too."

"That would explain his failings, then."

"What do you do here, Sister?"

"Call me Kitty. I work for the Pontifical Council for Justice and Peace. In the Palazzo San Callisto over in Trastevere. We promote justice, peace, and human rights throughout the world according to the principles of the Gospel. Simple. I expect our work will be completed by week's end and we can all go home."

"Good for you. Give me a call when you've wrapped it up, and we'll go out for a pint."

"Why wait? We could be out lifting one now."

"Sounds like a plan. Where should we go?"

"The Irish Monk." My questioning look earned an oblique reply: "It's livelier than the name suggests."

Twenty minutes later we were seated in Il Monaco Irlandese with pints of Guinness before us. The menus were done up like illuminated manuscripts.

"I'm travelling to your side of the Atlantic soon, Brennan, for a conference on social justice."

"Where?"

"Montreal."

"When?"

"January 10 to 15."

"Have you booked your flight yet?"

"No. I just got the word I'm going."

"Good. Monty, do you know your travel agent's number? Do you have her card with you?"

"I do." I pulled my wallet from my pocket and drew out the agent's card. Brennan took it and wrote the details on a Paddy Whiskey coaster and handed it to Kitty. "Get her to book you through Halifax on the way back. Spend a few days with us."

"Oh, I don't know now . . ."

"Roma locuta est, causa finita est."

"Rome has spoken, the case is closed. You're the voice of Rome now, are you, Brennan?"

"When was I not? I'll be expecting you in Halifax. Free room and board."

"Typical of this fellow," she said to me. "His way or no way."

"You've known him for a while, I take it, Kitty. You knew him when he was a starving student here in Rome?"

"Oh, I don't know if I'd describe him as starving. He kept lofty company, Brennan did. I'm sure he's told you all about it."

"There are great gaps in the history he's been willing to divulge to me, Kitty. If he spent his time anywhere but the Greg, the Angelicum, and the tomb of Saint Peter, I haven't heard about it."

"Ah, well, maybe he's right and it's my memory that's been playing fantastic tricks on me all these years. Himself in black tie at La Scala in Milan, in the private viewing box of the great diva Graziella Rossi, himself being screeched at by that same rossie — pun not intended but convenient nonetheless — when he offended her ladyship in ways never made public. Wasn't Cardinal Testa present in the Rossi apartments when that incident took place, Brennan, or have I been a victim of unfounded rumours?"

"Don't exercise yourself, Kitty. If I stumbled into the wrong quarters on occasion here in Rome, put it down to a young novice who didn't know his way around and was soon enough back on his knees before the altar of God where he belonged. How have you been, my darlin'?"

"Can't complain. As you know I had a rough innings in El Salvador a while back but that makes me all the more keen to get the justice and human rights file signed, stamped, and off the desk."

She spoke lightly, but Brennan didn't smile. He took her hand and held it. "Stay in Rome, Kitty. You've done your time out there. Nobody could ask more of you."

"You had some rough days yourself, Brennan, that stint you did in Brazil."

"My parishioners had the rough days; I didn't."

"Your parishioners being street children targeted for death by security agencies in the pay of —" She looked over at me. "This isn't what you came to Rome for, is it Monty? Shop talk. Sorry."

"That is what we came for, actually, Kitty. Shop talk of a different kind."

She took a long sip of her Guinness and said: "The death of Reinhold Schellenberg made great roaring headlines over here, as you can imagine."

"I was rather hoping the Roman grapevine had it solved by now. What's the talk?"

"Endless speculation, no resolution. None of it deterred in the least by the fact that there has been an arrest. Word is the fellow they arrested is just a patsy. So the rumours swirl unabated. It could have been this faction, or that faction. Liberals, traditionalists, the Germans, the Vatican, the Masons, it goes on and on. Nobody knows. You were there; I was hoping you could tell me."

Brennan shook his head. "Not a clue. You're right. They have a man on psychiatric remand, but we think they should be looking elsewhere. Most of the people at the schola were out of town when it happened. A few weren't, and I thought I'd ask if you know anything about them."

"Ask away."

"The fellow they nicked is Robin Gadkin-Falkes."

"Sounds like an English toff to me."

"You wouldn't be far wrong. He's a Brit and a Benedictine monk. Brother Robin."

"Never heard of him. Has he spent any time here?"

"Not that we know of. At least not since Vatican ii. What did he tell us, Monty?"

"He was covering the last session for an English publication. That was 1965."

"I wasn't here for the Council, so I can't help you there," Kitty said.

"We're taking a jaunt to the abbey in Praglia to ask about him. But our feeling is that he's claiming to be the killer for unfathomable reasons of his own. So, on to our other suspects. Enrico Sferrazza-Melchiorre."

"Enrico! You're having me on."

"No. All I'm saying is he's one of the people who doesn't have an alibi."

"Enrico's never had an alibi for anything in his life, God bless the sinners and the saints amongst us."

"Has he been in trouble before?" I asked.

"This is a rumour mill like none other on the planet, Monty. I have heard whispers about Enrico and a woman, but I honestly don't know what they were about. Though that would explain the call to Gino Savo."

"Gino Savo!" Brennan looked aghast.

"Yes. The arrest of this Robin fellow has had one benefit you may not be aware of, Brennan: Father Savo was packing his bags for Nova Scotia when word came that they caught the killer. So at least you've been spared that bit of aggravation!"

"What are you telling me now? Savo was going to land on me?" She may as well have told him Satan was taking over from him in the choir loft.

"Who's Savo?" I asked.

"He is the undersecretary of the Pontifical Congregation for the Clergy," she said.

"Which means?"

"The Congregation deals with priests around the world. It is made up of cardinals and bishops. The prefect — the chairman — is a cardinal appointed by the pope. Under the prefect is the secretary, who's an archbishop. Then comes Gino, who actually runs the office. And he has his spoon in many other bowls as well. The Vatican is a Byzantine organization, the Great Schism notwithstanding."

"And they were going to send this guy over to Halifax?"

"That wouldn't surprise you, Monty, if you knew Arturo Del Vecchio, the papal nuncio to Canada. And now that I've heard

Enrico's name in connection with this, I know why Del Vecchio got involved. A man can rise to dizzying heights in the Holy See — the Vatican is an absolute monarchy after all — if he has a champion, a mentor, a protector at or near the top. Enrico has a protector in the person of Arturo Del Vecchio. But the person at or near the top can falter badly and never recover, if he fecks up. Del Vecchio intends to settle for nothing less than the red hat. He plans on becoming cardinal prefect of the Congregation for the Doctrine of the Faith, when and if the grand personage who now occupies that position moves on. Or up. In case you don't know, Monty, that's the Holy Office, known in former times as the Inquisition. Del Vecchio has spent thirty years rising through the diplomatic service with that goal in mind. You can be sure he has no intention of letting his protegé Enrico besmirch his reputation by being publicly associated with a murder. Or any other class of . . . mishap."

"Mishap?"

"This woman trouble Enrico had, whatever it was. And Del Vecchio isn't the only one who sees a red hat in his future. There is talk about Gino Savo being appointed archbishop of Genoa; many of the archbishops in that diocese have gone on to become cardinals. Ambition runs through the veins here like the true blood, Monty! Anyway, Father Savo was up in Ars when he got the call from the nuncio. It's the only place Savo ever takes a vacation."

"Where's that?"

"In France, near Lyons. You must have heard of Saint John Vianney."

"Heard his name. There's a church named after him in Nova Scotia. And one of our suspects is devoted to him."

"As is Gino Savo."

"I was a little surprised to hear about all these people communing with the saints in this day and age."

"There he goes again about 'this day and age,'" Brennan said. "You're in the eternal city, Collins. Leave the day and age behind you!"

"Is this poor lad a heathen? If he's never recited the Apostles' Creed — 'I believe in the communion of saints' — you're not doing your job, Father Burke."

"I've tried, Sister, I've tried."

"Well, what about you, Kitty?" I persisted. "Do you count any particular saints among your closest confidants?"

"I have enough on my plate trying to make saints of the scoundrels I see around me every day. A woman's work is never done. But others are more in tune with the supernatural element of our faith. Some indeed —" she nodded towards Brennan "— are a strange mix of the worldly and the otherworldly.

"So. Gino takes his vacation every year at the home of Saint John Vianney, and Arturo Del Vecchio knew he could reach him there. He called, told him about the murder, no doubt told him Enrico Sferrazza-Melchiorre was on the scene, and ordered Gino to Halifax to investigate and control the situation. And control it he would. I believe the expression is 'control freak.' That's Gino all over."

"Does that mean he's learned to control his temper?" Brennan asked.

Kitty laughed. "Not that I've heard. He's still known for flying into a rage and terrorizing his staff. A bit of a tyrant, is Gino."

I brought the conversation back to the investigation: "So the Vatican is worried enough about Enrico Sferrazza-Melchiorre to send over this enforcer? It doesn't sound good for Enrico."

"I imagine Gino's mandate would have been broader than just checking up on Enrico. Del Vecchio would have wanted him to handle the situation no matter who committed the murder, given that it all centres one way or the other on the church. Del Vecchio is the pope's man in Canada, after all. And Gino himself would want the matter solved. Gino knew Schellenberg. He admired him, spoke highly of him whenever his name came up. Apart from all my blather about arse-covering manoeuvres by Del Vecchio and Savo, they both would have been terribly upset about Schellenberg's murder. So my advice to you, Brennan *acushla*, is to make sure the murder gets solved and stays solved! That way, no Vatican strongman shows up to complicate your life!"

"That's why we're here. We're hoping to find out what might have happened in the past between Father Schellenberg and our suspects."

"Can you picture Enrico as a killer?" I asked her.

"No! He is ambitious and he has had some obstacles in his path to the top. If he does not rise higher in the papal court, it could be seen as a disgrace to his family. After all, there have been Sferrazzas and Melchiorres at the pope's side for centuries. So if Reinhold Schellenberg was for some reason in a position to thwart him further . . . But Enrico is a dedicated priest. I can't see him doing this, or anything remotely like it."

"Was Father Schellenberg in a position to thwart Enrico's ambitions?"

"I'm not sure. They taught at the Lateran University at the same time. Schellenberg was head of the theology department back before he joined the Cistercians. It was the late 1970s, I suppose, when Enrico taught there. Just after you left Rome, Brennan. And there's lots of talk these days of new appointments to the diplomatic corps. So if Enrico is trying to get out of exile, and back on the road to a diplomatic career, and if he applies for a position, the powers that be would speak to Schellenberg about their time at the Lateran. Now, I do know Enrico spent a semester teaching at the University of Florence a couple of years ago, before he went to Africa. He would almost certainly have been in contact with Schellenberg when he was there. Whether Schellenberg was aware of any mischief Enrico got into, who can say? But killing a fellow priest to keep him quiet would not be in Enrico's bag of tricks, in my opinion."

"All right. William Logan. Does that name sound familiar to you?"

"The American?"

"*The* American? Is he well known?"

"He isn't. But his letters are." She rolled her eyes and signalled the waiter for another round. "If it's the same person."

"He left the priesthood in 1981 to marry one of your sisters."

She was nodding. "Him and thousands of others after Vatican II. Funny how they all fled when things lightened up instead of in the harsher old days. But it sounds like him. They know his handwriting here now. He addresses his letters to the Holy Father, though he's smart enough to know they never get within a ten-foot pole's distance of the pope. They go to the Secretariat of State with all the other letters from Catholics and crackpots around the world. Logan is one of the regulars known to the long-suffering Gary Sloane. He's an American priest who handles a lot of the English-language correspondence here."

"What does Logan write about?"

"Everything. Church doctrine, the clergy, this or that bishop who's pissed him off, the liturgy, a lay ministry he wants to start up, a counselling service or encounter group he's running, the moral teachings and moral failings of the church, Vatican finances, the choir at midnight Mass at St. Peter's as seen on television, the repairs they're doing in his parish. On and on. He's a figure of fun over here, at least among the few who have heard of him, but it's sad really."

"Sad how?"

"Well, he never got over it, did he? He left the priesthood. His correspondence at that time told the church to get stuffed. The church was the people. Priests and religious were unnecessary and irrelevant. The papacy was a medieval relic. Tear the whole structure down. Et cetera. But he can't leave it alone. I'm sure you've seen it yourself, Brennan. Catholics who leave. Or think they've left. If you're not Catholic anymore, what's the difference what jiggery-pokery we're up to here? Write us off and join the United Church! But they can't let go. No matter how far away they've gone, and how they've liberated themselves, what the church does still matters to them. Logan is one of those. You say he's with your group in Halifax?"

"That's right."

"There you go then. What's he doing there? I'll take you over to the Apostolic Palace to meet Gary Sloane. He knows more than he ever wanted to about Logan."

"All right. Thanks," I said. "Next one: Janice Ford."

"Never heard that name."

"Luigi Petrucci. A layman from New Jersey."

"No."

"He set fire to a church there in 1979."

"You're coddin' me!"

"Nope. How about Father Fred Mills?"

She shook her head.

"I know Fred," Brennan stated. "You can cross him off the list of suspects."

"I'll take your word for it. Almost. Final name: Kurt Bleier, a police officer in the former German Democratic Republic."

"Unless he was skulking around St. Peter's Square in May of 1981, I don't imagine such a man was one of our visitors."

"May of '81; that's when —" I began.

"The Holy Father was shot, yes. May 13."

We stayed at the bar for another round; then Kitty had to return to the Vatican for a meeting, so we walked her back.

"Treat you to a gelato at our old spot?" Brennan asked her.

"I wouldn't say no."

We stopped at a tiny place near the Vatican and ordered three cones of incomparable Italian ice cream: *amareno* for Brennan, *pistacchio* for Kitty, *fragola* (strawberry) for me.

When we got back to the Vatican City State, Kitty escorted us to the Apostolic Palace, familiar to anyone who has ever seen the pope appearing in the window of the papal apartments on the top floor. We walked down a long marble corridor and entered the office of Father Gary Sloane, who was barely visible behind the stacks of paper on his desk. Kitty introduced us, told him why we were asking about William Logan, and left for her meeting.

"Logan. Yes, I answer all his letters or, at the very least, acknowledge them. But I don't know how I can help him. I've suggested counselling, but I don't think he pays much heed to my poor attempts at advice. His marriage fell apart. The kids are with his ex-wife, who was a nun but now follows some new-age guru. Logan is upset because the kids have no religious beliefs at all. He goes from one job to the next; he seems to be in a spiral of poverty. He's fifty years old and nothing's worked out for him; he's sinking farther and farther from the reach of the American dream, so-called. Now he's got the second wife, and she wants to start a family."

"He tells you all this?" I asked.

"Oh, yes. He tells us what's wrong with the church, in minute detail, and gives us almost as much detail about his own life. Everything that goes wrong for him is, as you might expect, somebody else's fault. His correspondence to us suggests it's the church at fault. But, who knows, maybe he's a regular correspondent with the U.S. government and, when he's got them on the line, it's the CIA's fault. It's a sad case."

We thanked Gary, and left the palace.

"I've lined up somebody else for us to see," Burke announced as we walked through Bernini's colonnade. "I sussed out Graziella Rossi's schedule. Made sure she wasn't off to the Sydney Opera House or somewhere. She may have some information about Enrico Sferrazza-Melchiorre."

"You and Enrico are friends of Graziella Rossi?"

"Oh, 'friend' isn't a word I'd be tossing around with respect to herself. Woe betide anyone who thinks he or she is a friend of La Rossi. But we're both acquainted with her. It was through Enrico that I met her; he's known her forever."

"Will she talk to us?"

"She'll talk to us as soon as we get to her apartment. She's expecting us."

Thinking of that "woe betide," I asked him, "Were you on good terms with her when you left Rome?"

"Ah, well, good terms . . . I wouldn't say so exactly. But the woman loves to talk. And if she can pass the time slagging someone, she'll run on, you can be sure."

"What exactly was the nature of your relationship with this diva?"

"Am I on the witness stand now? Did I say 'relationship' or did I say 'acquainted'?"

I smiled, and he gave me a damning look in return. In fact, I knew he had been subjected to a screaming tirade by the great soprano, whose advances he had rebuffed. I had heard the tale from his brother in New York. Kitty Curran had confirmed that he'd been on the receiving end of the diva's fury. That's opera for you.

We were greeted by the doorman at the singer's sumptuous quarters in the upscale Parioli district of Rome. He alerted *Signora* Rossi, and sent us upstairs. The apartment had travertine marble floors, a grand piano, and enormous arched windows overlooking a broad avenue lined with similarly luxurious dwellings, palms, and plane trees.

I had heard Graziella Rossi on "Saturday Afternoon at the Opera" on CBC radio, and had a CD of her *Traviata*; this was the first time I had seen her. She was the very archetype of the dramatic soprano, and she had the operatic figure to match. Her black hair was swept back from her face and her upturned dark eyes flashed over a set of high cheekbones. Her large mouth was painted a flaming red.

"Ma che sorpresa! Caro Brennan! Can it possibly be?" She held out her arms and made a show of looking him over, then embraced him

and kissed him on both cheeks, leaving a smear of red like an open wound near each of his ears. I could practically feel the effort he made not to put his hands up and wipe the lipstick off.

"Whatever brings you back to Rome? A summons from the Holy Father? Or have you been desanctified? Settled down with a little hausfrau and a brood of runny-nosed children?"

Her eyes homed in on Brennan's face. *"Cosa è successo?"*

"Niente, Grazi, niente."

"Nothing has happened and yet your eye has changed. It gives you a tragic air, very minor key, shall we say. And who is this *angelo biondo?*"

"The blondy angel, whose appearance is deceptive, is Monty Collins."

She gave me her hand. I did not know whether I was supposed to shake it or kiss it. I opted for a shake.

Brennan listened to the latest developments in *Signora* Rossi's life, then explained our mission.

"We were all at vespers when the body was found," he concluded. "One of our guests in Halifax is Enrico Sferrazza-Melchiorre. Someone suggested there may be some bones rattling about in his closet."

"Oh, you must be referring to the intimidation charges. Have no fear, that was all hushed up."

"What do you mean, intimidation?"

"Interfering with a witness; is that what it would be called? My English!"

"Witness tampering?"

She gave Brennan a helpless look and shrugged.

"What's he supposed to have done?"

"It had something to do with the sex charges. You know. It was all too sordid. I paid little attention."

"Sex charges."

"Yes, yes." She flapped a bejewelled hand, as if it was of no interest. "Now, Brennan, did you know I made a film? You must see it. Though I warn you: you may be committing a sin by watching me in it. I am a long way from a good Catholic girl in this film."

"Are you now. Well, maybe I'll have the chance to see it some time."

"I have it here."

"Ah."

She turned her head and shouted at someone off stage. "Beppe! Set up my film!"

"What were those charges you mentioned, *Signora* Rossi?" I inquired. "Charges against Enrico?"

"There was a woman. Hasn't it always been so? *Cherchez la femme!* Who can say what happened? But dear Enrico found himself under investigation by the magistrates, and it was said that charges would be laid against him. False accusations? *Chissà?*

"Beppe!" she commanded again. "Are you setting up my film, or have you gone to Hollywood for it? He is useless!" she said to us then, not bothering to lower her voice. "I may have no choice but to dismiss him. Will you take him under your wing if I put him out on the street, Brennan, like poor Annunziata all those years ago? I am sure she was grateful for your assistance at that time. Ah, well, blessed are the poor, and Annunziata was blessed indeed to be the object of your attentions, Brennan, a man otherwise so —"

"The charges, Grazi."

"The charges went away! *Un miracolo!* Some day perhaps *Don* Enrico Sferrazza-Melchiorre will be named a saint, having performed such a miracle!"

"What accounted for the charges going away?"

She leaned forward and affected a mock conspiratorial pose. "That is more in your line than in mine, Father Burke: Vatican treasure, is what I heard!"

"What on earth do you mean?"

"Enrico Sferrazza-Melchiorre comes from a long line of Sicilian looters, my dear Brennan. Perhaps you didn't know. They bought their way into the aristocracy centuries ago with gold and art stolen from around the Mediterranean world. So what could be more natural to a Sferrazza-Melchiorre than to get his fingers on a priceless Vatican object and use it to bribe his former mistress — or victim, whatever she was to him — to drop the accusations? Jewellery is what I heard. Perhaps she's still flaunting it around the slums of Tirana! If she's still alive. If not, look closely — perhaps Enrico is wearing it himself!"

"You don't like Enrico? I never knew that."

"Oh! On the contrary! I have always held Enrico in the highest esteem. He partakes of a quality I cannot help but admire in others, a quality I recognized in you as soon as I met you, Brennan: a streak of utter ruthlessness."

He let that go, and continued with his questions: "Do you think he would have killed Reinhold Schellenberg?"

"Well, he missed his chance to kill *her*, didn't he? The Halili slut. Though one would think he had the opportunity. She trailed after him wherever he went. He tried to take a vacation in Venezia. She turned up there. He taught at the University of Firenze — Florence — she followed him there as well. I understand she caused a scene. Confronted him and made accusations. He eventually went all the way to Africa! But as for Schellenberg, if he knew about the scandal and if Enrico wanted him dead for that or some other reason, and didn't do the killing himself, someone in his family might have stepped in. Or perhaps they hired someone. Does anyone at your choir school look like a professional assassin, *Padre*?"

"This woman — Enrico's mistress — she's in Albania, you say?"

"As far as anyone knows. But she has been known to present herself in the streets of Rome."

"What are the chances of that happening in the next few days?"

"The odds are against it, but the odds could be improved."

"How?"

"Zamira always has her price. As I have explained to you."

"What would bring her to Rome?"

"Well, she already has the crown jewels. But the offer of a part in an opera would have her here quicker than you could grasp your wallet."

"She's a singer then."

"She is a screamer."

"So you're not likely to intercede on her behalf with the casting director of your next opera."

"Not in *my* next work, no. Perhaps she and Enrico can stage Verdi's *Sicilian Vespers* together. Do you know it?" She looked at me. "It is based on the massacre of the French by the Sicilians in the thirteenth century. The killing began at the time of vespers. Enrico can be one of the Sicilian tenors, and Zamira can sing the part of the maid!"

Brennan laughed, then said: "We can't pin our hopes on that, I'm afraid."

"No. Well, Alfredo Totti will be doing *Norma* next year. He is casting the opera now. Pia Franca will be singing the role of Norma, which of course should have gone to me." She gave Burke a significant look.

"You loathe Pia Franca."

"Yes, I do. I'll give Alfredo a call. Maybe he'll have a role for Zamira Halili — the role of Adalgisa perhaps? Bellowing alongside Pia on the stage. Come see me in a couple of days, to find out if she has taken the bait. *Ora*, my film! Beppe! Refresh our drinks."

Burke scrambled to his feet. "We have to go, Grazi. We're meeting someone at the Vatican about the murder. I hope to see your film another time. Will you be singing anywhere this week?"

"Alas, no. But come to my master class! I am teaching a new group of young sopranos, from all over Europe. The day after tomorrow at the Bel Canto Auditorium. Four o'clock. Consider it a free concert!"

We hailed a cab outside the apartment. It took us past the Borghese Gardens, past a multitude of trees, fountains, monuments, and statues. As I wrenched my head around to catch a fleeting sight of the Galleria in the gardens, I said to Burke: "We're not going to keep up this pace all week, are we? I want to relax and see the city. I was here years ago, but —"

"It hasn't changed. It's the eternal city, remember?"

"Still."

"Sure we'll see the city. It's time for a scoff now, though. Aren't you hungry?"

"Famished."

"Well, I know just the place."

✝

The Trattoria Benelli was a small, family-owned eatery a few blocks from our hotel in the Prati district. The aroma of garlic and freshly baked bread made me want to move in and live there. The walls, inside and out, featured frescoes of the Italian countryside. Everyone in the place was local — always a good sign — and they were having a marvellous time talking, laughing, and sharing food between tables. Italian folk music played over the sound system.

A young girl came over to take our order. *"Buonasera, signori."*

"Buonasera, cara. Dov'è Alberto stasera?"

"Papà è morto, tre anni fa."

Burke expressed his obviously genuine condolences to the girl on the death of her father, and asked her a number of questions, which I took to be inquiries about the current ownership of the restaurant. Mamma owned it now and Mamma was called to the table. Susanna Benelli had the kind of classic Italian face that should have been immortalized on a gold coin. Her rich brown hair was tied loosely back, and her deep brown eyes were lightly made up to show them to advantage. She was not in the least worn down by widowhood or the responsibilities of raising four children on her own. The three youngest, all boys, made their presence known in the restaurant as they carried out, or failed to carry out, the chores assigned to them. She introduced us to her sister, Isabella, who, except for being smaller and darker, looked exactly like Susanna.

We ate plate after plate of antipasto, pasta in mouth-watering sauces, fish, cheese, fruit, and sweets, and we washed down gallons of Chianti. By the end of it, I was playing the harmonica I always carried with me; Burke was singing a duet with one of the Benelli kids, a boy soprano; and Isabella was inviting us to a party the evening of the thirtieth at her place in a northern suburb of Rome.

The next day we walked all over the city, admiring the Renaissance palaces, baroque facades and fountains, the buildings in warm shades of ochre burnished by the sun. We retired to our rooms early and slept away our jet lag.

✝

Our third day in Rome was Sunday, which meant Mass with the cardinals in St. Peter's Basilica, an almost overwhelming experience given the immensity of the building and the enormous crowd of worshippers. In the afternoon we found our way to the Bel Canto Auditorium in the Termini district of the city. The old palazzo was surrounded by scaffolding but it was open, so we walked in. Graziella Rossi was on the stage with several women in their late teens and early twenties. They didn't see us come in and take seats in the back row. We listened as the young sopranos took turns singing arias from Puccini, Verdi, and Bellini. To me they sounded magnificent — a combination of natural talent and expert coaching from La Rossi. No doubt Graziella accepted only the top students. She issued gentle suggestions for improvement, and we heard the pieces again. Gentleness was the last thing I expected from the opera star. But it was clear from the genuine, unaffected delight she took in their accomplishments that she loved her pupils.

"Do you think we should announce our presence?" I whispered to Brennan, and he nodded. We got up and headed for the stage.

"Brennan! Monty! Come meet my girls! This is Melanie, Melissa, Annick, Anna, and Stephanie. You will see them in opera houses around the world some day. Girls, be good. This is *Don* Burke and *Don* Collins, the pope's legions!" She repeated it all in Italian, and we greeted the students, complimenting them on their performances.

"It's all from Grazi," one of them declared. "You are fortunate you did not hear me before!"

"No, *cara*, it is you." She looked with unselfconscious affection at the group, and said: "The daughters I never had!"

"Sing something for us, Grazi," Brennan urged her.

"Sing about love!" one of the students requested.

"Love — yes, the repertoire contains more than a few arias about love!"

Everyone left the stage but the diva, and she sang to us about *amore*. Puccini's "Chi Il Bel Sogno." She was in fine voice as she soared to an effortless high C. Brennan translated it for me later, but it was all there in the music: mad, intoxicating love, the kind of passion you'd give up all earthly riches to possess. She walked to the back of the auditorium with us, and turned to Brennan. "Do you know that kind of love, Brennan?"

"Yes. I do."

"I won't ask you who she was. Or *is*. But you will not pursue that life, will you? You belong only to God; you exist to glorify him with music. I have heard it said that most of us go to the grave with our music still inside us. That, at least, will never be said of you or me, Brennan. With our music we reach heights others can never reach. If we forgo other things in life, it is for this."

Everyone was silent for an extended moment. Then Brennan asked: "What will you be singing next?"

"*Tosca*. I don't know if I can do it."

"You'll be brilliant. Will it be here in Rome?"

"Oh yes, *Tosca* will be at home."

"I'll watch for it. Maybe I'll fly over."

"Let me know so I can get a box seat for you. Now, for sordid business. *La puttana Albanese* has swallowed the hook. She flies into Rome tomorrow. She believes Totti will be casting her in his opera this week! Here is where you will meet her." She handed him a slip of paper, turned, and walked back to the stage.

Brennan didn't say a word as we made our way to our hotel. He stopped to light up a smoke and seemed to inhale half of it before moving on.

He rallied later, though, and suggested an evening of musical theatre. He prepared me for the fact that most of the humour would go over my head, given that the bawdy jests and political jibes would be in a language I barely knew. Why go then?

"A feast for the eyes, Monty, a feast for the eyes."

So we queued for admittance to the Teatro Sistina, which should never be confused with the Sistine Chapel, and spent three hours gazing in wonder at a procession of extravagantly gorgeous women on the stage.

✝

Monday was devoted to sightseeing. We hiked to the top of the Janiculum hill and enjoyed a panoramic view of the eternal city. We toured the Capitoline Museum where we saw busts of the Roman emperors, and the famous *Dying Gaul*, the marble sculpture of a Celtic warrior who was magnificent even in defeat. And of course we saw some churches, including San Pietro in Vincoli (Saint Peter in chains) and San Pietro in Carcere (Saint Peter in jail).

In the evening, we returned to the Trattoria Benelli. Brennan asked me if I wanted to try a new place but, if you've made friends in Rome, and those friends can fill your every vinous and culinary need, why go elsewhere? The Benelli children were on the loose again, ensuring that Susanna and Isabella did not have a minute to relax, but that did nothing to cool the ardour of two men sitting at a table near the kitchen. One of them, big and blond, a German or a northern Italian, kept up a steady stream of conversation with Susanna whether she was in the room or not. She rolled her eyes in the direction of her admirer, and said something about him to Brennan in Italian. Whatever advice he offered was laughingly rejected. She headed off to the kitchen again.

"Who is he?" I asked Burke.

"Don't know. Whoever he is, she says he's been persistent. She's not nasty enough to tell him to feck off with himself."

When we had polished off two bottles of Badia Chianti and could no longer cram in another bite of food, Isabella came by with two cups of dark, rich, steaming hot chocolate so thick that gobs of it clung to the sides of the cups. I had never tasted anything like it. It was the chocolate equivalent of Turkish coffee. She went to get a tray of cigars, and offered them to us. I declined, but Brennan picked out a big fat stogie and fired it up. Isabella reminded us that she was having a party, then let go with a string of *sotto voce* curses when the northerner piped up from his table, asking for the time and place of the party.

Then it was time for the assignation arranged for us by Graziella Rossi. So, after emerging half-lit from the trattoria, we walked on unsteady feet to the Giulio Cesare Hotel, seated ourselves at the bar, and waited for our first glimpse of Zamira Halili, the woman who had stirred up so much trouble in the life of Father Enrico Sferrazza-Melchiorre. We knew her the instant she entered the room. Everyone in the bar marked her entrance. She may as well have been naked, her shimmering gold and black dress was so skimpy and tight. She wore four-inch stiletto heels as if she'd been born on them. Her thick dark hair was piled high on her head, with some curls escaping and framing her face. She had heavy-lidded dark eyes and a wide, unpainted mouth. I looked over at Burke and saw that his eyes were locked on her like some sort of heat-seeking guidance system.

"Divil take the jewellery," he said to me out of the side of his mouth. "If she's still accepting bids, I'll give her the Michelangelo *Pietà*." He rose from the bar stool and faced her.

Grazi had obviously given her an accurate description of Burke because Zamira headed straight for him and didn't stop until she was in contact with him on all fronts. She looked up and purred in a thick accent: "I am Zamira Lule Halili. You are an Irishman and a priest and you are looking for me. How can I help you?"

For a good fifteen seconds Burke neither moved nor spoke. Then he cleared his throat, backed up a bit, and said "Em, well," and cleared his throat again. She laughed up at him, then looked over and noticed me.

"Oh! Who is this? Your altar boy? What beautiful blue eyes you have, altar boy. I would like you to keep them open if we spend time together."

"I'd have no trouble with that," I assured her.

"I am very happy to meet you two gentlemen! I like whiskey and fruity wine, and I am thirsty now."

Burke tore his eyes away and called to the waiter. *"Cameriere! Tre Irlandese, per favore. Ed una bottiglia di vino Fenocchio Dolcetto d'Alba.*

"Tavolo?" he asked the siren.

Sì, she would like to get a table.

When we were all settled with glasses in front of us, Burke introduced me. "This gentleman is Monty Collins. Your name again is . . ."

He knew damn well what her name was. He just wanted to hear her say all those Ls again. So did I. "Zamira Lule Halili."

"And you have come to Rome in the hopes of getting a part in the opera being staged by —"

"I will have a part. Totti will give it to me."

"Ah. Yes. *Buona fortuna!* And you may also be willing to help us with some information."

"Maybe I can help you, but my English is not good."

"You're doing fine but if you want to switch to Italian, we can do that. I don't know any Albanian. I can't speak for Monty here." I shook my head stupidly. "Tell us about Enrico Sferrazza-Melchiorre."

Her features arranged themselves in a frown, as if the subject was painful or annoying to her. "Enrico disappointed me. Treated me very badly!"

"I'm sorry to hear that," Burke assured her.

"Yes. He assaulted me."

"Assaulted you how?"

"When a woman says to a man no, it is no!"

"True enough." Burke and I both nodded.

"And it is no even if before, when we loved, it was yes."

"Mm-hmm."

"Enrico made promises to me."

"What sort of promises?"

"That he loved me and would make me a home here in Rome. His family has apartments."

"And what happened?"

"One day he told me we must say goodbye. No home. No place for me in Rome. My heart was breaking. I tried to show him that it was me he wanted and he would be lonely when I was gone away."

She spread her arms out and downward like those of the Virgin Mary in a thousand statues, but, with her upper body thrust forward in the slinky dress, the effect was anything but virginal. She conveyed very effectively the message that anyone born with a Y chromosome would miss her painfully if she were gone.

"Enrico said it could not be. Then he moved on me and I said no, no more. He said I was seducing him again and he would not take no for the answer. I set the police on him. I charged him with assault."

"I see," said Burke. He took a gulp of whiskey, then asked: "Did the case go to court?"

"The case was going to court but it did not happen."

"Why was that?"

"I told Enrico if he gave me something lovely to help me remember him, I would go quietly and leave him to the life he wanted. Life without Zamira."

"What kind of gift did you have in mind?"

"A gift of the best quality. A woman loves jewellery, as you must know." Priest and altar boy nodded in unison. Zamira continued: "The Vatican, it is all men. What do they know of jewellery? It is meant to adorn a woman's body, but it sits in the Vatican museums. I said to Enrico: give me that necklace. It is gold, from ancient times. Older than Rome. An Etruscan bulla necklace, with a big round medallion and two other objects — they look like, how would you say it, vials — maybe for poison! — dangling from tubes of gold. I said to Enrico: 'Give me that and you will never see Zamira Lule again. Zamira will say she was mistaken about the assault. Enrico can become the pope. Some day the pope will make a visit to Albania, and see me in the crowd shining with gold!'"

It took a few moments for Burke to find his voice again. "So that was the plan. How did it go?"

"He tried to cheat me. The Sferrazza-Melchiorres are liars and cheats. I learned this from the goldsmith he hired to do his dirty work on me."

"Back up there a bit, Zamira," I said. "What goldsmith?"

"Enrico went into the Vatican museum at night. He knows his way around there. He had a key, or bribed a guard. This was a collection that was being stored then, not shown to the public as it is now. But he had taken me there and showed me. So Enrico took the necklace. Put some kind of card there, saying the necklace was being repaired. He gave it to his nephew's friend, who makes jewellery in Florence. I learned this because I followed Enrico there. Then I went to the friend. Enrico told him: 'Copy the necklace and give the *puttana* the copy, the fake!' He planned to put the real jewellery in the Vatican again. But Enrico did not know this young man would have sympathy for a poor woman abandoned and thrown away. I wept before the goldsmith. I promised him anything he desired if he would not cheat me like Enrico. The goldsmith fell in love with me; he told me he was giving me the real necklace and he gave to Enrico the fake to put inside the museum. A happy-ever-after end to the story!"

No so happy for Enrico.

"Where's the real necklace now?" I asked.

She leaned way over and said: "You can see it is not on me."

"I can see that. Where is it?"

"It is protected. It is priceless."

"Do you really believe you have the original?"

"Enrico believes it."

"How do you know?"

She just smiled and poured herself a glass of wine. She took a sip, and a drop of the ruby liquid ran down the side of her mouth; she scooped it up with her tongue.

"I am told the collection, Etruscan collection, is going to America for a tour." She smiled again.

Did she have the real one? Did her smugness mean she had had it evaluated and proven to be the original? If she was right, there was a fake artifact sitting in one of the Vatican museums, a fake soon to make its way to a U.S. museum, where a new set of experts would examine it. Did Enrico Sferrazza-Melchiorre know this? He would not be able to trust his nephew's buddy to tell him the truth; nor would he dare risk another theft and a consultation with an expert. I had little doubt that Zamira was using the necklace as blackmail, extorting money from Enrico with a threat to go public with her story.

Burke lit up a smoke and inhaled deeply. He looked at Zamira Lule Halili as if trying to figure out where the evening — where his life — was headed now.

Zamira spoke up. "But that is an old story, and Enrico is an old love. All in the past. I have been given another chance to stay in Rome now, in my opera. Will you gentlemen be here for a long time?"

"No. We're leaving soon," Burke replied.

"I must go to my room. I am drinking too much here." She stretched across the table and nearly all the way out of her dress and gave Burke a lingering kiss on the mouth, then favoured me with the same treatment. "My room is forty-three. I will be happy to see you there." It was not clear which one of us she meant, so I assumed the invitation was extended to us both. With that, she rose and glided sinuously from the bar.

"Fuck," was all Burke said. We drank silently for a few minutes.

"Tell me something, Brennan," I asked him finally. "If I walk out of here, are you going up to that hotel room?"

"No. She's bad news, as if you couldn't gather that from our little tête-à-tête here this evening. And that's bad news all around, not just for me, if you're thinking of sneaking up there yourself."

"What else would I be thinking, for Christ's sake?"

"Don't do it. Have yourself a long, cold shower."

We compromised. We didn't want to consign ourselves to the showers; nor did we want to stay within temptation range of Zamira Lule Halili in the Giulio Cesare Hotel. It was early, so we moved on to another bar Brennan knew, but I had taken only a preliminary sip of my drink when he turned to me and said: "It's tonight that Susanna is having her party."

"Isabella is having the party. And yes, it is tonight."

"Right. Where is it?"

"You're asking me?"

"Let me think . . . Tomba di Nerone district, north of here. The address had two fives in it and . . ." He searched his memory for a few moments. "I've got it. Let's find a cab."

Isabella's apartment had marble floors and marble door frames, and a wraparound terrace with a view of palm trees lit up in the courtyard below. But I didn't spend much time contemplating the view. The party was in full swing, with platters of food, carafes of tawny red wine, clouds of cigarette smoke, and dance music coming from the stereo. Susanna was trying to discourage the advances of the blond alpha male who had been pestering her in the restaurant. She saw her way out when Brennan greeted her with a little wave. It sounded to me as if she said "Brennan, darling, you're late!" and then gave the other man a "sorry, I told you so" kind of shrug. Brennan went along with the ruse and lied about why he was late, or at least that's what I think he did. Susanna took Brennan's hand, led him to the bar, put a glass of wine in his hand, and smiled up at him in a way that suggested perhaps he could be more to her than an excuse to avoid the attentions of another man. She had left her work clothes and her motherly demeanour behind her, and Brennan looked for all the world like a happy, happy man. Things looked promising for me as well. Isabella came up to me, two glasses spilling over in her hands, gave one to me, and pulled me onto the makeshift dance floor by the balcony doors.

"Com' è bello, eh Lina?" she called out to a friend.

"È carino, si. Come un angelo!" Lina agreed. If I heard one more person in my life say I looked angelic, I was going to grow a Mephistophelean goatee. But I'd do that later. In the meantime, if Isabella liked the look of me, who was I to complain?

The party went on till the small hours of the morning. My last sighting of Burke was him reclining on a sofa with Susanna kneeling beside him, taking sips of a golden liquid and transfusing it directly from her mouth into his. When I blearily asked him whether we had any duties scheduled in the city in the morning, all he said, in a languid voice I barely recognized, was "Let Rome in Tiber melt."

I woke up alone in Isabella's room when the sun rose, and went out to find her. She was in the kitchen making coffee. There was nobody else in the apartment, and I didn't ask where my travelling companion had gone. If Mark Antony had melted into the arms of Cleopatra, it was none of my affair.

✝

He did not turn up that afternoon for our planned excursion to the Vatican's Gregorian Etruscan Museum, so I made the short walk alone from our hotel in the Via Tunisi across the Viale Vaticano to the museums. I went inside and admired the gleaming treasures within. It wasn't long before I spotted a piece of jewellery that was exotic and yet familiar. Familiar from Zamira Lule Halili's description. It was a bright gold necklace with a round medallion and what looked like gold vessels — Zamira had suggested vials of poison — one on either side of the medallion. They hung from tubes of gold that were arranged in a semicircle as if they were tied around a woman's neck on a piece of string.

The information card told me this piece was from the Etruscan period, anywhere from three to seven hundred years before the birth of Christ. The Etruscans were described as brilliant goldsmiths, admired particularly for their elaborate technique of granulation: the side-by-side application of tiny beads of gold. This piece was acquired somehow by a Roman noblewoman. She gave it to her bishop along with all her other earthly wealth when she converted to Christianity. The woman was martyred for her faith; her jewels and other possessions were handed down through the centuries until they became part of the Vatican treasure trove. No one could say how much something like this was worth because its history rendered it priceless. I had no idea whether I was looking at the genuine article or a brilliant fake. But the write-up said the Etruscans' work had never been equalled; close examination by an expert would quickly tell the tale.

✝

Isabella had invited me to spend New Year's Eve at the trattoria and promised to save me a table on a night when many Romans partake of gargantuan servings of food and drink. There was still no sign of Burke, so I got scrubbed and spiffed up and went by myself. Lo and behold, Isa's sister, Susanna, was nowhere to be seen; it seemed she had taken a couple of days off. I ate too much, drank too much, played my blues harp, sang till my voice was gone, and joined in with the Roman revellers at the other tables. Isabella and I celebrated the arrival of 1992 together in a small, cramped room upstairs, to the sound of fireworks going off all over the city. We returned to the festivities and partied till it was time for me to roll back to the hotel.

Burke did not make an appearance on New Year's Day. There was no answer when I knocked on his hotel room door in the afternoon, but I noticed that the *Non Disturbare* sign never left the doorknob. Room service trays were stacked outside the door, piled with dinner plates and wine bottles. I did a bit more sightseeing in the city. I stood where Antony had stood when he cut such a *bella figura* at the Forum before losing himself in the sensuous East. I visited the Mausoleum of Augustus and his Altar of Peace, with its bas reliefs of Augustus, Agrippa, Tiberius, and the wives and children of the famous and infamous of ancient Rome.

I tracked down Kitty Curran and took her out for a ravishing, and ravishingly expensive, three-hour New Year's dinner at Les Etoiles, the rooftop restaurant of the Atlante Star Hotel. She didn't ask where Brennan was, which must have made her the most discreet person in Vatican City. The view of St. Peter's dome at night was magnificent, though Kitty made a crack about never getting away from the office. Like so many Irish, she was a born storyteller, and she kept me mesmerized with her tales of the Vatican and the wider world.

I asked her if she had ever met Reinhold Schellenberg. "I met him years ago, on more than one occasion, but we never had a conversation. I can't say I knew him. I wish to God I could help you solve this."

"Me, too. If the Vatican control freak you mentioned, Savo, isn't satisfied with the progress of the investigation he may swoop down on us yet. And Brennan won't be fit company if his reaction the other day is any indication!"

"Oh, Brennan will be crabbed indeed if he has Gino Savo breathing down his neck! The funny part is that, in some ways, they are two of a kind. Both very intelligent, good at what they do, men of the world. Brennan didn't come to Holy Orders a blushing virgin. Neither did Gino. He was married. His wife and daughter died. I don't know what happened. But Gino entered the seminary after that."

"And he's an ill-tempered, domineering despot who —"

"I wouldn't go so far as to say that, Monty! I don't think Gino ever intends to throw a tantrum; he just can't help himself at times. He had a bit of a nervous breakdown at one point, so people make allowances for him. He really is very highly regarded here. I mean, to be considered for the job of archbishop of Genoa, somebody has to like you!"

"Still and all, we'd be better off without Father Savo's intervention."

"Oh, my dear, yes!"

"Well, let's hope it doesn't come to that."

As we were finishing our espresso, she said: "I may not see you again before you go. Take care of him for me."

"Take care . . ."

"Of my dear friend Brennan."

"He doesn't seem to need much in the way of care; he's a pretty self-sufficient kind of guy."

"Do you think? Don't be fooled, Monty. Look around you." She nodded in the direction of the Vatican. "Observe the priests when you're over there. Some of them look twenty years younger than they really are. This is the life for some. The priestly life does not sit as easily on the shoulders of others. Like Brennan."

"All the more reason for you to come to Halifax and spend some time with him."

"I'll see what I can do."

✝

Our days in Italy were numbered, and I was anxious to get on with our investigation in other parts of the country. It was the morning after my dinner with Kitty and it was time I intruded on Burke. I knocked on his door. No answer. I went down for breakfast, took a walk around the block, went to the desk, told them I had forgotten my key, and went back upstairs with the key to Burke's room. I

183

ignored the *Non Disturbare* sign, unlocked the door, and pushed it open. The room of the normally fastidious priest reeked of booze, smoke, and sex. There were empty bottles on the tables, and an overflowing ashtray. The bed looked as if a cyclone had hit it, and clothing was strewn over chairs and lampshades. He obviously wasn't here, or he'd have cleaned — Jesus! My heart took a leap in my chest. He was on the floor; he wasn't moving. Was he . . . I started towards his body, towards him, then I hesitated. He was face down on the carpet, with his arms flung out wide on either side. He was wearing some kind of stole, part of his vestments. I looked up then and saw on an otherwise empty table a small monstrance, a gold receptacle shaped like a blazing sun, used for the consecrated host. He must have been saying Mass. Was he now prostrate before the sacrament in an act of adoration, humility, penitence? I watched him for a moment longer, saw his rib cage move, so I knew he was breathing. I backed out of the room.

I was concerned but I am also discreet, so I left him alone. He finally surfaced that evening, showered, shaved, and dressed in fresh civilian clothes. But he was half-blitzed when he came to my room to pick me up for dinner. We walked a few blocks to a tiny, quiet restaurant and bar, and sat by the window. We watched the parade of Romans go by, men in camel or black cashmere topcoats, women in party dresses and shoes that cost a month's rent. Dinner consisted of *antipasti, insalata caprese, linguini marinara alla pesce* with scallops, salmon, shrimps, and all kinds of other delicacies that, in Burke's case, went to waste. The meal, at least for us, also included copious amounts of alcohol. His face was drawn, and he had dark circles under his black eyes; he looked as if he hadn't slept in a year.

"Is guilt eating away at you, Brennan? Are you in fear of the fires of hell?" I asked lightly. "Kind of a *Portrait of the Artist* damnation scene?"

"Guilt? Of course I feel guilt, as I do any time I break my vows. And use someone else for my own ends."

"Well, it's not as if it wasn't mutual."

"And when you suspect you're using the person as a substitute for —" he paused for a mouthful of wine "— for someone else, then it's all the worse."

"You mean if you can't have Zamira Lule Halili!"

He looked at me as if he had no idea who I was talking about. Then he seemed to snap back into focus. "Zamira. Right," he said.

If it wasn't Zamira he really wanted, who was it? I didn't have time to speculate before he spoke again: "Anyway, all this is beside the point."

"Which is what?"

He waved my question away and lit up a cigarette. He blew the smoke out angrily, looked at the cigarette in his hand, and stubbed it out. "It's not guilt, fear of damnation, any of that. It's something worse."

"What could possibly be worse than burning in eternal hellfire?"

His exhausted eyes looked away from me into the darkness of the Roman night. I thought he had forgotten my presence but then he spoke again. "Oldest story in the book, a recurring nightmare."

"About what?"

"I dream of the Mass. But I'm cut off from it. I can't say it. I'm in the congregation, in the first row. I try to get up to the altar but I can't move. Ever. And I know it will be like that for me *per omnia saecula saeculorum.* For all eternity. The Mass goes on and doesn't reach me. I don't think it's a dream at all; it's too literal. It's more like I'm lying there thinking it when I'm awake. That I'll fuck up and lose my priest-hood. If that happened I couldn't —"

"No one's going to — what do they do? — fire you, or take away your privileges, over a couple of nights in the crib with a woman."

"Nobody would have to. I'd lose it on my own. I'd no longer be able to celebrate the Eucharist. The loss — it's beyond me to explain it to you, Monty. Only if you were a priest would you understand. Not even every priest would understand. When I say Mass — not every time but most times — it's as if — it's not *as if,* it *is* — the veil between this world and the unseen world drops away. The eternal, the ineffable, the heavenly, comes down to earth, is present on the altar, like beams of pure light, or unearthly harmonies, only more intense. Sometimes I can barely come back from it and finish the Mass. This is incomprehensible to you; it's not your fault. But your daughter knows. Normie sees it, she feels it. On those occasions when you or . . . or Maura bring her to Mass and I look at her, I know she's having a direct, an unmediated experience, even if just for an instant. Oh, Christ." He patted his pockets. "Am I out of smokes now?"

He muttered and cursed about that, got up and bought a pack of cigarettes, returned to the table, and said no more about the subject that was consuming him. We drank silently and excessively, then staggered to our hotel.

Chapter 9

Der Gerechten Seelen sind in Gottes Hand und keine Qual rühret sie an.
The souls of the righteous are in the hand of God and there shall
no torment touch them.
— Johannes Brahms, *Ein Deutsches Requiem*, Opus 45

When I awoke in the morning, there was a note shoved under my
door. "Mass 10:30 a.m., San Gregorio dei Muratori, Via Leccosa, 75.
Taxi. Bring camera."

I got ready and shoved my little camera in my pocket. Fighting
down the nausea induced by a night of drinking way beyond my con-
siderable capacity, I went downstairs for breakfast, then walked out of
the hotel and up the stairs facing the wall of Vatican City. A taxi
approached, and I sleep-walked towards it. I passed the driver the
paper Burke had left with the address of the church. The cabbie stared
at the address, jabbed it with his finger a couple of times, and looked
back at me: *"Dov'è?"*

I shrugged, leaned back, and closed my eyes. I felt the car surge forward and reel around several turns. My stomach followed suit. Then
we stopped, and I prepared to get out, but I saw that the driver had
pulled up beside a bar and was consulting a well-thumbed street directory. Leave it to Burke to come up with an address unknown even to a
Roman cab driver. I closed my eyes again and felt myself drifting off to
sleep, until the cab took off like a rocket. "Via Leccosa, *settantacinque*,"

I heard before we squealed to a halt. I paid the driver, got out, and only then noticed that there was no church in sight. The cabbie had left me at the entrance to a short, narrow alleyway lined with high tenements. I walked down the alley, hoping to ask someone for directions, but there was nobody in sight. One of the apartment buildings was number 75, so I pushed open the door and did a double take. There before me was a magnificent altar carved out of stone. Above the altar, light blazed in from an oval stained-glass window depicting the Holy Spirit in the form of a dove. There were only a few benches in the fore-shortened space of the chapel. I heard Gregorian chant and turned to see three priests in the choir loft, singing from large leather-bound books. Then Burke emerged from the sacristy, wearing his vestments, a biretta on his head. Two younger priests and two altar boys served at the traditional Latin Mass. I was handed a *Kyriale* and I chanted the responses along with the others in the small congregation. I was a bit late falling to my knees at the "incarnatus est" during the "Credo" but, other than that, my old altar-boy training came back, and it felt as if a quarter century of English Masses had never been.

For a few minutes afterwards, I sat basking in the incense, the remembered plainchant, and the beauty of the church, but Father Burke came and dragged me out. I had to sprint to keep up with him as he made his way to the Tiber and across the Umberto I bridge. A gurgling lump in my abdomen impeded my progress.

"Why are we running?"

"Angelus."

"What?"

"The papal blessing at noon; he appears in the window. We don't want to miss it."

"You run. I'll stay behind with my stomach."

By the time I had made my way past the Castel Sant' Angelo and up the Via Conciliazione, the pope had given his blessing to those willing and able to arrive on time, and had vanished inside his apartment. I shuffled around the Piazza San Pietro until I spied Burke. He bore down on me and handed me my next assignment. "I promised your little one I'd bring her a T-shirt with 'Angelicum' on it. Remember?"

"I remember something about it."

"She covets the one I have, and she seems quite interested in angels."

She thinks you're one yourself! All I said was: "The Angelicum is the Pontifical something of Thomas Aquinas, I take it."

"'Tis. Let's go. Camera?"

"Pocket."

He led me through the serpentine streets of central Rome until we reached the Pontifical University of Saint Thomas Aquinas.

"You studied here?"

"I did my doctoral work here, after getting my licentiate at the Greg."

"Doesn't look like the sort of place that sells T-shirts."

"It doesn't. I got mine when a crew of us had them done up."

"So how do you propose —"

"Take a picture and we'll have a shirt made up for Normie when we get back to Halifax."

I focused on the word ANGELICVM, which was engraved in a horizontal band of white travertine stone above the arched doorway and pillars of the building, and snapped a photo.

"I'm going to be sick from all this running," I complained.

"Me too, and it's not from running." I looked at him then and saw that he was in worse shape than I was. "But we don't have time for that. I've rented a car. Our investigation is going on the road."

Our destinations were two monasteries, one in Florence, the other outside Padua. The first had been home to Reinhold Schellenberg, the second to Robin Gadkin-Falkes. Brennan also mentioned an oratorio devoted to Saint Philomena in the town of Treviso, close to Venice. We left that open as a possibility. I don't think either of us held out much hope of being enlightened no matter where we went, but the prospect of a motoring holiday in Italy perked me up a bit. We returned to the hotel, picked up a sporty little rental car, and shoved our bags into the trunk.

"Andiamo," Burke said. "Flip a coin to see who drives?"

"You're driving. I'm the sightseer," I said.

"All right, but I'm not a well man."

"That makes two of us."

"I may have to pull over."

"We'll deal with that if it happens. Let's hope it doesn't. Christ, Burke, I've known you to put away vats of whiskey with no effects at all the next day. I've never seen you like this." He did not reply. I concluded that dark thoughts and brooding were doing more damage than the alcohol.

We travelled along the autostrada for about three hours, alternately roaring by the lines of eighteen-wheel trucks and being stuck behind them. But the highway was beautifully maintained and it afforded us a spectacular view of medieval hill towns, with high walls and towers that appeared to rise right out of the rock.

✝

Reinhold Schellenberg's home was the Monastero della Certosa del Galluzo in Florence, formerly run by the Carthusians, now by the Cistercians. Who apparently are Benedictines. I couldn't follow it, and Burke didn't elaborate. I had been in Florence several years before; good thing, because all I was getting this time was a white-knuckle ride through the streets on the way to the hillside monastery. City streets finally gave way to olive groves; when we reached our destination the sight was breathtaking. The monastery was a mix of medieval and Renaissance structures in the light earthy tones characteristic of Tuscany. We were met by Brother Giuseppe, who was wearing a white robe with what looked like a black apron over it; I learned later it is called a scapular. Brennan explained in Italian who we were, and the monk replied in a combination of Italian and English. He told us how devastated the *monaci* were about the death of Father Schellenberg, what a great, yet humble, man he was, and how he would always be in the community's prayers.

He led us to Schellenberg's room, which was spare in its furnishings but overflowing with books, binders, and pamphlets. Giuseppe took one of the binders from the shelf and showed us the contents, copies of papal encyclicals and other official church documents. The volumes were in several languages and covered theology, scriptural studies, liturgy, and the other subjects of interest to a Catholic scholar. Another shelf, inside the wardrobe, contained a number of books written by Schellenberg himself, all in German. They may have held a clue to the motive for his murder or they may not have. Burke succeeded in persuading the reluctant brother to hand over two boxes of personal papers, including correspondence to and from Schellenberg, and other documents that appeared to be in his handwriting. We promised to ship the items back once we had gone through them. Tucked away in the desk was a photograph of a very young Father Schellenberg with Pope John XXIII; the two men were sitting at a desk, examining a document.

"The Vatican Council?" I asked.

"No, before," Giuseppe answered. "In 1959 or 1960." It looked as though Schellenberg had been a trusted adviser well before the Council was convened. He had the appearance of a café intellectual then, hair quite long and brushed back from his forehead, black-rimmed glasses, and a short, trim beard.

"Brother Giuseppe, is there anything you can tell us about what may have led to Father Schellenberg's murder?"

No. He had no idea.

Guiseppe escorted us out, then asked us to wait a minute while he went to get something. He came back and handed us two bottles of the liqueurs made by the monks. I had the *Elixir di San Bernardo*, and Brennan had *Gran Liquore Certosa*. We thanked him, and he invited us to take a look around. After stowing the boxes in the car, we walked around the monastery, stopping in the chapel, where Brennan knelt and seemed to get lost in prayer. The silence was so profound and the place so peaceful I had no desire to leave.

But soon enough we were on the highway and headed northeast. We had reservations for the night in Fiesole, a town on a hill that rises over Florence. "I don't see any signs. How big is this place, Brennan?"

"Not all that big, but it's well known. There ought to be a sign, I'm thinking."

"Yeah, well, we'd better find it before we end up in Bologna."

"Did you know they had a law school in Bologna in the thirteenth century?"

"I wonder if they taught the lawyers to sue over badly marked highways. Damages for lost time and gas money. And mental anguish." I consulted my map and pointed to a turnoff. "We're beyond Fiesole now. Take that exit marked Barberino, and we'll work our way back."

We found ourselves skirting the Tuscan hills as we gained altitude, careening along a narrow mountain road with barely enough room to get by the cars that emerged suddenly from the blind turns ahead. It seemed we were mere inches from the precipice. Burke was unconcerned.

"The view here is brilliant, isn't it? These hills —"

"Keep your eyes on the road, Brennan, will you? And gear down. I wouldn't trust that guardrail to keep us from plunging to our deaths."

"Oh ye of little faith."

At that point I'd have preferred to be the wheelman myself but I had to admit he was a skilful driver.

Fiesole was a stunningly beautiful town, with crenellated medieval towers and extremely narrow winding one-lane streets — only to be expected, given the age of the settlement, which was noted for its Etruscan and Roman ruins. Mirrors were affixed to buildings on the corners; it was the only way to see whether another car was coming. We found a tiny hotel with cream stucco walls and green shutters on the windows; a white cat peered down at us from a windowsill. We registered and headed out immediately for dinner. It was the first time all day I could think of food without feeling queasy; now I was famished.

La Reggia degli Etruschi was, interestingly, a former monastery, up a steep hill from the town centre; it afforded us a panoramic view of Florence below us as the sun went down. Our six-course meal included such delights as noodles in black truffle sauce, beef filet flavoured with grapes, and mascarpone cheese cream with coffee-flavoured biscuits and chocolate. And then there were the Tuscan wines, which happened to be specialties of the house. Although by unspoken agreement we eschewed hard liquor for the evening, the wine selection was so spectacular we were both crocked by the time the *dolci* arrived. We yakked about our various travels in Europe and one-upped each other with war stories and mishaps. The brooding look returned to Brennan's face as the night wore on.

"Troubled by doubts again, about your vocation?" I ventured to ask.

"I have no doubts about my vocation," he replied with a certain tartness in his voice. Then, more quietly: "I just don't know if I'm able for it."

"You're able. You're having a dark night of the soul. It happens. Look at me. I'm a family man without my family. I don't know how long I'll be able for that." He looked at me for a long moment. In normal times, he would have started in on me by now: *Get it together, reconcile with Maura, don't be such a bonehead.* Obviously he didn't have it in him tonight. I drained my glass and signalled for the bill. Burke snatched it from the waiter and fumbled for his wallet. We stumbled back to the hotel with the enchanting lights of Florence beneath us at the bottom of the hill.

The next day brought us to yet another complex of magnificent buildings. The Benedictine abbey at Praglia, with its cloisters and Romanesque bell tower, was built between the eleventh and twelfth centuries. We walked through the loggia with a black-robed monk by the name of Brother Rodrigo. I understood much of what he said; Brennan filled me in later on the rest. There was not a lot he could, or would, tell us about Brother Robin Gadkin-Falkes. He knew Robin was in Canada, and we told him Robin had been ill, had perhaps suffered a breakdown. We said nothing about the murder and, if Brother Rodrigo knew what had happened, he did not let on. He seemed to accept that Father Burke and his friend were concerned about Robin and were looking for information that might help him. But all he could tell us was that Robin lived the life of work and prayer required of a monk. He particularly liked to toil in the gardens, and he loved the canonical hours, when the men gathered several times daily for prayer and the reading of Scripture. His was the voice with which the others sought to blend when the ancient plainchant was sung in choir. Did he ever speak of the death of his sister? The community was aware of it, and prayed for her soul.

Could we see his room? Brother Rodrigo hesitated, then seemed to find no harm in that, so he went to get the key and led us to the small, tidy room occupied by Brother Robin Gadkin-Falkes. But the room had little to say to us. There was a bed, a desk and chair, a bookshelf that did not contain anything unusual. Tacked to a bulletin board were some devotional pictures and prayers relating to Saint Charles Borromeo. Burke opened the door of a plain wooden wardrobe, and we saw nothing but robes and a couple of sets of civilian clothing. Three drawers contained underwear, socks, and toiletries. Brother Rodrigo looked as if he wanted to protest when the visiting priest yanked open the desk drawers and rummaged around. There were pens, pencils, writing paper, the usual things, and a photo of his sister,

Louisa. Brennan drew out a few sheets of paper and spread them over the desk. They were cartoons in black ink, well drawn, depicting Borromeo bowing low before a high altar; he was billed as the "Apostle of the Council of Trent." Another drawing lampooned Pope John XXIII as the "Apostate of the Council of Vatican II." The final cartoon depicted Pope Paul VI as a waiter, with a white cloth draped over his arm and a large menu in his hand, about to serve a motley group of people talking and laughing around a rectangular table. The menu said *"Novus Ordo."* The cartoon was a reference to the new Mass as a meal around a table, rather than the re-enactment of Christ's sacrifice at the altar.

That was it for Brother Robin's room. We thanked Rodrigo and stayed on for nones, the three o'clock prayer service. The chanting was ethereal. Brennan took part and he seemed, at least for those few minutes, to lose the careworn, hungover look that had marked him during our Italian road trip. When we came out of the church, Brennan tossed me the car keys, and I got into the driver's seat. We left the ancient monastery for the twentieth-century autostrada, where we merged with the traffic roaring along at one hundred thirty kilometres an hour.

"So," I said, "unflattering portrayals of Popes John and Paul. Did they deserve that sort of contempt?"

"Of course not. Anyone who grew up with 'Tantum Ergo' and now has to sit through 'They'll Know We Are Christians By Our Love' in the wake of the Second Vatican Council might cast a disapproving eye on Pope John. But to most people, he was a saintly and beloved man. He was in fact a funny, self-deprecating, sweet man. And the goofiness that infected the church after Vatican II is not his fault. As for Pope Paul, he was an intellectual and a profoundly spiritual priest."

"Next item of business," I said, "do we go on to Treviso, or back to Rome? I have to call Moody Walker from somewhere to see if he managed to set anything up for us in Frankfurt tomorrow."

"I'm thinking we won't learn much from the fact that there's a St. Philomena Oratorio in Treviso. We haven't done the rounds of St. Cecilia churches, because we're not likely to learn anything from those either. But Treviso is a lovely town. I'm happy to go along if you've a mind to check it out. It's not all that far, and we have another night before we fly out. But I'll probably sleep through it all."

"Let's go. We'll get a room, I'll give Walker a call, and we'll see if Saint Philomena speaks to us in a voice we can understand."

When we got to the outskirts of Treviso we stopped and procured a little map, and the man who sold it to us pointed to the Via S. Bona Vecchia as the street where we would find the oratorio. We made our turn and cruised along looking for the church.

"It should be just along here on the right."

We passed a food shop, a hotel, a tiny religious building of some sort, and then we were into a neighbourhood of white stucco houses with red or black scalloped roof tiles. "I don't know, Brennan. I don't see anything that looks like an oratorio."

"What? Pull over." He rolled down his window and called to an elderly woman going by on a bicycle. *"Scusi, signora, come si fa per andare all'Oratorio di Santa Filomena?"*

Her directions had us backtracking to the unlikely-looking structure we had just passed: a little cream-coloured octagonal building with two small spires and a red tiled roof. The tiny building, behind a wrought-iron gate, was virtually in the parking lot of the hotel next door, a building several storeys in height with a tiled roof like that of the oratorio. The Ca' del Galletto looked like a nice enough hotel, so the first thing we did was book a big room with two beds, an elegant bathroom and, to Brennan's delight, a trouser press in the corner. He flopped down on one of the beds and closed his eyes. I left him there and went outside.

I walked around the tiny church, and noticed what appeared to be bullet holes in one of the walls. *Somebody had strong feelings about this place*, I thought. There was a large plaque on the site, giving a detailed history of the oratorio. It was too much for me to translate, so I decided to snap a picture in case it contained anything of interest. If Burke did not get around to reading it during our visit, I could enlarge the photo and he could read that.

The man at the desk greeted me when I returned to the hotel, and I asked him about the oratorio. I began in his native tongue, but his English was much better than my Italian.

"Somebody doesn't like the oratorio, or the saint it was built for?" I asked.

He laughed. "It was nothing personal."

"Why do you say that?"

"It happened in the First War. An Austrian grenade from across the Piave. It exploded close to the oratorio."

"Battle of the Piave River, 1918."

"Yes. You know history."

"I'm a bit of a history buff." But not such a good detective; the flak damage did not reflect an attack on Saint Philomena. "Thanks for the information. I have to go see a sick friend."

"Your friend is in his room. I think he has maybe . . ." The man mimed a glass being lifted to his lips.

"Yeah, he needs to sleep it off."

I let the invalid nap for an hour, then shook him awake. We walked from the hotel into the medieval town centre, with its crenellated clock tower, arcaded streets, and shuttered stucco houses, which cast shimmering reflections in the water of the canals. The streets were narrow and winding, the crosswalks marked with white marble blocks. Burke had cheered up; he was clearly in his element.

"You're a man born out of time, Brennan."

"There's much to be said for the medieval world," he acknowledged.

✝

Our Italian sojourn ended the following day when we drove back to Rome and caught our flight to Frankfurt. Our first encounter in that city was with the world's most belligerent cab driver, who berated us for our inability to give him directions from the airport to our hotel, strangely named the Albatros. We tuned the cabbie out, and he finally located the hotel. We checked in and hired another taxi to take us to the Altstadt, the old town of Frankfurt. Luckily, this driver was much friendlier than the first one, so we asked him to give us a few minutes to walk through the old city. The town square was lined with tall, half-timbered houses that had been obliterated by Allied bombers during World War II, and rebuilt in exacting detail afterwards; even the original builders' mistakes were replicated. I snapped a couple of photos for Normie who, I knew, would love the fairy-tale houses, then we hopped back in the cab for the drive to Sachsenhausen, the apple wine district. Moody Walker's contact in Hamburg had set up a meeting for us with Helmut Oster, a retired police officer from the former East Berlin.

We got out of the cab and walked along the cobblestoned streets to a very Germanic-looking establishment called Zum Stern. Next to it was the Anglo-Irish Pub, which attracted a longing gaze from Burke on the way by. He told me the bar was a regular haunt of his brother Terry, an airline pilot who frequently flew the New York–Frankfurt route. Oster was waiting for us in Zum Stern. He was tall and broad and had very short bristly salt and pepper hair. German was one of the handful of languages Burke could speak, and I had taken a couple of courses back in my university days, so we were able to exchange a few pleasantries with the policeman in that language before he switched to heavily accented English.

Speaking of heavy, I looked at the menu offering — bratwurst, schnitzel, and hackfleisch — and wondered whether my tender stomach could take it. As if he had read my mind, Burke folded his menu, put it down, and said: "When in Rome, do as the Romans do." His stomach was in better shape than mine — no, apparently not. "Romans eat Italian food. I'll have the pizza Margherita." I had a salad. Oster laughed and ordered the hackfleisch.

Helmut Oster had been something of a dissident, at least to the limited extent possible for a police officer in East Berlin. He greeted with relief the disintegration of the Honecker regime in the German Democratic Republic, and did nothing to arrest its decline. He was of particular interest to us because, as Sergeant Walker had ascertained, he had been on duty for the state visit of Soviet President Leonid Ilich Brezhnev in 1971.

"Was Reinhold Schellenberg present at a demonstration against Brezhnev?" I asked him.

"Reinhold Schellenberg was shot and wounded at the demonstration."

"*What?*" Burke and I exclaimed.

"He was shot by the Stasi and taken into custody."

"What brought this about?"

"It is my understanding that he had been warned, and failed to heed the warning."

"Warned not to take part in the protest?"

"Yes. The authorities were anxious to avoid unrest and political embarrassment during the leader's visit."

"Who warned him off?"

"It was one of us, one of the *Volkspolizei*. As you may know, members of the *Ministerium für Staatssicherheit*, the secret police, worked closely at times with the VoPos, who were organized under the Ministry of the Interior. I believe it was Kurt Bleier who issued the warning. Bleier was involved in the operations surrounding the visit."

"Was Schellenberg known to Bleier before these events took place?"

"I do not know. What I do know is that the Stasi had been watching Schellenberg. He was a theologian. He had worked in the Vatican and was thought to be influential with certain liberal elements in the church. He was a priest in Magdeburg at the time, at St. Sebastian Cathedral. When it became known that he would be travelling to Berlin, at a time which coincided with Brezhnev, he was watched more closely. And, as I say, he received a visit from one of the VoPos, and I think it was Bleier. Then he turned up at the demonstration anyway. Someone rushed in the direction of the reviewing stand; it may have been Schellenberg and some others, it is not clear. But it was Schellenberg who received a bullet in his arm. He was detained for several days after that. His wound was treated; he was eventually released."

"What happened to him while he was in custody?"

"I do not know. I suspect he faced some rough treatment. He returned to his church in Magdeburg. He later became a professor and taught in several universities. Then he went to work in the Vatican again, and was quite an important man there."

"What can you tell us about Bleier?"

"I was not acquainted with him personally but what I know is that he was a dedicated socialist. He married a Polish girl, the daughter of a concert violinist. The family lived in Berlin. They were strong Catholics and were not in favour with the Party. The Silkowski home was known as a place of music and culture. The way I heard it, Bleier met the girl after going to the house to question the father. Perhaps he was seduced as much by the music and the spirit of the family as by the daughter!"

We were winding up our lunch and I asked Helmut: "Can you

think of any reason why Kurt Bleier would want Schellenberg dead after all these years?"

He shook his head as he balled his napkin up and placed it on the table. "If there is a reason, it is unknown to me."

We thanked him, and he went on his way. We had one more person to see. This was a woman suggested to Moody Walker by the policeman in Hamburg. I had called her, and we had arranged to link up at the Albatros where she, too, had decided to stay the night.

Frau Professorin Doktor Greta Schliemann met us at the door of her room leaning heavily on a cane. She appeared to be in her late seventies. The woman was dressed in what looked like old army pants topped by a blouse in a mod geometric pattern of tan and pink, which might have come from a shop in Carnaby Street in the 1960s. She bade us enter and make ourselves at home on the bed, while she sat in an armchair by the open window. Her room, like ours, had bright yellow walls and a blue carpet with a pattern of tiny yellow flowers. If Normie could see it, she would demand yet another renovation of her bedroom.

"You are interested to hear about Max Bleier and Father Johann Schellenberg. We were all interned in the same camp outside Berlin in the 1940s." Greta Schliemann picked up her cane and said: "This is not the result of old age but of Nazi brutality. I have been using this cane since I was released from the camp in 1945 at the age of twenty-two." That put her under seventy, considerably younger than she looked. "What would you like to know?"

Brennan said: "Reinhold Schellenberg has been murdered, as you know. We'd like to find out whether there was any connection between Father Johann Schellenberg, who was his uncle, and Max Bleier, in the camp."

"I was intrigued to hear that Max's son, Kurt, was in Canada at the time of the murder. What was he doing there?"

"I have set up a schola cantorum, a college of sorts for the study of traditional Catholic music."

Her eyebrows shot up. "Hardly the setting in which I would expect to see Max Bleier. But of course I do not know the son."

"It's hardly the setting in which *we* would have expected to see Kurt. He does have a reason to be there, an ostensible reason at least. His wife is a Polish Catholic and a musician."

"Well, well. One never knows. I can tell you only about the father and the uncle. Bleier was imprisoned, as was I, because he was a Communist, Schellenberg because he was a Catholic priest. They became acquainted with one another in the camp." Greta reached down to her left, rummaged in a large quilted bag, and brought forth a small tattered leather book. She flipped to the page she wanted and held it open on her lap. "My diary for my time in the camp. Comrade Bleier and Father Schellenberg passed time playing chess together. Many of the inmates did, of course, but those two played often, and I don't know whether they ever concluded a game."

"Why not?" I asked.

"They were distracted by other matters that interested them."

"Such as?"

"Debate, argument."

"They were antagonistic to one another?"

"They were German! They had a dispute going every time they came together at the chessboard. Arguments over politics, religion, philosophy. Johann Schellenberg was a big man, broad-faced, with thick fair hair. He was turning greyer by the day, of course, in there. Max had short brown hair; he was small and wiry. He was in constant pain from a beating he had received from the guards. But he tried to hide it, tried not to let on that they had hurt him. I can still see the two of them sitting out in the yard, in the shadow of the watchtower, their chess pieces forgotten between them. I was a student of philosophy before I was imprisoned; I was fascinated by their conversations and tried to remember them, so I could think them over. There were two doctors who were in the camp; I used to follow their talks as well. Anyway, Max and Johann . . . of course I had to reconstruct it later in the barracks, so I may not have it word for word." She consulted her diary.

"Here is Bleier, followed by Schellenberg:

> *Your church lulls the people into accepting their oppression here on earth, by promising a fantasy life in the hereafter.*
> *That is a cliché. You can do better than that, Herr Bleier.*
> *It is not a cliché, Comrade Schellenberg; it is the sine qua non of your religion.*
> *Hardly. Jesus exhorts us to feed the hungry, clothe the naked,*

visit the sick and imprisoned. This life is an important part of God's plan; otherwise, we would not be here.

Jesus also said the poor will always be with us. Marx assures us they will not. They will throw off their chains and take their rightful place as owners of the means —

We have had a quarter of a century of the revolution in Soviet Russia —

History takes time. No thinking man could expect otherwise, Comrade Schellenberg.

"He was right, you know," Greta said, giving us a direct look with her watery light grey eyes. "We need only look at our own era. Bad times for the left, a period of adjustment, of going backwards. But socialism will rise again. It is inevitable. Except in America, where political consciousness is not highly developed. How we used to laugh during the time of the 'red scare' in the United States! How we wished they really had something to fear! But no, what they have there is a huge underclass pacified by television. Goggling at the garish display of wealth and frivolous gadgets, which they believe they will some day acquire. They will not. They are fools."

"So Father Schellenberg and Max Bleier argued about religion, Communism . . ." I prompted.

"Yes, and then they would get on to Plato and Aristotle, Hegel and Kant, Hume, Nietzsche, Freud. It spiralled up to a level where the rest of us could not follow. It always reached the point where one of them would throw up his hands in exasperation and leave the board. Someone else would quickly fill in the seat, hoping for a match. But it wasn't the same. When one of them was absent, the other was out of sorts.

"Then came the escape attempt. A half dozen of the prisoners formulated a plan to dig a short tunnel under the farthest aspect of the perimeter wall. There was a crude but effective scheme to remove small bits of earth and weeds on quick passes by the corner of the wall, and take the dirt away in the prisoners' pockets. They had a clump or a berm or something they put back over it to hide the hole. One of them had to volunteer to forgo the chance to escape, to stay behind and cover up the tunnel, so it could be used again for a later group. Five of them made it out; the sixth stayed behind as planned, and covered up. The camp authorities were outraged. They proceeded to hunt down that sixth person. They did this by going into each of the barracks, taking one of the inmates at random, and beating him so that he would either confess or identify the conspirator. This happened twice. Then Johann Schellenberg stepped forward and confessed. He was beaten in front of the others, then taken away. Nobody knew where he was. But everybody knew he had nothing to do with the escape. That was the work of an older man, a Communist Party organizer from the north. There was great turmoil among the population after this.

"Max Bleier went through the camp calling out: 'Father Schellenberg! Where are you? Answer me!' And to the guards: 'Where have you taken Father Schellenberg? Are you torturing a priest? What kind of men are you?' He was told to shut up or he would get the same treatment. One of the guards roughed him up. He sat out in the yard, at the chessboard, half-heartedly playing with other inmates. This went on for several days. Every time a guard passed, he would look up: 'Where is Father Schellenberg? Let us see him.' Then, one day, there came Schellenberg, limping out of a shuttered building at the back of the yard. Gaunt, bruised, but alive. The expression on Bleier's face! Relief, joy, horror. All quickly masked. Bleier was not an emotional man. 'Where have you been, Comrade? I've been waiting.' Johann sat down, slowly, painfully, and they started up again."

Greta looked out the window, lost in her memories, and we were all silent for a few minutes. Then I asked: "What happened after that?"

She shrugged. "I was moved to a different camp in January of '45 and we were liberated in May. I don't know what became of anyone at the first camp."

"So you don't know whether Johann Schellenberg and Max Bleier kept in touch?"

"No. I never saw either of them again."

Chapter 10

There's a blaze of light in every word.
It doesn't matter which you heard:
The holy or the broken Hallelujah.
— Leonard Cohen, "Hallelujah"

Brennan and I rose early the next morning and boarded our flight to Halifax. It was Monday, January 6. Both of us were clean but bleary-eyed and unshaven; we looked as if we'd been on our road trip for a lot longer than eleven days. Slow lines at the airport had done nothing to make us more chipper.

An hour out of Frankfurt I brought up the murder case. "The chessboard at the schola, did that come from the choir school or the rectory, or from somewhere else?"

"I have no idea."

"You don't remember seeing it before?"

"I don't, but maybe I just never noticed."

"Be sure to ask Mike O'Flaherty. If you guys didn't put it there, who did? If Bleier brought it with him, does that mean he knew Schellenberg was coming? Or, if Schellenberg brought it —"

"We don't know, Monty. We'll see what we can find out. Now shut your gob and let me sleep."

But he couldn't sleep, and neither could I. We passed the time eating bad food, watching a bad movie, and having one too many drinks for the long overseas flight. Predictably we were jet-lagged, half in the bag, and feeling like hell when we finally landed on terra firma.

"I can't face the rectory like this," Brennan said when we fell into the back seat of a cab. "Michael will want to hear every detail of the trip, and I haven't the strength."

"We'll pick up something to eat and take it to my place. You can unwind there for the afternoon."

"Proper thing."

We got the taxi driver to stop at a grocery store and wait while I did some hurried shopping. It was chilly with the smell of snow in the air when we got to my place, so I lit a fire. I broiled a couple of steaks, baked some potatoes, and we had a mid-afternoon meal, which felt like a middle-of-the-night meal to us. Burke called Monsignor O'Flaherty to tell him we were back, poured himself a glass of Irish, drained it, then passed out in my armchair with the empty glass still in his hand. I called the kids and told them I'd see them tomorrow; I had a couple of things for them, and another item would be arriving later. I scribbled a note to myself about getting the Angelicum photo developed and transferred to a T-shirt for Normie.

I was just drifting off in my bed when the phone rang. It was Father Sferrazza-Melchiorre, telling me he had a couple of friends visiting from out of town. They were looking for something to do, and he knew Brennan was with me. Sure, bring them over. I gave him directions, then hauled myself out of bed and got ready for just what I didn't need: company.

A few minutes later I answered the doorbell and found Enrico standing on the step, fully caped, with two men who would be recognized even in a satellite reconnaissance photo as Americans. They each beamed a set of blindingly white teeth at me, and held out their hands for a shake. One had blow-dried blond hair and looked like the prototypical television preacher. The other was tanned and craggy and could have found steady work as an actor playing a cowboy or a farmhand. They were dressed in Sunday-go-to-meetin' suits. The cowboy introduced himself as Earl Slocum and the preacher as Eldon Pye.

"Brother Eldon and I are just in from Lutes Mountain," Slocum told me. "Up across the state line." *State laan.*

They had crossed quite a few state lines, in my estimation, if they were this far north; Slocum's drawl placed him in the deep south of the U.S.A. But he explained that Lutes Mountain was just outside Moncton, New Brunswick, and then I was able to place it, up across the *provincial* line.

"Big revival meetin' up there, put on by the Atlantic Baptist College, and they invited Brother Eldon to do some preachin' and some healin'. We're flyin' out tomorra mornin', and we wanted to make time to see Father Hank on our way through."

Father Hank — *Don* Enrico Sferrazza-Melchiorre — spoke up. "Mr. Slocum and Mr. Pye are from Mississippi, Montague. Their church is close to mine. Close geographically. They knew I was coming to Canada, and I gave them my address. Their flight to the U.S. leaves from Halifax, so they are my guests today."

"Come in, come in. Are you ready to go back to school tomorrow, Enrico?"

"Yes. In fact, I returned just after New Year's. I spent Christmas with my parishioners in Mule Run, but I wanted to come back to Halifax. I like the snow."

"You're lucky this year. We don't always have snow for the holidays."

"Yes, it is beautiful. I hope to ski."

"Right. We have Martock and Wentworth. It's not the Italian Alps though, Enrico."

"It is not Mule Run, Mississippi."

"I hear you. Make yourselves comfortable, gentlemen."

"I see my friend Brennan is here. Allow me to introduce . . ." Enrico began, then faltered when he saw his friend passed out in the living room, with a whiskey glass ready to fall from his hand. "Brennan is obviously exhausted. We shall wait for him to join us."

The two Americans stared at the tousled, unshaven man in the chair, looked at their watches, and exchanged glances with one another.

"Find a seat there, gentlemen. Can I get you anything? A beer? Guinness? Whiskey? Wine? Shine?"

Glances again. "Uh, no, Montague, thank you very much."

"Milk? Mountain Dew?"

"Mountain Dew would be real nice, thank you."

I got them ginger ale, and settled them in the living room. We all pretended there was nobody else in the room. Or that's what I thought we were doing. "This man," Slocum began, cocking a finger at Pye, "this man saved my life. I said to you he was up there in New Brunswick preachin' and healin', and that's exactly what I meant. He healed me, he can heal you, and —" Slocum looked with pity at Brennan and broke into song "— 'Amazing grace, how sweet the sound that saved a wretch like me.' He can heal that poor wretched man settin' in that chair."

"Think so?" I asked.

"I was lost, Montague. And Brother Eldon found me and brought me to the Lord. I have not touched a drop of liquor since I accepted Jesus Christ as my Lord and Saviour. Brother Eldon?"

"Thank you for that kind testimony, Earl." Pye's accent was not as down-home as Slocum's, but it was from the same latitude. "Let me ask you something if I may, Montague."

"Sure."

"Has this man been bedevilled by alcohol for a long time?"

"He is not drunk, but sleepeth," I replied.

"You're a loyal friend, and Jesus admires that. And I'm sure you are a great comfort to your friend in his darkness. Feed the hungry, clothe the naked, visit the sick. Inasmuch as ye have done it unto one of the least of these my brethren, ye have done it unto me."

The least of Jesus's brethren took that moment to moan in his sleep and mutter something in a language I did not understand; his glass fell from his hand, rolled across the rug, and stopped at the feet of Eldon Pye, who picked up the theme again. "I won't ask you, Montague, whether this man has been saved. He may have been baptized in the Lord as a child, I have no way of knowing. But to be born again —"

"Oh, you misunderstand, Eldon. Brennan is in fact a —" Enrico began, but I gave him a wink, and he fell silent.

"So what did you preach about up in New Brunswick, Eldon?" I asked. "Booze?"

"Many of those who came to me for healing came for that reason, Montague. Liquor flows freely in our society —"

"Hasn't it always?"

"— and I am only one man. I laid my hands on the heads of as many as I could, of those afflicted with whiskey and cigarettes and wild, wild women, to quote a song my daddy used to sing. My faith tells me those people who came to me have been healed. But, no, the subject of my sermons at that meeting was science."

"Oh, you're a scientist?"

"I am a scientist of Scripture, if you will. I am a creation scientist. And I am on a lecture tour, Montague, to warn Christian families of the evil of teaching Darwin's theory — theory, not fact — of evolution to our children. A close reading of the Bible tells us the earth is six thousand years old. God is never wrong, the Bible is the word of God, the Bible is never wrong."

"The Bible —" a groggy Irish voice had joined us "— is about 'the resurrection of the dead, the hope of eternal life, and the kingdom of heaven.' And not about 'the motion and orbit of the stars, their size and relative positions, and the predictable eclipses of the sun and moon.'" The Americans turned to gape at Burke, who spoke without moving or opening his eyes: "'Reckless and incompetent expounders of Holy Scripture bring untold trouble and sorrow on their wiser brethren when they are caught in one of their mischievous false opinions and are taken to task by those who are not bound by the authority of our sacred books.' Saint Augustine, *Literal Commentary on Genesis*. Written in 415, Anno Domini."

"Brennan, you're awake!"

"I'm in the middle of a feckin' nightmare here, Monty." He sat slumped over the arm of his chair, left hand massaging his temples. "Did I have a drink?"

"We have company, Brennan."

"Did I hear some class of horseshit about Darwin being wrong, and the earth being six thousand years old? The big bang happened thirteen point seven billion years ago. Plenty of time for us all to get over it." He opened his eyes, fastened them on our visitors, then shut them again. He fumbled in his pockets for a cigarette, then squinted as he tried to light it with shaking hands. "Ah!" he sighed, when the nicotine hit his lungs.

"Good afternoon, Brennan," Slocum said in his southern drawl.

"Mother of God!" Brennan exclaimed. His eyes found Father Sferrazza-Melchiorre. "Isn't this the crowd you dwell amongst, Enrico?"

"These are friends of Enrico," I explained. "They know him, however improbably, as Father Hank."

"I'm Earl Slocum, and this is Brother Eldon Pye."

Brother Eldon fixed Brennan with a smarmy, toothy TV–Christian smile. "Brennan, we are pleased to make your acquaintance. I was surprised to hear you say you were quoting Saint Augustine. My source is Scripture — Scripture alone — so I can't say whether you were quoting him correctly, but I suspect not, if —"

"Look it up."

"Forgive me for saying so, but you seem to have accepted the scientific fallacies of our day. The Bible clearly says —"

Burke was looking for something. His drink? Distracted, he mumbled at the preacher. "Pretend the universe is one year old exactly. Big bang happened January first. Our solar system didn't even appear till some time in September, the dinosaurs in late December. Our human ancestors just learned to walk upright in time for the party on New Year's Eve. As for modern man —"

"Now it's funny you should mention the dinosaurs. Let me say a word about them, if I may."

"Don't be telling us your grandfather used to hunt them. I haven't the patience for that kind of blather today."

"No, of course not. But our ancestors did. Called 'em dragons. And the Bible says —"

"The dinosaurs ceased to exist sixty-five million years ago. That's been established by science." Burke rose from his chair and headed for the kitchen. We heard the sound of glass on glass. "Get you anything?"

"No. Thank you," the southerners said.

Loyally, I said: "Sure. Whatever you're having."

Enrico asked for wine, and I got up to find a bottle of Italian red.

When we were settled again, Eldon Pye resumed his place in the pulpit. "Brennan. That's an Irish name, isn't it?"

Brennan didn't answer. He took a long swallow of whiskey, sighed with contentment, and said: "Cards?"

They shook their heads. Poker was not on the agenda.

Pye tried again: "Brennan, I think you'll find, even in the short time we have today, that Earl and I can help you with your problems."

"I haven't any problems."

"Now, Brennan, we all have problems. God made this world a vale of tears and it's up to us, with the help of Jesus, to assist each other as best we can. If you take the time to make yourself familiar with the word of God —"

"I'm a doctor of theology," he replied. The Americans goggled at him.

"Brennan studied with me in Rome, Eldon," Enrico explained. "In fact, he was at the top of his class and could have secured a position very high up in the Holy See, but he has chosen the life of a humble parish priest, like me. He is, of course, the head of our schola cantorum, and he —"

"Did I hear you right, Father Hank? This man is one of your *priests*?"

Burke let loose with a string of Italian then, and whatever he said made Sferrazza-Melchiorre choke on his wine. He apologized for his inability to translate; suddenly, his English was not up to the task.

"I have to get back to work," Burke announced. He got up, left the room, returned with his travel bag, headed upstairs. We soon heard the shower running.

"Well!" Pye exclaimed, but didn't follow up. We made small talk about the Americans' travel plans for a few minutes, then Pye said: "Uh, Hank, I've been meaning to ask you. Did you ever get to the bottom of that note?"

Enrico made a dismissive gesture with his hands. "All settled. Not a problem."

"You know, there was a report later about who delivered it."

"Non importa."

"Yeah," Slocum said, "somebody seen a big old Chrysler with Florida plates pullin' up to the church. The guy that stuck the note on your church —"

"A man just trying to express himself about one of the priests of the church. There is nothing wrong with that. So, would you like to see more of the city? Brennan is returning to work, and I am sure Monty has things to do."

"What's this about a note?" I asked.

Enrico started to answer but Slocum leaned forward and told the story. "Somebody nailed a nasty letter to the door of Father Hank's church in Mule Run. We know now it was delivered by two large dark-haired adult males. One male exited the vehicle carrying the envelope, a hammer, and a nail. He walked up to the church, crossed himself the way they do, then nailed the note in place and went back to the car. Then they skedaddled outta there." Slocum sat back and nodded.

"What did the note say?"

"It was something written in Eyetalian," Slocum said, "so nobody could read it except Hank. But I heard there were dollar signs in the message. Somebody bad-mouthin' Hank and lookin' for money at the same time. But Hank hightailed it over there, tore off the note, and wouldn't let anybody help hunt down the perps that did it."

"Crazy threats, Monty, against the church. It is known we are not popular there."

"Not popular with the locals, maybe, but surely that doesn't extend all the way to Catholics — Italian Catholics? — in Florida."

"Never mind. It was personal." It was said with an air of finality. He was not going to tell me. But I wondered whether the extortion that had been commenced in Italy had been extended to North America. This would suggest there were more hands in Enrico's pocket than those of a single Albanian prostitute. If so, the message was clear: they could reach him anywhere.

Would Reinhold Schellenberg, whom Enrico had been counting on to advance his career, have been aware of the trouble Enrico was in? Did Enrico feel that Schellenberg had to be silenced before the scandal became more widely known in Vatican circles?

The true picture existed somewhere, but all I could see was fleeting shadows on the wall of a cave.

Brennan reappeared among us, showered, shaved, and immaculate in his clerical suit and Roman collar.

"I apologize for cutting this short, Enrico, but I feel called to carry out the work of God."

"I'll give you a lift, Brennan," I said. "Enrico, why don't you make yourselves at home here till I get back. Find something to snack on, take a walk along the shore." I looked out the window. "Build a snowman."

The Italian looked uncertainly at his companions. Pye and Slocum opened their mouths to speak but were overridden by a higher authority.

"Bow your heads, gentlemen, and I shall give you God's blessing,"

Father Burke announced. The evangelicals gave each other a wary look. Then, perhaps not wanting to take this moment to quibble about God's blessings and who could or could not bestow them, they bowed their heads. But kept their eyes on Burke. Who knew what kind of foreign spell he might cast upon them?

He made the sign of the cross over them and said: *"Benedicat vos omnipotens Deus, Pater, et Filius, et Spiritus Sanctus."*

May Almighty God bless you, the Father, and the Son, and the Holy Spirit.

Only Enrico and I responded: "Amen."

†

The Schola Cantorum Sancta Bernadetta started up again the next day, which was Tuesday, January 7. My week at the office was hellish, with a backlog of work, emergency court appearances, and panicky clients. The most pressing matter was a murder appeal on the docket for the following week. I had a quick visit from Burke, who told me that all our suspects were back. And why not? All but one of them were innocent. There were only two people who did not return; I had never heard of either of them. One more thing: could I sing with the choir at a wedding Friday night? Yes, I could.

"Who's getting married?"

"Dave Forbes. Have you met him?"

The name was familiar. Was he one of the people roped into the Logan sales party? Yes, I remembered having a quick conversation with him when he came to the door. "The guy from Baltimore," I replied. "Old friend of yours, he told me."

"That's right. I've known him for thirty years. We were in the sem together."

"So he said. I assumed he was still a priest; he didn't say otherwise."

"He didn't?"

"No. He talked about knowing you in the seminary, meeting up with you again in Rome at the Gregorian University. Made some little joke about being your 'minder.'"

"He used to settle me down, tried to make sure I didn't get led astray."

"Is that right? So, when did he quit the priesthood?"

"Recently. He's the last fellow I'd have expected to leave. Completely dedicated, I thought. He was about to be made a bishop, according to what I heard."

"Why is he here? Is he still involved in the church, in music?"

"Oh yes. He's the organist and composer at the cathedral in Baltimore. The man is a walking encyclopaedia of sacred music, right back to the Hebrew psalms. In fact, I've sounded him out about my Mass. I can't understand why I'm stuck on the 'Agnus Dei.' It's just not good enough, the way it is. If that's all I can give back, maybe I should cancel the premiere. It's scheduled for a month from today, February 7, so be prepared for some intense rehearsal the week before. Unless I pull the plug on it."

"You're not going to pull the plug! From what I've heard, your music is wonderful. What do you mean, 'if that's all I can give back'?"

He looked at me as if I'd just got off the slow bus. "If that's all I can give back to God in return for the gift He's given me — the gift of music — I'm not worthy of wasting His time."

"God exists outside of time. A thousand ages in His sight are like an evening gone. You should know that, Father."

"True. So He deserves something timeless. Which my 'Agnus Dei' is not. I felt I was getting there just before we went to Rome."

"It's a wonder you have anything left in you at all, after Rome!"

It was just a throwaway remark, but he looked as if I had struck him in the face all over again.

"Brennan, I was joking."

He didn't reply. His thoughts were far away.

I brought him back to our conversation. "So. Dave Forbes. Why would he leave the priesthood at this point in his life?"

"*Cherchez la femme.* Did I not just say he's getting married?"

"You did. Shotgun wedding?"

"Wouldn't that be a sight now! The bride's old man marching a fifty-year-old former priest to the altar at gunpoint."

✝

The bride's old man appeared younger than the groom, I saw when the wedding Mass got underway Friday evening. Dave Forbes looked like what he was: a priest out of uniform. Thin, bespectacled, and ascetic-looking, he appeared to be happy but, at the same time, clearly shell-shocked. His bride, Barbara, had luminous dark eyes, freckles across her nose, and tangles of dark auburn hair, which could not be contained in the elaborate combs that were designed to hold it up; she had the voluptuous figure of a woman entering the third trimester of pregnancy. It was rumoured that she was carrying twins. The ceremony was magnificent, with Brennan celebrating the Latin Mass, and several of his fellow priests serving on the altar. I sang with the choir of men and boys in the loft.

After a brief reception in the auditorium of the choir school, the entire party headed to O'Carroll's Bar on Upper Water Street. There was an Irish band worth hearing, so we didn't talk. We listened and drank, none more so than the two old seminary companions, Burke and Forbes. Make that three priests or ex-priests with an extraordinary thirst upon them. William Logan planted himself on a bar stool and didn't leave it. When the band took a break, members of the wedding felt no compunction about borrowing their instruments to serenade the bridal couple. The mood was light, until Brennan went to the microphone and did a show-stopping rendition of Leonard Cohen's "Hallelujah":

> Now I've heard there was a secret chord
> That David played, and it pleased the Lord
> But you don't really care for music, do you?
> It goes like this, the fourth, the fifth
> The minor fall, the major lift
> The baffled king composing Hallelujah
>
> Your faith was strong but you needed proof
> You saw her bathing on the roof
> Her beauty and the moonlight overthrew you.
> She tied you to a kitchen chair,
> She broke your throne and she cut your hair,
> And from your lips she drew the Hallelujah

You say I took the name in vain
I don't even know the name
But if I did, well really, what's it to you?
There's a blaze of light in every word
It doesn't matter which you heard
The holy or the broken Hallelujah

I did my best, it wasn't much
I couldn't feel so I tried to touch
I've told the truth, I didn't try to fool you
And even though it all went wrong
I'll stand before the Lord of song
With nothing on my tongue but Hallelujah.

I stared at him. I knew how profoundly he related to the song. There wasn't a sound from the wedding party. Until we heard a crash as a bottle of beer hit the floor and shattered; William Logan had knocked over a table as he fled the bar.

Chapter 11

Inquisitors are not bound to give a reason to prelates
concerning things appertaining to their office.
— *Directorium Inquisitorum*, Rome, 1584

Burke came to see me at the office the following Monday, just after I
returned from court. His face was like a thundercloud.

"As if I didn't have enough to put up with . . ." The priest slumped
in my client chair with his head in his hands. He rubbed his temples
with his fingers.

"What is it?" I prompted.

He looked at his watch. "I have to leave for the airport in five minutes to pick up the last fecking person I want to see here."

"Who?"

"The Vatican's man. Rome is sending an 'observer' to monitor the
situation. This is all I need right now."

"Well, the police won't allow this guy to get in their way."

"He'll be in *my* way. That's the point. He won't be there with a
magnifying glass at the crime scene; he'll be loitering around the
schola making a nuisance of himself while I'm trying to do my work."

"Is this the fellow Kitty Curran was talking about?"

"Yes, yes. Gino Savo."

"It would be unusual for the undersecretary of the Congregation for whatever —"

"The Clergy."

"— to turn up in a place like Nova Scotia, I presume."

"It would be unusual for a high-profile theologian and former Vatican insider to be hacked to death while attending an institution established by, and catering to, members of the clergy."

"Point taken."

"And he's Del Vecchio's man. The papal nuncio. That's really why he's here."

"What's he like, from your perspective?"

"High-handed. Imperious." I smiled, and Burke caught it. "What?"

"Nothing. What time's he coming in?"

"Just after six o'clock."

"I'll go with you. It's not every day I meet a Vatican enforcer."

✝

Father Savo was impeccably dressed in a clerical suit, Roman collar, and black cashmere overcoat. A carry-on garment bag was draped over his arm. He was a slight man of medium height, with neatly trimmed black hair that was getting thin and turning grey. A sharp intelligence radiated from dark brown eyes behind a pair of wire-rimmed glasses. He had the look of a scholar or a bureaucrat. The two priests did not smile as they greeted each other in Italian. I was introduced, and we shook hands.

A female staffer came out of the baggage room, stopped, looked at Savo, and said: "Hey, there! Not taking any chances, eh?"

A look of annoyance crossed his face, and he raised his arm with the bag on it. "Right. Thank you."

She looked at me and made a little face, as if to say *there's no pleasing some people*. I gave her a shrug worthy of *Don* Sferrazza-Melchiorre, and she laughed.

Brennan said no more to Savo, but directed a whispered jibe to me: "That one in the baggage department was giving you the eye, Monty. Maybe you'd like to stay here for a while, try your luck."

I whispered back: "And leave you alone to face the Holy Inquisition? I wouldn't think of it."

The inquisitor wasted no time on small talk. As soon as we got into the car, Savo started questioning Burke in English.

"What security measures were in place here?"

"Security? This is Nova Scotia. Canada. It's a choir school I'm running, not a military establishment."

"Am I meant to conclude from your answer that there was no security?"

"Of course there was no security. The question is absurd."

"Not absurd. A man was murdered."

"That was not foreseeable."

"No? Reinhold Schellenberg must have been concerned for his safety. He travelled under a false name."

"I'm aware of that. But if he had specific concerns, they were not relayed to me. Or to anyone else at the schola."

"Have many left the schola? After the killing?"

"Only a couple."

"What measures have been taken to keep track of those who left?"

"The police have their names and addresses."

"Why were these people permitted to leave?"

"They weren't under arrest."

"Do you have a suspect in mind other than this Brother Robin?"

"No."

The atmosphere had not warmed up by the time we arrived at the rectory. I waited in the car while Brennan escorted his visitor inside and handed him over to Mrs. Kelly.

"Things seem a bit frosty between you and Father Savo," I remarked when Brennan returned to the car. "Why is that?" He dismissed my question with a flick of his hand. "You're going to have to cooperate with this guy, Brennan, like it or not. He's here and he's a guest, if an unwelcome one from your point of view. So, what's the story?"

"It goes back to a bit of a diplomatic flap when I was in Rome. Gino got a little miffed at me. Artistic differences. Nothing major." I let him off the hook for the moment; I'd get the story later.

✝

I didn't have long to wait. I was about to leave the office the following day when I got a call from Brennan. "What are you doing for dinner tonight?" I thought I detected a note of urgency in his voice.

"Ordering a pizza from Tomaso. As usual. Why?"

"Come over to the parochial house. O'Flaherty invited Gino Savo to have dinner with us."

"I should hope so!"

"I know, I know, but now O'Flaherty has to make a hospital visit. It'll only be me, Savo, and Mrs. Kelly. I'm just not able for it."

"Now there's an enticing offer. I'd better snap it up before somebody else does."

"You can smooth things over. Fill in the conversational gaps."

"What time?"

"If Mrs. Kelly had her way, the plates would be slapped down on the table at half five. But that's not on. Make it seven."

At seven on the dot I was ushered to a mahogany table in the Victorian dining room of St. Bernadette's rectory. Red-faced and flustered, Mrs. Kelly seemed to brighten when she saw me arrive. That may have had something to do with the brusque tones of the voices we could hear coming from the dining table.

"Here's Mr. Collins, Fathers!"

They both stood to greet me, then we sat and waited as Mrs. Kelly ladled soup into our bowls. Father Savo proceeded to say grace; perhaps he didn't trust his host with the job. After that, Savo sipped his soup, made a face, put down his spoon, and took up a quarrel that had obviously been raging before my arrival.

"All you had to do, Father, was direct the music for a group of American pilgrims. One Mass was all I asked of you."

"American pilgrims with more money than taste."

"Hardly a new phenomenon. They were filled with zeal on their first visit to Rome, and they were disposed to make a much-needed donation to the church of Santi Oliviero e Margherita. They wanted to participate in the Mass by singing the sort of music they understood."

"They wanted to sing something so atrocious — Mrs. Kelly!"

"Yes, Father!"

"Would you be kind enough to go into the library, open up that box of old discarded hymn books, and bring me one of them?"

Brennan and I ate our soup until the housekeeper appeared with a blue hymn book.

"This has never even been opened, Father. It's brand new! It must have been placed in the box by mistake, so I'll —"

Burke's black eyes made it clear that it was not he, but Mrs. Kelly and the book itself, that were mistaken. "Here's what they wanted to sing, Gino:

> Gift is you and gift is me, that is where it is today.
> Love and gift and peace within us, never let the doubts hold sway.
> Feel the presence in our selfhood, giving through the full new day.
> Fellowshipping with each other, in the brand new sharing way.
> Oooooooo, fellowship in a brand new way!"

He crossed his arms over his chest, sat back, and raised his left eyebrow at me. "What would you do?"

"Those have to be the worst lyrics I have ever heard, in any type of music!" I exclaimed. "What's the song supposed to mean?"

"Who the fuck knows?"

I heard a gasp behind me and turned. Mrs. Kelly was gaping at Burke as if he had just unzipped his pants and peed on the pope's leg.

"You refused to conduct the music for a group of Catholics —" Savo began.

"I refused, yes. I believe I told them that, as long as I was living and breathing, and had not been beaten by them into a pulp, or shot in the heart by whichever one of them might be packing a gun, that so-called hymn would not be sung in the church of Santi Oliviero e Margherita, or any other holy place dedicated to the Supreme Being, the Lord of Hosts. And that if they cared to look at a book I was about to pass around, the *Kyriale*, we could substitute a simple, beautiful hymn of praise to God in words He understands and appreciates. Or at least that's the way I remember it."

"Your memory accords with mine. And their bishop was enraged."

"He was, yes. I have to say the bishop sounded more like a stevedore than a shepherd of God's earthly flock."

"He is not the only priest we know who uses vulgar language, Father."

Burke continued as if he hadn't heard. "And a bigot as well, it pains me to say. According to him I was a conceited, insolent son of a bitch and my family should have stayed in the slums of Dublin where we belonged and given our place on the boat to someone who would appreciate America in a way I obviously didn't. And if I thought I was going to get one greenback American buck to use for that gaudy Italian church so a bunch of Euro snobs could sit and listen to the warbling of a band of boy sopranos with their nuts cut off, then I had fatally misjudged Bishop Wayne Carter."

"The bishop was understandably distressed. Who are you, Father, to snipe at the innocent failings of these people? They are not to blame if they are unsophisticated in the ways of the world. Such people do not have our advantages."

"European advantages, he means," Brennan explained in my direction.

"But that is the way they are," Savo declared. "I do not care if they sit there with banjos on their knees and keep time by that peculiar and vulgar American habit of chewing gum, Father Burke. When they come to Rome, they are to be treated as treasured members of the worldwide church, and accorded some latitude. They do not know any better."

"But that's all behind you now, gentlemen," I said. I engaged them in some inconsequential chatter, and we got through the meal. Savo left most of his untouched. Not up to Roman standards. Well, he wasn't far wrong there.

"Have you come up with any useful information on the murder, Father Savo? Anything that would cast doubt on Robin Gadkin-Falkes as the chief suspect?"

"No. I have not made any progress. Yet."

"How do you expect to make progress, Gino?" Brennan demanded. "You don't have a team of investigators here. But the police department does."

"Monsignor O'Flaherty was kind enough to say he will arrange a meeting for me with the police."

"They don't know anything themselves, beyond whatever they've uncovered about Robin."

"We can't assume that, Brennan," I cautioned. "They may have someone else in mind —"

"Oh?" Savo interrupted. "Do you think so?"

"I have no idea. I'm just saying we won't necessarily know what they're thinking unless and until they move forward with Robin, or clear him and arrest somebody else."

"Surely someone in the police headquarters can be approached —"

"They can't be bullied, even by the Vatican, if that's what you have in mind."

"No, that is not what I have in mind, Brennan!" Savo's voice had risen, and his face was flushed. "Please give me some credit! You have no reason to question my motives in this matter!"

"I had no reason to think one of our priests was going to be found at solemn vespers with his white vestments drenched in blood, a gaping wound in his neck, his head damn near off and —"

"That is enough!" Savo gripped the table with both hands, rose, and shouted at Brennan: "Do not sit there and recite to me in sensationalistic detail the horrible wounds the man endured! Have you no respect?"

"Respect for whom, Gino, you or Father Schellenberg?" Brennan asked coolly.

"For Father Schellenberg! I do not have to hear about his blood!" The Vatican's man trembled with anger. "I will not listen to any more of this!"

"Fine. Don't listen. But don't give out to us here as if the matter is of no concern, and say we're not doing anything to track down the killer. You didn't see it. The rest of us did. And we'll never get over the sight."

"None of us will get over it! It was not my choice to come here. But I have a task to complete. I want the matter solved so I can go back to Rome and give my report, a report which I hope will not provide the Holy See with any more consternation than it is already suffering over this terrible affair." He held Burke in his angry gaze, and Burke glared back at him across the table.

"Coffee, Fathers? Tea?"

We turned as one and glared at the interloper. Mrs. Kelly's hands wrung her apron into a ball as she stood there, knowing, I suspected, that her interruption was ill-timed, but knowing as well that she could no more forgo her routine than she could divine the identity of the killer of Reinhold Schellenberg.

I was in the Court of Appeal the next morning, making a pointless argument on behalf of a man who had been convicted of the murder of his infant son. The baby had been brutalized and left for dead; the accused man had tried to pin the killing on an elderly neighbour. I didn't have a hope on appeal, and I didn't really want one, but I did my best just as I did for all my clients. He had been represented by another lawyer at trial, so I made the usual argument about incompetent counsel. That didn't sit well with me, either, because the lawyer who handled the trial did an exemplary job. The whole sordid affair was in the papers again, and a local radio call-in show had started a campaign to press for the return of the death penalty. That wasn't going to happen. The death penalty had been removed from the *Criminal Code* in 1976; the last execution in this country had taken place in 1962.

At the end of the morning I lost the appeal, the client stayed in Dorchester Penitentiary, and I returned to my office on Barrington Street. I turned to other, less traumatic, cases and didn't look up from my desk till nearly four o'clock.

I heard voices in the street below and looked out my window. People with placards were gathering on the sidewalk, getting ready for a demonstration. Must have been planning to march to the federal Justice Department, or possibly disrupt rush-hour traffic heading home on Barrington. I had had enough for the day, so I left the office and went down to the street to have a look. It had snowed and then rained; the sidewalk was slushy and people were bundled up. There were two factions, those in favour and those against state killing. One of the women looked familiar, but I wasn't sure because she was bent over her placard, applying the finishing touches to her message. Yes, it was Jan Ford. I remembered Moody Walker's report of her arrest during a protest in Florida.

"Afternoon, Jan!"

She looked up. "Hello, Montague. I don't suppose I dare hope you're on the right side of this issue."

"I'm with you on this one, Jan. State murder has no place in a civilized country. It's wrong, it doesn't deter crime — just look at your own country — and too many innocent people have been executed. So, if I had the time I'd march along with you and try to out-shout the lynch mob. But my son has a basketball game, so —"

She picked up her placard and shoved it towards me. "Killers have no right to live!"

"You? In favour of state executions?" My voice cracked the way it had when I was thirteen.

"You really must move beyond stereotypes, Montague. I am a progressive woman. How can I sit back and watch women and children and innocent men being murdered every day, and let their killers spend a few years in jail and get out and do it again? How you can defend these people, I just don't know!"

"Don't you object to the death penalty on religious grounds, Jan? The deliberate taking of a life —"

"Don't get me started on religion and capital punishment, Montague. Now, as you can see, I have a protest to attend. So why don't you go back to making the streets safe for all the rapists and murderers and drug pushers you represent? Goodbye!"

Well, you just never knew.

✝

"Monty, I have to get Gino Savo out of my hair," Burke said on the phone that night. I had caught the call on the last ring as I came in from Tom's game. "I find myself wanting to proclaim the guilt of Robin Gadkin-Falkes to Savo's satisfaction so he'll fly back to Rome, present his report, and we'll be rid of him. But he won't budge. We have to solve this and have done with it, so I can get the schola back on track and get Rome out of my life."

"Let me have a talk with him, see if I can find out what he's thinking."

I found Gino Savo the next morning, having a cup of coffee in the dining room of the rectory. He greeted me with courtesy and invited me to have a seat. There was no sign of the anger he had exhibited at dinner. Mrs. Kelly hovered over us, offering me tea and coffee. I declined, and she appeared ready to remonstrate when she caught sight of Fred Mills passing by in the corridor.

"Oh, Father Mills! Would you like coffee and a biscuit? Anything for breakfast?"

"Thanks, Mrs. Kelly. Maybe I'll . . ." Fred peered into the dining room and saw me with Gino Savo. ". . . take up your offer another time. I think I'd better get over to the school. I left a couple of things undone." He said hello to us and kept moving.

"Do you really think you'll be able to solve this case to Rome's satisfaction, Father Savo? The police believe they have the right man. I've been doing some questioning outside official channels, and I'm not getting anywhere."

"I am here to monitor the investigation, not to conduct it myself. I am here to see that our interests are not compromised."

"You're here at the direction of the papal nuncio to this country."

"Correct."

"Does he have any theories about the killing?"

"He has a theory that no one connected with the Vatican has done this."

"You're not talking about priests in general."

"It may be a rogue priest. We all pray that it is not. We — I especially, in my role in the Congregation for the Clergy — are concerned with all priests. But Arturo Del Vecchio, the nuncio, concerns himself with those who have had, or may again have, a position in the Vatican itself."

"As far as I know that could only be Father Sferrazza-Melchiorre."

"There is also the matter of Father Schellenberg himself. Was there something sensitive in his background that might embarrass the church?"

"From what I understand, Father Schellenberg could have drawn fire from any number of directions."

"He is blamed by many for the loss of the old Mass and our musical heritage, and for all the other elements of disintegration that people attribute to the Second Vatican Council. Others, as you know, attack him for retrenching in more recent years. Liberals feel betrayed by one of their own, as they considered him to be."

"Did you know Schellenberg?"

"Yes, I knew him and worked with him in various capacities over the years."

"Were you an admirer?"

"Very much so. Of course."

"So you have a personal, as well as an official, incentive to see his killer identified and punished."

The priest's eyes began to fill with tears, and he blinked to clear them.

I returned to the subject of the silk-apparelled cleric who seemed to be living in exile. "I get the impression Father Sferrazza-Melchiorre may be doing a bit of purgatory before he returns to the gates of Saint Peter." Savo shrugged, and I continued. "Is the nuncio worried that Father Sferrazza-Melchiorre might be guilty?"

"He does not think that! Of course not. The Del Vecchio and the Sferrazza-Melchiorre families have known each other since the time of the Borgi — since Renaissance times. He knows Enrico is not a murderer. His desire is to make sure there is no misunderstanding that could lead to suspicions of Enrico if no other explanation is found. Or suspicions of anyone else who may be found to have a connection with Rome. That is all."

As simple as that.

"And you yourself are close to the nuncio?"

"He has always been good to me."

I suspected that it was a great boost to someone's career in the Vatican hierarchy if a powerful man was good to you. Savo would not want to let the pope's ambassador down.

"Do you share the nuncio's faith in Enrico?"

"Yes, yes, of course I do. My presence here goes beyond Enrico. I want to know what happened. I intend to find out. Then I shall present my findings and return to Rome. I shall also arrange to have Father Schellenberg's remains released and flown back to his home for burial."

"Well, let me know if you discover anything Brennan or Michael should know. And I'll do the same for you."

"I will. Thank you." Neither of us believed the other, but appearances were maintained, and I took my leave.

Chapter 12

He has besieged and enveloped me
with bitterness and tribulation.
— Lamentations 3:5

Two weeks into the new year, the schola participants organized a concert, presenting their own musical arrangements and, in a couple of
cases, their compositions. The music would be performed on Friday
night by the St. Bernadette's Choir of Men and Boys, of which I was
a member. This time, though, I would be in the audience, as I had not
been able to attend the daytime rehearsals.

Father Burke, dressed in his soutane, arrived and sat beside me. He
looked tense.

"What's the matter?" I asked.

"Who knows what we'll be hearing out of them tonight?" he
answered. "And, of course, I've got Savo in my house. There is a
glimmer of light in the darkness, however."

"Oh?"

"Kitty Curran flew in today. I'm expecting her here any minute."

"Wonderful! Where is she staying?"

"The parish house."

She arrived just as the master of ceremonies, Enrico Sferrazza-
Melchiorre, rose to welcome the audience. I slid over and made room

for Kitty, so that she was sitting between me and Burke.

The nun greeted me with a hug and kiss, then demanded in a whisper: "All right, lads. Tell me who's who. Which one's Logan?" We discreetly pointed to our suspects, giving her their names and a bit of background. She waved to Enrico Sferrazza-Melchiorre and, after a jolt of surprise, he smiled and made a little bow in her direction. Then we settled in to wait for the downbeat.

"He's not afraid to fly, but would you look at the white knuckles on yer man for this occasion?" Kitty said, pointing to Burke's hands, which were gripping his knees.

As it turned out, he had little to fear and much to be proud of. The choristers, looking deceptively angelic in their pre-Vatican II surplices, acquitted themselves well. Most of those who conducted the music were competent, and some exceptional. Father Sferrazza-Melchiorre, Father Ichiro Takahashi of Japan, and Soeur Thérèse Savoie, a Moncton, New Brunswick, nun, were in the latter category. The music had been chosen to represent the entire liturgical year, so we heard Victoria's beautiful "O Magnum Mysterium," honouring the pregnancy of the Virgin Mary and the birth of the Saviour; the very moving "O Vos Omnes" by Pablo Casals, in which Jesus asks passersby if their suffering is comparable to his; Victoria again on a similar theme, with the "Reproaches from the Cross" in Greek and Latin; and the "Exultet" and the "Alleluias" traditionally chanted at the Easter Vigil. The biggest surprise of the evening came under the baton of Billy Logan. The former priest, his abrasive manner held in check, managed to portray the exquisite longing of Palestrina's "Sicut Cervus":

Sicut cervus desiderat ad fontes aquarum ita desiderat anima mea ad te Deus.

Like as the hart desireth the waterbrooks, so longeth my soul for thee, O God.

The only low point was Jan Ford and her committee, who brought out a ukulele and tambourine and sang while a man and a woman pantomimed the actions they imagined went along with the words:

227

Sharing, caring, daring yet to be
At the Jesus table, friend to you and me.
Share Him, care f'r Him, we, Christ's bo-od-y,
Yea, His body and His light, His folk are we!

I sneaked a look at Burke and saw all too clearly how music could lead to murder. His Irish mouth was clamped down in a thin white line; his eyes were like the sun's rays boring through a magnifying glass at an insect about to be incinerated. Christ's folk were oblivious up at the altar. I thought he was set to shout them down. I leaned across Kitty and gave him a warning look.

But all in all, it was a success. Brennan rose at the end and gave a gracious tribute to the performers. Every one of them.

Maura had offered to host a reception following the performance. She had given me instructions as to what to bring, and I had dropped the items off earlier. Now I waited while Brennan made a quick trip across to the rectory to change into pants and a sweater. Then we all walked to Morris Street and a few blocks west to Dresden Row for the post-performance party.

"Where's Kitty?" I asked on the way.

"Monsignor O'Flaherty has appointed himself her escort for the evening. I think he's in love. He's been hanging on her every word since she arrived. A nun from Dublin is to Mike what a lap dancer from Brazil would be to you and, em, well, *you*, Collins. So what did you think of the concert?"

"Some of that was music to die for, Brennan. And Reinhold Schellenberg died on the feast of Saint Cecilia, patron saint of church musicians."

"That hasn't slipped my mind, Montague."

"Who would you single out as the most likely person to murder for music?"

"The most likely person for *me* to murder, you mean?"

"Excuse the lack of lawyerly precision. I meant the person most likely to commit murder."

"I knew that, Monty. I was taking the piss out of ya. Well, to answer your question, it wouldn't be Jan Ford."

"Don't be too sure. If Schellenberg's right turn has any lasting influence, and the old music enjoys a revival, her own efforts will be shunted to the sidelines."

"Nobody could harbour such strong feelings over that drivel," he said dismissively.

"So she's not worthy of being the murderer!"

"Hmmph."

"All right, who?"

"We can dismiss Colonel Bleier if music was the motive."

"What did we hear about him? He married into a very musical family. Jadwiga Silkowski's home was filled with music."

"Too much of a stretch. If he killed Father Schellenberg, it was for another reason. Something to do with their past in Germany."

"Logan?"

"I wouldn't know where to begin, to sort out what motivates Logan. Obviously he's never come to terms with his departure from the priesthood. Beyond that, who knows?"

"Enrico."

"He loves the music; he loves all the great art of the church. But I suspect if we find out he did away with Schellenberg, he did it for motives much more Byzantine than music."

"That leaves you, I guess, Brennan."

"Very amusing, Monty."

"So. Where were you on the afternoon of November 22?"

He stopped and looked at me. "You're not serious, I hope."

"No. Though maybe you have an acolyte — a groupie — somewhere who feels he or she is striking a blow for the music that constitutes a great part of your life's work."

"That must be it. Let me know when you've tied up the loose ends."

We arrived at the house on Dresden Row, and Maura met us at the door. It was the first time she had seen Burke since the trip to Italy.

"Brennan! Poor Collins was wrung out after his travels. Did you exhaust yourself as well? Quite the trip, was it?" No reply. "What happened to him?" she asked me. "Struck dumb at the throne of Saint Peter? Silenced by the Holy Inquisition?"

"No, no, amn't I still a little weary from the jet lag?" he said lamely. She gave him a penetrating look, and he made his way around her. "Step aside, MacNeil. I've a hooley to attend."

"Well, I intend to hear all the details of the journey, about which Collins has said very little. But which, I'm sure, produced the solution to the mystery we've all been living with here. Otherwise, you wouldn't have gone. Let me know if an arrest is imminent and whether it's someone under my roof right now." I knew from our previous conversations, of course, that it was her belief that the police had got it right — "this time," she had said to me, in order to show she was not a lackey of the police and was ready to second-guess them on the next occasion — and that Burke and I had affected to think otherwise in order to justify a road trip to Italy.

"We're still at the stage of helping the police with their inquiries."

"I see. Well, pour yourselves a whiskey or a glass of wine, and grab something to eat. Unless you're both sated for all time after your bacchanalian revels abroad."

"Where are the kids?"

"Normie's staying at Kim's, and Tom is with Lexie."

"Okay. Remind me later. I promised Normie I'd find her a little job to do in connection with the case. I had Tom do the newspaper research, so she wanted in on it too. I have something she can do —"

"Funny you should say that. She believes she knows where the answer lies, but it requires a trip to — Disney World!"

"All right, all right. You've made your point." I would take the direct approach, and ask Normie myself.

The house was soon full, and the gathering achieved what was almost a party atmosphere, but the strain of the murder thrummed beneath the surface, for some of us at least, like a sombre bass line. Gino Savo arrived with Mike O'Flaherty and Kitty Curran, Gino appearing to be in a less festive mood than his two companions.

"Now, Kitty, where would you like to sit?" Mike asked solicitously. "Would you have a little something to drink?"

"I'd have a whiskey if such a thing were available," Kitty replied.

"Oh, surely there's a drop of whiskey. I'll go and see. Now you just make yourself comfortable there." He was soon back with a glass of whiskey and a couple of chocolate treats in a tiny silver dish.

I left her in his tender care for a few more minutes, then brought Maura over and introduced her, noting Kitty's role on the Council for Justice and Peace. Keenly interested in social justice herself, Professor

MacNeil was soon in rapt conversation with the globe-trotting nun, while Mike O'Flaherty looked on adoringly. The smell of something burning in the kitchen reinforced the fact that MacNeil had found something much more interesting than tending to the stove. I went out, switched off the burner, and turned on the fan to suck up the smoke. I didn't bother to look at whatever remained in the pot, just opened the back door and pitched it into the snow. Maura didn't ask any questions when I returned to the living room.

The two women continued their intense conversation until the baby, Dominic, cried out from his room, and Maura excused herself.

I sat down with Kitty. "Well, you've got nearly half the cast in front of you tonight, Sister."

"In front of me and Gino Savo." I had forgotten that the Vatican's man was in the crowd; now I saw him standing against the far wall, looking tense and ill at ease. "He'll be more intent on observing them than I will. Nobody put me in charge!" She sipped her drink and popped a chocolate into her mouth.

"Maybe it would be best for everyone if Savo caught the perpetrator," I suggested. "Justice would be swift under his hand, I suspect!"

"Or mercy perhaps. He caught one of his staff members embezzling money. When discovered, the man claimed he needed it for his disabled son. Further investigation, however, revealed that the little boy had died years before, and the father had been using him as an excuse. But Gino Savo forgave him and kept him on. That's the priest in Gino. He tried to hush it up, but word got out."

"Commendable, but it gives rise to the suspicion that Gino may be hoping to cover up another crime, the one committed here."

"Kind of hard to do, unless he manages to fool the police along with everyone else."

She looked up. "Ah, the baby! Isn't he a dote!" Maura had returned to the living room with the bawling infant and busied herself with him in the corner. "Poor little thing; he can't understand why we don't know what he's miserable about!"

"Do you come from a big family yourself, Kitty?" Michael O'Flaherty asked.

"Seven brothers and sisters, Michael, and there's a tale about every single one of them."

"Don't leave out a word!" he urged her.

I left them to it, poured myself a ginger ale, and joined Fred Mills and Enrico Sferrazza-Melchiorre. "Brennan seems a little subdued this evening," Fred remarked.

"Well, it's not as if bubbly hyperactivity is his usual demeanour," I replied.

"No, there's something troubling him."

"He has been quiet since his travels," Enrico said. "Perhaps he fell in love in Italy! Tell us, Monty. Did he? Did you?"

I shrugged and started to issue a denial, but I was interrupted by Father Savo, who had joined us. He stated flatly: "Brennan is not a boy. It would take more than a glance at a pretty face, or even a night in the arms of a woman, to throw him off course, so . . ." His voice trailed off. I followed his gaze across the room, where Brennan was standing with a drink in his hand, listening to something Maura was saying. I stared at her. Lamplight bathed her face in a warm glow; despite a smear of something on her cheek, she looked beautiful. The baby was lying across her legs. No longer crying, he was all smiles, his big dark eyes on Brennan, his little legs kicking and hands reaching out to the tall man in front of him. The only move Brennan made was to lift his drink to his lips and down it. I did the same.

The scene receded from my mind with the arrival of Billy Logan and Babs. The former priest walked in just as Father Sferrazza-Melchiorre positioned himself before the fireplace and burst into song. He opened with an Italian folk number I thought I recognized from the Trattoria Benelli, then segued into "E lucevan le stelle," in which a man awaiting his own execution declares that he has never loved life so much as now. Enrico had a magnificent voice, and the party gathered around him, abandoning small talk and giving itself over to the music. All except Father Savo, who regarded Enrico stonily from the other end of the room.

"Brennan, join me!" Enrico urged. Burke waved him off. But the Italian was not to be denied, and Burke was half-corked by this time, so soon the two of them were singing opera in antiphonal mode, one doing one stanza and the other taking over. The showstopper, "Caruso," was a number written in honour of another operatic Italian who spent time in America. The song captured the embraces between a woman and a man who sees the end of his life approaching. Passions run high in the aria, and our performers rose to the occasion.

The audience applauded wildly. My wife fanned her face with her hand, and demanded of the duo: "That chorus means what, exactly? Let me guess: 'We can sing better than other men 'cause our testicles are bigger.'" This earned a hoot of laughter from Sister Curran.

Brennan seemed to have something caught in his throat.

A handsome and flushed Fred Mills tore his eyes away from Brennan, made a beeline for the bar, cracked open a beer, and chugged it.

But it was William Logan who notched things up to a higher operatic pitch. "Why don't you guys just fuck off and get over yourselves?"

The casually dressed Burke and the elaborately caped Italian turned towards Logan in astonishment. Before either of them could come up with a rejoinder, Logan launched himself out of the house. His wife gave everyone a mortified glance and stumbled after him.

I was shocked into immobility for a few seconds, then I decided to follow Logan and find out what his problem really was. I saw them down the street, standing by their station wagon. Babs was fumbling with the key, and Logan started in on her. "How long have we had this freaking car, Babs? Five months, and you still can't figure out the key turns counter-clockwise on the driver's side and clockwise on the passenger side!"

"Well, that's because it's never me driving it. It's always you."

"And it's going to be me now. I told you I'm fine to drive, so give me that key!"

"No, William, you're not driving. And it wasn't very nice what you said to Brennan and that other guy. Imagine what they think of you."

"What they think of *me*? I don't give a shit what they think. And I especially don't give a shit about that Euro-trash priest in the million-dollar cassock! It's Burke who sticks in my craw. That conceited prick. He's got it all and he rubs everybody's nose in it!"

"What are you talking about, Billy? For heaven's sake."

"He's got that voice, he gets people from all over the world to his choir school, he composes a Mass, he says he's going to write an oratorio, he speaks how many languages . . . Before he entered the sem he was getting more sex than Mick Jagger. Now he doesn't need it, doesn't need a woman, doesn't need a family. Doesn't need the United States of America! He's still a goddamn Irishman! His father was run out of Ireland because he pissed off his fellow terrorists in the IRA, he shoved his family onto a boat to New York when Brennan was ten years old, and the kid refused to give up his Irish citizenship, or he got it back, or he's a dual citizen, or something. So he lived in the U.S. but never became Americanized. He sneers at our government and our culture and the first chance he gets, he's off to Rome and all these other parts of the world. He's never even been to Florida! He's a fucking European! Now he's up here in this little Scottish outpost, loving every minute of it. Yeah, he's got it all. And to top it off, he still gets to celebrate Mass every day. In public. Unlike some of us. Now, give me that key!"

"Billy! You're not saying you wish you were still a priest! You wouldn't have met *me* if you'd stayed with that! You wouldn't have your kids."

"I don't have my kids, Babs. All I have is alimony payments and visits once a month. Remember?"

"But what about me?"

"It's not you, Babs. Obviously. It's just that nobody tried to talk me into staying. In the priesthood. Know what I mean? All these priests and nuns were leaving, and it was just so goddamn easy to get out. And it didn't matter because we were all Christ's holy priesthood anyway, Holy Orders or not. This all happened when the church went to hell in a handcart after Vatican II. Nobody was leaving when the church was strict, when being a Catholic meant something. Being a priest meant something. Back then, you told your bishop you were having doubts, he'd just tell you to get down on your knees and pray harder, then get your ass back on the job. And you did."

"Well . . . Brennan obviously still thinks it means something."

"He and God are singing in each other's ear. I don't want to hear another word about him. Get in — I'm driving!"

I melted into the shadows and returned to the party.

Chapter 13

Now therefore be ye not scoffers, lest your bonds be made strong,
For a decree of destruction have I heard from the Lord.
— Isaiah 28:22

Logan's harangue played over and over in my mind until I fell asleep, but it was his car that was in my thoughts when I awoke on Saturday morning. One of the few bits of information we had gleaned from a witness was that, right around the time of the murder, there was a car near Stella Maris Church with its wipers going on a sunny afternoon. Which suggested the driver was not used to the controls. Surely I was not alone in having that experience in a vehicle I was not accustomed to. A new car or a rental. Go for the light switch and you get the wipers. Or vice versa. Perhaps somebody had been in the parking lot near the murder scene in a car that was unfamiliar to him or her. I now knew William and Babs Logan had bought a car a few months ago, and she was unfamiliar with its locks because, she said, she never got to drive it. Lou Petrucci had come to town in his own car. Whether it was new or old, he would have had lots of time to get used to it on the drive from New Jersey. Kurt Bleier had a rental car. Enrico Sferrazza-Melchiorre had taken a car out for a test drive. It should be easy enough to determine whether the witness, the woman with the little dog, had noticed American plates, or a snazzy British auto, or maybe a car with a rental sticker in the parking lot that day.

I made a quick trip to my office and pulled out the notes of my interview with Clara MacIntyre. All I had was that she nearly got hit by a car with its wipers going in the bright sunshine. The car was nice and clean and did not appear to need its windshield wiped. Nothing about the kind of car or the driver. I hadn't pressed it, I remembered, because I hadn't been interested in the car. The near-collision was incidental to what I had questioned her about: voices she might have heard coming from the church. It was time to pay another call on Mrs. MacIntyre. I gathered up my photos of our suspects and called her number. "Come right over," she said.

But she put a damper on things right away when I told her what I was after.

"I don't know one car from another, Mr. Collins," she said, stroking Dewey's tawny head as he slept beside her on the chesterfield. "Last car I had was a Plymouth Valiant."

"They haven't made those in a while."

"No."

"Do you know what an Aston Martin looks like?"

"That's an English car. My husband didn't hold with English cars."

"One more thing and I'll leave you in peace, Mrs. MacIntyre."

"Oh, I don't mind at all, Mr. Collins. Dewey and I enjoy company."

"Can you remember anything about the driver?"

"I couldn't see a face at all. Not that I really looked. I just wanted to avoid getting hit. But the sun was blinding on the windshield. The driver could have been King Kong for all I know."

"That's fine. I understand. Here are the photos anyway, in case you saw one of these people lurking around the church."

She peered at the pictures, reached for a pair of reading glasses, and tried again. "No, no. Oh, I did see this fellow, I think."

My heart missed a beat. "Which one?"

She pointed to the photograph. Fred Mills. "It was either him or someone who looked a heck of a lot like him. But he wasn't as bright-eyed and bushy-tailed that day as he looks in this picture."

"You saw this man when you were walking Dewey on Friday, November 22?"

"I think so. No. No, it was the day before."

"He was at Stella Maris Church the day before the — on the Thursday?"

"No, not at the church."

I took a deep breath and willed myself to stay patient and calm. "Just tell me in your own words, Mrs. MacIntyre."

"Dewey and I had a walk at Seaview Park, which as you know is right there on the water, some distance east of Stella Maris, but you can see the church plain as day from the park. We walked around the park on Thursday until that man with the unruly Rottweilers showed up. The same rough owner and his dogs were there again on Friday, which is why Dewey and I decided to go to Stella Maris instead that day. But it was on the Thursday that we saw the young man in the picture. He was sitting on a bench looking at the church. Then he just sat there staring down at his feet. He was pale and shaky, looked as if he were about to be sick. In a way I wanted to ask if he needed help. But you never know — he could have been on drugs or something. Dewey ran up to him and sniffed his legs. He reached down and patted Dewey's ears but it was obvious his heart wasn't in it. He was unwell or upset, or had other things on his mind. Dewey left him alone. Then the fellow got up from the bench and headed for the parking lot. I never gave him another thought until now."

✝

Monday morning it was minus twelve outside, with a wind chill of minus thirty. Every muscle in my body contracted in protest when I sat in my frozen car. The heater finally afforded some relief just before I got to the choir school. I went inside and found Fred Mills, but he wasn't alone. He and Kurt Bleier were deep in conversation outside one of the classrooms.

"Achtung, Kolonel!" I turned just in time to see William Logan click his heels together and stand at attention facing Bleier. "Herr general wants to see you. *Schnell!* He says zere iss a large wall crumbling behind the compound and comrades are escaping to the West! Zere iss no discipline in the Fatherland anymore!"

Bleier looked up at Logan and replied in a deadpan voice: "Yes, many are scrambling to the West today. In America they are giving away free assault rifles to the first million people over the age of ten who eat the most wieners and answer a skill-testing question. The question is: 'Who is the guy who is not on TV?'"

"You've got some nerve laughing at American society!"

"It was you who started the conversation, on a decidedly offensive note, Mr. Logan. Until you burst upon us, I was having a courteous conversation with a very dedicated American priest, Father Mills here. But you gave all that up, didn't you? Couldn't bear the *discipline* of such a life, perhaps."

"How can you sit here and listen to this guy, Freddy?"

"Oh, give it a rest, Bill!"

"Father Mills is very well-informed about world history, unlike many of your fellow citizens, Mr. Logan. I think I have him persuaded to visit my country when I return."

"Maybe that should be *if* you return to your country. You could end up spending the rest of your life in jail here. Don't sit there and lap up all his propaganda, Freddy. German history of some kind probably accounts for the murder of Reinhold Schellenberg. You're probably thinking how spiffy Colonel Bleier would look in a tight-fitting leather trench coat with shiny boots and a great big stick but —"

"Bill? Go fuck yourself."

"There's the proof of what a bad influence this guy is, or maybe it's the influence of your other hero, Burke. When you start using the F-word, Fred, civilization as we know it is over."

Bleier gave him a level look. "If you knew the first thing about civilization, or civility, Mr. Logan, this regrettable conversation would not be taking place. And your efforts to portray me as the killer, while it is you who are incapable of controlling your resentments and your emotions —"

"Screw you, Bleier. You too, Freddy!" He stalked away.

"Hi there, Monty," Fred said to me. "Just another outburst of post-murder tension among the suspects. Do you think if we all accuse each other that means we're all innocent?"

"All are innocent except one, Fred. And you're right. It would serve that person very well to occupy the high ground and level accusations at one or more of the others."

"Well, I hope nobody seriously suspects me." He turned back to Bleier. "Monty and I both have kind of a boyish, not-guilty look, wouldn't you say, Kurt?" He put his hands together as if to pray. "I'll bet he gets away with all kinds of mischief on account of it."

"I don't get away with much. My ex-wife catches me out every time."

"Yeah, with me it's the church hierarchy!"

"But that doesn't get you really, really angry, does it, Fred?"

"No!"

"I shall let you get on with your interrogation, Mr. Collins," Bleier said. "It is obvious that you have not been taken in by this man's appearance of innocence. I look forward to speaking with you again, Fred. *Auf Wiedersehen.*" He left us, and I waited until I had Fred's full attention.

"Fred, were you up in the area of Stella Maris Church the day before the murder?"

He stared at me with unblinking grey eyes. "Why on earth would you think that? I was never in that church until we processed in for vespers, and found Father Schellenberg's body!"

"I didn't say you were in the church. Were you in Seaview Park, at the top of the Halifax peninsula, on Thursday, November 21?"

"No, I was not! What would I be doing there?"

"I have no idea, Fred. But we have a witness who said she saw you looking shaky and —"

"Your witness is wrong, and so are your accusations! I'm not going to listen to any more of this. Goodbye!"

Somebody else was having a bad day, I saw when I returned to the parking lot. Michael O'Flaherty was sitting at the wheel of his car, trying in vain to get it started. Even through the driver's side window I could see his agitation. Anguish, even. Then I saw why. Sister Kitty Curran was in the passenger seat. Right. This was Monday the twentieth, the day she was flying back to Rome. And Mike couldn't get his car going in the cold. I walked over and knocked on his window. He scowled in my direction and rolled down his window.

"Mike, you're going to flood the engine."

"Sure, I can get a cab to the airport, Michael," Kitty said. "Save yourself the trouble here. Cars weren't meant to operate in these temperatures, I'm thinking."

"This car's been working for a decade, Kitty. I'll get it going."

The scene took me back to my teen years. A date with a girl I liked and wanted to impress, and everything going wrong. Often with a vehicle. That's what Mike was going through now, with Kitty.

"Take my car, Mike. It's all warmed up. Here are the keys."

"Oh, now, Monty. There's no need of that."

But he let himself be persuaded, and his customary good cheer was restored. He transferred Kitty's bags to my trunk, got her settled in the passenger seat, even tucked my old plaid car robe around her. I said my goodbyes and promised to see her again in Rome if Mike wasn't over there monopolizing her time. He blushed, but said: "The three of us will go. You, me, and Brennan."

"All *right!*" I exclaimed.

Something in my tone called forth a clarification from Monsignor O'Flaherty. "*My* trip won't be like the trip you boys just had! I'm sure Kitty wouldn't want to know what you might have been up to!"

Kitty knew damn well what we'd been up to but wasn't about to say so, to me or to Mike.

They started out of the parking lot, then Mike stopped and rolled down the window again. "Monty! Where are my manners? Hop in, and let me drive you to your office!"

"No, a brisk walk will do me good. You kids get going. Take her straight to the airport now, Michael!"

Mike grinned, and Kitty gave me a wink as they pulled away.

†

We were having our regular Tuesday night choir practice, and this was probably our seventh take on the Saint-Saëns "Ave Verum Corpus."

"No, gentlemen. Somebody is still saying 'Mur-ee-ah' for Maria. The Virgin Mary was not a twin sister to Murray. It is 'Mah,' and the *R* is not like the *R* in Murray. You have to frap the *R*, make it almost — almost but not exactly — like a *D*. The way we do with 'Kyrie.' So. Maria."

"But you still want us to roll the *R* in *perforatum*, right, Father?"

"That's right, Rrrichard. Rrroll the second *R*. *R* is probably the worst sound in English singing. I could say more on this subject but

I'm sure we'd all rather get it right this time and go home. Once more. And come down to pianissimo when you get to *'Esto nobis praegustatum in mortis examine.'* It means: 'Be for us a foretaste in the trials of death.' Saint-Saëns has written it low and quiet, and it's all the more moving when it's done that way. So let's hear you one more time."

We sang it again, and he pronounced himself satisfied. Books were slapped shut and chairs rocked as the young boys made their escape from the choir loft. "Boys! You're in church! Take it easy."

I waited for Brennan and we descended the stairs together. Gino Savo emerged from the shadows as we entered the nave.

"Beautiful singing, Brennan. Of course it was beautiful the first time. Perhaps you expect too much of your choristers."

"I run a choir school, Gino. That's what they're here for. Now, what can I do for you?"

"I understand you removed some materials from Father Schellenberg's room at the abbey."

"Mmm."

"I would like to have a look at those materials."

"The police have all that now, Gino. It's out of our hands."

"That was not Monsignor O'Flaherty's understanding."

Nor mine. The boxes were sitting in my office.

"We had them at the rectory initially but we could hardly leave them there. For reasons of security. I'm sure you understand. And they may be evidence. We are trying to assist the police in any way we can."

"I see."

"If and when we get the boxes back we'll be happy to make them available to you."

Savo didn't believe a word Burke was saying. Burke didn't care. Savo left us with a curt goodbye.

"I guess we'd better have a look in those boxes, Monty."

"Before or after you go to confession for lying to a representative of the See of Peter?"

"Don't concern yourself about the state of my soul. Or my standing with the Vatican. Let's divide the workload."

"I'll sort it into three piles, Brennan. One for me, one for you, one for Michael O'Flaherty."

"I don't want the boxes over at the rectory. Obviously. If we let

241

Michael at them, his keen forensic eye will find something ominous on every page. And who's going to be hearing about it every five minutes? I'd as lief go through it all myself."

"But you won't. You haven't the time. I don't think we'll find anything at all. We already know the reasons Schellenberg became unpopular in so many quarters. But there could be some correspondence in there. Who knows? I have an idea. I'll speak to Mike on the QT, tell him we'd rather go through it ourselves before the Vatican does. Get him involved in a bit of intrigue. He'll enjoy that. I'll set Mike up in a conference room in the law office. You can come in and see the stuff when you have time. Meanwhile Mike and I will look it over."

"Mike doesn't know any German."

"A good deal of the material is in English — translations of Schellenberg's writings, or whatever. I'll give those items to Michael. So, how are you doing? Recovering from . . . the trip?"

"Oh, I'm grand, grand entirely."

†

I had other things I wanted to discuss with Michael O'Flaherty besides the Schellenberg papers. I wanted to check out the chessboard Colonel Bleier and Father Schellenberg had used. Then I hoped to do a little research into John XXIII and Paul VI, the two popes Brother Robin had lampooned in his drawings. I finally got away from the office in the middle of the afternoon on Wednesday. I made a trip to the choir school, found it open, and headed down the corridor to the little alcove where the chessboard was. Had been. It wasn't there. I wondered whether Brennan had come by and taken it, knowing it was of interest in light of our conversation with Greta Schliemann. But Brennan was out when I crossed over to the rectory. Maybe Monsignor O'Flaherty would know where he was. I proceeded down the hall to his room.

"Good afternoon, Michael."

"Good day to you, Monty! Is there anything I can help you with?"

"I was looking for the chessboard we used to see in the corridor at the choir school." Was that a blush I saw on O'Flaherty's cheeks? "Where did the board come from? Was it here already, or did someone bring it to the schola?"

"Em, well, I'm embarrassed to tell you, Monty, I have it here. And no, it doesn't belong to me or to anyone else here as far as I know. It appeared on that little table one day, and I used to see Father Schellenberg playing there, and, well, after what happened nobody seemed to use it anymore, so . . ." His cheeks flushed a deeper hue. "I took it. A little souvenir of the great man, you know. I thought maybe it was his."

"It may have been. So it's here?"

"There it is on my shelf, all set up. I didn't try to hide it, but I probably shouldn't have taken it."

"Oh, I'm sure nobody's going to rap your knuckles for that, Monsignor. Mind if I have a look?"

"Go ahead, Monty, please."

I looked at the board, which appeared to be quite old and worn. It was in the form of a box about three inches deep, with the squares painted in cream and brown on the top. I removed the chess pieces and put them aside, then picked up the box. It made a rattling sound, and I turned it over. Half of the bottom was a panel that slid open, so that the pieces could be stored. An inscription on the bottom showed that it had been made in Germany in 1913. Was this the same board that had been used by Max Bleier and Johann Schellenberg in the Nazi prison camp? I opened the sliding panel, and a broken bishop fell out. I saw something else inside as well. Papers.

"What have you got there, Monty?"

"There are papers stashed in here. Let's have a look. First, though, Mike, would there be a pair of rubber gloves anywhere in the building?"

The elderly priest's eyes lit up. "Evidence, is it?"

"Could be."

"You hold on. Don't touch a thing. I'll go down to the kitchen and get Mrs. Kelly's gloves."

He was back in sixty seconds, out of puff. "Here, Monty. You do it. I'm a bundle of nerves here!"

I snapped the gloves on and drew the papers out of the box.

The first was a message in English. "Reinhold Schellenberg. Stay in the monastery and say your prayers. I repeat, do not leave the monastery. You have destroyed the church. Do not tempt me to destroy you."

The second was in German. My rough translation was: "Father

Schellenberg. You have failed your homeland, you have failed your church, and you have failed yourself. You have caused others to fail in their faith. God damn you. If I am provided with the opportunity, I will kill you. Know that, and govern yourself accordingly."

There were no envelopes and no dates.

Michael O'Flaherty's face was white. "There were threats against him before! Someone must have been waiting for him to leave the monastery, to travel somewhere. If only we had known, we would have done something to try to protect him!"

"You don't remember when you first saw the chessboard?"

"The first time I noticed it was when I saw Father Schellenberg playing with Colonel Bleier."

"Exactly."

"So you think it was Bleier?"

"I don't know what to think, Michael." I filled him in on the conversation Brennan and I had had with *Frau Professorin Doktor* Schliemann in Frankfurt. His blue eyes were as wide as those of a child hearing a bedtime story.

"I'd keep that board out of sight for now, Mike. We'll turn it over to the police. But in the meantime, find a little hiding place for it."

"Oh, I will! You can be sure. That poor soul! We can't tell from the notes whether the threats relate to his time with Pope John at the Council, or his time afterwards when he returned to a more traditional stance. Change your position and you have double the enemies!"

"That reminds me of something else I meant to check. Do you have any information on the popes? I'm thinking of John XXIII and Paul VI."

"The popes of the Vatican Council. I have a little set of cards, Monty. Not a lot of information on each one, but here you go." He dug around in a desk drawer and pulled out a packet of cards the size of bookmarks, showing pictures and short biographical sketches of each of the popes.

I found Pope Paul. The photo showed a man with short dark hair on the sides, bald on top; he had black eyebrows and a long nose. It was a dignified, intelligent face. "Giovanni Battista Enrico Antonio Maria Montini was born in 1897 to an upper-class Italian family. After ordination in 1920 his studies included diplomacy and canon law. He spent some time in Warsaw, then returned to the Vatican where he worked for the Secretariat of State for thirty years. During World War II he was responsible for relief work and the care of political refugees. Montini was appointed archbishop of Milan and became known as the 'archbishop of the workers.' When he succeeded John XXIII in 1963, he was committed to continuing John's work on the Second Vatican Council. Paul's encyclicals on celibacy (1967) and birth control (1968) are still controversial today and tend to overshadow the other accomplishments of this gentle and brilliant man. He died in 1978."

Pope John, who knew our murder victim before and during the Vatican Council, was heavy, round, kind, and good-humoured, as his photograph attested. He was born Angelo Roncalli, in northern Italy in 1881. He was third in a farming family of thirteen children. He was quoted as saying: "There are three ways of ruining oneself: women, gambling and farming. My father chose the most boring." Roncalli entered the seminary at the age of twelve and continued his education until he spent a year in the army as a volunteer. He returned to his studies and received his doctorate in theology. Roncalli was ordained in 1904. He gained an understanding of the working classes, taught in a seminary, then served in the medical and chaplaincy corps in the army during World War I."

The First War. I thought of the holes in the wall of the Oratorio of St. Philomena, from the grenade that exploded during the war. It reminded me that I had not yet dropped my photos off to be printed. I had taken a picture of the plaque setting out the history of the oratorio. I got out my Schellenberg notebook and wrote: "Take film in."

I read the rest of Roncalli's biography: his ascension to the throne of Peter in 1958, and his convening of the Council in 1962.

"One more thing before I go, Mike. Those papers we brought back from Schellenberg's room in the monastery."

"Oh, yes."

"Brennan thought it might be prudent for you and me to go through them ourselves before we provide them to the police or to anyone else. Get a sneak preview, not that I'm expecting anything that will enable us to wrap up the case. But we'd like to know, right? Because if we hand them over to anybody else, we'll never know for sure what was in them."

"Right! Sort of like being the first archaeologists on the dig."

"Exactly. So I've put them in a locked conference room at my law office, and you can go in there and look through them privately whenever you have time."

"Good plan."

"Just call me at Stratton Sommers when you want to start. You have my number."

"Yes, I do. You'll be hearing from me soon, and I hope I find something revealing!"

When I returned to the office, I found a message from one Normie Collins. I dialled the familiar number, and my daughter picked it up on the first ring.

"Hello?"

"May I speak to Miss Collins please?"

"Daddy, it's me!"

"Hello, sweetheart. I know it's me. I got your message."

"Mummy says you have a job for me to do, on the murder case."

"That's right. I need a bit of research done."

"Okay."

"You have a collection of holy cards, pictures of angels and saints with little write-ups about their lives."

"I have tons of them. The ones I got from Father Burke, some other ones I got at the church fair, and a whole whack from Auntie Margaret when we were in Cape Breton."

"Perfect. Have you got a pen and paper there?"

"Just a minute." The receiver banged against the kitchen wall, then she was back. "I've got a pencil and paper."

"Could you look through your collection and see if you have any cards for these saints: Cecilia, Charles Borromeo, Andrew Avellino, Philomena, Joan of Arc, Clare, and John Vianney." I spelled out the names that could be confusing.

"Joan of Arc! I know about her. They set her on fire!"

"Yes, they did. And unfortunately, that's what I want you to concentrate on: how they all died. It's a pretty gruesome assignment, so if you'd rather not —"

"I want to do it!"

"All right, dolly. I'll leave you to it. Thank you!"

"You're welcome, Daddy."

†

Ulrike, the young receptionist at the Göttingen Gasthaus, was engaged in a lively conversation in German with Kurt Bleier when I arrived there after work. They were sharing a laugh over an article in *Der Spiegel*. There was merriment in his eyes when he turned to me. "Ah, *Guten Abend, Herr* Collins."

"*Guten Abend*, Colonel Bleier. Could I have a quick word with you?"

"I am at your service, Mr. Collins. A word about what?"

"Chess."

"Do you play?"

"I don't, but I know you do. And so did Father Schellenberg."

"Come up to my room."

The room had an elaborately carved dark wood bedstead and an even more elaborate cuckoo clock on the wall. We sat in two chairs facing each other across a small table.

"Yes, Reinhold Schellenberg and I enjoyed a few matches together before he was butchered." His voice faltered and he looked away from me. He was silent for a few moments before saying: "I hope you will soon make progress in finding his killer. Do investigations always move so slowly in your country?"

"Not always. But in this case we must be dealing with a very clever, cool-headed killer. It is trite to say it must be someone who had a connection with him in the past."

"Obviously."

"Well, it's not one hundred percent certain, of course. Father Schellenberg could have set off something in the mind of a fragile personality, causing that person to snap. But, if that's the case, why has the fragile personality held up so well throughout the investigation? I'm leaning more towards a cold, methodical type of person as the killer."

"It is hard to miss the inference that you are directing your comments to me. Do you find me cold and methodical?"

Not entirely, I thought, picturing the light-hearted banter between him and Ulrike downstairs. But I said: "I would imagine a police officer in a large European city, particularly one with the history of Berlin, would have to be methodical and cool under fire."

"So you think I slaughtered Reinhold Schellenberg in the most brutal fashion?" Bleier's voice rose in pitch and volume. "Then stayed around to dance on his grave? Why would you think this of me?"

"Why don't you explain the notes that were concealed in the chess-board?"

"I don't know of any notes."

"I think you do."

"I do not."

"Aren't you curious about them?"

"I have just learned of them now. Tell me about them."

"Did that chessboard belong to your father?"

That struck a nerve; he was unable to hide it. But he brazened it out. "That chessboard belonged to Reinhold Schellenberg. Or I assume it did. It was of German manufacture. He brought it with him when he came here."

"You're saying you didn't bring it yourself?"

"I did not see it until he produced it after his arrival."

"And you immediately began to play together."

"Immediately? I don't know. He may have played with others before me. I did not give the matter any thought."

"Do you really expect me to believe you did not know Schellen-berg before arriving here?"

"I have already told you what I knew, and did not know, of Schellenberg. I may have met him in Germany. I know he was detained by the police in Berlin, then released. I did not see him in custody. And, Mr. Collins, I had no reason — none at all — to want the man dead."

"Did your wife have a reason to want him dead?"

"My *wife*? What are you saying?"

"I remember hearing some time ago that Dr. Silkowski had run afoul of the authorities. I took that to mean, not the state authorities, because that would have been you, but the church authorities. Reinhold Schellenberg went through quite a period of retrenchment with respect to church doctrine, or at least church practice. Was he one of the authorities she offended?"

"As far as I know he was not sitting in judgement of my wife."

"Why did you rent a car and then return it?"

"That is a two-part question. Why did I rent a car? To orient myself in the city. Why did I return it? Because I am a retired policeman, not a rich man. I could afford to take the car for two weeks because they offered a special rate for two weeks."

"Did you have any trouble getting used to it?"

"What do you mean?"

"Hitting the wrong controls, for instance."

"Not that I recall. I am an experienced driver. Now, do you have any more questions, or may I proceed with my evening?"

"No more questions for now, Colonel. Open or closed?" I asked when I reached the door.

"Close it, please. I have some thinking to do, and I do that better without distractions."

✝

Michael O'Flaherty turned up after morning Mass the next day, eager to start going through Reinhold Schellenberg's papers. It wasn't long before he was at my office door. "Monty! I found something that may have a bearing on the case. Or, it may not of course, but —"

"What is it, Mike?"

"Well, it seems yer man was a bit of a wag. And perhaps somebody didn't appreciate his sense of humour! There's a set of limericks about the saints, scribbled on three pieces of hotel stationery. The Daphne and Steven Hotel in London! And there's a note stapled to them in German and I can't decipher it at all."

"Let's have a look."

We went into the conference room and Mike shoved the pages into my hand. A series of limericks was hand-printed in ink, possibly a fountain pen, in block letters. The lines appeared to have been printed in haste. A few words were smeared with a brownish stain, and I wondered if the poems had been copied down during a party in the hotel, or in the bar. I read aloud from the sheets:

> There was a young man from Aquino
> A student of Monte Cassino.
> A temptress was sent,
> Or should we say lent,
> By his family, the House of Aquino.

249

A handsome young man, Avellino,
Was troubled like Thomas Aquino
By the naughty behaviour
Of nuns of the Saviour.
He sent them away, Avellino.

His friend, the great Charles Borromeo,
While praying the Gloria Deo
Was attacked by a mob
Who, thank God, botched the job
And Saint Carlo continued to pray-oh.

"Here's a bunch of saints I've never heard of. Notburga, Botolph, Odo. They may have been considered martyrs just for going through life with those names. Oh, here we go, something more familiar. You must have appreciated this one, Mike:

Sure, Patrick and Dymphna and Kevin
Ensure there is Guinness in Heaven.
And Camillus de Lellis,
So they do tell us,
Is still rolling the dice for a seven.

"Camillus must have been a gambler."

"I believe so, yes."

"I don't recognize any of the other saints' names. How about you, Michael?"

"Some are unknown to me. But the ones we're interested in are the ones admired by our suspects."

"That's right. This sounds like something composed by a bunch of people sitting around a table. It seems harmless enough to me. What do you think, as a priest?"

"It doesn't seem particularly offensive to me, but I suppose if someone were very devoted to a saint and heard him or her being slagged, especially by a prominent member of the church, it could set the person off. This would have been in Schellenberg's more liberal days. It makes him sound like a smart-aleck."

Attached to the limericks was a note in German. It had obviously been produced on a computer. There was no signature. I read the note aloud to Mike, translating it roughly as I went along: "My dear Schellenberg. You have shown yourself to be a scholar and a wit. I imagine in my mind the sneers and laughter that greeted your beer-fuelled recitation. You wear the vestments of a priest and the honours of a theologian, yet I ask myself whether you are a Catholic. Would a Catholic denigrate the saints and martyrs in this way? And mock their suffering? Many names have been reviled, but one is missing. But, of course, it would not be there! Thanks to *him* and now, I learn, to *you*! Pray for forgiveness. Father."

"Well!" O'Flaherty exclaimed. "Somebody's unhappy with him!"

"We already knew that, Mike."

"Em, yes, of course, but now we have something in our hands that may lead to the killer's identity. Do you suppose the 'Father' at the end was a signature, or was the person calling Schellenberg 'Father'?"

"I was thinking the latter, and that he separated it from the preceding sentence for emphasis. There's something stilted about the writing, and I think there are a couple of errors in it. I'm not sure. We'll run it by Brennan. My impression, though, is that the writer of the note is not a native speaker of German."

"That leaves out Colonel Bleier, but it wouldn't be him anyway; he'd hardly be giving out to Schellenberg about mocking the saints of the Catholic Church."

"Right. But it could be any of the other people we have in our sights. The note writer says this is something Schellenberg recited, possibly in the bar of this hotel or at a party in one of the rooms. My guess is someone else jotted down what he said. Somehow it came into the hands of the person who wrote the note. Let's see if we can reach the Daphne and Steven Hotel. Find out if they remember a gathering of limerick-spouting theologians."

Calls to directory assistance in London got us nowhere; there was apparently no hotel by that name. But we found the number of a tourist accommodation service and spoke to a young woman with a thick Cockney accent. She informed us that the Daphne and Steven had been made over into the Chichester Suites in 1967.

"So Schellenberg's beery performance took place before 1967. The accompanying note in German was done on a computer, so it was written years after the verses. Was Schellenberg ever known as a drinker?"

"Oh, now, I never heard that about the man," O'Flaherty replied. "I did hear that he liked the occasional pint of beer and a feed of good German sausage. And he travelled quite widely in his earlier days."

"Do we know when Robin Gadkin-Falkes went into the monastery?"

"I believe it was in the late 1960s. I'm thinking 1969."

"That sounds right."

"Let's go through this again and see who he slagged," O'Flaherty said, taking the papers from my hands. "The only ones on our list are Andrew Avellino and Charles Borromeo."

"Saints Andrew and Charles. They were friends, Brennan told me. Enrico Sferrazza-Melchiorre is devoted to Andrew, and Robin to Charles. That accounts for two of our suspects, but someone might have been offended by any mockery of the saints, no matter which saints were named. And there could be something else. The note says: 'one is missing, thanks to him' — an unnamed third person — and to Schellenberg himself, apparently. I wonder who 'him' is. And who is 'missing'? But we'll work with what we have. Enrico or Robin might well have been moved to write this note in protest. We'll have to find out how much German they know."

✝

"Robin. *Wie gut kannst du Deutsch sprechen?*"

"You really must learn the art of making small talk, Brennan," Robin admonished him as we entered the hospital room. "How is my German, you want to know? I am competent in the language of the Hun, but barely so. Are you asking for any particular reason, or is it just idle curiosity? Do have a seat, won't you? What a pleasure to have visitors. Well, it's part of your calling, isn't it, Father Burke, to visit the sick?"

"Did you write this?" Brennan handed him the German note without the limericks attached.

Robin did not take the time to read it. "No, I did not. Is there any

252

other way I can be of assistance to you gentlemen today?"

"Have you seen this before?"

"No."

"How about this?"

He handed over the three pages of limericks, and Robin read through them.

"Very droll, Brennan. Are you the author? I can't help but notice the anachronistic references to Guinness being swilled by the Irish saints, though that bit of doggerel is not quite as clever as some of the other verses. If you did write it, you may want to rework —"

"I didn't write it. Or, to be more accurate, I didn't take notes while it was being recited. I wasn't there."

"You weren't where?"

"I'm glad you asked. The Daphne and Steven Hotel in London."

"London. Is that why your inquiries have brought you once again to me?"

"I'm asking myself if you might have been there that night."

"How should I know, if I don't know what night it was?"

"So, you've been to the Daphne and Steven Hotel."

"Not that I recall. Can't say one way or the other. When was this, and why are you here disturbing the rest of an invalid about something so silly?"

"We don't know exactly when it was, but it was before 1967. Though the letter of complaint is more recent."

"I see. Why is this of interest?"

"We believe Reinhold Schellenberg was the author of these verses, perhaps with help from others around a table in the bar."

"He did like to lift a beer stein from time to time, or so I heard. And I do have it on good authority that he was fond of a jest. I wish I had been there. Sounds like fun. But no. I'd never met Schellenberg until he made his entrance here. Or, there." He pointed out his window to Halifax across the harbour.

†

Once again, Brennan and I were none the wiser after an encounter with Brother Robin. We had nothing to say on the ride over the bridge from Dartmouth. I thought of all the saints who were named in the limericks. Most were names I had never heard. In fact, the saints I knew probably constituted a very small proportion of the realm of the sanctified. I had been surprised to learn there was a Saint Reinhold, but I shouldn't have been. Weren't all Catholics in former times named after saints? Saint Reinhold, like the more recent Benedictine monk by that name, had been murdered. Normally, I would find it difficult to write that off as coincidence. But, given the number of saints who had suffered frightful deaths at the hands of others, I was forced to conclude it likely *was* a coincidence. I wondered if Schellenberg's choice of the Benedictine order was influenced by his namesake. The first Reinhold had been drowned. No, that's not what Mike O'Flaherty had told me. Wasn't there something about a construction site? When I was back in my office, and had cleared some work from my desk, I got Mike on the phone and asked him to refresh my memory.

"He was done in by masons, Monty. God rest him."

"Masons? The guys with the secret handshakes?"

"No, real masons. Stonemasons, back in the tenth century. The story is that he was supervising the building operations at an abbey being constructed in Cologne. Reinhold was more industrious than his workers, and made them look bad in comparison. They beat the poor man to death with their hammers! Then his body was thrown in the Rhine River. Legend has it the body was found through divine revelation. Reinhold is the patron saint of stonemasons. I'd advise them to take a humble approach when they pray for his intercession!"

"I don't know about you, Mike, but I was never taught this kind of stuff in Catechism class!"

"Nor was I. The dear old nuns didn't want to frighten us off!"

"Isn't Lou Petrucci a stonemason?"

"Oh, I don't think so, Monty. I believe he's an electrician."

"That may be it. But I remember him telling me generations of his family built the church that he eventually torched in New Jersey. Kind of hard to overlook him under the circumstances."

"Yes, but wasn't he able to give a good account of his whereabouts?"

"He didn't have a watertight alibi, but he had a witness to say he was in a tavern that afternoon. He was a little sketchy about the times. I think I should talk to him again."

"I'll let you get on with it then."

"Thanks, Mike. Bye for now."

I searched my notes for Lou Petrucci's phone number. I remembered meeting him at the Park Vic on South Park Street. A young woman had answered when I called to set up the appointment. I wondered whose apartment it was. Probably his nephew's, and the woman may have been a girlfriend. It might be more instructive for me to talk to the nephew, Giorgio; after all, he was Petrucci's alibi witness. I dialled the number, and again it was answered by a female voice. I asked to speak to Giorgio.

"Just a sec. Georgie! Phone!"

When he came on the line, I explained who I was and asked whether I could stop by and talk to him for a few minutes. He hesitated, then suggested we meet in the Victory Lounge at the Lord Nelson Hotel.

He was waiting for me with a beer in front of him when I got there ten minutes later. I ordered one for myself and sat down. Giorgio Spano was over six feet tall and must have weighed two-fifty. He had black hair parted in the middle and falling to just below his jawline.

"Hi, Giorgio. Thanks for meeting me. What position do you play for Saint Mary's?"

"Defensive tackle. I didn't have a very good season."

"I'm sorry to hear it."

"Yeah, well, better luck next year maybe."

"I just wanted to check with you about the afternoon of November 22."

"My uncle was with me at the Bulb."

"The Lighthouse Tavern."

"Yeah. We were watching this old guy do a coin trick. He put it in his fingers and squeezed and water dripped out. There's a picture of the Queen on it, right? Well, he said he was making the Queen pee. So that guy was there, and he can say he saw us."

"That guy's always there, Georgie. Now, can you remember what time you got there, and what time you left?"

"Uh, well, not exactly. I think it was around noon hour when we got there, but then . . ."

"Then what?"

"I'm not sure how long we were there."

"Do you remember where you went afterwards?" He looked at me without responding, then took a sip of his beer. Then took another. "What's the matter, Giorgio?"

He laughed uncomfortably. "The alibi was as much for me as it was for Lou."

"What do you mean?"

"Well, see, I left kind of early. I left Lou there. I was meeting this girl and, uh, I didn't want Alice to know. Alice and I are living together, but I saw this other girl Tracy a few times. Not anymore, but I was with her that afternoon. So I said I was with Lou the whole time."

There goes the alibi. I said: "I understand. So, what time did you leave the Lighthouse?"

"I was meeting Tracy at two o'clock. So I would have left the tavern a few minutes before that."

"And what did your uncle do?"

"I don't know. He still had a draft in front of him when I left."

I thanked Giorgio for his help. I got up to go, and he stayed in the lounge. It wouldn't take long to confirm his version of events. I drove down Spring Garden Road to Barrington and turned right. The old Lighthouse Beverage Room was near the end of the street, south of downtown. I went in and asked around. One of the waiters had been on duty that day and he remembered Georgie Spano, because he followed the fortunes of the Saint Mary's football team. Georgie had been drinking with an older fellow. Georgie left first, and the waiter had a bit of conversation with the older guy, who turned out to be Georgie's uncle. They talked about the football season. Then the uncle finished his draft and left the tavern.

✝

I was able to track Petrucci down at the schola later that day. I decided to do a little bit of covering for the nephew, so I didn't mention my conversation with him. As far as Petrucci was concerned, I had come

256

by some unwelcome information in conversation with a waiter at the Lighthouse. Lou's face went grey.

"Did you know how Saint Reinhold died?" I asked him.

"Who? I never heard of Saint Reinhold."

"Are you sure? He's the patron saint of stonemasons."

"First I heard of it. I'm not a stonemason."

"Somebody in your family was, though. Your grandfather? Your father?"

"So what?"

"So Saint Reinhold was beaten to death by stonemasons, using their hammers as weapons."

"You're shittin' me!"

"No, I'm not. And here we have the descendant of stonemasons who's so upset with the activities of the Catholic authorities that he set fire to a church. Then he shows up in Halifax, and a monk named Reinhold is murdered."

"I didn't kill Schellenberg! You're crazy with this stonemason stuff! You're probably making it up."

"Why did you lie?"

"Because I was sticking up for the kid. He took off to meet some girl. He didn't want Alice to know, so we fudged the times."

"No problem. Now, where did you go afterwards?"

"I don't know. Nowhere! Fuck off and leave me alone!" With that, he shoved me aside and ran from the building, nearly taking out a group of choir school kids in his haste to flee.

Chapter 14

Omnes sancti martyres, orate pro nobis.
Sancta Philomena, ora pro nobis.
All ye holy martyrs, pray for us.
Saint Philomena, pray for us.
— "Litany of the Saints"

"Police were at Logan's place last night, the house he's staying in."

I was in the office Friday morning and was so intent on my medical malpractice file I didn't hear Moody Walker come in. My secretary must have let him through.

"What happened, Moody?"

"Had a break-in."

"Oh?"

"Yeah, Logan and his wife were out. Went to dinner with a bunch of other Yanks from the choir school. When they got back they found black ice in their driveway, so Logan went into the shed to get some salt. Things didn't look right in there. Some tools had been moved around. Whoever did it was a good locks man. He picked the lock, went in, did whatever he wanted to do, and locked up again when he left."

"Was anything taken?"

"Not that Logan could see. He and his wife checked through the house and didn't notice anything wrong in there till they got to the basement. There was a small hatchet and a larger axe that had been hanging on hooks along the wall. Somebody had put them side by side on the workbench. The back door of the house was left open. Looks as if the perp was real careful about the way he got in, then had to leave in a hurry. May have heard something, thought it was Logan coming home."

"Did the neighbours notice anything?"

"Guy next door saw lights in the basement. Flashes of light, he said."

"But he couldn't see in?"

"No, it wasn't the basement light going on. It was more like a camera flash. Happened a couple of times, then nothing. He didn't think any more about it."

"What time was that?"

"Around nine o'clock. And a few minutes after nine, a cabbie met a small car peeling out of Logan's street, jumping the stop sign. The neighbour never saw any car in front of Logan's. So if it was the perp, he had enough sense to park farther up the street. But there's no way to know whether it was connected. Could have been anybody."

"What happens now?"

"Forensics are out there, looking for prints on the axes and the doors."

"What does Logan have to say?"

"He's in a snit. Says somebody's out to get him."

"Out to get him why?"

Moody shrugged. "He clammed up when they questioned him. This may be about the Schellenberg murder, but who knows? It may have nothing to do with Logan at all. It's not even his house. Just a house with nobody home. Random hit."

"But it looked like a pretty skilled operator."

"We do have our professionals, you know. You see some of the messes I've seen in houses that have been hit, you come to appreciate the pro, the guy who takes pride in his work."

†

My malpractice case kept me tied up for much of the weekend; I had a blues gig on Saturday night, and the rest of my free time I spent with the kids. But I found a bit of time Monday afternoon and made a point of locating William Logan in one of the classrooms at the schola. "Heard you had a burglar out at your place, Bill."

"Yeah, right. A burglar. Somebody taking pictures of the axes in the basement. What do you think that's about?"

"What do *you* think it's about?"

"Obvious, isn't it? I'm being set up for the murder."

"How have you been set up? Those axes, they were already at the house, weren't they?"

"Yeah. But think about it. The cops never found the murder weapon. Now they find axes in the house where I'm staying."

"Did the police take the axes?"

"No."

"Well, then. They must not have seen anything suspicious about them."

"They were clean."

"Clean in what way?"

"Every way."

"How do you know? Did they sparkle or —"

"I cleaned them!"

"You cleaned them. When did you do that?"

"Before the police arrived."

"Why did you do that, Bill?"

"Because I was afraid somebody came in and put something on them. Contaminated them. Blood or something."

"Did you share your fears with the police?"

"No way."

"Yet you called the police in, knowing their attention would be drawn to the axes if you described what had happened in the basement."

"I didn't call them. It was Babs. She freaked out and called them before I had a chance to calm her down."

"So then you did the cleanup job."

"What are you looking at me like that for?" His voice was suddenly too loud for the room. "What would you do if you'd been in my place, Collins?"

"I wouldn't have kept the murder weapon in the house, Bill."

"It's not the murder weapon!!"

"Which one?"

"What? Neither of them!"

"Then you had nothing to hide."

"I did if somebody came in trying to frame me!"

"Who do you think is trying to frame you?"

"I have my suspicions."

"Obviously. Who?"

"That commie!"

"Bleier?"

"Of course Bleier! How many other commies do you know?"

"Well, my father-in-law for one. And there's my buddy Miguel; I was at a party at his place recently. He's the current leader of the Communist Party of Canada, and —"

"You can't be serious!" He looked as if Beelzebub had materialized before his eyes. "These people are communists and you know them?"

"You have to get out more, Bill. Anyway, you were talking about Bleier."

"Yeah, a cop from Communist East Berlin! Don't tell me the Folks Police or whatever they called themselves didn't work hand in hand with the secret police."

"I'm sure they did, before the Berlin Wall came down. But how does this relate to Schellenberg's murder? And to you?"

"Why is Bleier here, Collins?"

"Good question. Why do you think he's here?"

"To murder Schellenberg and then pin it on an American? Could that be why an atheist from an Iron Curtain country suddenly shows up in Canada at a Catholic choir school?"

"Why do you think he's framing you in particular?"

"Why not? I'm an American. I'm the enemy."

"You're not the only American here. Why you?"

"Besides the fact that he knows I'm on to him and I call him on his bullshit every chance I get? He knows I wasn't out of town on that bus tour when the murder happened. Convenient for him."

"Where were you that day, Bill?"

"I've already answered that question, and I don't feel like answering it again. Okay? It's pretty bad when you believe him over me. But I guess I shouldn't be surprised, given the company you keep."

"I never said I believed Bleier. Do the police know you wiped down the two axes?"

"Not unless they were assisted by Bubbles, the detergent-sniffing dog."

†

There was no sign of Kurt Bleier at the schola. I remembered seeing an announcement of a speaker on Polish Catholicism, and I thought perhaps his wife would be in attendance for that one. I went back to work, then returned to the school a few minutes before the lecture, and caught my first glimpse of Jadwiga Silkowski. She had a handsome Slavic face; her salt and pepper hair was done up in a French twist, and she had black-rimmed glasses on a chain. She skipped up the steps of the building and went inside. Her husband followed at an unhurried pace.

"Colonel Bleier," I said.

It had started to rain. January in Halifax: it may snow, it may rain, it may do both.

"Mr. Collins. Montague. No questions for me today, I hope."

"Let's step inside." We entered the building and positioned ourselves off to the side of the entrance. I looked him in the eye. "What were you doing at the Logans' place last Thursday night?"

Not a muscle in his face or body moved. But his mind was working furiously. I could almost feel the concentration of energy. I of course wasn't certain he had gone out there. But he didn't know that. A trained interrogator like Bleier knew how counterproductive it could be to lie about something the questioner might already know.

"I was trying to find evidence."

"Against Logan."

"Yes. Evidence that your police have failed to unearth."

"They have a suspect on psychiatric remand."

"They have the Englishman. I think they should be looking elsewhere."

"You realize that if our police find out you broke into a dwelling house, you could be facing a maximum sentence of life imprisonment."

"You're a lawyer, Montague. I'm a policeman. You and I both know the crime is break and enter with intent to commit an indictable offence. I had no such intent, I committed no such offence. I did no damage, committed no theft." He was no fool and he was right, for the most part. The law *presumes* a criminal intent in the absence of evidence to the contrary, but maybe the German cop would be able to raise a reasonable doubt and beat the rap. I let it go.

"Logan knows it was you," I said, and let it sink in for a moment. "He thinks you were trying to frame him for the murder."

"I believe there is evidence, somewhere, of his guilt."

"You're telling me you truly believe Logan killed Schellenberg."

"I do."

"Why Logan?"

"I think the man is unstable."

"And the Englishman isn't?"

"Logan flies into a rage with the slightest provocation. He bears ill will to a number of people in the Roman Catholic Church. Schellenberg was receiving threats —"

"How do you know that?"

"We have — our police force has information about these threats. At least one of them came from America at a time when Schellenberg was planning a trip to the United States. He cancelled the trip."

"Because of the threat."

"Correct."

"Why didn't you share this information before?" He didn't answer. A novel and unwelcome experience for a career policeman, being on the other end of an interrogation. "What else can you tell me about Schellenberg?"

"Nothing. Let us return to Logan. Of all the people here, of all those who cannot give an account of themselves for the time of death, Logan is the one I suspect."

"He suspects you."

"No. He does not. He pretends to suspect me to divert attention from himself. When I went out there —"

"How did you get there?"

"It is a simple matter to rent a car and read a map. I intended only to look around in the garden shed."

"How did you know there was a shed?"

"I knew. I hoped it was not locked. But it was, and so I picked open the lock. Did no damage. I did not see anything of interest to me in the shed. There was no one about, so I decided to enter the basement."

"You're a pretty skilled man with a lock."

"One learns things over the course of one's career. I went into the basement and looked around. I saw a small axe and then a larger one. I took them down from the wall to examine them, to photograph them. I took two photographs, then I heard a sound, so I left them on the work table and got out."

"Where are the photos?"

"I have them."

"Do they show anything on the axes?"

"I could not see anything."

"Logan wiped them off."

"The action of a guilty man."

"He wiped them after the break-in, not before."

"How do you know that?"

"He told me."

"And you believe him."

"You want me to believe *you*. Logan claims you went out there to plant evidence, that you might have put blood or something on one of the axes."

"Whose blood?"

"Well, it wouldn't work unless it was the victim's blood, would it?"

"Where would I get Schellenberg's blood?"

"From the real murder weapon?"

"You are reaching, Montague. You have no grounds for suspecting me."

"I wouldn't say that, Kurt. But I'll be off now. You and Logan have given me a lot to think about."

✝

"And so, my Lord, the defendant submits that the plaintiff is a crumbling skull plaintiff and not a thin skull —"

"What are you *saying*, Montague?"

I turned off my dictaphone and looked up. Brennan was standing in the doorway of my office late Monday afternoon, staring at me as if I were a witch doctor.

"Sit down, Brennan. In tort law," I explained, using the tone of voice he himself used when instructing those who just will not catch on, "a thin skull plaintiff is someone with an underlying condition or weakness that becomes manifest only after his new injury. If he has degenerative changes in his spine or is emotionally unable to deal with adversity, and his reaction to the injury is worse than another person's would be, too bad for the defendant. We have to take the plaintiff as we find him. But if the person already has symptoms from his underlying condition, that means he would have had problems even without the accident, and so we only pay for the portion of the damage we caused. His skull was already crumbling, so to speak. Crumbling skull plaintiff. Thus endeth the lesson."

"A lesson I'm not likely to forget."

"Good man. Now, what can I do for you today?"

"I just took a stroll over to see if we could sit down and talk about grisly death scenes. But, hearing all this about crumbling skulls, I'm not so sure I'll be able for it."

"Sure you will. Give me an hour and come back. I've got a trial starting on Thursday, a medical negligence case. So I have to get some other stuff cleared away. Like this file, a minor claim. Somebody looking for 'monetary bandages,' if you know what I mean. I'll meet you downstairs at six-thirty."

I finished my work and met Brennan on Barrington Street outside my building.

"I thought we might talk about the sanctified again," he said. "And how they died. I can't escape the notion that there's a connection between the murder and one or more of the saints."

"If you had told me a year ago, Brennan, that I'd be looking to the dead heroes of the Catholic Church for clues to a murder, I'd have thought you'd gone simple."

"No, no, just stepping back and forth between one world and another. Nothing to it."

"If you say so. Anyway, what we should be looking for is a depiction of their death scenes."

"I asked Mike, but all he has is Butler's *Lives of the Saints*, which, as you saw, is not illustrated. The information is out there if we need it; we'll just have to do some digging."

"Well, I do have somebody on the case. I asked Normie to look through her collection of holy cards to see if she has any of the people we're interested in. She'll be home from school by now. Maybe it's time to ask for her report."

"Let's hope the death scenes aren't shown in any detail! You wouldn't want the child seeing that."

"They're holy cards, Brennan. Not slasher films."

So we walked to my car and drove to Dresden Row, where Tom and Normie were just finishing a meal of spaghetti and meatballs, and butterscotch pie for dessert.

"Evening, Stormie. Mr. Douglas."

"Hi, Father."

"Where'd you get the pie?" I asked, ogling it.

"Mummy bought it," Normie answered.

"Can we have some?"

"Okay, but if you take the last piece you have to buy a new one. I didn't mean you, Father Burke!"

"Why not him?" I demanded. "I'm giving him the smaller piece, then." I cut modest slices for myself and Brennan.

"Where's Mum?"

"At Fanny's with the baby."

Tom asked: "Are you guys going to be here for a while? If I can have the car, I can go get Lexie and bring her over."

"Sure. Go ahead, Tommy."

I handed him my keys, and he took off.

"Okay, Normie. Time to get to work. We need the results of your research."

"It's all done! I have cards for some of the ones you asked for!"

"Great. Let's move into the dining room. Put your cards on the table."

She pounded up the stairs to her room, ransacked the place by the sounds of it, then came flying down the stairs and didn't stop till she hit the dining room table. Her cards were clutched in her fist. Seeing her with them reminded me: I had not yet taken my film in to be developed. I wanted the photo of the Angelicum for her T-shirt. I made a mental note to get it done. She put the cards on the table in a pack, then squinted at the one on top.

"Where are your glasses?"

"I don't know. I don't need them." This battle had been going on for five years, but now was not the time for fresh hostilities, so I let it go.

"All right. What did you find?"

"Saint Joan of Arc."

"The saint beloved of Jan Ford," I noted for the record.

"Saint Joan led the French army in all kinds of battles and did a really good job. Then she was captured and they said she was bad and burned her to death! They said she was a heretic. That means somebody who's not a good Catholic. But they found out it wasn't true and she was really a saint." The card showed the maiden warrior in armour; fortunately, she was not depicted going up in flames.

"Who else have you got, Normie?"

"You wanted Saint Clare; I have two Clares!"

"Brilliant!" Brennan exclaimed. "Lou Petrucci rescued the statue of a Saint Clare, Santa Chiara, from the modernized church in New Jersey. Before he set fire to it. Give us your Clares."

"Clare of Rimini and Clare of Assisi. The Rimini one was dis-so-lute," my daughter said. "Dissolute?" She stumbled over the word, then looked up at me. "What's that mean?"

"She probably partied a lot."

She turned to her priest. "It was a sin to go to parties back in the thirteen hundreds?"

"Em, well, there's partying, and then there's *partying*."

She waited for enlightenment but none was forthcoming, so she went back to her card. "She enjoyed *sinful pleasures*, it says here. Then she stopped sinning and opened a convent. And it says —" she bent over until her face was about eight inches from the card. "'She practised penances that would have been thought extreme even in medieval times.' What do they mean by that?"

"I have no idea," Burke lied.

"Okay."

"How did she die?"

"Of natural causes," Normie read from the card.

"Or unnatural penitential practices," the priest muttered.

"What does 'natural causes' mean?"

"It means nobody killed her," I replied.

"But you want someone to kill her, right?"

"Well, that's probably what we're looking for."

"Let's see," Burke said, peering at the card. "Oh, this Clare has been beatified, but not canonized. So she's called 'blessed,' not 'saint.' Who's the other Clare?"

"Saint Clare of Assisi," Normie answered and showed us the card. The saint was pictured in the brown and black habit of a nun. "She liked music. She was born rich, but started a group called the Poor Clares. Natural causes again," she said with disgust, and pushed the card away.

"All right. Who else is on our list? Do you have Saint Andrew Avellino there?"

Normie looked as if she had just been given a D on her math exam. "No! I kept looking but he's not here."

"No problem," I assured her. "We know a bit about him already. Do you have Saint Charles Borromeo?"

"No." She shook her head, and looked as if she might burst into tears.

"It's okay, sweetheart. We didn't expect you to have every holy card in the world. We know Saint Charles was shot by a member of a society, the *Umiliati*, who resented his reforms. The attempt took place while he was praying at the altar. He survived for another fifteen years, then died of a fever. Andrew Avellino was Borromeo's friend. Andrew was attacked by a crowd of people who resented *his* efforts at reform." I turned to Burke. "He was attacked by the johns he booted out of the convent-brothel in Naples."

"Funny how that stuck in your puerile mind."

"I'll bet it stuck in yours too."

"It did."

"A reformer, a lawyer who committed perjury, a priest — Andrew must have died of exhaustion."

"He suffered a stroke while celebrating Mass and died soon afterwards."

"Borromeo is admired by Brother Robin, and Andrew by Enrico

Sferrazza-Melchiorre. Who else have we got?"

Normie shuffled the deck as if one more bad card would cost her the house. Then she found the ace of spades. "Cecilia! You asked for her, and here she is!"

"Of course! Thank you, sweetheart. Her feast day is November 22, day of the murder."

"Here you go." Normie passed the card to Burke.

"All they show here is the sculpture in the Catacomb of St. Callixtus in Rome. The figure of a young girl, carved in white marble, lying on her side; you can see a cut on her neck. We know her killers tried to drown or suffocate her in her bath, then tried to cut her head off . . ." Burke's voice trailed away as he looked at my little girl, her eyes as big as butterscotch pie plates.

"Attempted decapitation," I responded, "as was the case with Father Schellenberg. It's hard to avoid the conclusion that the killer was trying to re-enact Cecilia's death."

"Patron saint of church musicians. Everyone at the schola would be keen on her, I'm thinking. Of course a couple of our suspects have no saintly devotions at all, namely Kurt Bleier and Billy Logan."

"From my own observations, Brennan, and from our researches in Rome, I'd say the ex-Father Logan is more attached to Holy Mother Church than he lets on."

"No doubt."

"All right. Back to the holy dead. We mustn't forget Saint Reinhold himself," I said, "beaten to death by masons. And Saint John Vianney."

"I've got him!" Normie exclaimed. "Right here!" She waved his card in our faces. John was shown with long white hair and a kindly face; he was vested as a priest and had a halo around his head.

Brennan looked at the card. "The great confessor and patron saint of priests."

"Isn't there another one who's patron saint of priests?"

"There are many, but Saint John is a particular favourite. What does it say about his death, Stormie?"

"Another one who died of natural causes." She gave the appearance of one who was letting down the side.

"Fred Mills is devoted to him," Brennan said, "but I don't think we have to spend much time wringing our hands about Fred."

"Why not?"

"He doesn't have a motive."

"He doesn't have an alibi."

"Not one of them has an alibi, Monty. They didn't all kill him."

"That is probably a safe assumption," I agreed, with only the slightest lawyerly reservation. They may indeed all have killed him. But it was unlikely.

"Who else?" I asked. "Philomena, obviously, since it was a Philomena chaplet I found in Robin's room. Normie, did you —"

"I have a card for Philomena! I'll read it to you. 'Philomena's death was extraordinary even when measured against the bizarre torments suffered by other saints. The Roman Emperor Dio — Dioc —' How do you say this?"

I looked at the text on the card. "Diocletian."

"He wanted to marry her but she refused, saying she had promised to be the bride of Christ. The emperor had her scourged — What's that mean?"

Burke gave me a look across the table. "It means they hit her with something," I said.

"They were really rough in those days! Like those police in Germany back in the 1970s. I'm glad I wasn't around then."

"This was even before the dark ages of the 1970s."

"Way back," she agreed. "Anyway, then they tied her to an anchor to be drowned in the Tiber River. There's a legend that angels cut the rope, the anchor fell, and she was transported up to the bank. The soldiers then shot her with arrows! Again she was saved by heavenly in — inter — intervention. Then they —"

I gently slid the card away from her and read the rest of the gruesome tale to myself. They tried heated arrows on her, but the arrows miraculously turned back and killed the archers. Finally, the emperor had her head cut off. I stared at the card, at the image of a young girl with long dark hair crowned with a circlet of flowers. In her left hand she held a bouquet; in her right she clasped a sinister collection of items: a scourge, an anchor, an arrow.

Anchor. Arrow. The swizzle stick and valentine cards left on Father Schellenberg's body, after the killer tried to cut off his head.

"It was the death of Saint Philomena that was being re-enacted!"

Burke's eyes were riveted to the card. Normie looked from one to the other of us, and stayed silent.

When I recovered, I said: "We don't know of any devotions to Saint Philomena on the part of our suspects. She's the patron saint of what?" I consulted the card. "Priests, babies, children, sickness, lost causes, desperate causes — I see as well that there are miraculous cures attributed to her. We're getting there. I know it."

Normie couldn't hold it in: "Did I help you solve the murder?"

"You may have, Normie. Your work has given us something we didn't know before. And I think it's something important."

"Wow! Wait till I tell — No, it's a secret. I know that."

Brennan turned to me. "The Saint Philomena chaplet. Someone put it in Brother Robin's room, with the note saying 'let me grieve with you.'"

"That story Robin told us about his sister, a young girl who died of some sort of disease or infection in Africa. Does somebody think Robin blames Philomena for failing to save the sister? Could anyone's mind work like that?"

"You tell me. You defend murderers for a living. How do their minds work?"

"I defend people *accused* of murder, Brennan," I replied. "But let's get back to Robin. There was nothing like this in his statement to the police; it dealt with Schellenberg and the changes after Vatican II."

"He's led us around in circles," Brennan said, "and I'm sure in his own mind, he has his reasons for all this daft behaviour."

"The heart has its reasons, which reason knows not of."

"True enough. It was my understanding that Robin didn't do it. But now, seeing this, I don't know what to think."

"Somebody knows," I interjected. "Somebody put that chaplet and note under his door. And we know Enrico's fingerprints were on the note, along with Robin's."

"Let's pay a visit to Enrico again."

✝

But Enrico only shrugged once again when we called upon him that night, and denied having anything to do with the note.

"Your prints were on it, Enrico."

"I cannot explain."

"But you must realize this puts you in a very difficult position."

"I did not see this note. What kind of a note was it?"

"It was a piece of paper torn from a larger sheet of writing paper, and it said: '*Fac me tecum plangere.*'"

"Perhaps this was writing paper that I had touched. But how can I know if I have never seen it?"

"I can tell you it was beautiful marbled paper. Probably quite costly."

Sferrazza-Melchiorre leaned over and opened a drawer in his desk. "This paper?"

It was a pad of marbled paper matching the one on which the note had been written.

"Exactly like that."

He shrugged again. "My paper. My fingerprints."

"Now we're getting somewhere. Did anyone borrow this, or take a sheet from it?"

"I do not know. Perhaps someone did."

"Who was in your room?"

"Many of the people here at the schola. I cannot say who. Or, to be more correct, I cannot say who was not in here."

Great.

✝

I retrieved my pictures from the one-hour photo place on Tuesday and headed straight to the T-shirt shop in Scotia Square, where I handed over the ANGELICVM picture and ordered a shirt for Normie. Then I sifted through the other snapshots. There was St. Philomena's Oratorio. The plaque containing the lengthy write-up of the building's history was perfectly legible in the photo, so I drove to the rectory. Burke was in, and he took out a pair of half-glasses, perched them on his nose, and swiftly translated the Italian text.

"In 1908, the parish priest of St. Bona, *Don* Natale Reginato, decided to create a tangible sign of his devotion to the holy virgin and martyr Filomena, whose cult had become popular around the middle of the nineteenth century, following the wondrous recovery of the Curé d'Ars, San Giovanni Maria Vianney, thanks also to —"

"Vianney!" I interrupted. He looked at me over his reading glasses and waited. "A connection between Saint John Vianney and Philomena. We have the Philomena chaplet placed in Brother Robin's room with the note attached. Which one of your students is devoted to Saint John? Fred Mills. A connection between Fred and Robin?"

Burke did not reply.

"What else did you just read there? Let me see it. The '*guarigione prodigiosa.*' What's that again?"

"The wondrous recovery. Saint John must have been cured of something dire, and attributed the cure to Saint Philomena."

"So. Sickness and cure. Robin's sister died of illness. No cure there. Would someone maintain a devotion to a saint who fell down on the job? 'My saint came through for me,' or 'my saint let me down.' Would any rational person think in such crass terms, haggling with the supernatural?"

"People do it every day, Monty. 'Dear God, if you cure me of this liver ailment, I promise I'll never let a drop of whiskey touch my lips again.'"

"I know, I know. But I can't figure out what point the sender of the chaplet was trying to make with Robin. I'm way out of my league here, Brennan."

"We all are, Monty. You saw the butchery visited upon Reinhold Schellenberg. Don't expect the killer's motivations to make sense to you."

"True. Well, I'd like to find out where the chaplet came from. I know of only one religious supply shop in town."

✝

F.X. McMurtry Ecclesiastical Supplies was an obscure little place tucked in between two antiques shops on Agricola Street in the north end of Halifax. Red and blue votive candles flickered in the left-hand window; a plaster statue of the Virgin Mary oversaw a collection of rosaries on the right. There was an elderly man presiding at the counter.

"Good afternoon, sir. Major day out there."

"Beautiful," I agreed. "I'm wondering whether you might have any medals of Saint Philomena."

"Not likely, but I'll check."

He pulled out a drawer and rummaged in it. "What do you know? We've still got one." He held it out to me in shaking fingers; before I could grab it, the medal fell out of his hand.

"Poor old Philly. Dropped again. Sorry, my hands are a little shaky. Doctor says there's not much to be done except I shouldn't fill my teacup to the top." He bent down behind the counter and retrieved the medal. "Here you go."

"Thanks." I looked it over but didn't gain any insight from the tiny piece of metal. "Have you had anyone else asking about Philomena in recent weeks? I'm thinking of a chaplet I saw, with red and white beads. Did you sell one of those?"

"I don't remember selling one, but we had a table of leftover items. If someone purchased a chaplet along with some other things from the table, I would not have noticed."

"I'm going to show you some pictures, if you wouldn't mind, and I'd like to know whether you remember any of these people coming into the shop."

"Okay."

I brought out photos of Sferrazza-Melchiorre, Logan, Ford, Petrucci, Mills, and Bleier, although I didn't seriously imagine the East German cop had given the British monk a chaplet of an ancient Roman saint. It was all for nought anyway; the proprietor didn't recognize any of them.

"Sorry I can't help you. This must be about the murdered theologian."

"Yes, it is. My name is Monty Collins. I'm the lawyer for the schola cantorum, and I'm doing a bit of detective work."

"Good luck!"

"I'm going to need it. You may be able to tell me something about this: apparently, Saint John Vianney was devoted to Philomena, something about a miraculous recovery?"

"The way I heard it, it was his friend, not John himself, who was cured of a hopeless disease. But John had a well-known devotion to Philomena. He called her the 'new light of the church militant.' Pope Pius x, himself canonized as a saint, named Saint John Vianney the patron of something called the Universal Archconfraternity of Saint Philomena. I won't define that for you, but you get the picture. John and Philomena were an item. Never mind that they were separated by fifteen centuries of history! Though I suppose they're together now."

I wondered then about something he had said. "What did you mean a minute ago, 'dropped again'? Did something happen to her medal, or a statue?"

"Don't you know?" I shook my head. "She got dumped from the calendar of saints."

"So that means what? She's no longer a saint?"

"No, it's not quite that bad. But she's no longer publicly commemorated in the liturgy of the church. She doesn't have a feast day anymore. She hasn't been decanonized, and people can still maintain their devotions to her. But she took a hit, no question."

"Fans of Philomena and John Vianney must have been upset."

"I suppose so, yes."

"Why was this action taken against her?"

"Not enough known about her, and some of the evidence they had didn't stand up. They just couldn't come up with sufficient historical information to keep her on the official calendar."

"I never heard that. Of course, I can't claim to know much about the saints. I saw a write-up about her in a book, though, and a holy card. There was nothing about her demotion."

"There wouldn't be, if it was a holy card. And there would be nothing in the book about it if the book was old enough."

"It was a fairly old book. Butler's *Lives*, I think it was called."

"Right. Probably the 1956 edition."

"When was she delisted?"

"Early sixties, during the time of Pope John. Just before the Vatican Council."

Chapter 15

Cessent iurgia maligna, cessent lites.
Et in medio nostri sit Christus Deus.
Simul quoque cum beatis videamus,
Glorianter vultum tuum, Christe Deus:
Gaudium quod est immensum, atque probum,
Saecula per infinita saeculorum. Amen.
Let evil impulses stop, let litigation cease,
And may Christ our God be in our midst.
And may we with the saints also,
See Thy face in glory, O Christ our God:
The joy that is immense and good,
Unto the ages through infinite ages. Amen.
— "Ubi Caritas"

Just when the Philomena revelations promised a new avenue of inquiry, I had to suspend my investigation. Temporarily. My excursion to F.X. McMurtry Ecclesiastical Supplies took place on Tuesday, January 28. Two days later, my medical malpractice trial got underway in the Nova Scotia Supreme Court. I stayed in touch with the schola cantorum in the evenings, but not for forensic purposes; I was at St. Bernadette's for choir practice. The premiere of Brennan Burke's new Mass was scheduled for February 7, three weeks before the inaugural class of the schola was to complete its studies. Brennan was, by turns, excited and apprehensive. The Mass, the "Missa Doctoris Angelici," meant the world to him as a priest and musician. Somehow, he managed to avoid infecting the choir with whatever tension he was feeling, and the rehearsals were joyful occasions. The boys were very much aware that they were breaking new ground, singing something nobody had ever sung before. I thought the Mass was exquisite. The polyphonic parts sounded as if they had been composed in the sixteenth century; the Gregorian-style "Credo" could have been over a thousand years old. The composer was still not satisfied with his "Agnus Dei," but it sounded fine to me.

†

On Friday night, February 7, after a successful week in the law courts, I resumed my role as choirboy. The St. Bernadette's Choir of Men and Boys was in place in the choir loft two hours before the premiere of the new Mass. Burke had insisted on our early arrival, on pain of eternal damnation. But now he himself was missing. The little fellows in the choir were getting restless and finding diversion in horseplay. The men were looking at their watches.

"I'll see if I can scare him up," I offered, and pounded down the stairs and across to the rectory.

Mrs. Kelly met me at the door, looking fretful. "He never came down for supper, so I finally trooped up there to get him and, well, he won't come out. Didn't even hear me enter the room, then he looked right through me. Seemed like he was looking at something over my shoulder. I turned around. But there was nothing there. Sometimes that man . . . I don't know. When he isn't scary, he's spooky! I just gave up and left. He hasn't eaten."

"I'll go up and see him."

The door was unlocked so I gave a perfunctory knock and walked in. He made no sign he was aware of my presence. He was dressed in a soutane, and was hunched over his desk, writing furiously. He finished a page, gave it a shove, let it waft to the floor, and grabbed another. It wasn't writing; it was musical notation. I asked him what he was doing; he didn't hear. A moment later he stopped his pen, raised his left hand, and shook his head, almost if he were asking someone to slow down. Then both hands came up and he conducted an unseen choir. He returned to his page and wrote some more. Without breaking stride he issued a command: "Rehearse them." He didn't say another word. He wanted me to conduct the rehearsal? I'd never conducted in my life. But somehow I knew it would be a mistake to interrupt whatever was going on. I turned and left the room, closing the door gently behind me.

"Father Burke's going to be delayed for a bit," I announced to the choir when I returned to the loft. I ignored the questioning looks. "He's asked me to handle the rehearsal, so please bear with me. Luckily we already know it so it should just sing itself."

We went over the composition at half volume, because the church was already filling up below us. Once again, I marvelled at what a lovely and evocative setting of the Mass he had produced. Then it was time to get into our black cassocks and white surplices, and wait for showtime. Nervous glances were exchanged as we dressed.

Finally, we heard someone bounding up the steps two at a time, and Burke appeared before us in the loft. He gestured for us to sit, but didn't speak. His eyes sought out certain members of the choir, guys I knew to be the best sight-readers and musicians in the group, including one superb boy soprano, and he handed them photocopied sheets of music. One had my name on it. It was music I'd never seen before. Nobody had. A new "Agnus Dei." Why was he handing it out now, minutes before the performance? I stared at it in astonishment. It was legible, but just barely. Had he actually been composing this when I was in his room? He seemed unfocused, distracted. We usually opened our performances with a prayer but he must have forgotten, because all he did was signal to us that it was time for our procession to the altar.

The church was nearly full, and I saw many of the schola people sitting in the congregation. Enrico Sferrazza-Melchiorre was in the second row in his shoulder cape; the buttons of his soutane glittered like black diamonds. Next to him sat Gino Savo in sombre dignity. On the other side of the church were Kurt Bleier and Jadwiga Silkowski. A pissed-off William Logan clambered into a seat, late, and glared at his wife. My own spouse was there with Tommy Douglas and his girlfriend, Lexie. Normie sat on the aisle, dressed in her ANGELICVM T-shirt, and grinned at me as I went by.

We shuffled into place and faced the congregation. Burke gazed above our heads as if he'd forgotten why we were there. Then he brought his eyes down to us, raised his arms, and we began his dark, austere "Kyrie Eleison," followed by the exultation of the "Gloria," the conviction of the "Credo," and the beauty of the young boys' voices in the "Sanctus" and "Benedictus." Without thinking I turned to the last part of the Mass in our binders. A quick half shake of Burke's head brought me back to the strange situation that had presented itself earlier, when he arrived with a different "Agnus Dei." He picked up his new composition and waited for the selected choristers to open their copies. He quietly sang us our notes and signalled the beginning of the piece we had never rehearsed, never seen. Father Burke — the taskmaster, the perfectionist, the man of endless nitpicking rehearsals — appeared unconcerned. And somehow, for the most part, we got it right. Like the Allegri "Miserere," it was a mix of plainchant, polyphony, and a soaring soprano line that cried to heaven for the Lamb of God, who takes away the sin of the world, to have mercy on us, to grant us peace. Brennan Burke's "Agnus Dei" was stunning, ethereal, out of this world. If any music was "the harmonious voice of creation; an echo of the invisible world," this was it. The congregation rose to its feet as the last note floated up from the altar, and Burke turned to face the applause.

I saw Maura staring at him as if she were seeing him for the first time. Normie's eyes were riveted to him; she left her seat and came forward as if in a dream, extending the forefinger of her right hand till it grazed his own. I almost expected a spark to fly between them. The applause went on and on. He just stood there. Finally, he gave a little bow. The people filed out of the church in silence; nobody chattered.

Afterwards, in the mundane world of a church basement reception, the effect had not worn off. Normie loaded a paper plate with chocolate squares and brownies but forgot to eat them. She drifted to a quiet corner and sat by herself, staring into space.

I made my way over to Enrico Sferrazza-Melchiorre who, I saw, was consoling a distraught Gino Savo. The Vatican's man had tears in his eyes. *"È come Montini, è come Montini,"* he whispered, then walked away.

"What does he mean?" I asked Enrico.

"They used to say of Montini — Pope Paul vi — that he seemed to have shutters over his eyes to mask the light within. That sometimes you would catch him with the shutters open just for an instant. And you would see a light, a luminous, radiant brilliance behind his eyes. That is what Gino saw in Brennan tonight after his Mass. I do not think Gino is the only one who saw it. Your little one was very much affected. She seems like a person open to — what would we call it? — the mystical realm."

"People say she has the sight."

"Yes, I believe she does." His eyes followed Savo as he left the gathering. "I think Gino has seen more in Father Burke than he ever thought was there, and regrets the way things have always been between them. Perhaps he will make an overture to Brennan when he settles down."

William Logan brushed by us then, Babs in tow with an apologetic look on her face.

"What did you think of that, Bill?" I asked him.

"God works His wonders through the damnedest people," he muttered, and left the room.

When I finally saw a gap in the well-wishers around Brennan, I walked over and made to shake his hand. But the evening seemed to call for more, so I went way over the top in male-to-male intimacy, and clapped him on the shoulder.

"When did you start writing that 'Agnus Dei,' Brennan?"

"I don't know," he said in a quiet voice.

"When we got back from Rome?"

"No, not that long ago."

"You didn't just write it today."

"Some time today, I think . . ." He wandered off, distracted.

"Wasn't that something, Monty?" It was Monsignor O'Flaherty, delight written all over his face.

"Yes, it was, Mike. Magnificent. And I'm glad there were so many here from the schola. A great inspiration for them, I'm sure."

"Yes, indeed. And it isn't just those in consecrated life who have been affected by Brennan's masterpiece. I saw Mr. Petrucci sitting in a daze at the back of the church. Still there, as far as I know. He wasn't moving when people were filing out. Maybe he'll sign up for another session of the schola, to see how Brennan can top what he did tonight!"

"Perhaps he will."

"Or we may hire Lou to do a bit of repair work, Monty. He was saying to me the other day we need some rewiring done; I walked into the church and saw him poking around the electrical outlets. We're not up to code, he says. Well, I knew that."

"True, but that's a problem for another day. Excuse me, would you, Mike?"

"Surely. I'll have Mrs. Driscoll pour me a nice cup of tea."

Lou Petrucci poking around at the electrical system and now alone in the church? I could not imagine that this beautiful old building would activate his fire-starting impulses, but I decided to go and see what Petrucci was doing.

I was halfway up the stairs when I met him rushing down. He grabbed me by the arm.

"Monty!"

"Evening, Lou. I was just on my way up to see —"

"I was at the back of the church. There's an outlet I'm concerned about, so I was — Anyway, I overheard Father Sferrazza-Melchiorre and Father Savo!"

"What did they say?"

"They were sitting knee to knee, having a very intense conversation in Italian."

"Which you can understand."

"Yes. I heard Savo pleading with Sferrazza-Melchiorre. 'You have responsibilities! Don't let this agony go on any longer. Do your duty, Enrico, I beg you!' All Enrico was saying was 'I don't know, I don't know.' He was really upset. Looked like he wanted to disappear. Father Savo told him: 'I will make it as easy for you as I can. I promise you.' It may be about something else, I know that. But I got the impression it was something big. They must have heard me or sensed my presence because they stopped talking and looked around. Startled, like they got caught at something. When they turned to each other again, I slipped out. I gotta get back to my wife and my sister. They're waiting at the apartment and they're gonna kill me if I'm any later."

I had to decide. I had one suspect casting suspicion on another. Should I try to detain Petrucci, or confront Sferrazza-Melchiorre? Either way, if something was going on, the answer was in the church. "Thanks, Lou. I'll see what's happening."

I headed upstairs. Was I going to find the church in flames, or Father Savo in danger of his life? I quietly pushed open the door to the church and went inside. There was nobody there. I stood for a couple of seconds, then walked on silent feet to the confession box on the left. Nobody inside. Crossed to the right. Nobody. I sprinted towards the altar and didn't hear a sound. Had Lou Petrucci led me down the garden path? I took a quick walk around the church and saw nothing amiss. But would I know what to look for, if an electrician set something up to catch fire later on? I tried to think back to the arson cases I had worked, but I couldn't focus.

Lou may have been perfectly honest with me, but he could have misinterpreted the scene between the two priests. Enrico may have been falling apart about something else altogether, and had chosen his fellow Italian as a confidant. I left the nave and returned to the reception in the hope of finding Lou and asking him to describe the confrontation again. But Lou was gone. And there was no sign of the two Italian priests. I decided to go to the rectory; if Gino was in his room, I would attempt to pry some information out of him. Not that he would reveal anything said to him under the seal of confession.

I heard an engine start up just as I reached the top of the basement stairs. There was a wrenching of gears, a screeching of tires, and the sounds of a car taking off. I launched myself out of the church. Just in time to see a pair of tail lights turning right onto Morris Street. I could make out two heads in the front seat.

I ran to the rectory and pounded on the door. No response. I pounded again. Finally, a pale-looking Mrs. Kelly peered out the window, then opened the door.

"Mrs. Kelly, did Father Savo or Father Sferrazza-Melchiorre just come in here?"

"Oh, I don't know, Mr. Collins. I've been in bed with a headache. I get them every once in a while, and I just take a pill and hit the sack. But I heard somebody making a racket. That must be what woke me up. Or maybe it was you knocking."

"A racket?"

"Stomping up and down the stairs, it sounded like. But I was so groggy — Oh, it must have been Father Burke."

"Why do you say that?"

"His car keys are gone." She pointed to the hooks where the keys were kept.

"I have to go upstairs. Excuse me, Mrs. Kelly."

I brushed past her, took the stairs two at a time, and went straight for Enrico's room. The door was wide open. Clothing was strewn across the bed, and his desk drawer had been pulled out. It was empty. It looked to me as if he had grabbed whatever he needed in clothing and had taken his papers from the desk. Papers and, I was willing to bet, his passport. I made a beeline for Gino's room. His door was closed, but it opened when I pushed. He had been a bit more methodical. But there was no travel bag in sight, and a quick check of his desk showed that it was empty.

What now? Drag Brennan from his reception? Call the police? And tell them what? That two priests had an argument, according to hearsay from one of my suspects? Should I report a stolen car? I thought I knew where Enrico was going, and I was not a believer in police chases. The last thing we needed was Father Sferrazza-Melchiorre, the Grand Prix fanatic, driving at breakneck speed to outrun the police, and driving himself and Father Savo off the road. I would call the police from the airport. Not for the first time, I wished I was more of a gadget man, the kind of guy who had a car phone. But I wasn't and I didn't. I jumped in my car, wasted a couple of precious seconds debating whether Barrington or Robie street would be quicker, decided on Barrington, and took off in delayed pursuit.

I tried to reason like a killer desperate to flee the country. If I were Enrico, what would I do with Gino Savo? I was pretty sure Savo was in the car with him. Had he forced Savo into the car? My take on the situation was that Savo went along willingly, that he was going to try until the bitter end to keep the situation under control. Get Father Sferrazza-Melchiorre back to Italy. Back inside the walls of Vatican City. If Enrico could make it that far, he might be safe forever. Canada has no extradition treaty with the Vatican.

I now knew the identity of the killer. I should not have been surprised, yet I was. I liked the flamboyant Roman-Sicilian priest. I had no idea what had driven him to murder. Was the killing of Father Schellenberg linked to the sex charges, the witness tampering, the extortion over the Vatican treasure? If so, where was the connection between all of that and the Philomena death scene? Imagination failed me when it came to the web of intrigue that marked the life of *Don* Enrico Sferrazza-Melchiorre.

I stopped trying to reason it out and concentrated on getting to the airport. It's twenty miles north of the city, and there are no shortcuts. The fugitives had a good head start, particularly if Enrico was at the wheel.

I skidded to a halt when I got to the terminal, parked the car illegally, and ran inside.

The monitors told me the next European flight was Air Canada 860, the regular night flight to London, set to depart in forty minutes. Had they begun boarding? I saw no sign of Enrico or Gino Savo. Had they gone through security already? There were queues of cranky-looking passengers at all the checkout counters. And I knew I'd have no luck asking Air Canada or airport personnel about the passenger lists. They would tell me to get lost, or they would call security. Did I know anybody out here? I tried to think. Wasn't there someone I had spoken to recently? One of the baggage handlers, when Brennan and I met Gino Savo here. She might recognize Savo. Of course, everyone in the building would know if someone fitting the description of Enrico Sferrazza-Melchiorre had just gone through security. But the baggage handler sounded like my best chance. Especially when I remembered Brennan ribbing me, saying she had been giving me the eye.

On my way to the baggage area, I ran the previous airport scene through my memory again. We had met Father Savo when he emerged from the arrival area. He was wearing a top coat and he had a garment bag, the kind used to carry suits, over his arm. A woman came by and greeted him. How did it go? "Hi, Father." No, she just said "hi there" or "hey there." Then she asked if everything was all right, or whether he had everything straightened out, or something like that. He had given her a pissed-off look, completely uncalled for, I was sure, and indicated with his arm that he had his bag with him. I had a clear picture of the woman in my mind.

I went to the baggage carousels and looked around. No sign of the woman. I peeked into the office but there was only one person inside, a man. "Excuse me. I'm looking for one of your baggage handlers, a woman, about five foot two, a little, uh, on the heavy side, hair in a ponytail."

"Oh, you mean Rhonda. She'll be back in a second. I won't tell her you said 'heavy.'" He laughed, and I thanked him.

Sure enough, she came in less than a minute later. "Hi, Rhonda.

My name is Monty Collins. I'm hoping you can help me. You were here last month, the middle of January. I was meeting a passenger, and I'm wondering if you remember him. He flew in from Rome. He's a priest, and he was wearing a black coat. Tonight I —"

"Yeah, I remember you. And I remember him, because I was surprised. I didn't know he was a priest."

"Oh, well, yes he is. I was just — What do you mean, you didn't know he was a priest? You mean you didn't notice his collar?"

"Oh, yeah, I saw it that time."

"What time? That night, you mean?"

"Yeah, I noticed it that night. But he wasn't wearing it the first time."

The first time? What on earth was she saying?

"Are you all right, um, Monty?"

"Are you saying you saw this man before mid-January?"

"Yeah, first time he came through here. He just had on regular work clothes and a ball cap, so when I saw him in a priest's outfit, I was a little surprised."

Gino Savo in a ball cap? In the Halifax airport? "When was this other time you saw the man, in work clothes?"

"Couple of months before, I guess."

"He arrived in Halifax a couple of months before the night I saw you here."

"Right."

"Then he came again dressed in black."

I must have looked brain-dead, the way I was staring at her, but my mind was fully alive and scrambling to assimilate the new information. "So tell me what you said when you saw him arrive again, as a priest."

"I was probably asking if things went smoothly this time, with his luggage. Which was stupid of me because the second time around, the time I saw you here, he had a carry-on. He kind of lifted his arm that second time to show me. Like he was saying *I'm carrying my bag because I can't rely on you guys!* The first time, he had checked his bag through, then it didn't show up on the carousel. And was he pissed! He was so uptight you'd think he had the crown jewels in there. He hung around till the bag arrived — turns out it had just fallen off the cart — but he gave us a lot of grief until he got it! So when I saw him coming through again, I remembered him all too well. But we have to be friendly to our passengers, no matter what they're like, so I asked him if everything was all right this time around."

"Rhonda, can you get me upstairs to the departure lounge?"

"I —"

"I know it's irregular. I'll take the blame. Here, I'll show you some ID. You can pat me down if you like. This is urgent, and I'm going to call the police when I get up there."

"I can't let you go by yourself, Monty." She hesitated for a moment. "But I'll take you up. Hold on a second."

She disappeared inside the baggage office for a moment, then reappeared with a walkie-talkie in her hand and some other gadget on her belt. She gestured for me to walk ahead of her.

When I entered the departure lounge, I looked to my left and saw the gate where AC 860 would be boarding. No sign of Savo or Sferrazza-Melchiorre at the gate. I looked right. There they were, at the far end of the lounge. Enrico was staring straight at me. Gino was doubled over in his seat. I noticed as I walked towards them that they were the object of curious glances from the other passengers.

A voice came over the PA announcing pre-boarding of Air Canada flight 860 to London. Enrico looked to the gate.

"This isn't going to end if he leaves the country tonight, Enrico."

"I cannot speak to you about this, Monty."

"I already know what happened. I know Gino was here in November."

Father Savo raised his tearstained face to his fellow priest. "It is too much of a burden for you, Enrico. I am sorry."

The burden of confession. That's what Savo had wanted Enrico to do in the church, hear his confession of the murder. Enrico knew instantly what was going to happen and he did not want to hear it, to have to keep the secret. Lou Petrucci said Savo had offered to make things as easy for Enrico as he could. What did Savo mean? That he would turn himself over to the authorities and bring the investigation to a resolution, rather than leave Enrico to carry the burden alone? If so, Enrico was not going to let that happen here in Canada. His instinct was to get Savo out of the country, back to the Vatican. Never mind that they'd almost certainly be intercepted before they made it;

desperation blots out logic every time.

Savo spoke again. "Montague knows the truth. They all will know. As they should."

He looked me in the eye. "Reinhold Schellenberg was a mentor to me, ever since I first met him at the Vatican Council. Thanks to his influence, I was able to prosper in my career. But now, there is talk — everyone knows, in fact — that the archbishop of Genova will soon be made a cardinal, a prince of the church. Many of those who have gone to Genova as archbishop have returned to Rome as a cardinal. And my name is on many lips as a replacement for the archbishop."

I remembered Kitty Curran telling me this in Rome. So it all came down to ambition, after all.

"As soon as I heard about my possible appointment, I called Schellenberg at the abbey. I asked if I could be assured of his patronage, his recommendation of me to the Holy Father. He said no! He knew of certain . . . difficulties I have had in my life. I have at times let my troubles interfere with my work; sometimes I have been unable to control my emotions and have lashed out at my colleagues, my staff. But I have tried to remedy this! I am under psychiatric care. I told this to Schellenberg. But he was unmoved. 'If I am asked, I cannot in good conscience recommend you, Gino. I am sorry.' This man, who had been like an older brother to me, was now going to deny me advancement in the hierarchy. I do not seek promotion only for myself, but for the good of the church. But no, he would not hear of it." Savo stopped speaking and looked at the floor.

"What do you mean by your 'personal difficulties,' Father Savo?" I asked quietly.

He raised his head and stared at me intently. "You have children, Montague. I had a little daughter. Cristina. She was the light of my life. She died. And the loss was too much for my wife, who died of grief. I, too, was nearly destroyed by it. I buried my wife and entered the priesthood."

"Do you see some connection between your loss and Saint Philomena?"

"Philomena is a wonder worker, as the Curé of Ars, John Vianney, well knew. When I was a child, one of seven in our family, my mother was dying. She was cured, miraculously, through the intercession of

Philomena, to whom the whole family prayed night after night. There was no other explanation for her recovery. The doctors said such a reversal was impossible. My daughter, Cristina, contracted the same illness, a hereditary disease, that had beset my mother. We were told there was no hope for Cristina. But she survived and grew stronger. In the loving care of Philomena. Until Pope John XXIII struck Philomena from the calendar of saints. And here is where my guilt begins. I examined the so-called evidence of Philomena's life. I found the gaps and errors others had found in her biography, in the archaeological findings. I too was filled with doubt. Could it be that my mother owed her life to one of the other saints? Should I research the saints to see who else may have interceded for her, if not Philomena? As a result of all this, I ceased praying to Philomena! By the time I came to my senses and resumed my prayers to her, it was too late. Within six months, my child was dead."

Gino Savo, a highly intelligent, capable man, had been unhinged by grief. He had never got over the death of his wife and child, and his personality had been shattered as a result. Little wonder Schellenberg had refused to lobby the pope on his behalf. I could not bear to think of losing a child, and I could not be sure I would recover if it happened to me.

"Why did you stage the death scene of Reinhold Schellenberg to reflect Philomena's death?"

He looked at me in horror, as if seeing for the first time the bloody tableau of Schellenberg's body in the church. He was silent for a few seconds, then shouted at me: "Because Schellenberg was one of the group who told Pope John that Philomena should be removed from the calendar! I found this out years ago. I brought it up to Schellenberg. He dismissed what I had to say. I sent him an anonymous letter about it, and he discerned that it was from me. He told me my concern with the saint was an unhealthy obsession. But no, there is nothing unhealthy about devotion to the saints! I know he would have used this against me in my campaign to be named archbishop of Genova. When word reached me that Schellenberg was coming here, I began to plot his death. At that moment I fell into mortal sin." Savo began to tremble.

I heard the call for regular boarding of the overseas flight.

Passengers gathered their things and headed for the gate. Some straggled behind, apparently hoping to witness a little more of the drama.

Savo did not seem to be aware of them. He took a deep breath, then spoke rapidly. "I was in France when I heard that Schellenberg was coming here. That gave me only a few days, not sufficient time to obtain false documents or whatever else a professional assassin would do. I thought about staging the death scene of Saint Philomena. I found the axe I intended to use as the weapon. Naturally, I did not know where to locate a scourge, the whip she holds in her pictures. But I remembered something else. Children come to Ars from time to time, to pay homage to Saint John Vianney. They leave little gifts and cards. I recalled seeing valentine cards there. They stayed in my mind because they showed hearts pierced with arrows, and arrows are a symbol of the tortures that befell Philomena. There is an irony here as well: it was on February 14, Valentine's Day, 1961, that her dignity was taken from her by the church. I stole some of the cards and packed them in a duffle bag with the axe. I flew here from Paris. The baggage people could not find the duffle bag when I landed here. I was upset, and drew attention to myself when in fact my goal was to slip in and out of the country unnoticed. We lose our ability to function intelligently when we are under extreme stress."

I remembered Rhonda then and turned to look at her. She stood without moving, her eyes fixed on Gino Savo.

"I rented a car here at the airport, purchased a map, and found my way to a hotel across the harbour in . . . Dartmouth? Is that what it's called? Yes. I went into the Anchor bar and found the little anchor stick and added it to the heart-and-arrow cards. I made calls to the schola and learned something of the schedule. The feast day of Saint Cecilia would set the investigators' minds in the wrong direction, giving me time to escape, so I planned my attack for that day.

"I telephoned Schellenberg in his room at the rectory to lure him to the church. I did not identify myself, but I got the impression he may have recognized my voice. I told him I required his assistance for a personal crisis and I suggested we say Mass together at the old church where we would not be disturbed. I drove to Stella Maris Church in the rental car. I went into the church. I put on gloves and a raincoat even though it was a bright sunny day. Father Schellenberg greeted me with his arms open wide. I raised my axe and killed him. I put the anchor and the arrows on his body. Then I cleaned myself at a basin at the back of the church, cleaned the floor, cleaned the weapon, put it in the duffle bag, and drove away. I drove out to the ocean and sat with the car heater on until all my clothing was dry where I had washed away the blood. I returned to my hotel. Only then, with all the actions completed, could I contemplate the evil of my deed. I was sick in body and in soul. That night I flew back to Paris, discarded the murder weapon, then went on to Ars."

I asked Savo: "Why on earth did you come back here after you had escaped detection?"

"The papal nuncio to this country, Arturo Del Vecchio, called me in Ars the day following the murder. I had not yet arrived there, of course, but I received his message when I got back. I returned his call with fear in my heart. He demanded that I come here, that I investigate and make sure nothing would rebound on the Holy See. I was near panic. I would have to revisit the scene of my crime, monitor the situation like a normal bureaucrat, protect the church and protect myself. And of course I was exhausted from travel and was barely able to think. But then Brother Robin was arrested. I was able to convince Del Vecchio there was no need for me to come. A few weeks later, he was not satisfied of the Englishman's guilt, and demanded yet again that I travel here and handle the crisis for him."

"Brother Robin —"

"I composed in my mind the message I intended to send from the Vatican, asserting his innocence. Now all I can hope for is the opportunity to thank him for his sacrifice. Whether he knew it was for me, I do not yet know. But I am undeserving of his kindness, the more so as I did nothing to relieve him of the burden he took on. I regret with all my heart what I have done."

It was a matter for the police after that. I called them from the departure lounge, and waited with the two priests in silence until they arrived in force. Father Savo put up no resistance when they arrested him for the murder of Reinhold Schellenberg, and took him into custody.

†

Enrico Sferrazza-Melchiorre and I went through some hoops to get the two illegally parked cars back — my car and Brennan Burke's. We stood for a few minutes outside the airport before driving into the city.

"Enrico, you must have been stunned to hear of Father Savo's guilt."

"Oh, yes."

"How come you didn't want us to know you test-drove a car on the day of the murder?"

"Having a car, it would not look good for me. Easy to get to the church, easy to get away. Though I must say it was not a car to pass unnoticed anywhere! A car for speed but not a car for secrecy and stealth."

"What was it?"

"An Aston Martin V8 Vantage. It was called Britain's first supercar when it was produced in 1977. Very powerful. It was a 1987 model they had."

"Where did you take it?"

"Out on the highway."

"All you had to do was tell us where you really went in the car and we could have verified it."

"I could not get her to verify it."

"Who?"

"The woman I was with."

"Why couldn't you get her to stick up for you?"

"I could not find her again."

"Why not?"

"She was a prostitute, working on one of your streets. Agricola Street? I took her for a ride."

"I see."

"No, you do not. I did not have relations with her. I cruised by, she was on the corner, she admired the car. I asked her if she wanted to go for a very fast ride on the highway. She said yes. And we went. We particularly enjoyed the curving roads that run beside the ocean. The only laws I broke that day, Monty, were the speed limits!"

"Weren't you worried that you were a suspect in the murder?"

Shoulders, hands, lips, and eyebrows rose in an elaborate shrug. *"Sono innocente!"*

It was late but I headed straight for St. Bernadette's. Nobody would be sleeping on a night like this. I had telephoned Moody Walker after the police came for Savo; Moody said he would report to Monsignor O'Flaherty in person. When I got to the rectory, Mike was in the kitchen with Mrs. Kelly and some of the schola people, including Fred Mills, William and Babs Logan, and Kurt Bleier. Teacups, whiskey glasses, and beer steins were raised and lowered as they discussed the murder and its denouement. I recounted the scene at the airport. Just as I wrapped up my story, we heard a car outside, then a knock at the back door. It was Robin Gadkin-Falkes, dropped off by his lawyer, Saul Green.

One by one, our previous suspects took me aside and had their say. It was almost like confession.

†

"Robin, you're a free man."

"Montague. Yes, I am. Would you like to know where I really was the day of the murder? One of the drawbacks of confessing up front is that nobody asks for your alibi, and I would have adored giving mine."

"Okay, let's hear it."

"I was rehearsing with the local Gilbert and Sullivan society. We were going to put on a performance of *The Mikado* just around the time the schola course was to wind up. I so wished someone would ask, so I could say I was playing Pooh-Bah at the time!"

"That I would love to have seen." We were quiet for a few moments, then, more seriously, I asked him: "Robin, how far were you prepared to go with this?"

"I would like to think I had the stuff that would have seen me through to the end. But you and I both know I didn't have it in me. I confessed, I un-confessed, I was guilty, I was not guilty. I was, and am, a bloody fool." He was quiet for a few seconds. "I knew Gino Savo had lost his daughter, and then his wife. I know what grief can do to a person. My heart went out to him."

"When did you learn of Savo's loss? Did you know him before?"

"This is ironic indeed: I met him during the Second Vatican Council! I doubt he would remember. I was there in the role of Vatican II correspondent for the *English Catholic*, covering the final session in 1965. I saw Gino Savo. He was a seminarian, and was attending a few of the sessions of the Council. He had no official role there; I assume he was listening in for reasons of curiosity. Anyway, I introduced myself to the group of seminarians and tried to interview them. I didn't get much out of them, as I recall. I was not a very imposing presence as a foreign correspondent, young and unsure as I was. But at one point I overheard Gino telling another man about the death of his wife and daughter a few years earlier. And of the miraculous cure of his mother, which he attributed to the intercession of Saint Philomena. As you might imagine, given my own bereavement, I was all ears. I did not hear Gino mention Schellenberg, or even Pope John, by name, but it was clear that he was angry with the powers-that-were, and that this had something to do with the loss of his family.

"My natural sympathy with the bereaved is multiplied sevenfold when it comes to Gino. I heard something about him years ago that made me love and admire the man. I once attended a retreat on the subject of redemption. One of the speakers was a man, Franchi, who had in the past been caught stealing money from the Vatican, where he worked as a low-level functionary. He claimed he had stolen the money to support a crippled child. Turns out his son had been killed in a car wreck at the age of two. Franchi had been driving, and it was his negligence that caused the accident. Anyway, it was Gino Savo who found the man stealing; it was Gino to whom Franchi poured out the sob story about the disabled son; it was Gino who heard the real story later on. And forgave him. Kept him on staff. What Gino did for the least of his brethren, so the least of his brethren — I, Robin Gadkin-Falkes — tried to do in turn for Gino Savo."

"How did you know for sure that it was Savo who killed Schellenberg?"

"Reinhold Schellenberg and I chatted a couple of times after we met here, fellow Benedictines and all that. I didn't light into him about his actions during the Second Vatican Council — that was much easier to do on paper than in person! He was a very pleasant chap, actually. I happened to see him just after he received the phone call that led to the cancellation of his lecture and of course led him to his death. He was puzzled and he asked me if I knew who Gino Savo was. I said yes. He said he thought he recognized Savo's voice on the telephone, even though the caller did not give his name. Father Schellenberg cautioned me not to say anything because Savo, or whoever, was in the depths of a personal crisis and obviously wanted the matter kept confidential. Schellenberg still had his lecture notes in his hand, for the talk he was supposed to give. I asked to read them, and he gave them to me. These were the notes I burned — incompletely! — when I decided to make myself look guilty.

"As soon as I saw Schellenberg's body at vespers I thought of the death of Saint Philomena. This was confirmed when I caught sight of the anchor stick and the valentine arrows. I had researched Philomena way back when I first heard of Gino's plight; I had considered writing an article, but my editor wasn't interested. I knew it was Gino."

"When did he slip you the Philomena chaplet with the note?"

Robin looked at me with some amusement. "My dear Montague. It was I who wrote the note, and affixed it to the Philomena chaplet. I went out the day after the murder and found a chaplet among some other bargain items in a shop."

Hearing this, I remembered I had not shown Robin's photo to the shop owner; there was no need to, I thought. Just one of the many things I had missed.

Robin continued his story: "I helped myself to a couple of sheets of Father Sferrazza-Melchiorre's writing paper and wrote the note saying let me grieve with you. It was meant for Gino. I was careful to avoid leaving my fingerprints on it. I had not yet hatched the plan to pose as the guilty man, you see. Then Gino slipped away, escaped to Europe, before I could find him. So I kept the chaplet. It was nowhere in sight when the police received an anonymous call from a phone booth — so very *Boys' Own Adventure* — and came for me. I must have put on a fairly convincing Canadian accent. Anyway, I realized later that the housekeeper had taken some of my clothes to be laundered. The chaplet was in the pocket of a pair of my trousers."

So that was why Mrs. Kelly had been so mysterious; she had inadvertently removed evidence, then replaced it after the fact.

"Robin, if you acted out of sympathy with Savo's grief, why the big long rant about the changes to the Mass after Vatican II?"

"Why not? I meant every word of it. It was my one and only chance to make a speech from the dock, denouncing the wreckage caused by the Second Vatican Council!"

✝

Next I spoke to William and Babs Logan.

"So you really were shopping the day of the murder, Bill."

"Shopping?" Babs queried. "No, we weren't shopping."

"Never mind, Babs. They know we didn't ice Schellenberg, so who cares what we were doing?"

"But we did pretty darn well that day, Bill. Do you ever go to flea markets, Monty?"

"Uh, well —"

"Of course he doesn't. He's a lawyer. The man can afford to buy retail."

"I may not hit the flea markets, but we sometimes go to a chain of second-hand clothing stores called Frenchy's where you can get —"

"Save it, Montague. He's just trying to spare our feelings, Babs, because we're so pathetic. We scoured the flea markets the weekend we arrived here, and went around to the second-hand shops to sell what we could. The home sales racket isn't paying the bills for us. We needed a bit of extra cash. Yeah, I know. Losers. If I'd stayed on as a priest, I'd at least have room and board!"

"I wasn't thinking that."

"You're not a bad guy, Monty. And I'm glad you know I'm not a killer. I still have all the other problems in my life to deal with, but at least I'm not going to fry for murder."

"We don't fry people in this country, Bill."

"I'll keep that in mind if anybody really cheeses me off before I leave town!"

✝

"Fred, where were you at the time of the murder? We know you

295

weren't really at the Atlantic School of Theology."

"Tell me this first, Monty. Where did Jan Ford tell you she was that afternoon?"

"That's easy. She refused point blank to say where she was. Told us she didn't need an alibi, and we could all get lost."

"She was with me."

I stared at him in astonishment, and he laughed. "Yeah, I know. Fred Mills with a woman; it doesn't compute. She came along with me for support."

"Came along where?"

"Monty, I was seeing a shrink!"

"Oh?"

"Yes. Well, not a shrink exactly, but a psychologist. I have an anxiety disorder. A phobia. And it flared up when I arrived in Halifax."

"Okay . . ."

"You're going to laugh. In fact, I don't know who is likely to find it funnier: the people here or the folks back home. In Kansas."

"You've got me curious, Fred."

"Have you ever heard of thalassophobia?"

"Thalasso —"

"Fear of the sea! I've had a morbid fear of the ocean since childhood. Childhood in Kansas. About as far away from the sea as you can get. It really got out of hand when I came to Halifax, teetering on the brink of the Atlantic Ocean! St. Bernadette's is about a sixty-second walk from the harbour. I started getting worked up as soon as I mailed my application to the schola. I even called Brennan to ask — casually, I thought — exactly where the schola was located. But I guess I wasn't quite smooth enough, because he replied: 'We're on a houseboat, Freddy. And I can't remember the last time the waves crashed over the top of us. Jazes,' he goes, 'gotta bail!' So he was no help. He doesn't take it seriously, tries to jolly me out of it."

"And so you didn't want him to know you were seeing a psychologist the afternoon of the murder."

"Exactly. I should seek professional help again, to find out why I gave a false alibi in a murder investigation rather than risk ridicule from my old professor! That speaks volumes about my character. Sad, I know."

"Oh, we all have things we want to keep private. And look at it this way: you knew you were innocent of the murder, so you figured your real destination was nobody's business."

"Right. The irony is that it was fear of going to Stella Maris Church — Star of the Sea Church, overlooking the water — that set me off. I even went up near it the day before, to see if I could handle it — that's when your witness saw me at Seaview Park. Then I had to listen to Monsignor O'Flaherty's enthusiastic promotion of the bus trip to Peggy's Cove. How huge the surf is there, how people have been swept off the rocks by rogue waves, the whole bit. Hearing that, and knowing we were going to Stella Maris after dark, was enough to propel me into Debbie Schwartz's office for treatment. Wonderful woman. My psychologist in Kansas looked her up and smoothed the waters for me, so to speak, before I got on the plane to come here."

"Yes, I know Debbie. I frequently hire her to assist my clients. Well, nobody has to know."

"Oh, hell, I'm a big boy now. I'll own up to it, even if Brennan won't be as sympathetic as Jan Ford. She may be guilty of atrocious music, but she was a great help to me when she noted my symptoms that Friday and offered to accompany me to Doctor Schwartz's office."

"Well, there you go. If we find out anything else happened that afternoon, you and Jan are off the hook."

✝

When it was Kurt Bleier's turn he leaned towards me and spoke intently. "On the afternoon of the murder, I was out looking for Reinhold Schellenberg. I was concerned — justifiably so — when he suddenly cancelled his lecture. Reinhold was a priest at St. Sebastian Cathedral in Magdeburg, in the German Democratic Republic."

"East Germany."

"Yes. You may not believe me, but I had great respect for him and for many other churchmen. And I was not alone in that. During the war, the second war, many priests were imprisoned by the Nazi regime. They sat in prison with other enemies of the state, including members of the Communist Party and other socialists. And so it was that my father, Max, came to know Reinhold's uncle, who was also a priest. Johann Schellenberg. An honourable and courageous man, he took the place of another inmate in the prison and let himself be abused by the authorities, so the other man would be spared."

I recalled the story as told to us by Greta Schliemann. Father Johann Schellenberg had confessed to an escape attempt in order to protect the guilty party. Kurt Bleier's father had demanded his release.

"My father admired him greatly. Whether he ever told him so, I could not say. But they respected one another, and met often over a chessboard. The chessboard you saw here at the schola. Yes, you were right: it was my father's, and I brought it here. The notes concealed in it were threats that I knew about through a contact in Reinhold Schellenberg's abbey. I copied them out to show him. But I am getting ahead of myself.

"When I was growing up in Germany after the war, my father spoke to me often about Johann Schellenberg, whom he admired more than any other man he had ever met. Oh, he thought Johann was in error, philosophically and politically. But the Schellenberg name was revered in our home. When I joined the *Volkspolizei*, I became aware of the nephew, Reinhold. Another man who, although suffering under the delusions of religion, was a man of honour. He was in fact a principled opponent of our regime. There were many things about our regime I myself did not agree with, Montague, but I always hoped the revolution would purge itself of those errors in years to come. I still believe it would have, but we ran out of time. For now, anyway.

"In October 1971 the Soviet leader, Leonid Brezhnev, made a visit to Berlin. There was a young man, a seminarian named Lukas Vogel. He was a student and friend of Reinhold Schellenberg, and he was a dissident. We received information that Vogel was planning to disrupt the state visit. I travelled to Magdeburg to speak to Schellenberg. We had never met before. I did not speak about my father and his uncle at that time. I told him I knew of the planned protest, and I urged him to take Vogel in hand and make sure it did not happen. Schellenberg claimed he knew nothing about the demonstration, did not know where the seminarian was, and had nothing to tell the *Volkspolizei*. I warned him. If he could not guarantee the young man would drop his plans to disrupt the visit, I would have to inform the security apparatus. He would not agree. But I heard from sources that he did in fact try to warn Vogel and his group away from the visit. Obviously, they did not heed his advice.

"Reinhold Schellenberg came to the event himself. The Stasi were on the lookout for Vogel. They found him and closed in on him, but he broke away and ran towards the stage where Brezhnev was speaking. Schellenberg emerged from the crowd and moved to block Vogel. He threw himself in front of the young man just as the Stasi drew their weapons and fired. Schellenberg was hit and went down. He was taken into custody along with Vogel and two others. Schellenberg was treated for a bullet wound in his arm. All four were interrogated. Reinhold was made of the same stuff as his uncle, Johann. I admired him, but I let him down. If I had been more efficient, the whole thing could have been prevented.

"I have told you about the threats against him in later years. He cancelled a journey to the United States because of a threat years ago. But he was not out of danger. This is the first trip he ever made to North America. When I heard of it, I arranged for my wife to sign up for the schola cantorum. She is very musical, and agreed to the plan. I had notes of the threats — copies I wrote out — in the compartment of the chessboard, and I showed them to Reinhold. For the first time, I told him of my father and his uncle in the camp. We became friendly in the days before his death. I urged him to be careful. I asked him about his movements around the city here. He shrugged off my concerns. When he suddenly cancelled his lecture that Friday afternoon, I was worried. I tried to find him. But it was my failure. Again."

$$\dagger$$

There was somebody missing from the gathering. "Where's Brennan?" I asked Mike O'Flaherty when I finished speaking with Kurt Bleier.

Glances were exchanged, then Mike said: "He doesn't know any of this yet."

"What? Where is he?"

"Come with me."

He reached for a set of keys, went outside, and crossed to the church. I followed. Mike put his fingers to his lips for quiet, then worked some heavy-duty locks to get into the nave. Was Burke in the church, down on his knees giving thanks to God for letting him express the inexpressible in his music? Was he prostrate before the Blessed Sacrament, the way I had seen him in Rome? We tiptoed in. The church was lit by the warm glow of candlelight. Burke was sitting in one of the pews, in his Roman collar and an ancient leather jacket. His head was resting on the back of the pew, his eyes were closed, his left arm was flung out to the side. Sleeping in heavenly peace. He looked about eleven years old. Curled up next to him, holding his right hand, was my daughter Normie. She too was sound asleep, and someone had covered her with a blanket.

"Your wife thought she'd be all right here," Mike whispered.

I looked at her for a long moment. "Yes, she will."

We left them, and Mike locked up.

"You know, Mike, she's investigating him to see if he's an angel! I suspect tonight tipped the scales in his favour. What are you going to say if she asks you?"

He smiled. "'Christ Jesus came into the world to save sinners, and I am the foremost of sinners.' That was either Brennan's slurred speech to the Romans or Saint Paul's first letter to Timothy. I expect our friend will go and sin no more!"

"Do you think so?"

"I know so. He's a new man, Monty. A new man."

Acknowledgements

I would like to thank the following people for their kind assistance: Dr. John Macpherson, Rhea McGarva, Joan Butcher, and Edna Barker. All characters and plots in the story are fictional, as are some of the locations. Other places are real. Any liberties taken in the interests of fiction, or any errors committed, are mine alone.

The following books and publications proved invaluable in the writing of *Cecilian Vespers*:

Benedict XVI. *Summorum Pontificum.* Apostolic letter issued *motu proprio data*, on the use of the Roman liturgy prior to the reform of 1970. July 7, 2007

Chesteron, G.K. *St. Thomas Aquinas: "The Dumb Ox."* New York: Image Books/Doubleday, 1956 (first published, 1933)

Day, Thomas. *Why Catholics Can't Sing: The Culture of Catholicism and the Triumph of Bad Taste.* New York: Crossroad, 1990

Maritain, Jacques. *St. Thomas Aquinas.* New York: Meridian Books, Inc., 1958 (first published, 1931)

Martin, Malachi. *Hostage to the Devil.* San Francisco: HarperSanFrancisco, 1992. This is the source of the passage about the "Montini experience", to which I refer in the last chapter.

Reese, Thomas J., SJ. *Inside the Vatican.* Cambridge: Harvard University Press, 1998

Rose, Michael S. *Ugly as Sin: Why They Changed Our Churches from*

Sacred Places to Meeting Spaces – and How We Can Change Them Back Again. Manchester: Sophia Institute Press, 2001

Saint Thomas Aquinas. *Summa Theologiae*

Second Vatican Council. *Constitution on the Sacred Liturgy, Sacrosanctum Concilium,* 1963

Walsh, James J. *The Thirteenth: the Greatest of Centuries.* New York: Catholic Summer School Press, 1924 (first published, 1907). This is the source of the comments on the "Great Latin Hymns" in the first chapter. The quotation on the "Dies Irae" is from Prof. George Saintsbury, cited in Walsh at page 197.

Wiltgen, Rev. Ralph M., S.V.D. *The Rhine Flows Into The Tiber: The Unknown Council.* New York: Hawthorn Books, Inc., 1967

I am grateful for permission to reprint lyrics from the following:

"Hallelujah"
Written by Leonard Cohen
Published by Sony/ATV Music Publishing
1670 Bayview Avenue, Suite 408, Toronto, ON, M4G 3C2
All rights reserved. Used by Permission.

Here's a sneak peek at Anne Emery's
next Collins-Burke mystery

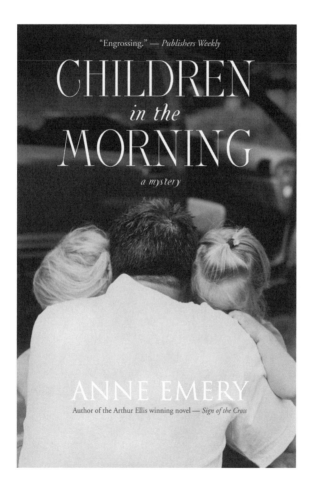

"Engrossing." — *Publishers Weekly*

CHILDREN
in the
MORNING
a mystery

ANNE EMERY
Author of the Arthur Ellis winning novel — *Sign of the Cross*

Chapter 1

(Normie)

You should know right from the beginning that I am not bragging. I was brought up better than that, even though I am the child of a broken home. That's another thing you should know. BUT — and it's a big but — (I'm allowed to say "big but" like this but not "big butt" in a mean voice when it might be heard by a person with a big butt, and hurt their feelings) — but, about my broken home, Mummy says people don't say that anymore. Anyway, even if they do, it doesn't bother me. It kinda bothers my brother Tommy Douglas even though he's a boy, and a lot of times boys pretend they're tough. Tommy never says, but I know. We have another brother, Dominic, but he's a little baby so he's too young to know anything. However, the whole thing is not that bad. That's probably because we don't have the kind of dad who took off and didn't care and didn't pay us any alimony. When you've been around school as long as I have — I'm in grade four — you know kids who have fathers like that. But not my dad. We spend a lot of days with him, not just with my mum.

And they both love us. They are in their forties but are both still spry and sharp as a tack. It's stupid the way they don't just move back into the same house together but, aside from that, they are great people and I love them very much.

Mum is Maura MacNeil. People say she has a tongue on her that could skin a cat. She is always very good to me and never skins me. But if I do something bad, she doesn't have to stop and think about what to say; she has words ready to go. She teaches at the law school here in Halifax. My dad is Monty Collins. He is really sweet and he has a blues band. I always ask him to sing and play the song "Stray Cat Strut" and he always does. It's my favourite song; I get to do the "meow." He is also a lawyer and he makes faces about his clients. They're bad but he has to pretend they're good when he's in front of the judge so the judge won't send them down the river and throw away the key. Or the paddle, or whatever it is. It means jail.

I forgot to tell you my name. It's Normie. *What?* I can hear you saying. It's really Norma but you won't see that word again in these pages. Well, except once more, right here, because I have to explain that it comes from an opera called *Norma*. Mum and Dad are opera fans and they named me after this one, then realized far too late that it was an old lady's name (even though the N-person in the opera was not old, but never mind). So they started calling me Normie instead.

I am really good in math and English, and I know so many words that my teacher has got me working with the *grade seven* book called *Words Are Important*, which was published way back in 1955 when everybody learned harder words in school than they do these days. And I have musical talent but do not apply myself, according to my music teacher. I am really bad at social studies but that's because I don't care about the tundra up north, or the Family Compact, whoever they are. But it was interesting to hear that we burned down the White House when we had a war with the Americans back in 1812. Tommy says we kicked their butts (he said it, not me). You never think of Canadians acting like that.

Anyway, I must get on with my story. As I said, I'm not bragging and I don't mean about the math and English. I mean I'm not bragging about what I can see and other people can't. Because it's a gift and I did nothing to earn it. And also because it's all there for other people to see, but they are just not awake (yet) to these "experiences" or "visions." I'm not sure what to call them. They say about me: "She has the sight." Or: "She has second sight, just like old Morag." Old Morag is my great-grandmother. Mum's mother's mother. She's from Scotland. And she is really old; it's not just people calling her that. She must be eighty-five or something. But there are no flies on her, everyone says. People find her spooky, but I understand her.

I am looking at my diary, which says *Personal and Private!* on the cover. I hide it in a box under my bed. Nobody crawls under there to spy on my stuff. The diary is where I kept all my notes, day after day, about this story. I am taking the most important parts of it and writing them down on wide-ruled paper, using a Dixon Ticonderoga 2/HB pencil, a dictionary, and a thesaurus. I am asking Mummy about ways to say (write) certain things, but I'm not telling her what I am writing. All the information you will read here is my own.

✝

It all started in the waiting room of my dad's office. He came and got me from school at three thirty on the day I'm talking about, Thursday, February 13, 1992. He still had work to do, so he took me to the office. I sat there with a kids' magazine, which was too young for me really, and the bowl of candies Darlene keeps behind the reception desk. There were two other kids there around the same age as me, a girl and a boy. They looked sad and scared about something, so I tried to cheer them up. They were staring at the candies, and I shared them. They said thanks. Since Daddy was taking such a long time, I decided to work on my poster.

I go to a choir school. It goes from grade four to grade eight. Me and my best friend, Kim, are in grade four so this is our first year at the school. Kim is taller than me and has long blond braids and no glasses. We wear a uniform that's a dark plaid kilt, white shirt, and bright red sweater. The boys don't wear a kilt, but they could, because there are a lot of Scottish people around here and they would think it's normal. But the boys wear dark blue pants.

Anyway, I was making a poster for our new program to give free music lessons to kids in the afternoons when regular classes are

3

finished. One of the teachers came up with the name "Tunes for Tots" ("tots" means little kids), but Father Burke put his foot down and said no. He said that name was too "twee." Another teacher said we should call it "Four-Four Time," and he went along with that. Four-Four Time is a good name because we have it four days a week, Monday to Thursday, and it starts at four o'clock. It goes for an hour and a half. So, four days at four o'clock. "Common time" in music is four beats to a measure and the quarter note has one beat; a whole bunch of songs are written in that time, and it's called four-four time. I didn't go to it that day, but I usually went. Anyway, about the program. The teachers at the choir school take turns staying after school for it, and we, the students at St. Bernadette's, can go as often as we want and help the kids who come from other schools for free music lessons. We also provide healthy snacks. It is really to help poor kids, but nobody would say that to them, because it wouldn't be polite.

I mentioned Father Burke. He runs the school, and he also runs a choir school for grown-ups, including priests and nuns; it's called the Schola Cantorum Sancta Bernadetta. Father Burke's first name is Brennan and he was born in Ireland, which you can tell from the way he talks. People think he is stern, aloof, and haughty. The thesaurus also says "lordly," which would be true if it means he works for the Lord but he doesn't think he's the Lord himself, so I'll leave that one out. But he's not. Or at least, deep down, he's not. He can seem that way to people who don't know him. But I do, and he is very kind, especially to children.

Anyway, I got out my paper and markers, and got down on my hands and knees in Daddy's reception room to work on the poster.

"What's that?" the little girl asked.

"Oh, it's a thing they started at my school. They're giving free music lessons to kids, plus treats, books, stuff like that."

"Can anybody come to it?"

"Yeah! You guys should come!"

"What school is it?"

"St. Bernadette's Choir School, on Byrne Street. Do you want to come?"

"Maybe. It sounds good."

"What's your name?"

"I'm Jenny and that's my brother, Laurence."

Jenny had wavy brown hair down to her shoulders, and she had it pulled over to the side of her forehead with a white barrette shaped like a kitty-cat. Laurence had short, dark brown hair and was bigger than Jenny.

"I'll write your names down on the back of the poster, in pencil, so I can tell Father Burke you're coming." I asked her how to spell their names and I printed "Jenny" and "Laurence" on the paper. "What's your last name?"

"Delaney."

"I know how to spell that," I told them. "I saw that name somewhere."

They looked at each other but didn't say anything. I wrote it down.

Then Daddy came out, and a woman came out with him and took the kids with her.

Later on, I found out why they looked sad and scared. They had a family tragedy!

(Monty)

I was in the courtroom when they came for Beau Delaney. I was early for my own court appearance, and walked in during Delaney's summation on behalf of his client.

"And yet again, My Lord, we witness the spectacle of the state's jack-booted goons trampling the rights of an innocent, law-respecting, own-business-minding citizen of this province. A man to all appearances secure in his home. I'm sure Your Lordship holds dear, as do I, the dictum of the great English jurist, Sir Edward Coke, that a man's home is his castle. That a man should be safe and secure in that castle, however humble an abode it might be. That he should not have to quiver and quake, tremble and twitch lest he hear that most fearsome of sounds, the knock on the door in the dead of night, perpetrated by the rednecks in red serge, poster boys for a nation that has sold its soul for peace, order, and good government, Renfrews of the Mounted, goose-stepping into history over the bodies of those whose rights they are sworn to uphold."

It was vintage Delaney. The mild-looking, bespectacled Mountie who had led the raid on Delaney's client's trailer rolled his eyes as the diatribe went on. He'd heard it all before. Then the Mountie's attention was drawn to something happening at the back of the courtroom. I followed his glance and saw two Halifax police officers coming in the door, looking tense. They sat in the back row, and leaned forward as if ready to spring. Justice MacIntosh made quick work of Delaney's argument that the search of his client's property was illegal, and found the man guilty of cultivating marijuana contrary to Section 6 of the Narcotic Control Act. Sentencing would proceed at a later date. Delaney gave his client a "you win some, you lose some" shrug, stood, and packed up his papers. The two Halifax cops got up and went out the door.

Beau Delaney was the best-known criminal defence lawyer in Nova Scotia. He was probably the only lawyer whose name was a household word across the province. A giant of a man at six feet, five inches in height, with a long mane of wavy salt-and-pepper hair brushed back from his forehead, he wore glasses with heavy black frames, the kind you often saw on Hollywood movie moguls. Delaney was known for his flamboyant manner and courtroom theatrics; he was the object of envy and barroom bullshit. He greeted me after he snapped the locks of his enormous briefcase, and we left the courtroom together.

The minute the courtroom door closed behind us, the cops moved in.

"Beau Delaney?"

"Yes?"

"You are under arrest for the murder of Peggy Laing Delaney." His wife of nearly twenty years.

†

I heard from Delaney that night. He asked me to represent him on the murder charges, and I arranged to see him at the Halifax County Correctional Centre the following day. So we sat down and faced each other across the table in a lawyer–client meeting room at the Correc. Delaney looked as if he had been there a month.

"What's the story, Beau?"

"I wasn't there."

"You weren't home when Peggy died?"

"No."

"Did you give a statement to the police?"

"I told them I wasn't there. Period."

He shouldn't have said even that much.

"Why do the police think you were home?"

"Because it fits with their theory that I killed her!"

"They must think they have evidence that you were at the house."

"I was out of town, and I came home —"

"— Just after your wife fell down the stairs."

"Save your breath, Montague. I'm a professional so I'm not going to say what Joe Average Client would say: *If you don't believe me, I'm getting another lawyer.* You and I are grown-ups. We're lawyers. Whether you believe me or not, I wasn't there. That's my defence. Take it to trial and get an acquittal. Now I'm tired, having been kept awake by a near riot in this place last night, so let's talk bail."

That could wait.

"Where were you the night she died?"

"I was in Annapolis Royal for a three-day trial. I drove home rather than stay another night when it was over. Didn't bother to call Peg; I just got in the car and headed home."

"Who can we get to say you weren't there?"

"I'm not sure. The kids were all in bed."

"How do you know?"

"Because if they were up, they'd have been looking for their mother and probably would have found her. But they didn't. I did. They were asleep when I got home."

"Where do you park your car? You have a garage, right?"

"Yeah, but we never park in it. It's full of junk."

"So you leave your cars in the driveway."

"Yeah."

"The Crown must have somebody who claims you were there."

"Well, it will be your job to find out, and discredit them."

"Let's hope the Crown doesn't have a pile of will-say statements from your neighbours stating they looked out and saw your car there just before they sat down to watch the evening game shows."

"Won't happen. You'll be interested to hear that the medical examiner did not conclude Peggy was murdered. He said the facts were consistent with an accident or an assault; it was impossible to make a conclusive finding either way. The Crown couldn't hope to prove murder beyond a reasonable doubt with that, so they shopped around for a second opinion. They got lucky with Dr. Heath MacLeod. Ever heard of him?" I shook my head. "He's a new pathologist in town. It's clear he's got a bright future ahead of him as a prosecutor's expert. In his opinion, Peggy was struck on the head with a large rock, and then fell — or more likely was carried by me and placed at the bottom of the stairs."

"A rock? In the house?"

"Yeah, unfortunately, we did have some big rocks in the house. One of our neighbours had a stone retaining wall. He replaced it with a new brick one, and our kids asked if they could have the old stones to build a castle. He said sure. The kids started their building in the backyard. They managed to lay half a dozen stones before a freezing rain storm blew up. End of the season for outdoor construction. They began hauling the rocks inside, with a view to building their castle in the basement. Peggy and I told them to move them out of the way, and wait for spring to do it outdoors. But they never got them all out of there, so some rocks were still on the basement floor when Peggy fell."

"They were piled at the foot of the stairs?"

"No, off to the side a bit. But the way she fell, she hit her head on them."

"And the Crown sees this how?"

"They say I picked up one of the rocks, bashed Peggy's head in with it, then carried her down the stairs. She was found on the basement floor and her injuries were consistent with a fall, so, since the Crown can't get around that fact, they have to say I went down there, picked a rock from the pile, and brought it back to the top of the stairs, where I hit her with it. Then, since the rock was under her head, they say I panicked and arranged her body so her head was lying on the rock that fractured her skull. Panicky but precise is what I'm alleged to have been. I'm sure they'll leave open the alternative theory that I pushed her down with such force that she fractured her skull."

"That's it? That's the Crown's case as you see it?"

"The Crown doesn't have a case."

"What do you say happened?"

"She obviously fell down the stairs."

"Backwards."

"Apparently so."

"How do you suppose that came about?"

"I don't know. I wasn't there."

"You must have given it some thought."

"Of course I have!"

I was silent for a long moment, then said: "Let's talk about the show cause." The bail hearing. We discussed the ins and outs of that, then we dealt with housekeeping matters, that is, fees and payment, and I left to drive back into town.

So. The guy wouldn't say anything beyond "I wasn't there." You'd think Beau Delaney would know better. That may look like the best defence in the world: *My client didn't do it, My Lord; he wasn't even there.* But in fact it's often the worst defence of all, because if it turns out the police can place him there, it's over. With other defences — insanity, self-defence — you have room to manoeuvre. The fact that he was there doesn't kill you on day one. Or day two.

But right now, I had to get him out on bail. I started preparing for that as soon as I got to the office on Barrington Street. I also asked my secretary, Tina, to track down any news stories she could find about Peggy Delaney's death. She had something for me by noon, from the January 17, 1992, edition of the *Chronicle Herald.*

"Selfless Mother" Dies at Home
Margaret Jean ("Peggy") Delaney, 48, prominent children's rights advocate and mother of ten, died in her
south-end Halifax home two nights ago. She was the
wife of well-known criminal defence lawyer Beau
Delaney, and the daughter of Gordon and Margaret
Laing. Mr. Delaney said he returned home late on

Wednesday night and found his wife at the bottom of the basement stairs. Foul play is not suspected but Mr. Delaney expects that there will be an autopsy because this is an unexplained death. Mr. Delaney said: "Peggy was the love of my life, and the most giving, the most selfless woman and mother I have ever met." The couple had a family of ten: two biological, two adopted, and six foster children. "They are all our children," Mr. Delaney said. "They are devastated. I don't know how to get them through this. We're going on a wing and a prayer at this point." A funeral will be held at St. Mary's Basilica once Mrs. Delaney's remains have been released.

I didn't like our bare-bones defence that Delaney wasn't there. But we had one thing going for us, and it was no small thing: Delaney's character. Loving father of ten children, BCL (big Catholic layman), top-notch lawyer working above and beyond the call of duty for his clients. Part of the Delaney legend was that he had been known to work above and beyond the call even for people who were not his clients, people who had in fact refused his offer of pro bono — free — legal services. This was the Gary's General Store case, which had propelled Beau Delaney to national fame.

Fourteen years ago, in 1978, two men robbed Gary's General Store, a family-owned store in the tiny community of Blockhouse, an hour west of Halifax, shooting the two young employees who were on the night shift. Scott Hubley, the owner's seventeen-year-old son, died on the floor behind the counter. Cathy Tompkins, the other clerk, sixteen years old, was shot in the head and left with permanent mental and physical disabilities. Police arrested two suspects the following day. They went to trial and each pointed the finger at the other, saying the other guy had pulled the trigger. The evidence showed that both men had handled the gun at some point, so it was not clear who had done the shooting. What was clear was that both planned and perpetrated the robbery. Beau Delaney represented one of them; another Halifax lawyer represented the co-accused. Beau gave his client, Adam Gower, a brilliant defence and, to use layman's language, "got him off on a technicality." The co-accused was convicted of the second-degree murder of Scott Hubley and other charges relating to Cathy Tompkins.

Understandably, feelings ran high in the small rural community. So high that Beau and the other lawyer received threats against their lives and were warned never to set foot in Blockhouse again.

It didn't end there. Delaney's client, Gower, left the province but decided to move back a year or so after the trial. Within days of his return to Nova Scotia, he was found in the woods off Highway 103 in Lunenburg County, beaten to death. Only his dental work identified him as Gower; his injuries were so severe that he was otherwise unrecognizable. Cathy Tompkins's brother, Robby, who had a minor criminal history himself, and who had been heard uttering threats against Gower, was picked up and charged with the murder. Beau Delaney entered the picture again. He contacted Robby Tompkins after his arrest and offered to defend him free of charge. But the Tompkins family, still outraged over Beau's successful defence of Adam Gower, refused his help. Robby Tompkins vehemently denied involvement. He went to trial with another lawyer. The jury took four days but eventually — one can presume reluctantly — found Robby guilty of second-degree murder. He was sentenced to life in prison with no chance of parole for ten years.

Beau worked the case like a cop for two years, trying to find something that would exonerate the young man. His efforts were noticed, and they paid off when he received an anonymous phone call that pointed to a shady character named Edgar Lampman as the real killer of Adam Gower. Lampman was a middle-aged man who had a record of violent offences, and who had been a frequent customer in the convenience store when Cathy was working. She had apparently been uncomfortable in his presence; the suggestion was that he was attracted to her. Since the killing, Lampman had died of natural causes. Beau passed the tip on to the police, who checked it out and found that it was legitimate. The upshot was that Edgar Lampman was posthumously fingered as the killer, and Robby Tompkins was exonerated and set free.

Delaney was lionized after his triumph. There was even a movie about the case, titled *Righteous Defender*, with Jack Hartt starring in the role of Delaney. Known in the tabloids as the Jack of Hearts, the tall, handsome actor was a Canadian raised in a suburb of Toronto. He had gone on to fame and fortune in the United States.

So. I had a hero for a client, and I would make the most of that fact in defending him against the murder charge in 1992. I wished I could play the feature film for the jury. No such luck.

Not surprisingly, Delaney's arrest was front-page news in both of the daily papers, and even earned a spot in the national media. The *Chronicle Herald* showed Delaney in his barrister's gown and tabs, holding forth in the plaza of the Nova Scotia Supreme Court building. Gown and mane of hair lofted by the wind, arm raised to make a point, the lawyer proclaimed a client's innocence to the throng of reporters and cameras. The focus of the piece was a history of Delaney's courtroom triumphs. The *Daily News* showed him waving from the driver's seat of his customized Mercedes twelve-passenger van. Several of his children gave toothy grins from behind the car windows. The story centred on the Delaney family's well-known practice of holding weekend events, such as picnics and sports tournaments, in public spots like the Halifax Commons, Point Pleasant Park, and Dingle Park. Any children who happened by were welcome to join in, pick up a ball glove, have a hot dog or an ice cream cone, take part in a sing-along.

The Delaney kids were now split up, staying with various relatives of Peggy and Beau; they were in a holding pattern until the completion of the trial. None of the relatives was in a position to keep the children indefinitely, and certainly not all ten of them. One of Peggy's sisters broke down and wept — and terminated the interview — when asked if only the Delaneys' "own" children would find a permanent home with relatives. It was clear that if Delaney was convicted, at least some of the kids would go back to government care or foster homes. The family would be ripped apart.